Praise for
Heidi Wessman Kneale

All romance stories need a little magic, and Heidi Kneale has told us a romantic story brilliantly.... [MARRY ME] deserves to be on the top of your TBR pile.

—Kayden Claremont, author
"Timeless Passion"

"I enjoyed [AS GOOD AS GOLD], well written and with well-rounded characters."

—Long and Short Reviews

"...Kneale succeeds in reversing reader expectations in more ways than one."

—Chris Butler, The Fix:
Short Fiction Review

"Heidi Kneale has so much imagination. She's one of the best I've seen."

—Anne Wingate, author
Deb Ralston series

"...the world introduced [in AS GOOD AS GOLD] was intriguing and there seem to be more possibilities to be explored, always a sign of a strong tale."

—Margaret Fisk, author
Uncommon Lords & Ladies series

For their Ladyships,
Lady Sarah and Lady Amy.
Go forth and be mighty.

God of the Dark

by
Heidi Wessman Kneale

Of The Dark—Book 1

Enjoy.

God of the Dark

Book 1 of the "Of The Dark" series.

Other titles in the **Of The Dark** series:
- Bride of the Dark (Book 2)
- House of the Dark (Book 3)

Cover Design: HW Kneale and SR Kneale
ISBN: 978-0-6484228-1-5
IngramSpark version 1.0—[date]

Printed on planet Earth by human beings.

This book is also available in a digital edition for those who adore carrying hundreds of books on their smartphones.

License Statement

Table of Contents

⸜◉⸝

Chapter 1

Adrastea descended into the dark. As her feet touched the cellar's stone floor, the scent of brandy enveloped her. It was stronger here, smelling of peaches and hot summer days and possibly forbidden kisses. Oh dear. Something had broken.

Up in the stillroom Ari Healer peered into the cellar, her anxiety palpable. Her skinny hands gripped the top of the ladder and she sniffled. "Was it my barrel? Please tell me it wasn't my barrel."

"I don't know." Something shimmered at the edge of Adrastea's vision. The auras? Everything had an aura. She pushed away Ari's worry and squinted into the darkness. Was it a bottle of new brandy that broke, or the barrel of old brandy? Please, not the new brandy. Adrastea had worked so hard distilling enough. Her heart ached at the thought of losing even one drop.

But if it had been Ari's barrel, the one that had sat in this cellar for twenty-five years, its precious contents aging to perfection, that would be a greater loss.

She drew a breath and coughed. The alcohol stung her lungs too much to tell which one had spilled.

A warm light wavered above the cellar door. "Here. Take the lantern."

"No. Too risky." It would do Adrastea no good if the flame of the lamp ignited the brandy fumes.

Ari's voice shuddered. "It is my barrel, isn't it?"

Again, Adrastea caught a shimmeriness out of the corner of her eye, flaring then fading. Now that was interesting. "Could be the barrel," she ventured.

Ari let out a whimper.

There! The glimmer brightened at the far end of the cellar. How fascinating. Ari's grief had illuminated the location of the brandy barrel, a pulse along the thread that connected her aura to it. That was new.

For Adrastea, everything had an aura of connecting threads. Mira Priestess once told her they were the Lines of Deeper Power, which bound Creation together. She also said that not everyone could see them all the time. So, Adrastea had never given it much thought until now.

When up in the world, out in the light, she could barely tell they were there, just gossamer webs out of the corner of her eye. Down here in the cellar they came to her much stronger. She relaxed and focused inward, drawing a deep breath. Lines from dried herbs and potions she'd prepared lit up and connected to her. She'd made all this. It belonged to her and brought her deep satisfaction. How comforting to know that something she created with her own two hands did some good in the world.

There was the lavender she'd harvested a month ago. That would go for calmatives. Next to that, the rosemary hanging from the rafters, waiting to be pounded into powder. Her fingers brushed against it in the darkness. Later she'd turn it into an antiseptic. Scents of all kinds filled her nose as the Lines of connection wrapped about her. So much down here was hers. But the brandy barrel? That was purely Ari's.

Ari loved that barrel. Adrastea didn't know how but she did. Now the Line between them grew brighter, so bright it was as if she could touch it.

Could she?

Adrastea reached out a tentative finger and stroked along a Line. It felt like touching the surface of warm water. She teased at it, making it arch up like a kitten, its warmth wrapping about her hand. Impressions of apples came to her, spicy and speaking of autumn. If she pushed too hard, her hand went through it. But when she concentrated, it responded to her touch. Fascinating! Who knew you could touch them? An idea blossomed in her head.

"Ari?" Adrastea called out.

The ladder under Ari's hands rattled. "What?" It came out as a wail. Her anxiety strengthened a Line, thickening it to stand out from the rest, connecting Ari to her barrel.

That worked better than she'd hoped. When Adrastea laid her hand upon it, she felt the ripples of Ari's panic. "Twenty-five years' worth of brandy..." Her grief pulsed powerfully through all the Lines. How distracting. Now everything was illuminated.

"Stop panicking." Adrastea lifted her hands and centered herself.

"Just focus on the barrel. I'm almost there." Soon the thread between Ari and the barrel reappeared, separating itself from the rest—ethereal, yet strong. She let it guide her past shelves and boxes, bundles and casks.

In the darkest corner of the cellar she found the barrel. As her hands roamed over its ancient oaken surface, she discovered the hoops and staves completely intact. "It's all right," she called back to Ari.

"Thank the Light." Ari broke into noisy tears of relief. The worry line between Ari and the barrel relaxed but didn't fade completely; Ari loved that barrel so much. Why?

Adrastea extended her senses. So, if it wasn't the barrel, what spilled? Adrastea's heart sank. It had to be the new brandy. She and Ari had been distilling for weeks and weeks in anticipation of emptying the big barrel. Soon, they would take out the mature brandy for bottling and a new brandy would be oaked. Until that happened, the new brandy would have to remain stored in multiple bottles on shelves, awaiting their next step of the journey.

She inhaled, letting the familiar scent in—fruit and fermentation and disappointment.

There was something else. Adrastea smelled an undercurrent of beer. She felt about until her fingers found what she was looking for—beery dampness. An over-brewed beer bottle had popped its cork, the projectile knocking several precious bottles of new brandy off their shelves. She knelt to the cold stone cellar floor, her fingers dabbing into spilled brandy and poking at bottle sherds. Adrastea's guts ached over weeks of her hard work lost.

Upstairs, someone called out, "Ari! Ari!" Adrastea's brother Mikal, his adolescent voice cracking with urgency, ran into the stillroom. The floor creaked over her head. "Come quickly. Little Peter fell into the tank."

The ripple of Ari's urgency vibrated along the Lines. The healers were needed. Ari's feet pounded on the floorboards as she followed Mikal outside.

By the time Adrastea climbed out the cellar into the warmth of summer's light, they were gone. She grabbed her healer's cloak and medicine bag and dashed after them.

The village of Sacred Spring sat about the rectangle of the green, a collection of clapboard houses lining the dusty roads. Pines and quaking aspen ringed the edge of the village, silent in the summer heat. Adrastea followed Ari and Mikal, now distant figures running to the tall smithy.

The smithy had a huge water tank, stone on the bottom, wooden on top like a barrel, cooped up with heavy steel bands. At the end of winter, it held gallons and gallons of water. As it was now reaching the end of summer, that water level had dropped somewhat. Still, it would have been well over Little Peter's head.

Someone had turned on the spigot of the tank. Water gushed out at a furious rate, turning the ground dark and muddy. A crowd of villagers gathered, desperate and edgy in the summer heat, staying just beyond the growing puddle. It was as if they were afraid the water might grab them.

Ari pushed her way through the crowd. Adrastea wasn't far behind, prickly sweat dampening the back of her bodice.

"How'd he get up there?" Ari called out. That tank was a good two stories high. Little Peter Smithson wasn't more than three years old.

Big Peter Smith was up on the smithy roof with two other men, Jak Carpenter and Rop Storekeeper. Jak and Rop held Big Peter as his head and arms disappeared into the tank. Little Peter must still be alive.

Sheelagh Smith, Big Peter's leather-clad wife, smashed a mighty axe against the side of the tank. Thumps rang loud across the green as she chopped at the wooden staves. Despite her efforts, she'd barely made a dent in the thick hardwood.

Adrastea shook her head. There was no way Sheelagh would chop through in time, not by herself. Why wasn't anyone helping her? She looked around.

The other villagers hovered nearby, murmuring one to another and wringing their hands. Most stood about, their gazes fixed on the tank before them.

Someone returned with a coil of rope. This, he tossed up to the men on the smithy roof.

Ari paced back and forth through the mud, her eyes upwards at the men on the roof. "Is he alive? How is he?" No one answered her.

Adrastea looked about. Dozens of villagers were here with more arriving, drawn by the drama. Their web-like auras were all but invisible here in the summer sun, but the collective anxiety made them shimmer.

"Peter!" Sheelagh cried between blows. Was she urging her husband on, or calling out to her son? "Hang on!" Her blonde hair had come loose from her bun, sticking to her sweaty skin. She blew it out of her face before raising the axe again.

Adrastea caught up with her brother. "What happened here?"

Mikal swallowed, his adolescent Adam's apple bobbing. "Dunno how but Little Peter climbed up there. Lid must've been rotted. They tried draining the water. It wasn't going fast enough so they thought they'd fish him out."

"How'd he get up there?" Adrastea muttered more to herself than to her brother. A ladder leaned against the smithy. Was it there before, or had the men thrown it up to get to Little Peter?

Sheelagh called out to her drowning son. "Stay with me, Petey! Keep kicking!" She did not give up her axework.

"Damn it!" Big Peter Smith, his face still sooty from the forge, rose up from his prone position on the roof. "This pole's too short!" Peter threw it to the ground, heedless of the people below. "Gimmie a longer one!"

Adrastea clenched her hands. Her heart ached. If they got Little Peter out alive, he'd need medical attention. If they didn't get him out alive... Adrastea swallowed. Nothing hurt worse than the death of a child.

Ari looked about "Wait. Where's Natan?" She called out. "Natan!"

Mikal reached out and plucked at Ari's sleeve. "Uncle Natan's in the tank with Little Peter."

Adrastea covered her mouth with her hands. Did Uncle Natan even know how to swim? How were they going to get them out?

"They tried lowering him on a rope. Then the rope broke."

"What was he thinking?" Ari raged. Natan Mayor was a large bear of a man. No doubt his sense of responsibility drove him to such foolishness. "Why didn't they send Tam, or someone smaller?"

Adrastea looked at the tank, tilting her head. The threads around it were thicker towards the bottom; the tank was nowhere near empty.

Then she saw them flex as if someone pulled on them.

On the other side of the rain tank, almost hidden from sight, a petite mud-covered figure placed her hands on the tank. Adrastea squinted. Was that a child?

As she drew near, her nearsightedness resolved. It was no child but the diminutive figure of Mira Priestess. Mira was shorter and slimmer than Adrastea. The size of the tank dwarfed her even more. "Mira, what are you doing? It isn't safe."

The priestess wiped her muddy hands over her dark hair, streaking it with filth. Then she placed a hand on her forehead and exhaled in exasperation. "Go away. Let me concentrate!"

"Sorry." Adrastea backed away, the mud sucking at her feet.

Mira put her hands together in prayer before her face. The frustration around her faded as calmness took over.

Mira reached out and grasped the Lines that held the tank together.

Adrastea drew a breath. Mira knew about touching the Lines? She never said anything before. Did everyone know or only priests?

At first her hands fell straight through them. She took a deep breath and tried again, this time, laying gentle hands on the ethereal filaments that bound about the tank. What did she feel through them?

Adrastea's heart skipped a beat. The Lines extended out, to wrap themselves about Mira's arms in a shimmery, faint web. The priestess closed her eyes and pulled.

The staves of the tank bowed out, enough to leak a little bit of water. Then the Lines slipped away from Mira's grasp. The tank returned to normal.

On the other side, Sheelagh continued her assault with the axe, her voice now hoarse from her audible grief.

Mira tried to pull the Lines again. Once more, they slipped from her grasp. "Oh!" She kicked the tank.

Adrastea saw what Mira had done wrong; she had let her focus waver. That's when the Lines eluded her.

When Mira tried a third time, Adrastea watched closely. "I can do that," Adrastea murmured to the priestess. She twisted her dark curly hair up out of the way.

Mira didn't turn, so focused was she. "They're too slippery, Crozie. I can't."

Adrastea ignored Mira's name slip. She removed her cloak, knelt down next to her and placed her hands on the tank just as Mira had. The Lines moved under her hands, almost sticking to them. What happened if she released the Lines around the tank?

They were like the threads that her mother, Lillybet Weaver, strung on her loom. Lilly pulled those threads all the time. Why had it never occurred to her before now that these Lines could be handled in the same way? Her heart thumped harder.

Ari pounded on the side of the tank. "Natan?" she shouted. "Do you have him? Do you have Peter?"

Uncle Natan's voice came from within the water tank. "I've got him," he called out, his voice echoing unnaturally. "But—"

Adrastea closed her eyes and pushed the world away from her. She focused on the Lines and how they wrapped the tank. They were strong; they had to be, to keep that much water in. As Mira had done, she let the Lines connect to her. She imagined her hands pulling on them to free them.

At first, they didn't respond. She put her sheer force of will into it.

The tank grew too hot, then too cold under her touch. The iron cooper bands broke, and the wood fractured. With an almighty crack, the stone base of the tank split open. A wave of water flooded out. Sheelagh's feet washed out from beneath her and she tumbled to the ground. The falling barrel staves splattered mud everywhere.

Adrastea felt this, felt every single splinter of wood, every little piece of stone, every drop of water, through the Lines. Such power! The force of the water had also pushed Adrastea back into the mud, washing over her, soaking her clothing. Then it flowed away, to create muddy puddles in the dust, its energy depleted.

She lay there, staring up at the clear blue summer sky, breathless. The loud murmuring of the crowd also washed over her, though it didn't make any sense. Her whole body hummed in reflection of the energy from the Lines.

She did it. She had saved a life.

Mira lay against the side of the smithy, her shoulder injured. Adrastea felt Mira's pain through the Lines between them that hadn't faded completely. Were they connected now? Is that what these gossamer threads did if you touched them? What was happening?

The crowd had broken apart like so many panicked ants. No one had expected the tank to split like that.

Sheelagh scrambled forward through the mud to gather the limp body of her son from Natan's huge hands. "Peter!" she shrieked.

Ari was there, only the hem of her skirts damp from the flood. "It might not be too late." Removing the cloak from her shoulders, she dropped it on Sheelagh. Ari took Little Peter and turned him upside down. She whacked him a few times on the back. Water trickled out of his mouth then he coughed before emptying the contents of his stomach into the mud.

"Mama!" Little Peter held his muddy arms out. Sheelagh gathered him up, crying and thanking the Light.

As the people cheered Peter's rescue, Adrastea shook the mud from her hands. A Line, hot enough to send a thrill through her, wrapped around her heart. She looked back to Mira, who cradled her injured shoulder.

"Light save us all," whimpered the priestess, her eyes haunted and staring at Adrastea. "Oh no, Adrastea. Not now."

N atan Mayor slumped at side of the smithy. What a ride! And what a stupid thing to do. What had he been thinking, jumping into the rain tank like that?

Little Peter's life had been at stake. It would not do to have had Big Peter jump in as well. What if he'd failed? They both could have died in there.

He looked over at Ari, the love of his life, as she tended to Mira's injured shoulder. She would give him grief later. He deserved it.

Earlier Ari had wrapped a cloak and a disapproving glare about his wet form. He still shivered but didn't care. He'd saved a life! So what if things went pear-shaped? Everything had turned out well in the end.

He was never doing that again.

His back ached. After all his efforts to stay afloat, he would sleep well tonight, if the concerns of the day were shoved deep into his personal worry-box. As Mayor of Sacred Spring village, he worried about everything. It was his job to worry.

Mira leaned against the wall of the smithy, her eyes closed and her skin pale. Would she be all right? Adrastea was with her earlier.

Ari inspected her medical tools of trade, her forehead wrinkling as she tut-tutted over their filthy condition.

"That was amazing!" he said as he flicked at the mud on his damp trousers. "Did you see—"

Ari scowled at him as she tied her healer's bag, pulling the drawstrings harder than necessary. He didn't finish his thought.

Ari went over to Mira and laid a hand on her shoulder. Mira looked up, murmured something, and looked away. Hers were a pair of haunted eyes. The Mayor in him recognized something wrong, something deeper.

"What's the matter?" he asked the priestess.

Mira said nothing. Perhaps too many thoughts tumbled through her head. He saw a heaviness on her shoulders, possibly grief. Natan looked about. Was he missing something?

A cold shiver ran down his spine. "Mira? Are you all right?"

At first Mira did not reply. Then she turned her gray eyes upward. "No, Natan," she said in a too-smooth voice. "I am not." Those were rather chilling words. "We have a problem."

With Ari's help, Natan got Mira home to her tiny cottage. The priestess drew the heavy curtains across her four windows, blocking out the afternoon light. She closed and locked both doors. "Ari and I have a terrible secret. It is time you knew."

More out of habit, Mira swung her kettle over the fireplace and prepared a pot for tea. Ari sat at the tiny table, tapping her steepled fingers against her lips.

Natan looked from woman to woman. Both avoided his gaze. Something tightened in his heart.

The fire provided the only light, and the heat from the fireplace made Natan's skin prickle against his damp clothing. "Well?" he asked the two disconcerted women. "This must be some secret." Especially as they didn't let him go home to change into dry clothing. At least Ari plunked a cup of tea in front of him.

Mira and Ari looked at each other, hesitating. "Twenty-two years' worth," Mira said. "It concerns Adrastea."

A niggling little fear he normally associated with his sister Lillybet rose under his heart. Lilly had not had it easy growing up. She had always been a little odd, claiming to see and hear things the others didn't. He loved her—when few would—despite her quirks. All his life he had protected his little sister, defending her against those who would mock her.

When his niece Adrastea was born, Natan worried that she would suffer the same way. But as she grew up a perfectly normal little girl without a lick of the madness that dogged Lillybet, his fears eased.

He noted his niece's absence. "Where is Adrastea?"

"I—" Mira started. "She was filthy. I told her to go to the Sacred Spring to clean up. She doesn't know what we are about to tell you."

Natan twitched. An itch of sweat rolled down his back. The cup of tea dwarfed by his big hand cooled, forgotten, as he listened.

"I've read the Lines of Deeper Power," Mira said, "but I've never seen anything like this."

He furrowed his brow at Mira's lack of context. "What do you mean, 'Lines of Deeper Power'?"

Mira's jaw dropped. "Are you serious? Don't you listen to a single thing I say every week?"

Ari put a finger into the middle of her forehead and shut her eyes. "Natan…"

He spread out his big bear paws. "What? Oh, you mean the religious stuff."

Ari rolled her eyes, while Mira dropped her head into her hands.

"Sorry," he apologized again. "My head's still on the Smiths." He reached out and patted Mira's tiny hand with his big one. "Really, I do listen to your sermons." He took a sip of tea, mainly to buy himself more time. Once a week he and Ari had Mira over for supper, as did most villagers. In exchange for a good meal, Mira Priestess would offer blessings upon their homes and teach them about the Gods and Creation. "Deeper Power. Binds Creation together. Right?"

That seemed to mollify her. Barely. A tremor niggled in Mira's hands. "Then, when Adrastea was born…" She bit her lip. "At first I didn't know if it was just my imagination or not—"

"Only I saw it too." Ari helped herself to the last few drops of Mira's delicate teapot. She frowned as they did not fill her cup. She filled the kettle before swinging it back over the fire.

"Saw what?" Natan asked.

"Lillybet had given birth," Ari said, not answering his question. "You know how Mira is."

He nodded. Mira had a weak stomach. He couldn't recall a single birth she attended where she hadn't thrown up, poor thing.

Ari leaned on the mantelpiece, staring into the flames. "After Lilly was settled to enjoy her new baby, I slipped out to check on Mira. That's when it happened."

"What?" Natan demanded again.

"It was a vision. Like in the Book of the Light. The air around us crackled like the dry wind before a storm." Ari sketched in the air with her hands. "Pictures that moved through the air and followed my eyes wherever I looked." She looked at Mira as she said, "We saw the same thing." Mira nodded in agreement and Ari continued. "We saw the baby, only in the vision she was a woman full-grown. It was night and she stood on a hill."

She paused, in case Mira wanted to add something but the priestess remained silent.

Ari took that as consent. "There were people on the hill, people in pain. They climbed the hill, begging to be healed. And our Adrastea stretched forth her hands and touched them, healing them."

A few things came together for Natan. "So that's why you offered apprenticeship for Adrastea when she was still a baby. I always wondered why you leapt in." Why had Ari never told him any of this?

"Well, about that..." Ari scratched through her dark hair, knocking out specks of dried mud. "I thought it would be a comfort to Lillybet to know her daughter was spoken for, seeing..."

She didn't need to say any more. Natan remembered full well how no one in the village would take strange Lillybet as an apprentice. So, Lilly ended up a weaver, like their parents. Terribly embarrassing, being apprenticed to one's parents.

Another sobering thought: when her husband Joe died and grief overwhelmed Lilly, it was only natural that the girl went to Ari's care until Lillybet recovered. Her son Mikal was only a baby. When Lillybet's milk dried up he went with Marta Innkeeper, the only other nursing mother in town. In the space of a week, Lilly had been all but deprived of her whole family.

He'd been thinking about that tragedy for a while now. But that was an issue for another time. Natan made a note to stick that one back into his worry box for later. After all, he had a plan.

The kettle whistled over the fire. Ari prepared a second brew. Mira didn't move.

"So, everything in the vision came true?" Natan asked. "Adrastea was apprenticed to you and she became a skilled healer."

"But..."

Mira's voice was so soft. He felt that cold chill up his back again. "There's something you're not telling us, isn't there, Mira?"

She nodded.

Ari returned to the table, full tea pot issuing steam from the spout. "Mira?"

"The water tank..." Mira sobbed. "There is so much I should tell you, about the Deeper Power, about the Gods, about everything. So much..." She made fists of her hands and pressed them to her forehead.

Ari stared at her best friend. "Mira, why didn't you tell me there was more to the vision?"

Mira ignored her question.

"But what about our Adrastea?" Huh. Ari didn't know everything after all. "There was more to the vision, wasn't there?"

Mira nodded. "Everyone belongs to Creation. Therefore, everyone, to some extent, exerts some influence on Creation. We make our own luck, for good or ill, we form our own destinies. Our potential is infinite, limited only by our own motivations. But sometimes, Creation has something else in mind." She put her hand over her mouth for a moment. "Sometimes... how do I explain this?"

A log popped and collapsed in the fireplace. Natan swirled his tea and took several sips. Mira sniffed and fought her tears.

Natan burned to know what Mira saw. "Our Adrastea's destiny? It was good, was it?"

"No." Mira sniffed again, then wiped her nose on her cuff. "Adrastea looked just a little older than she is today. She stood on a hill and stretched forth her hands." Her voice grew high and rapid, as if she had to force out the words as quickly as possible. "She healed people, not even touching them. I didn't understand then, but I do now. She did it with the Deeper Power, like she opened the tank today. Oh dear." Mira wiped her nose again. "In the vision, she was not alone."

"Mira," Natan probed. "Who was there?"

"I...." Mira closed her eyes as if to recall the vision better. "She stood on the hill, and a man stood behind her. He touched her in a way that—" She drew in a breath. "It—" she hesitated, not sure what to say. "He..."

"Who?"

Another breath. "Mor-Lath, God of the Dark. I think."

The teacup in Natan's hand went 'tink' as it cracked under the pressure of his hand. The dregs dripped onto his trouser leg. "Are you—" began Natan. "But you're not sure." He abandoned the remains of his teacup and wiped his damp hand on his shirt. "Perhaps you are wrong?"

"Perhaps," Mira replied, though in a way that made Natan feel her vision was not in error.

Healing without touching? Presence of the Dark God? "But what does it mean?" he asked, shoving the thought that it might mean Adrastea turning from the Light.

Mira did not answer but Ari sat upright. "What do you mean, 'what does it mean'? I think it's obvious."

"Is it?" Mira hunched over, staring past Natan into the fire, its light flickering.

Natan shook his head. "Our Adrastea's a good girl. She's always walked in the Light."

Mira shuddered. "But now." She shook her head. "I've been

pondering this for more than twenty years. You're right, Natan. She's a good woman. Not always the brightest but her heart's in the right place.

However," she lifted a finger for emphasis, "something is going to happen. In the vision, he wrapped his arms around her and said, 'Mine.'"

The thought Natan had pushed down came back up. She was Lillybet's daughter. Symbolic or not, Adrastea's possible future seemed to include a path to darkness.

Mira pulled herself together. "Look. However we choose to interpret this, it all boils down to one thing: evil is coming. When you play with the Lines of Deeper Power, it attracts attention. Adrastea's demonstration of her new talent is bound to attract that sort of attention."

"Attention?" Natan asked.

"New talent?" exclaimed Ari.

Mira's head bowed under the weight of knowledge. "The water tank? Adrastea did that."

Natan forgot to breathe. Did one woman split open a tank that size?

"How?" Ari gasped, her question more a whisper.

Mira slowly shook her head, more in denial than ignorance. "I've never known a priest with enough talent to do what she did. If I knew she could influence the Lines like that, I would have sent her to Crossroads, or even Feown—"

Natan shivered as a draft rolled around his damp ankles. "For what?"

"Training! Anyone with even a glimmer of talent is best given over to the priesthood." Her head fell into her hands. "I'm such a fool."

Natan felt like he was missing something. "What's this about talent?" She'd never demonstrated anything before, that he knew about. Lillybet sometimes talked about being able to see angels and demons. But Adrastea? Nothing.

Mira sighed. "Don't you ever listen to my sermons?" She leaned forward, and the others followed suit. "In the vision, Adrastea used the Deeper Power. But I never thought it would have a literal interpretation. So, if that's literal, then..."

"What does this mean for her?" Natan voiced his primary fear.

Mira licked her lips. "Darkness will come, in one form or another. Does she stand against it, or does she succumb?"

Natan felt a tightness behind his eyes as a new worry settled onto his shoulders. "Is there anything we can do?"

Mira did not answer but lifted her teacup and pressed it to her lips in prayer.

Adrastea grumbled as she marched up the hill, away from the village. Up in the foothills, nestled in a meadow of wild grass, the sacred spring flowed from the mountains. Stories spoke of how the Light Herself once stood there. A spring erupted from Her footsteps, to bless any who sampled its waters, or to purge them of their sins. Mira had been most insistent Adrastea wash the mud off there. "Don't you go anywhere else. You must wash off in the spring! Nowhere else."

She wasn't sure why. Mira hadn't explained. There were lots of things today that didn't make sense—but she obeyed... at first. The spring was quite a hike from the village.

After breaking the tank and saving Peter, Adrastea had thought Mira would have been pleased. She was only trying to help. Mira would have been devastated had she failed to burst the tank and Little Peter died.

"I did a good thing," Adrastea told herself. "Why is Mira so unhappy?"

The priestess had shaken Adrastea, leaving muddy handprints on the sleeves of an already dirty blouse. "Do you realize what you've done?" she had cried.

"No..." replied a stunned Adrastea.

Mira sent her off like an errant child to clean herself up. She most likely would have dragged her to the spring herself, had her shoulder not been injured. "You must wash in the spring!" As if it was the most important thing in the world.

Once, long ago, the sacred spring had been the destination of pilgrimages. The waters could heal, protect and bring good luck.

Pilgrims no longer came in droves but in dribble—a mere handful in the year. Had the spring lost its power, or were people no longer interested in its bounty? Either way, the village named after the spring suffered.

As for it being a source of water, it tasted as good as any other spring to come out of the mountains. A stream brought water to the village. From there, it flowed out to the town of Crossroads. By the time it reached there, the water was no longer sacred.

Adrastea huffed up the path until she needed a rest. Breaking that tank took a lot more energy than she realized. Peering back through the quaking aspen that covered the hillside, she could no longer see the village.

So, why the spring? It was so cold it stung. The mud on her skin had dried, leaving her skin feeling tight. Water was water; the stream was good enough, and probably somewhat warmer. She left the path and waded through the undergrowth until she reached water. Mira wouldn't know.

She found a small pool not too far away, surrounded by brush and trees. Here she could wash in peace. After she kicked off her shoes, she removed her bodice, her blouse, and her cotton overskirt, which crackled with dried mud. These she dropped into the water. Her petticoats were not in better shape. They, too followed, leaving her standing in her chemise and pantaloons.

After she washed the mud from her clothes, she draped them to dry on the slim branches of the quakies.

Mira often spoke about the Deeper Power as part of her religious duties. Everyone knew about it. Adrastea had seen the Lines her whole life. So, when she saw Mira struggle to free Little Peter from the tank by pulling on them, it had been the most natural thing to step in and help her.

Mira's reaction had surprised her. Adrastea never meant to overstep her bounds, whatever they were.

Kneeling on the bank, she scooped the cool water onto her muddy face. Would she ever be clean?

A twig snapped behind her and she turned around. "Who's there?" she hissed. She covered herself with her arms.

No one answered. A breeze began to rustle the round leaves of the quakies, they sounding like the whispers of a hundred people. Then she heard her name.

Adrastea...

She drew a shuddery breath. "Who's there?"

A man came out from behind the trees, moving silkily towards her. She squinted. He looked familiar.

He wore black, from the fine shirt laced across his chest to his well-fitting pants and high-topped boots. Nobody in Sacred Spring dressed like that. A black cloak draped his shoulders, the hood thrown back. His hair was also dark, tendrils brushing the edges of his face. His skin was pale, his features fine. His eyes startled her the most, for they were lighter than they should have been, possibly green. Those eyes bore into her soul.

The Lines of Creation flickered about him, stronger than she had ever seen, even in the cellar. They created an aura about him so strong the trees themselves appeared to bend down under the weight of it. That same aura reached out to her. Adrastea retreated into the water, her feet slipping on the stones. The Lines wrapped about her and drew her back.

"Adrastea." His voice was a rich baritone that woke a dormant hunger in her.

Her heart hammered in her chest. Why was he so familiar? "I know you," though she didn't know how. The Lines around her reached out to him, linking them. They wanted to pull her to him.

He held out his hand. "I am Mor-Lath, God of the Dark. I have come to claim you, Adrastea, as my Bride."

Chapter 2

What did he say? Adrastea shivered. The gentle afternoon breeze sent the round leaves of the quakies shaking, their song a soft whisper. Mor-Lath held out his hand to Adrastea.

She should not take it. The water of the stream bumbled against her legs as if to push her towards him. She fought it.

As the wind shifted, rippling across her skin, she remembered her undress. Blushing, she crossed her arms before her chest and stepped back. Her foot found a moss-covered rock and she slipped. Mor-Lath reached out and caught her in time, saving her from a rather cold dunking. More gently than she would have expected of the Dark God, he helped her to ground.

"I've been waiting for you all your life," he told her as he took her face in his hands.

Adrastea shivered, not only from the cold but from his touch. His hands were warm. They slid to her shoulders, then her back, then her waist... She gasped as they roamed lower, to pull her intimately against him.

Panic rippled through her. "Wait!" She pushed away from him. This was no figment from Mira's evening tales. She snatched her hands away from his warm chest. Touching him would not do.

The Lines between them increased. They wrapped around her, drawing her closer to him. Yes, the Lines told her, he was the Dark God. That alone frightened her more than any mortal man ever could. She struggled with the Lines, attempting to free them from her. They refused to comply.

Mor-Lath simply waited. Then with a wave of his hand, the Lines dissipated. "Relax. I'm not going to ravish you. I intend on wooing you properly."

Adrastea paused on the brink of stepping back into the water. "Why me?" After all, she walked in the Light.

"Why not you? Today you have touched your true potential for the first time. I cannot tell you how pleased I am." With a single hand, he unclasped the cloak about his shoulders. He swept a corner of it around her, enveloping them both. Adrastea gasped as the soft fabric settled around her. Her heart thumped as her breath caught in her throat. As his arm wrapped about her waist she felt, to her dismay, a thread of desire rising within her. She pushed it away.

"You are destined to be my bride," he murmured in her ear. His hand caressed her face, sending another thrill through her skin.

Adrastea should have pulled away. She cursed that knot of longing that had sprung up under her heart, a knot that ached for her to collapse into his arms, to inhale his fragrance and taste his skin with her lips. Another shudder rolled through her, one of yearning.

She had to resist. With reluctance, she said, "No. I cannot be your bride." Why couldn't she walk away? The Lines grew stronger, wrapping about them both. She found herself pressed close to him as if her skin wanted to melt into his.

As she drew in a breath, she could smell him, spicy and masculine. No, no, no. This would not do. She focused her thoughts on the coldness of the water. Yes, cold water to fight the warmth that threatened to consume her.

"You will be my bride. The Light has given you to me." Even his voice wrapped about her and she felt dizzy again.

Panic in her stomach wrestled with the knot of desire and won. She tried to pull away but his strong arm around her waist prevented it. Although his cloak enveloped her, she felt naked, pressed to him. The fabric of his shirt rubbed against her nipples through her chemise. Her knees began to tremble. She had to get away.

It took all her willpower. She slipped out from under his arm and backed up until she hit a tree. It held her up when her knees wavered. "That is not true! The Light would never... I have a choice, and I—" Her voice faltered as his eyes hardened.

"I ask you to marry me. Say yes and come to me willingly." He held out his hand once more.

She clenched her fists to her chest, lest they betray her. "I can't." She cast her gaze about her. Was there something she could use as a weapon? A rock maybe?

He gave a small chuckle. His hand closed, and he withdrew it. "Maybe not today, for today is but our betrothal. In the end, you will."

Faster than she thought possibly, he crossed the distance between them. He wrapped his hand behind her head, bringing her face close to his. "So you do not forget, and so others may know who you truly are, I leave you a betrothal gift."

He raised his hand, the back of it to her right cheek and stroked it once. Her skin sang under the contact. He lifted his hand once more and traced a line down her cheek.

A searing hot pain followed his finger. The heat spread through her face. So great was the pain, she could only gasp.

He secured his cloak about her near-naked shoulders. A blink of an eye, he was gone.

She pulled the soft cloth close and sank to her knees.

Only then could Adrastea cry.

Natan Mayor stood on his sister's porch, hand raised to knock but hesitating. Did Lillybet know about Mira's vision? What about its implication for her daughter Adrastea? Surely something like this couldn't have lain dormant for this long. Ari might not have known Adrastea had talent. Did Lilly? If anyone did, it would have been his sister.

Had Lillybet come out to watch the rescue of Little Peter? Her thatched home lay on the outskirts of the village, up the hill from the smithy. Clever Joe Weaver had chosen a most ideal spot to build the house for his wife. From the front porch, one could gaze past the trees of the village of Sacred Spring and over the patchwork quilt of farms to the plains beyond. Small hazy patches of smoke marked where other villages and towns stood. They seemed so close, when seen from the porch but Natan knew it was hours by horse to the closest, Crossroads, and days to the rest.

The smithy tank was not visible from this side. Unless Lillybet had been in town, she couldn't have known.

She would know eventually. Sooner or later, gossip would reach her. He worried, too, about how much the villagers knew about Adrastea's involvement and how much of it was the truth?

Natan, as Mayor, worried about gossip. The village council was supposed to control it, suppress it but could never stop it. Who else saw what Adrastea did? Who guessed the true reason the tank had split? Mira said nobody saw but Natan knew better.

Lillybet had to hear it from him first.

He reached the door and heard a muffled sobbing from within. His heart sank. Lillybet had always had bad spells, when the darkness of the soul enveloped her. Nothing could bring light to it again for days. She became useless then, barely able to care for herself, much less anyone else.

The villagers found Lilly's oddness disconcerting.

She once confided to him, just before Joe came to the village, that it was demons that visited her, taunting and mocking her. He didn't believe her, not really, until now.

For those few golden years when Joe lived, her demons stayed away but returned upon his death. Sometimes she could go for months without being plunged into darkness. As soon as Natan thought he'd seen the end of it, something would happen, and she'd fall into depression.

She'd been so good recently, having gone nearly three seasons without an episode. Alas, it seemed the good spell was over. If so, she would need him, not as Mayor but as a brother.

Before he could knock, he heard her voice.

"Would you like another one?" a calm Lillybet asked.

The sobbing had not been her.

"There," she said. "Try that. I only wish it was winter."

He knocked.

Immediately the sobbing ceased as Lillybet hissed a warning to her mysterious guest. "Who is it?" she called out.

"It's Natan. I must speak to you."

Lillybet opened the door but a crack, her brown eyes peering out of the darkness. "How did you know?"

"Know what?"

Lillybet admitted her brother to the house and closed the wooden door. Like Mira, Lillybet had shuttered the windows and drawn the curtains, despite the heat of summer. The common room was large enough to accommodate Lilly's looms and baskets and everything that had anything to do with weaving. Unlike Mira, Lillybet had no fire burning today, so the house felt cooler. Spots of sunlight escaped onto the floor from the thinning thatch on the naked ceiling. It would need rethatching soon, at least before winter came. Aside from a fly buzzing indifferently, the only sound was a soft sniffling. It came from a figure wrapped in a black cloak, sitting on one of the only two chairs Lillybet owned.

The figure removed a compress of cloth from her face and dipped it into a bowl of water on the table. "Oh, Uncle Natan, I'm so sorry," she said.

"Adrastea?" He came forward and peered at her. "What happened?"

His niece turned to look at him with eyes full of sorrow. Her tears started again. A black line trailed from cheekbone to chin. Had she been injured when the rain tank broke?

"Wait. I thought you knew," Lillybet accused her brother.

Natan looked from his sister to his niece.

He gestured at the mark. "Is that from..."

Lillybet folded her arms. "You do know something about it, don't you?"

Natan's insides sank. Trust his luck that his sister was in one of her more lucid moments. "You tell me what's happened here, and I'll tell you why I came."

Lillybet pulled no punches. "My daughter—your niece—has picked up a suitor, or rather, a betrothed."

Natan blinked. That was the last thing he expected.

"Mother, please," begged Adrastea. She rose. The cloak she pulled close about her drew his gaze. It couldn't be hers, or Lilly's, for it was long enough to trail along the ground. Her voice pitched higher as she began to plead. "Please, Uncle Natan. It's not my fault. I promise I'm a good girl and that I walk in the Light. I never meant this to happen."

Two and two came together. Everything Mira told him and now this. He scooted backwards until his back hit the door then he slid to the floor.

"Bugger me!" he swore.

Lillybet stood by the table, arms folded, watching, as if expecting him to fix the matter.

"I'm sorry," Adrastea squeaked. "It happened so quickly. He didn't give me a chance."

"Bugger me," Natan repeated, softer now. "It was the God of the Dark, wasn't it?"

Lillybet dropped her arms. "So, you do know."

Adrastea reapplied the cold compress to her cheek.

"Bugger me..." Natan let the curse dribble from his lips.

Lillybet approached. "Will you stop saying that? I want you to tell me why my daughter has just been claimed by a god. A. God. What could he possibly want with her?" Her eyes narrowed. "Why didn't you tell me before?"

He risked looking into her light brown eyes. They blazed with fire. If he didn't act soon, she could very well break out into a glorious fit of anger and then there would be no reasoning with her.

"I only learned this afternoon. I came directly to tell you."

"How? From who? I only just learned. Adrastea hasn't seen anyone since it happened."

Natan rose. His head spun. Too much had happened today. His legs ached from his water-treading in the Smiths' tank. Mira and Ari's secret weighed heavily in his heart. And now this.

Even though he towered over his sister he knew nothing could compare to her towering temper, should she not take the rest of the news well. Was there any good way to put it?

"When Adrastea was born, Mira had a vision."

Lillybet wiped her mouth. "I thought Mira threw up outside."

Natan shook his head. "Mira was having a vision. Ari witnessed it. Well, some of it. And it was..." how to put this? "Let's just say that it wasn't something she felt needed sharing."

"So, Mira and Ari know about the Dark God too? Why didn't they stop it? Why didn't they say anything earlier?"

Natan shook his head. He dared to reach out his hands and take his sister gently by the shoulders. "I know nothing more except that Mira had a vision." He looked over Lillybet's shoulder. He saw his niece sitting at the table, huddled in a dark cloak, a wet cloth pressed to her face. Cold dread filled him as if poured from a bucket. There was more going on than he knew. "Adrastea, what happened?"

She shook her head in embarrassment.

His gut froze. "Was... was he here? He didn't... That is...." He'd never dealt with anything like this before. "He didn't... rape you, did he?"

Adrastea shook her head. "No. He was all kind and gentle... until this." She removed the compress. Natan studied the straight black line that marked her. She turned the compress to the cooler side and pressed it again to her skin.

He knelt down beside her. "Tell me?"

"After the barrel incident, Mira sent me up to the Sacred Spring to bathe. It must have been some ritual or something. I don't know; she never told me. So, I was there at the stream and I'd taken... I'd started washing the mud off when he showed up." She shuddered. "Oh, you should see him. He's..."

Natan felt the thrill run through her body. He pulled back. "Then what?"

"Well, it's like, he wasn't there, then he was. He told me that I was supposed to be his bride. I told him no, but he didn't listen. He said it was my destiny. Then he marked me. Said so everyone would know. He branded me." She turned her face away from him as if she was crawling into herself like a pillbug.

Natan sat back. What an odd turn of events. Not quite the way he'd declare his romantic attentions. Then again, he was not a god.

His hand brushed over the fabric of the cloak. It was softer and finer than anything he had ever seen his sister or Joe weave. "Where did you get this?" he asked, as he rubbed the fabric between his fingers.

"It's his."

Natan snatched his hand away. He beat a hasty retreat. "I've gotta talk to Mira." His heart thumped, and he fled.

As he ran down the hill, he heard his sister cursing behind him. "Damn it, Natan! Get back here. I need you!"

Adrastea sighed in relief as Ari's cool fingers smoothed ointment on her cheek. The alcohol had stung almost as bad as the line but then the sting went away, as did all sensation until her cheek was pleasantly numb. Her face felt better but her heart still ached.

After Uncle Natan ran off, Lillybet had given her brother's back a severe tongue-lashing. But he had returned quickly with an anxious Ari and a pale Mira.

While Ari attended her journeyman, Natan took his sister and the priestess into the bedroom.

Adrastea frowned. "They're talking about me in there."

"Of course," Ari replied as she replaced the lid on her ointment jar.

"Why not out here? It's not like they're being quiet about it."

"They need space to sort things out." She rubbed her fingers in annoyance. "Sometimes this stuff works too well." She tamped her numb fingers against each other before washing them off in the bowl of cold compress water.

The door failed to muffle Lilly's voice. "You don't think they'll notice?"

Ari wiped the sweat from her slender neck. "Can I open a window? It's hot in here."

Adrastea shrugged. It seemed her brain had gone numb as well.

Bright daylight filled the common room as Ari pulled back the curtains and opened the shutters of a window. Adrastea raised her hand to shade her eyes. "Why didn't you tell me Mira had a vision at my birth?"

Ari returned to the table and sat down. "Not much to tell. I didn't get to see the whole thing."

She pulled the cloak on her shoulders around her tightly then leaned forward. "You saw it?"

"I saw you standing on a hill."

"Like the one with the sacred spring?"

Ari didn't answer. "You stood on the hill and people were climbing it, coming to you. You stretched forth your hand and healed them all."

Now this was interesting. "And?"

"And that's all I saw."

Adrastea slumped back, disappointed. "So, was that why I was apprenticed to you?"

Ari let her fingers dabble in the bowl of water. "One of the reasons, yes."

"One?"

A small smile played on Ari's lips. "That, and you're Natan's niece. I've always had a soft spot for you. You're not the brightest lass but your instinct is good."

Adrastea didn't know if she should thank her or not.

"There were protests when I took you on..." Ari kept rubbing her numb fingers.

Adrastea grimaced. "Marta, right?" Marta Innkeeper was Lillybet's biggest critic. Then again, few people met Marta's ideal of a good person.

"Their opinion doesn't matter. You know the healer craft well." Ari frowned, more to herself. "You're a good journeyman."

From the bedroom, the voices crescendoed, Mira nearly shouting. "Lilly! We must."

Lillybet shrieked back. "No, I won't let you! She's my daughter! I've all but lost my son; I won't lose her too."

Then Natan, much calmer, said, "Now, Lilly. See reason."

Adrastea wiped at her damp brow. It was getting too warm. "What are they going to do with me? Get rid of me?"

"Get rid of is probably not the gist of the conversation. More like..." she hesitated, weighing her words. "You are a journeyman. Traditionally, they travel."

"You mean, send me away?" Her stomach tied itself in knots. "They can't send me away! I've done nothing. I won't let them." Adrastea slammed a fist onto the table, making the bowl of water jump.

"What are you? Twelve?" Ari laid a hand over the fist. "There are other options."

"Is leaving me alone one of them?"

Ari's eyes tightened. "No. Leaving you alone is the last thing we should do." She gripped Adrastea's fist. "There is no way in Creation we are letting the Dark God have you, you stupid girl! Don't you realize there's a reason behind his declaration? He's not just chasing you so he can tumble you in the barn like a wench. He's got a plan for you. We don't know what it is, and that's what scares us."

"How do you know he's got a plan?"

"Creation knows. Otherwise, why would there have been a vision, if there wasn't a reason for it?"

Her grip tightened. Adrastea squirmed. "Ari," she protested as her hand started to hurt.

"You listen here. Stop acting like a child. Let us be adults and decide what to do with you."

"Can I decide for myself?"

"There is more than just you at stake. Don't you realize what this may mean for the rest of us? As children of the Light we plan on resisting the Dark God. He's not going to like that. I don't think he is the sort of person to give up so easily."

The conversation in the bedroom ended, sparing Adrastea from more of Ari's lecture. Natan came out first, a look of determination on his face. Lillybet came next, her eyes blazing with triumph. Mira followed last, looking decidedly ill.

Adrastea pulled the dark cloak tightly around her as she rose. "I guess I don't get a say," she loftily stated.

"Doesn't matter at this point," Natan replied. Adrastea knew better than to stand up to her uncle. She sank back to her seat.

Natan kneeled down by her chair and laid a large hand on her shoulder. "Adrastea, do you know the extent of the situation?"

She studied her uncle. "This about the tank? What I did?" And about the Dark God?

"This affects everybody, not just you. This will have an impact on us all and not in ways we could imagine."

Mira's arms wrapped about her stomach. Was she going to be ill again? "The Dark God's presence may draw demons. His little visit will affect everyone's luck, including ours in trying to keep this a secret. Nobody that powerful can be somewhere without leaving an imprint on the Creation around them."

"A secret?" inquired Adrastea.

Mira licked her lips. "Do you really want to tell the visitors about your betrothal?"

"There is no betrothal. I never said yes."

"Good," growled Natan. "Let's keep it that way."

Mira held out her hand and ticked off the aspects. "There was a vision at your birth. Common people don't get visions at their birth. That vision foretold something very bad. Today you demonstrated a skill that most people don't have." She swiped her hand over her forehead. "Even I can barely see the Lines most days, never mind pull them as you did."

She held out her other hand and continued with her points. "That attracted the attention of the gods. One of these gods—and not the Light— has declared you as his intended. Did I mention that laypeople who display the sorts of skills you displayed today tend to be accused as witches? If we do not keep all of this a secret, the wrong sort of people are going to get spooked. There is a good chance you could end up on your funeral pyre before you're properly dead."

She held up her hands, fingers extended, as if she were going to bless or curse Adrastea. "We must not speak of Adrastea's actions today at the rain barrel. We should not mention the Dark God's presence here, nor his intentions towards Adrastea."

Adrastea gestured to the line—now blissfully numb—on her face. "What about this?"

"Easily explained. Enough people saw you close to the barrel when it exploded. You caught a splinter of wood, as did several other people this afternoon. Ari will bandage it up in an obvious manner and that will be that."

"But the line won't go away. Not ever." She didn't know how she knew that, but it was true.

"Scars never do." Mira turned to them all, spreading her arms wide. "All of you, promise."

A moment of silence, then Natan bowed his head. "All right." The others mumbled after him. Even Adrastea, though her eyes burned with rebellion, agreed.

Mira pointed at Adrastea. "And you, you have a further promise."

"Another one?"

Mira's hand hesitated over Adrastea's shoulder. "You have a talent, one we didn't expect. Therefore, you must be schooled. I need to teach you everything I can about the Deeper Power, about Creation, about it all.

"But we have to keep it a secret. If any should find out, they will question why I have taken you on. Nobody must know if we can help it."

Everyone in the village knew about Mira's lack of an apprentice. It worried them. Should something happen to Mira, they would be left without a priestess—without protection. For a few years now, the village council had been pressuring her to take on an apprentice. Mira had resisted for reasons known only to her. If they learned she was teaching Adrastea, questions would be asked.

Adrastea considered this. She'd never given a second thought to the Lines until today. If she'd known what would have happened, she would never have laid a finger on their spindly little brightness in the cellar. The events of the day left her overwhelmed and unprepared. Could Mira help?

"I promise."

"That's that," declared Mira.

Adrastea pressed her knuckles to her mouth. Now what?

Chapter 3

It was easy for Lillybet to keep the secret. She just did what she always did and stayed home. The door of her tiny cottage kept the disapproving stares of neighbors at bay, and the clandestine protections that her beloved late husband Joe had laid across the thresholds kept demons out. Here she could stay safe.

But what about Adrastea? Lilly worried about her daughter. Sure, Joe's protection could keep out demons. But could they keep out a god?

Not everyone could see demons, she had learned. Unless one was a priest by trade, anyone who claimed to see such supernatural things was regarded with caution. Only madmen saw strange things, like wispy beings who flew along invisible lines. What would they say about this? Lilly completely believed Adrastea's tale, as did Mira and Ari.

The rest of the village might not be so magnanimous.

Small communities had a way of shunning those they considered "not normal". Lilly, with her wild imagination and helter-skelter temperament, had fit their definition. How did the Weavers produce both strong, solid Natan and flighty, mad Lilly? That was a question many a villager had asked at one time or another.

When Joe died, Mikal had been fostered out to the Innkeepers, much to Lilly's chagrin but he proved to be normal, thank the Light. Adrastea had been old enough to be apprenticed out. As her daughter grew to adulthood under the safe eye of Ari Healer, she'd shown no trait that would paint her with the same brush that had stained Lilly.

Until today.

Lilly had intended to spend the day weaving, as she did every day, losing herself in the patterns of her fine cloth and ignoring the fabric of Creation that glimmered out of the corners of her eyes. It whispered of the

Dark God's need for her daughter. How could she focus on something so everyday when this event threatened her family?

With the scent of Ari's ointment still in the air, Lilly forsook her warp on the loom. She would find no comfort there. She paced the room, from the front door to the rear door, and back again. She passed the table, the breakfast dishes forgotten there.

Why today? Of all the days for the Dark God to propose—and Lillybet did not doubt her daughter's story—why did he have to propose today?

Today was the day Lilly planned to get Mikal back.

From afar, Lillybet had watched her son grow into a strapping youth. Sure, it was under the foster parentage of Marta Innkeeper, possibly Lilly's worst enemy but she could not fault Marta or Tam Innkeeper for raising her son into a decent human being.

She did wholly blame Marta for poisoning the Council against her. At least twice a year, Lillybet applied to the council to support her in the return of her son. And always something happened that prevented them from agreeing.

It was as if the demons wanted her to fail.

Weeks could go by without a single angel or demon showing up. Lilly could relax, maybe too much. Then, when she'd dropped her guard and became complacent, they'd appear, sliding along those gossamer Lines that connected everything and everyone. They'd rush in and startle her, and she'd scream.

That was how she'd learned, as a child, that not everyone could see demons.

And now Adrastea had seen the Dark God himself. At the very least, she'd inherited her mother's abilities. At worst? This, Lilly could not see. Why would the Dark God want her daughter? She was a country lass who, until today, had not displayed a glimmer of talent. Surely Mira would have sensed something before now, had that been true? And if she had, would Mira have offered to take Adrastea when Joe died?

Would the village have let her? Lilly had always believed that Ari took on Adrastea because of Natan. She'd never considered there might have been another reason.

It was not until the shadows of the afternoon lengthened that Lilly settled her determination. She would not let this strange turn of events disrupt the rest of today. She had a plan, one even Marta couldn't counter with an argument. There wasn't much she could do about her daughter's situation at the moment but at least she could act on behalf of her son before anyone else learned about Adrastea.

Sunset came. Village Council would be starting soon. There, people shared their good news, aired their grievances, and put forth their petitions. Today was the day she planned on presenting hers. She had rehearsed her approach, going over potential arguments in her head, time and time again, coming up with solutions to any 'concern' Marta might have.

Lillybet had proven herself stable for the past year, without a single incident that could be held against her. It had been difficult, not jumping in startlement when demons or angels appeared.

The village had to grant her petition now.

Maybe. If it wasn't for the events of today... Lillybet shoved that to the back of her head. Part of keeping a secret meant not thinking about it. Focus on Mikal, not Adrastea. And by all means, do not think of the Dark God, she admonished herself. The last thing Lillybet wanted was another visit from demons.

Natan Mayor held Village Council one evening a week in the common room of the Inn. Tam and Marta Innkeeper made a special point of letting everyone know how generous they were in allowing everyone to meet there. They went so far as to have dinner on offer, for those who wished to pay for it.

The inn was the tallest building in Sacred Spring, boasting a whole three stories of well-kept clapboard. A porch spanned the whole front. The inn dominated the village green, looming even taller than the smithy. Lilly could see the inn from her front porch, though most other houses were hidden by the trees on the hill. She took one final breath for courage and left her cottage.

The sun had sunk beyond the mountains, yet twilight lingered. As she walked down the dusty road to the village green, Lilly watched the bobbing lights of lanterns draw nigh. Many villagers were coming tonight, converging on the brightly-lit inn. Lillybet knocked the dust off her shoes before she climbed the steps of the porch and entered the building.

Trestle tables and their chairs crowded the common room of the inn, every seat taken. People crowded the benches along the walls, shoulder-to-shoulder. Even the staircase was full of people too slow to score a seat at a table or bench. Was nearly every villager and outlier present? Lillybet swallowed her anxiety.

An empty fireplace dominated one end of the room. In front of it a few Farmers and the Millers huddled together, their loud conversation a too-bright contrast to Lilly's anxiety. Two doorways stood opposite the front, leading to the kitchens in the back. The doors remained open to catch the canyon breezes once the sun went down.

No children attended, for this was not their business. The only children present were the Innkeepers', to serve refreshment to those who wished it, and to collect their coin.

Lillybet approached Natan's table and scratched her name the best she could. Joe tried to teach her letters, but it never really sank in. Anything else she had learned had left her long since. Natan sat there, dressed in his official robes as Mayor. During these times, he was not her brother.

"Lilly," he warned, "is this about...?"

Lilly sniffed. "Oh, please. I am a woman of my word." She drew herself up straight. "I have issues about my son."

Natan nodded. "I meant to talk to you earlier today about Mikal. But with what happened with..." He couldn't say his own niece's name.

Lilly frowned. Of all the people here, he should have supported her the most. "Does that mean I should stop fighting? I've been good for years now."

He shook his head in resignation. "It's not about that—"

"Whose side are you on, Natan?"

His answer was ready. "Mikal's."

Lilly turned away from him, so he couldn't see the tears welling in her eyes.

"Lilly, wait."

Unable to face the Mayor, she held up a hand to his face. It wasn't fair. Marta had had her son for more than ten years now. And always some excuse as to why she wouldn't give him back. He wasn't Marta's son! She had plenty, so why would she want one more? Lillybet stalked off.

Natan should have been her brother—and Mikal's uncle—before he was Mayor.

But then, he was Mayor. Mayors were not to show preferential treatment for anyone, even family. This was why Mayors never married. Her gaze flickered towards Ari, sitting on a bench well away from Natan.

Ari sat on the other side of the room. For official functions it would be unseemly for her to sit with Natan, considering their unofficial relationship. As long as they didn't openly flaunt it, the others were willing to turn a blind eye.

Mayors never married but that didn't stop her brother from loving Ari. Lillybet felt Ari's gaze on her. The Healer beckoned for her to come over and join her on the bench—an offer Lilly gratefully accepted. Ari would support her, even if Natan didn't.

Lillybet scowled as she passed Marta, who was filling her reluctant neighbor's ear with poison. Natan hadn't mentioned as much but Lilly would be very surprised if Marta hadn't been trying to pressure him into taking one of her sons as apprentice. She had already tried pushing her daughters onto Mira. She once toyed with the possibility of making an offer to Marta to claim one of her children as a weaver's apprentice, not in seriousness but just to annoy the woman.

Even Ari was not safe from Marta's insistence. Adrastea had been a journeyman for several years. Ari should have taken on another apprentice by now.

Adrastea wasn't present, although she had every right as an adult. "Where's Adrastea?" Lilly asked Ari.

Ari sat up and looked about. "Took her time over dinner, so I left her behind. Thought she'd be here by now."

"You took her away so quickly, I..." Lilly sighed. "Is she all right?"

Ari shook her head. "She needs time."

Lilly saw Mira on the other side of the room. As village Priestess, she had a right to sit next to the Mayor. Mira would support her petition this year. Mira had no clue of what Lilly was going to say but Lilly knew that this time Mira would stand for her.

Natan rose and knocked on his table. "I welcome you all to the Village Council," he shouted.

Immediately the buzz of neighbors chatting with neighbor settled down. People shuffled in their seats to face the Mayor. He repeated himself, his voice much lower.

Natan consulted the slate. "Because of the sheer number of petitions, ooh, about twenty, I ask that you please be succinct. I have yet to cook my dinner and would like to do so before I must cook my breakfast." This brought a few good-natured chuckles, and a snort of disapproval from Marta. No doubt she's insulted, Lilly thought, that Natan did not choose to eat supper here. Good.

"First name on the slate is Willem Tanner."

"No, it's not!" spat Marta. "We put our names down first!"

But old, frail Willem Tanner, with the aid of his journeyman Jon

Tanner, had risen, making his way forward. "That it may be that you put your names down first but I put my name at the top of the list," his voice creaked. "I thought it best we start with some good news."

Lilly allowed herself a bit of smugness at Willem's cleverness. She'd always liked him.

Jon Tanner escorted his old master to the front of the room, where Natan provided him with a chair.

"I'll be brief," Willem said without sitting down. "I'm retiring." Jon helped him back to his former seat.

"What?" scoffed Marta, jumping to her feet. "That's it?" Tam, still remaining silent, put out a hand to his wife but she ignored him.

Willem didn't rise to her anger. "I could dress it up in flowery language, but Natan Mayor said to keep it short. I'm old. I'm retiring. I want to spend what time I have left with Amarice." His granddaughter was the only living family he had left, her mother and grandmother having died in childbirth.

"That's not what I meant!" Marta did not back down. Tam tugged at Marta's skirts to no avail. Lillybet rolled her eyes. Would the woman never shut up?

Lilly saw Amarice, Willem's granddaughter, a portly lass who resembled her dead mother so very much. She leaned over to her grandfather and hissed in his ear.

He whispered back.

Whatever he'd said, she was not happy about it. More secrets, then.

Amarice sat back, turning into the arms of her husband Marlon Poulter for comfort.

Lillybet glanced over to Ari. Marlon was her nephew; did Ari know what was going on? Ari studied Amarice with a slight frown on her face. Lillybet's own thoughts began to tumble. Why would he want to spend more time with Amarice? He could have said the whole family. But he just said Amarice.

Natan's voice broke through Lillybet's thoughts. "I refuse to hear any protests over his retirement. It's not something we vote on. It's something we accept and congratulate." Lillybet watched his hands clench tight on his patience. He really should have eaten dinner before he came. "Jon Tanner is more than capable of carrying on the work, as he's got several apprentices and another journeyman to help him."

"I didn't mean that either!" Marta snapped.

"Marta, we shall speak of this later. Sit down."

She didn't but she did keep her tongue. She turned away with a sound of impatient disgust.

Natan looked at the list. "Anyhow, it seems you're next. And this had better be more important than whether or not you approve of the retirement of an old man."

"It is," replied Marta coldly. "It concerns Peter's incident in the rain barrel."

Natan consulted the list. "Big Peter and Sheelagh are later on the list. Defer it until then."

Sheelagh spoke out of turn. "We just wanted to thank everybody—"

"It's not about Peter," Marta spat at them. She looked over to where Lillybet sat. "I have issue with Ari."

Ari looked up, startled. "Me?" Her face flushed.

Marta pointed an accusing finger at her. "Peter's life almost didn't get saved because of the interference of your apprentice."

Lilly's breath caught in her throat. What did Marta know? And where did she get off calling Adrastea an apprentice? Her daughter was a full journeyman, thank you.

Mira spoke. "This is a serious accusation, Marta. What are you implying?"

Marta glanced at Mira, surprised. She hadn't expected Mira to protest Marta's actions.

While Marta's voice was a bit quieter, her words lost none of their sting. "When you were at the rain tank trying to help Peter, Adrastea interfered. She shoved you away from the tank." Marta turned to the village. "Peter could have died because Adrastea stopped Mira from doing her job."

Lilly sprang to her feet. "That's not true!"

Ari also rose but to pull Lilly back. She whispered in her ear. "Let it be. Mira will take care of this."

Lilly whispered back, "Marta knows!"

"We don't know that."

"Then why is she saying this?"

"Spite, of course. Nothing more."

"I won't let her." Lillybet turned from Ari but Ari grabbed her arm.

Ari said, louder, "Lilly. Sit down." She forcibly pulled her back down to the bench. Then she hissed into her ear. "Just watch."

"But—"

Ari surreptitiously pointed at Mira. "Watch and listen."

Lilly followed her finger, to see the diminutive priestess facing off against broad-hipped Marta, who stood more than a head taller.

Mira didn't back down. "What makes you thinks she interfered? Quite the contrary; she saved me. That is her job. If she hadn't pushed me out of the way before the barrel broke, I could have been seriously injured. Did you see the injury on her face? She got that saving me."

Lillybet put her fingertips over her mouth. If she'd hedged the truth like that, and got caught, her mother would have spanked her.

"That's not how it happened," Marta accused Natan. "You know it. You're letting family get in the way of being Mayor."

Natan rose. "Marta, I'm not defending anybody."

Everyone became silent.

Natan pointed a beefy finger at her. "Look. You made your accusation and Mira, the true aggrieved party, answered it. Now be silent or I shall throw you out."

"You can't throw me out of my own inn!"

"Yes, I can. Tam can speak for you on any other issues you may have."

Marta's brother, Mutch Miller, who had been sitting with the rest of the Innkeeper clan, groaned. "Aw, Marta, shuddup!"

Marta whirled and punched her brother in an uncharacteristic loss of control. Marta never punched anyone in public before. The villagers gasped and shuffled back. Heated discussions sometimes happened during council but actual fisticuffs?

Something was not right with Marta.

The hairs rose on the back of Lillybet's neck. As her heart thumped, she fought the urge to leap to her feet, flee the inn and retreat to the safety of her protected cottage.

Lillybet knew that feeling—something or someone lurked along the Lines. As soon as she had the feeling, it disappeared, and the world settled into a sense of peace. That wasn't a demon. Lilly knew demons. An angel then? At a fistfight? Why?

Ari drew in a sharp breath of realization. "Of course. Stupid woman. She should have told me. Save us all some aggravation," she muttered to herself.

Lillybet studied Marta. What did Ari mean? Marta and Mutch squared off, neither one backing down.

Non-participants backed away, but Millie Miller joined the

argument, siding with her husband against her sister-in-law. Maybe if she was lucky, Natan would throw Marta out. Lillybet could get on with her petition without any interference.

Natan strode over, after stumbling on the hem of his robes, and grabbed Marta's dark braid. "Tam!" he roared. "Marta! Outside, now." Marta stumbled as Natan yanked on her braid again. But Mutch and Millie did not pursue the advantage for Natan glared at them. "You stay right here. I have issues with you!"

With that, he escorted Marta outside, followed by Tam, who did not look too pleased.

Nobody followed them to the door but those sitting next to the windows leaned closer to hear what might be said. A few family members comforted Mutch, as did Ari, who pronounced his bloody lip not too bad.

Mira, meanwhile, had taken Natan's seat at the table. She rapped smartly, then when nobody paid attention, shouted at them. "Everybody! Sit down!" Reluctantly, they returned to their seats. If anyone had authority in the village after Natan, it would be Mira. "This is no way to conduct council!" She took Natan's chair. "Now, let us behave like civilized people.

Civilized people? Hardly. Lilly looked around. Natan had refused to support her. Ari was still muttering under her breath. Marta starting an actual knock-down-drag-out fight, and Natan shouting. Was this the Dark One's influence?

Mira drew up as much as her short height would allow her. She cleared her throat. "Willem Tanner. We are all pleased to hear of your retirement and know that Jon will do well as Master Tanner."

The villagers nodded in agreement, some even saying, "Hear, hear."

"Fine!" shouted Marta outside, and all fell silent in Council. Then a red-faced Natan and a subdued Tam returned, without Marta. Mira relinquished Natan's chair, and he sat down as if tired. "Marta is hereby banned from weekly Council for the next two weeks. Tam, I've a good mind to dismiss any further petitions you may have today."

Tam, who had returned to his seat, rose again, penitently. "Please, Mayor. I have only one thing. I feel you will agree we need to talk about it." He hurried on, just in case Natan was going to cut him off. "Mira needs an apprentice."

Lilly hissed low and turned to Ari, but Ari waved her finger before her mouth.

Natan said, "I'm listening."

Tam held up his hands to ward off bad luck. "I am saying nothing more of the situation at the smithy, but we could have lost Mira." He turned to the priestess. "We have discussed this before, but you need to train an apprentice. We lose you, we're all lost."

Others murmured assent.

"Mira," said Natan, "I'm afraid I must agree. Will you take on an apprentice?"

Mira stood. "You have pressured me before to take on an apprentice, and I haven't." She drew in a breath. "In light of, er, recent events," her eyes flickered to Ari and Lillybet, "I may acquiesce to your requests. However," she held up a hand at their collective sigh of relief, "I refuse to choose an apprentice from this village.

That got people murmuring. A chuckle of pleasure rose in Lilly's chest. How wise of Mira.

The priestess continued. "Have you never wondered why I didn't choose an apprentice, even though I've had everyone's daughters and sons offered to me? Being a priest requires a certain talent, a gift from the Light. I've known you all my life. I'm sorry to say I've never found any child with enough talent."

Lillybet knew that if Marta was here, she'd protest what level of talent was required. And before the rain barrel incident, Lillybet, too, would have been hard-pressed to accept Mira's judgement. But she knew differently now.

Natan suggested, "Mira, could you ask Carles from Crossroads? Perhaps he could offer one of his apprentices."

Mira considered this. "I'll write to him tomorrow."

And that was the end of that discussion.

For the rest of council, everyone kept their petitions succinct and discussions kept to a minimum. Even Big Peter and Sheelagh kept their thanks short. No one else wanted to risk Natan's wrath. Marta had created enough trouble for them all today.

Lillybet was last, before Natan's final words.

She rose when bidden and approached the front of the room. She drew a deep breath, not so much from nervousness but to slow down her racing thoughts. "My son Mikal will be fourteen soon. He's been available for apprenticeship for three years now, but nobody has made an offer for him." She sucked in another breath. Now was it.

Now, she would issue a petition that nobody could deny without good reason. Marta was gone, and Tam would not risk further mayoral wrath.

The path cleared. She had found a way of getting her son returned to her.

"I hereby request that if nobody makes an offer for my son before his fourteenth birthday, I shall take him on as a weaver's apprentice and he can join the family business."

She did not look at Tam but looked at everyone else, half in dare, half in warning.

Nobody said anything, pro or con, except Natan.

"Oh." His voice carried disappointment.

She turned to Natan, anger rising in her chest. "What?" She balled her fists. For a moment, she understood why Marta had attacked Mutch. Sometimes brothers needed a pounding.

He hesitated, licking his lips. "I'm sorry, Lilly. I meant to tell you earlier. It's been a busy day." He glanced around at all assembled. "I was thinking of making an offer for Mikal. If he is willing, I would take him on as mayorprentice."

Well, she hadn't been expecting that. "You?" How long had this been on his mind, and why hadn't he said something earlier?

"Assuming he agrees. You do know what this means."

She did. Mayors, like priestesses, served the community and none else. At the end of their apprenticeship, mayorprentices had to make their final oaths. They were not allowed families, lest they put the good of the family above the good of the community. Even though everyone looked the other way when it came to the situation between Natan and Ari, should Ari have ever fallen pregnant, things would have changed. But that had not been a problem.

"It would mean the end of our family line," Natan said.

"But there's still Adrastea," Lillybet blurted, then in horror she covered her mouth. "Oh, I'm sorry Natan. I shouldn't have—"

"That is not the issue," Natan said too quickly. "This is about Mikal. The point is whether or not he would accept. He would then come live with me, you know."

Lilly shrugged. "I am used to an empty home. Though I, too, should consider taking on apprentices." She glanced towards Mira, then back to Natan.

Natan spoke: "I ask your permission to ask Mikal for this apprenticeship."

"I give it," Lilly said with breathless relief. In joy, she flounced back to her seat and eagerly grasped Ari's hands. While he would not be returning to her, he would be returning to family. Mikal was away from the Innkeepers.

Natan did not ask if anyone wished to discuss this and nobody protested this obvious oversight of protocol.

"Since that was what I wished to discuss, this Council is— No, wait." Natan rose and jabbed his finger at the villagers. "Everyone's behavior tonight as been appalling. I will brook no bullying and no brawling in further meetings. Anyone who cannot behave as adults will be banned from the meeting like the squabbling children they are. Mutch, Millie and Tam, I wish to speak with you privately, after. This council is dismissed."

Chapter 4

Adrastea sat alone at Ari's dinnertable, her bowl of food before her untouched. Ari had pestered her all afternoon with questions until Adrastea finally snapped and told her to go away. Eventually, Ari gave up getting any response from her journeyman and departed for Village Council. Adrastea remained behind, her head full of questions and her heart empty.

No, she was not all right. She'd met the God of the Dark and he wanted her for his bride. The whole afternoon had passed in a haze. Evening fell, taking all natural light with it. Only the lantern on Ari's table illuminated Adrastea's world.

For as long as she could remember, Adrastea had been raised on a steady diet of Mira Priestess' weekly sermons, all delivered personally at this very table. The village of Sacred Spring did not have a chapel like the town of Crossroads, so every house became its own sanctuary. Many times had Mira stood at the head of this table, her sacred glass lifted high. "As the light shines through this water, let the Light shine through me," she would say.

She had grown up to believe in a God of the Light, a benevolent She/He who blessed the world. She'd heard whispered tales of a God of the Dark but had dismissed them as ghost stories, told only to scare children.

Until now.

The God of the Dark was real. If he was real, then so was the Light, she reasoned. He wouldn't have called himself the God of the Dark otherwise.

She stared at the lantern. Let the light shine through me?" she wondered. Even now, the pool of light from the lantern on the table seemed unreal. Adrastea lifted her hand, passing it between her and the light, to cast a shadow across her eyes.

He wanted her. Why? Ari kept pestering her for answers. She had none to give.

She stroked a thumb along the black line that marred her cheek. Ari's bandage hadn't been needed. Her wound wasn't a laceration or even a burn. It was as smooth as her unmarked cheek. The blackness didn't wash off but appeared to be embedded in her very skin.

While it had stung when he had given it to her, the pain did not last long, if one could call it pain. It had been more of a pressure, a throbbing, as if the line wanted her to know it was there. He said it would mark her, so she would not forget, and others would know.

What would people say when they saw it? Would they know what it meant? Did Mira know? She moved to the door and out onto Ari's porch. As the sun set, the canyon breezes blew, lending a distinct touch of chill to the late summer evening.

Adrastea reached inside for a cloak hanging on the peg rack by the door. Her hand closed on soft fabric—Mor-Lath's cloak. She hesitated. Her mother had never woven anything so fine. So soft and warm.

She drew it out and studied it. She'd never seen such a fiber before. She lowered her face into the folds of the fabric. And the scent. Her heart beat faster as she inhaled. Spicy, masculine, addictive. Her hands clenched the fabric closer.

She should never have brought it back to Ari's house. Reluctantly, she put it back on the peg. Tomorrow, she'd do something about it, though it panged her to imagine the loss of the item. Maybe she'll give it to Ari and let Ari take care of it. Better that way.

With a touch of resignation, Adrastea selected her common brown healer's cloak. With the chill warded off her shoulders, she stood on the porch and watched the villagers gather. In the distance, under the twilit sky, lanterns bobbed along. Everyone would come today, those who had witnessed Little Peter and the water tank. There would be much to say about that.

Adrastea looked down the road that led out of the village. Next to Ari's house sat Willem Carpenter's modest workshop. Beyond that lay Mira's cottage, then a few more houses, and that was the end of the village. The Millers lived further down, where the sacred spring creek tumbled down a hill to power their mill. Had anyone been out to tell them the happenings of the day?

Once she was old enough to attend, Adrastea had always gone to

Village Council. If one wished to know the true business of the villagers, that was where one went. Matters were discussed, and decisions made. Any villager could have his say, provided he write his name on Natan's slate. Natan kept an orderly Council.

Adrastea debated. Should she stay, or should she go? No doubt there would be questions if she showed her marked face. But would her absence raise more questions?

No. Better to know what was said, than to rely on fickle ignorance. Besides what would happen if she stayed home? What if he found her there? There was no one to stop him, should he decide to whisk her away.

The thought made her shudder. It propelled her feet off the wooden porch and through the honeysuckle-scented front garden. There was safety in numbers.

As she hurried along the dusty road, she regretted not bringing the lantern. The sun had set, leaving the land in darkness. No other lights bobbed about; everyone else had shown up to Council on time. She hastened along.

Several lanterns hung on the porch of the Inn, guiding her to the meeting. As she approached, she saw quite a number of figures gathered at the inn. That was odd. Had so many people shown up there was not room to receive them?

No. As she squinted, she recognized the group. Several youths, old enough to be on their own but too young to attend council, lurked about the porch, listening at the open windows. Did their parents know they were here?

Adrastea slowed. When she was underage, she had lurked by those windows from time to time, keeping as still and quiet as she could. She'd never been caught. Few children thought to eavesdrop then.

Today, there were plenty.

A few saw her approach. They scattered, in case she grassed on them.

But not all ran. Martine, off the porch and near the alleyway between the inn and the shop, paused. "It's only Adrastea," she called.

Only Adrastea? Martine Innkeeper was only a few years younger than she. By the end of summer, she would be old enough to attend Council officially. Until then, the only time she got to know what was going on was when her mother drafted her into service for the night. At least Adrastea could walk right in through that door and not be turned away.

Her stomach clenched. But what if they knew about him?

A few of the braver children came out of hiding and resumed their eavesdropping.

Before Adrastea could step onto the porch, Martine moved in front of her. Martine's little sister Salle clung to her skirts, a thumb in her mouth.

Adrastea stopped. How much did they know?

Martine didn't bother with niceties. "How'd you get that?" she asked, gesturing at the black line. Her voice was low.

Adrastea raised a hand to her face. "Standing too close to dangerous things."

Her brother Mikal was there, crouching low beneath a window with his foster brother Tom. When he saw his sister, he came down off the porch. Tom remained huddled under the window to catch the gossip.

Mikal nodded to her in greeting. He gestured at the door of the Inn. "Uncle Natan's not happy with Mother. Think she'll petition for me again?"

"Of course. It's the end of summer, isn't it?" Every summer around Mikal's birthday, their mother put forth a petition to have her son returned to her, instead of living as Marta's foster son. Every year, for some reason or another, she was denied by the Village Council. "You know, you could always just come home."

"Home?" He sounded genuinely confused. He'd known no other home than the inn.

She looked up at the tall, cold building. "You don't have to live here, you know. We all know what Marta's like. You can just leave."

Mikal squirmed. "I dunno." He refused to meet Adrastea's eyes. Mikal stood out from the Innkeeper brood, for he shared the same dark coloring Adrastea inherited from their father Joe, whereas all the Innkeepers sported the same light brown hair that streaked with blonde in the summer.

"You know how much Mother misses you."

"But... she's strange. Ma—er—Marta thinks she's a witch."

"She's not— Wait. You call Marta 'Ma'?"

"Sorry," he mumbled, shoving his hands into his pockets. "Habit."

"She's not your mother!"

"Yeah, she is!" This came from Salle. "Ma is our ma."

Adrastea frowned. "But she's not Mikal's."

Little Salle looked all perplexed. "Course she is."

Martine shoved Salle behind her. "Salle, this isn't your business."

Spite blossomed in Adrastea's heart. Adrastea lived with Ari, had always lived with her since her father died but she devoted time to her mother. Lillybet loved her daughter, sometimes to smotherness but Adrastea could never deny how much she'd been cherished. It was as if every hour she spent with her mother enveloped her in a warm, tangible blanket of love.

But Mikal had been denied to Lillybet. Adrastea had felt a pang from her mother whenever Mikal had been mentioned. "What if my Mother wants Mikal to live with her now?"

Salle shook her head. "But Mikal's supposed to live with us. Ma said so. She said that Li'bet couldn't keep her eyes up and—" Salle cut off short when Martine gave her sister a cuff on the head. Salle began to howl in protest.

Raised voices from the Inn caught the Innkeeper children's attention. Martine applied a hand to Salle's mouth to quieten her. Salle obliged, not because she listened to her older sister but because she probably heard what all the others had.

"That's Ma," said Tom. "Let's go see what's up."

Adrastea hadn't heard anything, but she followed along. No doubt the others were so attuned to their mother's voice, that they learned those subtle danger signals that told them to either pay attention or make themselves scarce. Marta's impatience and resulting temper were as famous as Lillybet's bouts with darkness.

Adrastea joined them. Why didn't she go to council with Ari? She felt like a youth again, skulking about like this. Walking in late as one's ears were burning was very bad form. "What have they been talking about?"

Martine shrugged. "Arguing, mostly. I think Little Peter's accident has made everyone short-tempered."

By now other youths gathered around the inn. Those present murmured gossip to the latecomers.

"Hey," whispered Tom, in a prime window position. "They're talking about you, Adrastea."

Oh, this she had to hear.

Martine waved to everyone else to be quiet. They all gathered around the windows. Inside, Mira gave Marta a dressing down over the events earlier that day. Marta was right; everyone was short-tempered. Mira's anger floated out the window, little sharp lines of barely-reigned temper. Very much unlike the diminutive priestess. Then again, Mira's faith had been shaken today.

Martine whispered to Adrastea. "Did you really save Mira? Is that how you got that?" She gestured to the line on Adrastea's face.

Before Adrastea could answer, they heard someone shout for Marta to shut up, an altercation, then the angry voice of Natan.

"Uh oh," said Adrastea. She recognized the angry, mayoral voice of her uncle. "He's coming."

All the children bugged out, disappearing around the corners of the inn. Some even dived under the porch. Adrastea and the Innkeepers scrambled into the narrow alley between the inn and the storehouse, sliding into the twilight shadows just as Natan burst out of the inn door. A furious Marta and a subdued Tam followed. Adrastea, who had the best vantage, watched as her uncle spun his large frame to face Marta.

"Now you listen here," ordered the Mayor. Natan Mayor was far scarier than Uncle Natan. Even Adrastea still shook when she faced his wrath. "I've had it with your bossy ways and your stupid accusations. You have no foundation. Adrastea did nothing, you hear me? She did nothing. You leave her alone or you and I will have more than words."

Adrastea glanced back to the others hidden in the alley. Not only were the Innkeepers there but a few more children as well. They all looked at Adrastea, their unspoken questions in their eyes. As burning as their curiosity was, it did not yet outweigh their fear of discovery. Nobody made a peep.

Marta was not to be cowed. "It is my inn and I shall say what I will!"

"But it is my Council. You will obey the laws of this village and this Council. Just because we meet here does not give you sovereign rights over this village. We can just as easily meet elsewhere.

"And as for your other actions, I hereby ban you for two weeks."

A susurrus broke out among the alleyway children. What had she done to warrant a banishment?

Marta let out a squeak of indignation. "Ban me, and I shall refuse you entry to my inn!"

"So be it. We can always meet somewhere else." He turned to Tam, who quickly put up his hands.

"I have no quarrel with you, Natan."

"Control your wife, Tam Innkeeper, or I shall ban her permanently."

Beside her, Martine drew in a sharp breath. Adrastea had never seen her uncle so angry that he'd ban someone permanently. Why was he in such high dudgeon?

With that, he pushed past Marta and stalked back into the meeting. Adrastea let out her breath.

"Bastard!" Marta shrieked. She made to follow but Tam grabbed her forcefully, spat some words at her that Adrastea couldn't catch. Marta stalked off, away from the inn. She paused long enough to pick up a rock to hurl, but her husband had already dodged inside. The rock slammed against the side of the Inn.

So much for going to Council. To show up now would be unthinkable. Of what had Marta accused her?

The children waited until Marta had moved far enough away from the scene before emerging from their hiding spots. But instead of gathering in front of the inn, they all scurried to the darkness of the storehouse porch, where they could possibly overhear any more interesting items, yet stay out of the way of both trouble and being seen.

"What was that all about?" someone asked through the darkness. It sounded like Truesie Taylorprentice, who was Martine's age. "What did you do, Adrastea?"

"Nothing," she replied too hastily. "Why do you think I did anything?"

The children gathered around her.

"Because of what your uncle said," replied Tom.

"Because of what Marta said to Mira," said Truesie.

Adrastea swallowed. "I helped Mira. Nothing more. The tank—" she caught her breath.

Martine didn't say anything but stood by her brother, Salle's hand held tightly. Mikal stayed back, as if afraid the taint of his sister-by-birth would affect him.

Truesie wasn't about to drop the subject. "My ma says that Martine's ma says that your ma..." she leaned forward, as the other youth did too, "dabbles," she whispered dramatically.

"I don't know what you mean." Adrastea truly did not.

Tom grabbed Martine's sleeve. "Ma!" he warned. Tom had been keeping a watch out for wherever his mother had gone. They knew she'd be back. And if she hadn't yet found a scapegoat on which to vent her anger, she would no doubt vent it on one of her children.

Faster than the rest, the Innkeeper children had vanished. The others left almost as quickly. Adrastea slipped out around the store, only to see the angry shadow of Marta stalking this way.

Suddenly a man's hand closed around her face. He jerked her back against his chest and held with his other arm around her waist. Her heart quickened in panic. She struggled to free herself. Her scream came out muffled against his warm hand.

"Shh," warned Mor-Lath into her ear. "Stand still and she won't see you."

A vibration rolled over her skin. It was as if every speck of her either wanted to sing, or to dissolve into nothingness. The warmth of his body pressed against her. "I will protect you," he promised. His aura flowed about her, making the hairs on her skin stand up.

Her fearfulness ebbed away. She nodded her head.

Only then did he release her mouth and pull her back against him. He stood there against the front of the storehouse, holding her. She clutched at his arm about her waist as if to still her wildly-beating heart.

They were in plain sight. Marta would see them, and then what would she say? Adrastea's fear squeaked in her throat. She swallowed it down.

But Mor-Lath murmured reassuringly in her ears. "She won't see you. There's nothing she can do to you. I would move the whole world to protect you."

Marta came around the corner and stalked right past them. Adrastea let out the breath she didn't know she had held. She'd been so sure they would have been caught.

All the youths had scattered, so there was not a soul to be seen. Marta slowed her stalking. She approached the window of the Inn. She slunk along the wall to eavesdrop at the window. Her fists gathered tightly against her chest as she overheard the Council from which she'd been banned.

"She's up to no good," Adrastea finally whispered, for she could bear the silence no longer.

"I know." His other arm slipped around her waist and pressed his face into her hair, inhaling deeply.

Adrastea wanted to tell him to stop his distracting behavior and focus on the matter at hand." Why does she hate my mother and me so much?"

"Your mother is unpredictable. That is all. Oh, and she objected to your father."

"Why? What was wrong with my father?"

"He was unpredictable too. Your Marta hates that. She is a woman who prefers order to her world." Then he pointed to the Inn. "Meeting's over."

Marta lit out, disappearing into the alleyway between the inn and storehouse. Woe betide the young who had sheltered there.

Mor-Lath released Adrastea. He grasped her arm before she made good her escape. "I have a gift for you, my dear. I trust you can read?"

She nodded. He placed a black-leather book into her hands. "Read this and keep it our little secret." His finger brushed gently across her lips.

In a breath he was gone, leaving nothing but the darkness of night where he once stood. Light fell from behind her. She turned, to see people emerging from the Inn, their lanterns casting stark glares of light across everything.

Adrastea hid the book under her cloak and fled home, all the way back to Ari's house. If what Martine had said was true, the villagers were turning against her as they had her mother.

Once inside the house, she turned up the lantern, dispelling all shadows. She sat at the table, placing the book before her.

What to do with it?

Mor-Lath wanted her to read it. What was it? Evil spells? The secrets of the universe?

This book, with its fine leather cover and gilt-edged pages, must be worth quite a bit. Her hand hovered over it. Maybe it was best to let Dark things be. The God of the Dark was Dark for a reason. No good could come of it.

Best to hide it for now. Adrastea climbed a few rungs of the ladder that led to the loft.

Ari returned before she could finish her ascent. "Adrastea, I'm back."

Adrastea jumped, fumbling the book as she grabbed the ladder to steady herself. The book fell to the floor with a loud thump, practically at Ari's feet.

The healer picked it up and opened it. Her eyes grew wide. "Adrastea?" she squeaked. "Where did you get this?"

Adrastea froze. "I..." She shrunk back down the ladder.

Ari's hands shook. "Have you been reading this?" Her voice tightened in her throat.

"It— it's not mine." The moment those words passed her lips, she knew it was an untruth. Of course, it was hers. He'd given it to her, hadn't he? But that didn't mean she wanted it.

"It has your name in it." Ari thumped the first page with her finger.

Adrastea leaned forward. There, on the first page, a beautifully-written dedication etched in gold. "To Adrastea, a betrothal gift for you, Mor-Lath."

Adrastea shrunk back against the wall, bumping into the cloaks that hung there. "I only got it tonight." Her fingers closed around a cloak. The fineness of the fabric told her which one she'd grasped. She let go of it as if it burned her skin. It fell off the hook.

"Mor-Lath was here?" Ari wavered as the blood drained from her face. "You let him into my home?"

"No." she protested. "It happened outside."

Ari hastened to the stove, jerked open the door and threw in the book. She slammed the stove door harder than she meant, the impact ringing through the iron.

"First, you will never allow Mor-Lath inside my home. Second, you will not go outside should he come calling. Third, you will refuse each and every gift he gives you." Her eyes narrowed. "He hasn't given you anything else, has he?"

Adrastea kicked the black cloak on the floor. "Um..." The word 'no' was on her lips but she couldn't let the lie out. In guilt, she picked up the cloak.

Ari scowled at her journeyman. Her gaze drifted to the bundle in Adrastea's arms. "What's that?" Fear tainted her voice. She snatched it from Adrastea's hands.

"No, Ari! Please!" She clung to the cloak.

They wrestled over the cloak. "You must have nothing to do with him, do you hear me? Nothing. It's too dangerous."

Adrastea could only nod. She let go. Ari was right.

Ari stuffed the cloak into the stove and closed the door. Only then, did she relax.

Adrastea retreated to the loft and her bed. Ari was right; Adrastea knew that. Still, it stung how she, Adrastea, wanted to keep those gifts.

In the loft it was still and private. The front of the loft Ari used for storage. The back she had curtained off and given to Adrastea all those years ago.

Adrastea couldn't sleep but lay awake in her low bed stuffed with straw. The cool evening breeze ebbed in through the window she'd opened earlier to let out the heat of the day.

Adrastea had never got a chance to see the title of the book. No doubt it was not anything good. It had frightened Ari something fierce. Still, for brief moment, it had been hers.

And why was Ari in a bad mood? Had something gone wrong at the meeting? Surely it wasn't because of the Marta incident, was it?

What had Marta said?

As sleep eluded her, she rolled out of bed to sit on the floor near the low window, staring out at the starry sky.

If the man who wanted to marry her hadn't been the God of the Dark, would Adrastea have accepted his attentions wholeheartedly?

It was not fair. Her head warred with her traitorous heart. A man finally takes enough interest to propose marriage, and he's the bloody Dark God.

She missed the luxurious cloak, no doubt ashes in the stove by now. "Really," she told herself, "I liked it because it was of fine make." Not because it had belonged to Mor-Lath. That was a silly thought, a foolish one. Even dangerous.

Ever since Ari had brought her home that afternoon, that cloak hung forgotten on the peg with all the others. Ari had never noticed it wasn't Adrastea's usual brown cloak. She and Mira had been too distracted by the events of the day to notice this new addition to the rack. A healer's cloak was not so much an item of clothing but a tool of the trade. Often, they were used to keep an injured person warm. Once, in Adrastea's experience, Ari had used it to staunch a serious hemorrhage and save a life.

Her cloak—Mor-Lath's cloak—which had hidden her state of undress at their first meeting, was gone, consumed by the fire. And the mystery book, also gone. Ari was perfectly in her rights to destroy these items, but it didn't make Adrastea feel more protected. If anything, she felt more vulnerable. Would Mor-Lath be displeased they had so readily disposed of his gifts?

Ari had fixed herself a tisane of who knew what and had retired to bed. So skilled was the healer with her lotions and potions that she would soon be fast asleep, despite the events of the day.

At the very least, she could have thought to have offered something to Adrastea.

She felt so lonely. As she watched the stars in the firmament, she cried her heart out to them. "Oh, Light!" she prayed. "What has happened to me?"

But She did not reply. Adrastea felt even lonelier than before.

ornament

A rooster crowed. Adrastea awoke cramped and chilled from having fallen asleep on the floor by her window. Only a rough blanket kept her warm. Dawn brightened the sky and her bedroom. Last night's crying had left its swollen footprints on her eyes.

She hurried down the ladder and finished lacing her bodice by the stove. Her fingers slowed as she tied her laces. She reached out tentatively to the stove.

It was still warm. That was odd.

Adrastea opened the cast iron door to rake out the ashes, only to find the stove full of an unburnt black cloak. She teased the cloak out with the fire poker, shaking the ash from it.

It had not burned. Quickly folding it and hiding it on the seat of a chair pushed under the table, Adrastea peeked again into the oven.

The book, likewise, remained undestroyed. It took up half the oven and had banked the fire naturally.

She inspected it after she pulled it out. It, too, had no mark. Ari would not be pleased.

What to do with it? Adrastea listened carefully to Ari's steady breathing through the door. It would not do to keep it here in Ari's home, where she could chance upon it again. There was only one place Adrastea could guarantee easy access to the book yet keep Ari and any other curious soul from discovering it—Lillybet's home.

Adrastea placed the book in the ash hod and stuffed the cloak around it. She covered them both with ashes from the fire. This, she set outside the back door, to await a time when she could carry it safely away. Ari would never think to look under the ashes of last night's fire, if she happened to see the hod before Adrastea could dispose of it. For the first time, Adrastea thanked the Light Ari hadn't taken on another apprentice, whose job it would have been to empty the ashes.

Adrastea built up a fire and filled the kettle with hot water for breakfast. She'd get all her morning chores done before disposing of the book and cloak.

A soft knock came from the back door. It startled Adrastea. She dropped the canister of tea she had fetched from the pantry. It hit the floor with a thunk but didn't spill open.

"Ari?" called a familiar voice.

Relief flooded her. Mira. "Door's open," she called but not too loud to wake Ari.

Mira eased herself in and gently shut the door behind her. She carried a bundle under her arm. "I saw the smoke from the chimney and knew someone was awake."

"Ari's not. She's... suffering." Adrastea glanced at the bottle on the table. "Tea?"

"Yes, please. I did not sleep well last night either."

"Did something bad happen at council last night? "Adrastea set three cups on the table. "One could hear Marta shrieking through the whole village. And Ari came home in a bad mood last night."

Mira thought for a moment, then shrugged. "On the contrary. With the exception of a scuffle, I thought things went..." Mira let her words trail off. "You should have been there. How are you feeling?" Mira sat down, placing a cloth-wrapped bundle on the table.

Adrastea ignored her question. "What's that?" Adrastea scooted an empty cup before Mira.

The priestess unwrapped it. "The Book of the Light. I've brought it for you to read."

Adrastea ran a hand over the brown leather cover of the book. She'd seen it once a week, always in the protective custody of Mira. As her source of knowledge, she used it to spiritually guide the village. When Adrastea's hand lit upon it, she could feel the same strength of power as had Mor-Lath's book, but it felt different, almost as if it were another flavor. If this was the Book of the Light, then was Mor-Lath's book the Book of the Dark? "I—" she hesitated. "I don't know."

"Adrastea, you need all the help you can get."

"Oh, it's not that. It's just that I know this is your prized possession. I know how expensive books are." She sighed, thinking of the book that Ari was so willing to burn. What Mira would have thought of Mor-Lath's book? Would she have burned it as well? When Ari had taught Adrastea to read, as part of her duties as a Healer, the apprentice learned her letters from pencil and slate. Only when she had mastered those, was she allowed to ink notes to the paper Ari made.

If she could make enough paper, could she could bind a book together? Not that she knew what she would put in it. Books were things of profound knowledge, of marvelous wonders beyond her scope.

Her heart yearned for a book—not the one before her but the one in the hod, the forbidden one. It disconcerted her. She'd not wanted a book before. Why that one?

Mira caressed her beautiful treasure. "I do desire that you read this, rather than my just telling you what's inside. Although," and Mira smiled, "I do confess that I will not be letting it out of my sight." She inspected her empty cup. "You make us some tea. Then I want you to read it to me."

Adrastea hesitated.

Worry lines creased Mira's forehead. "Adrastea, please. You must read it."

"I—"

The door to Ari's bedroom crashed open, startling them both. Ari stumbled out the door, hair wild, her clothes from the night before looking like she had been dragged through the underbrush backwards. She scrambled up, desperately reaching for the table. "She doesn't have to read anything!" She seized the book.

"Ari! No!" Adrastea shrieked.

Mira let out a cry of surprise.

Adrastea tackled her mistress to the floor. The Book of the Light hit Ari in the chin, before it went flying across the room to hit a shelf. The jars and sundry rattled but nothing fell and broke.

Mira sobbed and ran to her precious book. Too late; the damage was done. One page was horribly crumpled and had a tear near the spine.

Adrastea let up her mistress unapologetically. "What are you doing?" she cried at the older woman. "That was Mira's book, not mine." She had never dared to stand up to Ari before like this but something within her urged her to defend the truth.

Ari rose to her feet, her eyes shining brightly. She slapped her journeyman across the face. Adrastea spun from the force of it, crying out.

"Stop it! Stop it!" cried Mira, who cradled her open book as if it were an injured animal.

Ari breathed heavily but did not advance on her journeyman. Adrastea had collapsed into a chair, hand to offended cheek. That slap stung, almost as bad as the line on her other cheek had when she received it. What was wrong with Ari?

"You don't understand!" cried Ari. "It... I—" Her eyes fell on the worn brown cover of Mira's Book of the Light. Ari looked mortified. She sank to the chair.

Mira sat down opposite Adrastea and smoothed out her book on the table, best she could. She let out a little sob of her own when she inspected the unfixable tear.

Wordlessly, Adrastea pushed the canister towards Ari. With the same silence, Ari took it and spooned leaves into the teapot.

Adrastea fetched the kettle before it whistled.

"Mira, I'm sorry," Ari said, more to her teacup. She cradled her head in her hands. "It has not been a good night."

"Can't you stop drinking? "Mira asked. Seeing that the page was as smooth as she could get it, though it would never be as good as it originally was, Mira closed the book carefully, to help press it back into shape. She laid her cloth over the top of the book and folded her hands over it. "Now, what is going on here? I swear, the whole village has gone crazy. I thought at least you would have been spared."

Neither Ari nor Adrastea said anything. Mira waited. Minutes passed and still nothing. "Well? "

Ari drew deep breath. "The Dark God was here last night."

Mira let out a slow breath. She checked the bottle. Empty. "Ari? Any more of this?"

Ari went into the stillroom and returned with another bottle, cool from the cellar.

Mira had poured them all tea. After accepting the bottle from Ari, she poured a healthy dollop into Ari's cup. "Hair of the dog." Ari stared at Mira with shadowed, grateful eyes. "But no more," the priestess cautioned.

Mira had her tea plain. She made a face; unsweetened tea tasted flat. Alas, there was no honey pot on the table. "It is upsetting to find the two of you at odds."

Ari, having drunk most of her tea, glared at Adrastea. "She has been consorting with him again. Alone, I might add."

Adrastea returned her sullen look. "I did not ask for it."

"I would be more concerned," interjected Mira, "if you had."

"He gave her a book, Mira." Ari poured herself a bit more tea and sweetened it with the bottle. "He came into my home and gave her a book."

"He didn't come in," Adrastea insisted. "I was outside, on my way to Council."

Ari frowned. "I thought you said you didn't want to go to Council."

Mira drew on her store of patience. "Ari, finish your tea. You'll feel better. Adrastea, tell me what happened."

Adrastea licked her lips, then rubbed her nose. "I thought it best I go to Council. I was late. After Uncle Natan banished Marta, I knew I couldn't go in.

"Mor-Lath came to me." She said nothing of his hiding her from Marta. "He... gave me a book and told me to read it. Then he left, and I came back inside. Then Ari came home." Adrastea sniffed and did not meet anyone's eyes. "She found the book. She got all scared and stuffed it into the stove before I even had a chance to look at it."

Ari stared at her empty cup. "I thought it best that we discourage gifts. This is not a courtship, you know."

Mira sighed. She eyed the bottle on the table. "Ari, this is exactly what it is. But I agree. We should discourage gifts as much as possible."

Adrastea felt some disappointment. Mira was right; this was a courtship, even an unwelcome one. But a small corner of her soul questioned its status. Part of her wanted to fling herself into his arms. Why? She let out a small sigh.

Mira reached across the table and took Adrastea's hands. "I know this is tough, but it is all for the best. If he was anyone else, I would be more than happy to encourage his suit. I want to see you happy. But this is Mor-Lath, God of the Dark. No good will come of it. The value of your soul is too great."

"You can't stop him from giving me things."

For a moment, silence lay between them, only the popping of a log within the stove and another crow of a rooster outside could be heard.

Then Mira smiled. "Oh, yes we can."

Ari raised her head. Adrastea looked doubtful. She didn't like the sound of this.

"We can protect her by not leaving her alone."

"What?" Adrastea protested. "All the time?"

"All the time. Every waking moment during the day, and even at night—especially at night. We don't want any suitors coming to you in your bed."

Adrastea blushed and silenced her protests.

"I don't know if I can handle all the time," Ari said. "I've got too much to do. Adrastea has too much to do."

"Well," Mira hesitated while she came up with a plan. "Perhaps she can spend some time with you, some time with me. Maybe some time with her mother, and... I don't know. Natan, perhaps? I'm sure we can find other company for her."

Adrastea balked. "I don't think treating me like a child is going to help." Until Mor-Lath came along, she had greatly valued her privacy. It gave her time to really feel like herself, without having to guard her every move. The people of small villages had ways of finding out each other's business and taking things the wrong way.

Mira shot Ari an unfathomable look. The one Ari returned was full of resentful knowing.

What had Adrastea missed? "I guess I don't have much of a say?"

"Not if you want to keep your soul." Mira rose from the table. "I see today is not the best day to start our lessons, Adrastea." She wrapped up her precious book. "I shall come by later when I have a better idea of what we are going to do." To Ari, she said, "Thanks for the tea. See you later. I'm going to go talk with Natan."

Mira let herself out.

Ari gently rose from her chair and wandered over to the stillroom door. "I'm getting started on the morning chores, then... well. We'll see how I feel. I wish I could go back to bed but..." She slipped insides the stillroom for a drink of water while Adrastea cleared up teacups. When she returned, Ari said, "I'm going to lay down on the bench with a cold compress. Do not—" she hesitated, not sure what to say. Eventually, pausing in her doorway, "Just be a good girl, Adrastea. I know this can't be easy. Please. Stay in the house where I can hear you. If anyone comes to the door, don't answer it."

◦❦◦

Chapter 5

Mira slipped out of Ari's house as quietly as she could, into the back garden. The Dark God wasn't going to make things easy. Mira felt a twinge not only for the damage of her own book but the complete loss of the other one, even if it had been a gift of the Dark God.

So Mor-Lath proposed marriage to Adrastea. Why? And if he wanted her to be his bride, why didn't he simply take her?

Mira's brow furrowed in thought, her hand lingering on the door handle. He didn't take her. What was his reason?

As she latched the door, her skirt brushed the ash hob. It fell over, scattering ash across the path. Something else spilled out of the hob. Cloth, by the looks of it. Quite a lot.

Mira pulled the bundle of cloth out. Something hard was wrapped inside. Could it be? Her heart fluttered in guilty anticipation. Could both items have survived the fire?

Take it.

Mira shivered from a sudden coldness running up her back. Glancing back at the shut door she carefully scooped up the hod and its contents and hastened home.

Smoke ebbed from a few chimneys of the houses that encircled the large village green. Cat-a-corner to the inn stood Natan's small house. From the wisps of his chimney, she knew he was awake. The smithy, likewise, issued smoke.

Mira did not go through her front door but ran to the back of her cottage. From here, she had a spectacular view eastward, over the plain. The sun had risen fully, to spread its light across the waking world. Patches of smoky haze marked where other villages stood along the Great Western Road. While she could not see the actual Road, she could see the gash that separated the patchwork fields of distant towns. How small Sacred Spring village seemed compared to the rest of the world.

Yet the Dark God stopped here.

Mira dropped the hod on her back step.

Sacred Spring might be small, but Mira wished she had someone to share the burden of her calling. She wanted someone to speak with, as a colleague, a fellow priest. Someone who understood why it was so important to remind her flock of the positive consequences of walking in the Light.

Even in the best of times, she worried about her village. Fewer pilgrims came to visit the shrine every year. No pilgrims, no money flowing in. Unless the families could make a living through farming, often they left the village to seek work elsewhere.

As the village diminished, so did the talent pool. Among the youth in Sacred Spring there were no suitable candidates to serve as her apprentice.

Carles, the Priest of Crossroads, had several priests serving with him. Did Carles have any apprentices, or even some journeyman priests who would be willing to move to her village? She'd have to write him a letter.

Mira brought the hod inside and set it by her fireplace. Oh, for a stove like Ari's! She kissed her own Book of the Light rather hastily before stowing it on its usual shelf, along with four other treasured books and a few sacred items, including her holy water glass.

She hesitated for a moment, then let her hand close around the glass. She lifted it down and filled it with water from the bucket on her sideboard. Opening a curtain to let in the newly-risen sun, Mira held the glass up in its rays. "As the light shines through this water, let the Light shine through me."

"Forgive me," she murmured, as she pressed her lips to the glass. "I do this only to gain further wisdom." She sipped the blessed water. The cup she set back on the shelf, still full.

Now, what was Adrastea trying to hide? With careful hands Mira lifted the cloak from the hob and shook the ashes into her fireplace. The cloak needed further brushing and it smelled of smoke and spice. Otherwise it was undamaged. Mira felt the softness of the fabric next to her cheek. If only it wasn't the Dark God's. But then, perhaps that would work in her favor. She gave it a quick brush to remove the ash. She folded it up carefully, laying it on the table.

What would the Lines tell her about this cloak or its owner? Mira held a hand over the cloak, closed her eyes and opened her heart. Would she feel the Deeper Power today? Mira could not rely on her weak talents to sense the Lines every time. With strong emotion, like the other day at the smithy tank, she found she had better luck in hearing what the Universe had to say to her.

The vibrations of the Lines came easily to her. Mira sensed comfort and protection from the cloak. She felt strength. Mira gave in to these feelings, letting them wash over her.

She could sense a faint trace of Adrastea, possibly because the girl had also let her emotions rule. No wonder her talents in the Deeper Powers had come to the fore, if she'd been letting her heart rule her head during a time of great crisis. Strong emotions made one more sensitive to Creation.

So why now? How did Adrastea make it through the tumult of adolescence without calling her talent forth? What had changed?

Mira pushed back that line of reason and focused on the cloak. The free yearnings of youth and their spontaneous ways rolled over her. She whimpered with the longing of it. Beneath the cloak she could sense the table, old and polished black from the priestesses before her. Her mixed emotions and old memories rolled forth onto the stage of her mind.

Mira had been a youth, about Mikal's age, when she became old Crozie's apprentice. Crozie claimed her two years into Mira's embarrassing apprenticeship to her own Baker mother.

She had been the second of the only two apprentices the old woman ever had.

The first apprentice died of illness not less than four years into her journeyhood, when Mira was but a little girl. Crozie resisted taking on another apprentice; some people thought this was due to grief. When Mira was eventually taken on, she was told the truth. Crozie had been pressured to take another apprentice, just as Mira was being pressured now.

"I take you on with great reluctance," said Crozie, "for I would get no peace otherwise. There is precious little talent here in this village. It's been bred out of them. Nobody can touch the Deeper Power any more. It's like they've all gone numb." After teaching Mira the basics of priestcraft, Crozie reluctantly accepted Mira's ability to sense the Lines of power that bound Creation. But that was it. Any time she attempted to pull them like the strings of a puppet, they evaded her grasp.

"No matter," said Crozie. "You can see them, and you can read them. You know what they mean and that's enough for a priestess of the Light. To actually pull them for your own selfish desires is the way of the Dark."

No sooner did Mira reach the end of her apprenticeship, then Crozie's twin sister died.

Crozie grieved after the death of her sister until it affected her mind. She disappeared into the forest, presumably to die herself. No one ever saw her again.

Crozie never met Joe, Adrastea's father. She was gone several years before he showed up. What would she have thought of him, this young Feowan man with a talent he could hide from all but Mira? The Lines ran strong with him. While he never admitted as much, she wondered if he had run away from a priesthood apprenticeship. Then again, Joe knew something about everything. He could have been anybody.

His Lines tied in strongly with Lillybet's, binding them so closely together that nothing could separate them, except perhaps for death. Maybe not even then.

Mira ran a hand over the fabric of Mor-Lath's cloak again. No wonder Adrastea kept it. Since the death of her father, she'd had little in the way of male attention, aside from her uncle Natan. As he was Mayor of the village, there wasn't much he could do other than the occasional uncle-ish things. He could not be a father as well. Anyway, now that she was more than old enough to consider marriage, no doubt her heart yearned for a male attention of a different kind.

There weren't many boys Adrastea's age who weren't of the Innkeeper clan. They avoided her, Marta's influence no doubt being the reason. As Adrastea grew older, her marriage prospects grew slimmer. Mira shook her head. Sometimes the Council had discussed if Adrastea should spend some time in Crossroads. She was, after all a journeyman. They were supposed to go off, see the world, practice their craft, then return home to settle for good. Ari had fled Sacred Spring and spent a couple of years abroad when she was Adrastea's age. Then she returned, unable to stay away from Natan.

Then again, some journeymen never came home, having found someone to marry elsewhere. Was that Joe?

It had taken an unusual outsider to marry Lillybet. And now a most unusual outsider wanted Adrastea.

"Why does it have to be the Dark God?" Mira sighed out loud.

She drew a deep breath and calmed her soul. Each breath brought new clarity of mind. It was not so much the Dark God she had to contend with but Adrastea's past as well. If Joe had lived, would his fatherly love have been enough to strengthen Adrastea against temptation? No doubt Mor-Lath would seek out those empty spots in the young woman's life.

In her younger days, Adrastea had not been so focused in her healer work that she hadn't noticed the fine young men of the village. She'd had a few silly crushes, as girls were wont to do. Nothing came of them, for the young men were not as interested in her. While she had not spoken of it in these later years, Mira doubted Adrastea's heart had grown cold. Deep down, she still yearned to be loved.

If he discovered this, he could lure her to his side with empty promises.

With reluctance, for Mira found the softness of the fabric infatuating, she put the cloak away in the bottom of her linen chest, where nobody would find it.

The cloak had nothing more to share with her that she didn't already know. As seductive as the cloak was (Mira was tempted to wrap herself in it) other treasures waited. From the bottom of the hod she pulled the black book.

She opened it and gazed at the beautiful script on the first page. "To Adrastea, a betrothal gift for you, Mor-Lath." Rather sure of himself, wasn't he? Had Adrastea felt this same compulsion? Is that why she opened the book and discovered its secrets? Yet Adrastea had not opened the book, or so she said. Perhaps Adrastea had been telling the truth.

Mira turned the page and began to read.

A drastea had been true to her word; she did not leave the house. All she did was open the back door.

The hob was gone.

Panic welled within her. While much of the village couldn't read, if that book fell into the hands of someone who could, what would they think?

She scoured the back garden, ere it should have fallen off the porch.

Not a trace, other than a small scattering of ashes leading nowhere.

She paced the porch, tapping her forehead. "Think, think, think." Had it simply gone missing, or had it been stolen? How could she know?

"Adrastea?" Ari's voice, from inside the house, sounded weak. "Something wrong?"

The healer had woken. She had a hand to her forehead and she leaned against the kitchen doorjamb.

"No, nothing wrong." Adrastea slunk back into the house and closed the door. "Just looking outside." Something irked inside her. Rebellion propelled her to say, "I can do that. I'm not a child who's been grounded to the house."

Ari blinked heavily and settled into a sigh. "I know. You're an adult who's wise enough to realize that when she's left the safety of the herd, the black wolf hunts her down."

Adrastea opened her mouth but thought better of it. Curse Ari for being right.

Ari sat at the table, cradling her head. Delicately, she said, "I made a mistake last night." Her finger traced the dry rim of the bottle. "I don't know if I'm in any condition to bear you company."

Or rather, Ari would prefer the quietude of an empty house. And what would Adrastea do all morning? None of her morning chores would suffice, for she knew from long experience they were too noisy for the house of a hungover healer.

Furthermore, Mira would not be a suitable companion this morning. She'd been rather withdrawn since the barrel incident. Adrastea didn't know what bothered the priestess more—the presence of the Dark God, or the fact that Adrastea could touch the Deeper Power.

"What if I go visit my mother?" Of all the people in the world, her mother would be the most understanding. But could she help?

Ari lifted her heavy head and blinked her bloodshot eyes. "Perfect." She rose with great effort. "Let's go."

Mor-Lath must really frighten Ari if she was willing to risk a morning walk through the village with a hangover.

Heat shimmered across the dusty roads as the sun rose higher. Summer insisted on squeezing out every last bit of heat before autumn chased it off. Most everyone remained inside, their doors thrown open to allow the faint breeze to cool their homes. Adrastea led a delicate Ari through the village and up the hill. The trees provided some cooling cover but not much. Soon they reached the small cottage at the top of the hill.

Adrastea paused at the open doorway. Lillybet sat at her loom, her hands sending the shuttle back and forth, her back to the door. "Hello, mother. I'm home."

Lillybet looked over her shoulder, her hands never slowing. "Come in." Click-clack went her shuttle.

When Adrastea crossed the threshold, a feeling calmness infused her. It always felt like this when she came home to her mother. It always felt safe and welcoming here. Perhaps she should come home more often.

Ari, massaging her temples, brought Lillybet up to speed. She told her of Mor-Lath's little gift last night and how she had acted quickly to dispose of it. "This is what happens when we leave her alone."

Lilly's shuttle never slowed.

Ari huffed. "Keep her safe, Lilly. Keep her inside and don't let her leave your sight."

Lilly's clacking shuttle slowed. "You staying with her?"

Ari leaned against the doorframe and put a hand to her forehead. "I'm not feeling well."

"Ah." Lilly put much meaning into the word. Ari ignored it, for once.

Lilly tried another tactic to needle the healer. "And what should I do, should the Dark God show up?"

Ari turned her back to her. "Don't let him in." And so, she departed, in no mood for sparring.

Once Ari left, Lillybet abandoned her weaving to embrace her daughter. "Oh, my dear! You had a busy night last night."

Lillybet smothered her enough to make up for all the hugs she'd missed. After she had hugged her fill, Lillybet held her daughter out at arm's length. "You have circles under your eyes."

"I didn't sleep well."

"Nor did many people. I shall tell you more later. Here. Sit." She shoved twisted skeins off a kitchen chair. "Would you like something to eat?" Without waiting for an answer, she turned to her cupboard. Her foot caught on her rag rug and she stumbled. "Always tripping over that thing," she muttered as she rummaged in her larder. "Ah, here we go." Lillybet produced bread and cheese. For Adrastea she provided a cup of tepid milk. Was there no tea in the house? Adrastea's stomach grumbled. She'd forgotten about food in her anxiety over the hob. She slivered off some cheese with the sharp knife while Lillybet pulled the loaf apart.

Her mother craved gossip. "Did he really give you a book?"

"Yes." She took a breath. Best to start with honesty. "I was going to bring it here but..."

"I'm sorry," her mother said, without sounding like she meant it. She looked around, as if afraid of being spied upon. "You know," she confided, "I was so proud of you when I learned what had happened."

The bread and cheese in Adrastea's mouth felt dry. She couldn't swallow. She laid a hand to her lined cheek. She was proud Mor-Lath had singled her out? "How can you say that?"

Her mother's enthusiasm was not to be deterred. "I knew it was you who pulled the Lines at the rain barrel. I wasn't sure at the time, but I felt it."

"What…?" Adrastea shook her head. She hadn't been expecting that.

"Oh, my dear! You have the talent." Her mother looked fit to burst. "I have a secret to tell you."

She lifted her hands and, as if stroking a cat, stroked the air in front of her. She caressed the Lines of the Deeper Power between them. Adrastea felt a thrum as if the strings of her own body had been plucked. Then her mother folded her hands in front of her, satisfied.

Adrastea's chest tightened. "You can touch the Deeper Power?" she whispered.

Her mother only smiled mysteriously.

"How come you never told me?"

"I haven't told anyone, really."

"But you could have told me!"

Lillybet shrugged one shoulder. "Why? Until now, you never showed a single glimmer of talent. If you had, I'm sure Mira would have snatched you up, if only for your protection. See, not everyone can see the Lines."

Adrastea blinked. "They can't?" She looked about the room. How could anyone miss the shimmeriness that connected Creation together? Sure, they were difficult to see, especially when light was bright, but they were unmistakable, like the trees and the dirt and the walls of the house. "But still…"

"What would the others say if they knew? Then I really would be a witch, for I was not trained as a priestess."

Adrastea hesitated. A cold thought had occurred to her. "You're not Dark, are you?"

"No," Lillybet replied. "Nor was your father. But do you think that would have mattered to the others if they knew?"

"But… couldn't you have protected yourself?"

Her mother's smile faded a little. "No. I can send ripples, that's about it." She bit her lip. "But to do what you did the other day…?" She shook her head. "I could no more protect myself than Ari could.

"I can feel the Lines and they feel me. There's not much I can do about it." She reached out a finger to dab at the crumbs on the cheeseboard. "I see angels, I see demons. They leave their own wakes. It affects me. I can't always fight it."

Adrastea nodded. Her mother's mood swings. "Why do they affect you like this?"

"I don't know."

Adrastea pondered this revelation. "Does Mira know about..?" She gestured to the Lines that she and her mother could see, and no one else could.

Lillybet shrugged. "I'm sure she suspects. If she knows, she has kept my secret."

Adrastea pushed the crumbs of bread and cheese around the board. "And nobody else knows?"

"Besides yourself? Nobody who lives."

"So why were you never apprenticed as priestess?"

Lillybet laughed, more bitter than jolly. "It takes more than talent to be a priestess, daughter. It takes acceptance. And who in the village would accept me as their spiritual guide?"

Adrastea didn't answer. A priestess had to be calm. She had to be strong. Her mother was neither of these, with her heart and her head going willy-nilly. Or so she had appeared.

Lilly's eyes met Adrastea's. "Your father had a secret as well."

This caught Adrastea's attention. She knew so little of her father, so any information was valuable.

Her mother drew a slow, deep breath. Her sorrow vibrated along the Lines, to ripple across Adrastea's skin. "He, too, had the talent. Nobody knows this but before he came here, he was a journeyman priest."

She couldn't help but blink. Her father, a priest? An actual priest? No wonder they kept that tidbit of information a secret.

"I don't think his heart was in it. His blood was too passionate to devote himself to serving others and nothing for himself. So, he wandered, as a journeyman does, and saw the world. He saw the great city of Feown and more beyond. Since people there have priests aplenty he had to find other ways to earn his bread.

"Your father's talent was more like mine. He could touch the Deeper Power, send waves through it but could not pull on it like you can.

"But there was one thing your father could do; he could create his own luck. Everyone can do this, to some extent." She drew in another deep breath. "Oh, but not like your father!"

Adrastea picked up a piece of cheese and nibbled it. Both parents, talented. So that's where she got it.

"The reason your father was so good at the things he did was because he was always lucky. He originally came here on a pilgrimage to the Sacred Spring, yet something told him to stay. He told no one he was a priest, not even me, at the time." She sat back and folded her arms before her. "If I had known I would never have done what I did."

"What did you do?"

Smugly, Lillybet replied, "I seduced him."

Adrastea felt a flush warm her cheeks.

Lillybet nodded, affirming what her daughter wouldn't—couldn't mention aloud.

"You were born of great passion, Adrastea. And I am not sorry I did it. It wasn't until much later that I learned the truth.

"See, your father had half-given up his profession by the time he met me, and I guess I was the deciding factor in him completing his choice."

Adrastea pressed her knuckles to her mouth as she listened to this new story about her father unfold. He was a priest? And he gave it up for love?

Lillybet continued. "Did he regret it? I don't think so, for we loved each other passionately until he died." She stifled a sob. "It seemed his luck went when he did. Mikal was taken from me and no matter how hard I tried I could never get him back. You had gone to Ari, but I had expected that. The demons came back. It took all my energy to fight them off. Only here in the house am I safe.

"Since your father died, luck has not been on my side." Then, to Adrastea's surprise, a small smile crept across her mother's lips. "Until now. I think you have your father's luck, Adrastea. I hope it serves you well."

Right. Proposals from the Dark God. Very lucky.

Lillybet changed the subject. "Did Ari tell you what happened last night at council?"

Adrastea shook her head. Ari had not said a word. Adrastea and the others had caught everything up to the point of Marta's expulsion but very little after that.

Lillybet reached out and tapped Adrastea's hand as way of emphasizing her news. "Instead of petitioning for the return of my son, I announced that he was ready to be apprenticed. If nobody presented me an offer, I said I would take him into the family business."

This was news! "So? What happened?" Adrastea asked. No doubt the only reason her mother got this through was because Marta was absent. A dark little niggle in her heart made Adrastea wonder if this was something Marta had overheard in her own eavesdropping session. What did it bode for the future?

"So, your uncle stands up and says that he'd been busy this week, but he'd been meaning to speak with me about Mikal. Can you believe it?"

Adrastea looked at her mother blankly. "Uh, believe what?"

Lillybet's hands shook in her excitement. "Natan's going to take on Mikal as his apprentice!"

"Oh."

Lillybet stood up. "Don't you see? I've won! I've secured my son away from Marta. There's no way she can have him back now. He belongs to me again."

"But he'll live with Natan and that's only if Mikal agrees."

"So? He's not living with Marta anymore."

"But what if he says no?"

"Then he comes to live with me. I am his mother and he cannot refuse a family apprenticeship if no others came knocking."

Her mother seemed so proud of her successful petition that Adrastea couldn't bear to point out the flaws in her plan. Natan Mayor was Mikal's uncle. Was the shame of being apprenticed to one's uncle be as bad as being apprenticed to one's mother? Let time see what Natan and Mikal would do. Perhaps he would accept and perhaps the family would be reunited again.

But then there was Adrastea herself. She had her own problems. Big ones.

As if Lillybet knew what her daughter was thinking, she said, "You don't really care, do you?"

"No, no," Adrastea hastily replied, flushing a little. "I know how much you want him back."

Lillybet traced her finger around the edge of the wooden cutting board. "I'm sorry," she said with all contrition. "Here I am telling you about my petty problems when yours are infinitely worse.

"I confess a curiosity towards this Dark God. As we are of the Light, we hear about him from time to time. Tales, really." Lilly dropped back into thought for a moment. "Never thought we'd actually get to meet him."

Adrastea swallowed. Did her mother really want to meet him? "You don't want to."

"What? Not meet the one who is, ultimately, responsible for all the bad things that's happened to me? I have been called witch before."

Adrastea knew of this. As a child she'd defended her mother a few times with some hair-pulling and a few well-placed kicks before the other children learned not to say such things in front of her. Didn't mean they stopped saying them entirely.

"And because of that," her mother continued, "I, perhaps more than anyone else, know the stories of Mor-Lath, if only to be sure I'm not behaving as a witch.

"When one is thought to be of the Dark, one must work extra-hard to prove that one is of the Light. But I could never have been a priestess. I was too young to be Aunt Crozie's apprentice. By the time Mira became Priestess, well, it was too late for me—reputation, you know.

"And it's a shame you couldn't be as well." Lillybet's voice went husky. "Oh, Adrastea, I want to cry. When I was a child, not only could I see the Lines of the Deeper Power, but I could see demons and angels. Unfortunately, I was too young to know discretion or to know that not everyone saw those things. I blabbed out the first silly thought in my head. And that is why everyone thinks so poorly of me. But when one is young, and a demon pops out of nowhere scaring you to bits and nobody else sees a thing, one gets called mad.

"And now you've seen Mor-Lath himself."

Adrastea interlinked her fingers and clenched her hands together on the wooden table. Her face ached. "I didn't ask for this."

"We never do. Not one day goes by that I don't wish I never saw demons, or even angels, or even the Lines. I just wish I could remain in my ignorant way and kiss the glass once a week when Mira stops by, with half a heart and less than half a brain towards the faith we all grew up in. I wish I could see it as just a simple tradition with little meaning and then go about my life the other six days.

"But I know better. I know for sure that this is all real. The words Mira preaches have meaning. For if there are Lines and there are angels and demons, then there must surely be a God of the Light. And if there is the Light, then surely there must be a God of the Dark. When you say he is come to you, I believe you."

Lilly came around the table and knelt down before her daughter, taking her hands into her own. "Now. As we all know very well, the Light is goodness and truth. Therefore, the Dark must be the opposite. Whatever his purposes, I doubt they are honorable. He says he wants to marry you, but I have a hard time believing him."

"So, what does he want?"

Lillybet shrugged her skinny shoulders. "My biggest concern—and I believe Mira and Ari share this—is that he will say anything so he can seduce you. When he has sated himself on you, he will abandon you. After all, you're just a country girl."

That stung more than Adrastea was expecting. So, what if she was a country girl? Did that make her any less likely to have talent?

Lillybet patted her daughter's hand. "Don't take this wrong, for I love you dearly but what would some big powerful God of the Dark want with you? There are far more powerful and higher-ranking women he could ask to be his bride."

Her heart sank. So much for her mother being proud of her talent. She blinked and sniffed. Until the other day, she'd been all right with her ordinariness, for it meant she was accepted in society.

The Dark God had noticed her. Surely, he wouldn't have noticed her if she was truly ordinary.

Lillybet shook her head. "No. This is all a game to him. He's playing with you. I don't want to see you hurt."

"What do you mean?" Why did her throat have to feel so hot and tight?

"I got lucky when it came to your father. Sure, we did things a little backwards, but he was always a man of honor. He loved me. I doubt the Dark God loves you."

Adrastea pulled a hand free from her mother's grasp to wipe her nose. "When did my father ask you to marry him? Was it because of me?"

Lillybet's eyes filled with tears. "No. He asked me to marry him a few months after I'd seduced him but five minutes before he learned about you. That is how I know it was love and not obligation."

"Mor-Lath says I will marry him."

"Will you?"

Adrastea had the word 'No' on her lips, but it didn't want to come out. She forced it out anyway.

"Hmmm," her mother grunted. "If marriage is truly what he wants—though I don't know why—so be it. But until he has promised his troth before a priest, you keep your skirts down, girl. I doubt your Mor-Lath will be as noble as my Joe.

"This I know; you have attracted the attention of the Dark God. I don't know the whole story, but I do know one thing: stay strong, stay true and the Light shall protect you.

"Now," said Lillybet, her lips twitching, "tell me about this book of yours."

Chapter 6

Adrastea looked at her mother, whose hazel eyes burned with a desire to know. "Uh, there isn't much to tell," she confessed. "Mor-Lath visited me last night and gave me a book. I didn't even get to look at it before Ari threw it in the fire."

Her mother's countenance fell. "Oh. How disappointing."

Adrastea felt a twisting in her stomach. Did her mother crave the book as well? If only the book had been burned. "No. Ari tried to burn it—the cloak too—but it wouldn't burn. In the morning, when I went to clean out the stove, there it was, undamaged."

Lilly leaned forward. "So, where it is now?" She clenched her hands together.

Adrastea's shoulders tightened. "I don't know. I put it in the hod outside the door, because I wanted to hide it somewhere—later when Ari wasn't looking—but it disappeared."

Lillybet looked away. Her forehead wrinkled with worry. "Oh no."

Then the whole story came rushing out, along with Adrastea's fears. The book could be in anyone's hands. Hods did not walk off on their own. "What if someone figures out it's mine?" Her hands tightened over her mother's.

Lillybet's ran a tongue over a tooth. "Well, perhaps whoever found it can't read. Maybe they don't know whose it was."

"It was left just outside our back door!"

Lillybet rose to pace in front of her loom. "Let's be rational here. Who in the village can read? You, Ari, Mira, Natan."

"And Marta. And Tam, and probably the rest of the family too."

Lilly nodded in assent. "Who else?"

"Um... Rop Storekeeper. And...?" In truth, Adrastea didn't know. Most villagers didn't have a need to read, so they didn't bother learning.

"So, half of those people already know our secret." Lillybet smiled broadly as if the problem was solved.

"It's the other half I'm worried about. I don't want to be called a witch either."

Her mother sobered. "Ah, yes." She rose, and sat down in the other chair, steepled her fingers and tapped them against her lips. "There is that. They're not the most tolerant of people, our village. They fear anything strange. You could say I almost fear them more than I fear Mor-Lath." Lillybet shivered. "We've got to get that book back."

"How?"

"I don't know," she murmured. "Give me time. I'm not as clever as your father was." Lillybet said nothing more but sat on her loom bench to think.

"Assuming one of them has it." Adrastea prayed they didn't.

"I doubt it's an Innkeeper who's got your book. After all, why would one of them be sneaking about Ari's place, stealing her ash hob?"

"But the ash hob is gone."

Lilly shared another thought. "Have you considered that maybe Mor-Lath took the book back, after it had been discarded?"

Ah, no. She hadn't considered that. "But it wasn't me who burned it."

"No. It wasn't. Maybe he knows that and is keeping it safe for you. Until it shows up again, there's nothing we can do." Lilly leaned forward. "You do want the book?"

Adrastea had no answer for her. She knew what Mira would say; get rid of the book. Stay away from the Dark. So why did her heart ache at the thought of its loss? "But what if someone else has it?"

At this her mother gave a little snort. "Really, child. You have met the God of the Dark. I hardly think a mere mortal is worth being frightened over."

⁂

For the first time, Mira understood Adrastea's challenge. She had meant to put the book away, but it called to her, sweet and seductive.

Mira had never been seduced in her life, being a priestess but in her youth, she had had her share of crushes—one of them being Natan, once. She thought she had outgrown that sort of thing, until now. As she laid a hand on this book, she felt the same puppy-sick yearning. It weakened her limbs and her mouth tasted of iron. A burning hunger gnawed at her heart, a hunger satiated only by that book.

She had only meant to have a look. What sort of book would the Dark God have given Adrastea? Unlike her own faith with the singular Book of the Light, she had heard of other religions with multiple holy books. Even so, would Mor-Lath's followers called theirs "The Book of the Dark"?

Now that she thought further upon it, Mira had no idea what Mor-Lath's followers called themselves. The Avelians to the south were rumored to be devotees, as were a few of the Tredan tribes to the west. Were they even aware, like followers of the Light were, of the Dark God's evilness? Or had they been completely beguiled and consumed, having lost the battle against the Dark?

Perhaps she could read just the first chapter—know one's enemy.

There was no title page. On the blank page before the book began, Mira found a handwritten dedication: "To Adrastea, a betrothal gift for you, Mor-Lath."

Why would he want her to have this book?

Unlike the Book of the Light, which consisted mostly of fables and stories and exhortations, this was more like an instruction manual. The first few pages described the nature of Creation and the relationship of the Deeper Power with everything. Mira knew some of this already. But as she read on, the book revealed the extent of her ignorance. The Book of the Light explained what Creation was, but it had never taught her how it worked.

Mira learned more about the Lines of the Deeper Power, that force of relationship between every element, every object, every living being. The Deeper Power explained everything from why things fell down to why people fell in love. She learned more about Creation in that one sitting than she had her whole life. A growing corner of discontent in her soul irked her. Did Crozie know about this before she went? Did Carles from Crossroads know? Why was none of this in the Book of the Light?

It taught her not only about those Lines and how they affected the world but also that Creation could be made to serve her.

Mira slammed the cover of the book closed. Her heart thumped. Here was the dangerous part.

In guilt, Mira closed her eyes. Of course, the Book of the Light was sparse on the nature of Creation. Every priest knew that by the wisdom of the Light, Creation acted on you. You did not act on Creation. Mortal men have an imperfect understanding of the world in which they lived. They were prone to making hasty decisions before gathering all the facts. Of course, anyone with enough talent could see, feel or even affect the Lines of Power but would they have wisdom enough to use it for the better?

For the best, priests were discouraged from using the Deeper Power for their own purposes. It should only be used for the benefit of others, and even then, governed with wisdom.

Mira pressed a closed fist against the leather cover. Her heart ached to know more. But should she know more? What would she do with such knowledge?

Then again, knowing was one thing, doing was another. Clearly one could not do if one did not know. But if one knew, that didn't necessarily mean one had to do.

Mira whimpered longingly. She loved books. She read every single book she could get her hands on. She'd made regular forays into Crossroads just so she could devour anything she found in Carles Priest's ever-growing library.

Here was a book that Carles had never read, possibly no one in Feown had ever read. As if of their own volition, her fingers lifted the cover and turned the pages.

If she were to go up against the God of the Dark, wouldn't it help to know more?

The book explained how one could come to grasp them and use them to one's own ends... with detailed instructions on how to use these Lines for one's own purposes. How to keep secrets, how to bind secrets to others, how to discover secrets and more. Sometimes it was a simple as making a request of Creation—granted your will was strong enough to compel It.

Mira's fingers itched to pull the Lines, to twist the world to her ways. She pushed that feeling away. This was where she would draw her line of integrity. Learn, yes. Use? Never.

Well, not unless she had to.

A knock sounded at the door, startling her. She had only enough time to throw the book to a chair under the table before Ari came in. Even though it lay out of sight, the book drew her senses. Had she, simply by learning more about the nature of Creation, improved her Talent already?

Had she made a connection along the Lines to the book? Is that why she knew it was there? Or was this the monkey of guilt clinging to her back and chattering in her ear?

Ari had her own problems and needed the other ear of the priestess. Mira half-listened to Ari's contrition about her out-of-character actions with her journeyman. She thought it would be best, for Adrastea's protection if Adrastea was escorted at all times. Mira nodded and agreed, hoping that Ari would leave soon so she could finish reading the book. Then Ari said something about Natan and Lillybet, and if they agreed. (Agreed to what?) "So, can you take her first?"

"Yes. Er, what?"

"Mira?" asked Ari. "You feeling okay?" Ari advanced, her hand raised to feel Mira's forehead. "You're looking flushed."

Mira hopped up, more to keep Ari from the table. "No, I'm fine. I'm just…" Her cheeks burned even hotter as she thought of the book hidden near her lap. She prayed Ari wouldn't find it. Was there some secret in the book that would enable her to hide it from the gaze of others, even though it be in plain sight?

Ari nattered on about maidens needing protection and how some people might sleep too deeply to prevent said maidens from possibly sneaking out.

Mira's thought strayed back to the book. What did he truly want?

Ari had one last request. "Mira. Please let her stay with you tonight. You're the priestess. You'll have the protection of the Light."

Mira brought herself back to the present. "Adrastea, here?"

"Yes." Ari's eyes narrowed. "You can do that?"

"I will." And with that, Mira forcefully ushered her to the door. She shut it behind her, locking it.

Mira couldn't get the book out fast enough. She started to read again.

Throughout the day, knocks and calls came on the wooden door and she ignored them. The sun soon set, and she tore herself away to light a lantern. Night fell, and she had to refill the lantern once. She moved the chamber pot into the kitchen with her so she wouldn't have to be away from the book long.

She read until the words swirled and her head thudded. She read until she had finished the book. As the rooster crowed and she closed the back cover, only then could she collapse onto the table to sleep.

How long had it been since Adrastea had spent an entire day with her mother? Ever since her apprenticeship at a rather early age, she'd pretty much been living with Ari. Sure, she'd spent a few hours here and there with her last living parent but not a whole day and certainly never long enough to hear all the stories of her mother.

Lillybet had talent. Adrastea never knew. Joe, likewise, had talent. Of course, he had, if he had once been a priest.

Her mother forwent weaving for the afternoon and told Adrastea anything she wanted to know. Oh, did she have questions. Adrastea remembered her father as a dark-haired man with a ready laugh. Now that she thought about it, it did seem a bit of a waste for him to be a priest, when he had so much more to share. "Does Uncle Natan know about this?" she asked as the shadows of the evening grew long.

"Some." Lilly's eyes looked sideways. "Enough to sate his curiosity and prevent questions, or rather, enough to encourage your uncle to not ask the questions he's always had. My life was never more stable than when Joe was around." She sighed over this one. "Natan's questions have always been there. I think he will start asking them now."

Soon the sun sunk below the horizon and Lilly had to light her lamp. Adrastea looked at the newly-forged Lines between her and her mother. She stroked a finger along one of them. When she did, she felt a ripple of trust. Her mother believed in her. She would support her.

In a different place and time, Lillybet could have been a priestess—a powerful one.

Adrastea wasn't sure how she felt about that little revelation. "But if you were a priestess, you would never have gotten married. Never had me."

"I know." Lillybet smiled as her thoughts settled into pleasant memories. Her momentary contentment rolled along the Lines, warming her daughter. "In the end, I got the best bargain."

Lillybet had no meat but she had vegetables and plenty of bread. At her mother's bidding, Adrastea concocted a soup from potatoes and the summer vegetables she had gleaned from the garden. It wasn't the most sumptuous fare, but Adrastea didn't care. The knowledge of her parents' lives more than satisfied her soul.

The thatch of Lillybet's roof rustled. The canyon breeze had arrived, bringing the scent of wood smoke and pine trees.

"Open the door, love, and let's get some air in here," her mother asked.

Adrastea opened the back door then went to the front door. A cold shiver of air, far colder than any to be found in summer, rushed in and curled about the ankles of both women.

"Good evening, my betrothed." Mor-Lath stood in the doorway, leaning against the doorjamb.

Adrastea let out a squeak of surprise and jumped back. "I— I'm not supposed to talk to you."

Lillybet stood and clamped both hands over her mouth. She stared at the personage in her doorway.

Mor-Lath straightened. "And who will stop me?"

Between her fingers, Lillybet muttered, "I know you now." She stared at something above Mor-Lath's head, something Adrastea couldn't see. She pulled her daughter out of her way. "You can't come in to my house!"

Adrastea's skirt caught on the doorknob, pulling her out of her mother's grasp and back towards Mor-Lath. She reached out a hand to stop her ricochet. It fell on his chest. As he laid his hand over her, his touch brought sinful ripples of pleasure across her skin.

Lillybet disentangled the skirt and once more, pulled Adrastea away. Adrastea's contact with Mor-Lath broke and her hand twitched in restlessness.

"Oh, really?" scoffed Mor-Lath, then he took a step forward.

Or tried to. The moment he reached the threshold of the house, he stopped. A flash of bafflement lit his features, then was gone again, replaced with the same cynical mask he always wore.

Where did her mother find all this courage? Why did she think she could stand up to him? "As long as I live," Lillybet declared, "I will fight you, Dark One. I won't let you take away my daughter. Get off my porch, you bastard."

For a moment, Adrastea thought he'd explode in a fit of temper, but he only smiled wryly. "So be it." He turned to go, then paused. "Oh, by the way, my parents were married."

And he was gone.

Lillybet stood there for a moment, chest heaving, not sure that he had truly left.

Adrastea also drew in deep breaths. As her legs gave way, her mother jerked her up into a hug.

"Oh, my precious girl!" Her mother hugged her and hugged her, and Adrastea let her, even though her ribs threatened to break. "Was... was...?

That was him, wasn't it? I— I mean, I knew it—him. The moment I saw them. He is real."

Adrastea nodded, as much as the tight embrace would let her. Lillybet released her and held her at arm's length. "And did I really face him off?"

Adrastea nodded again.

Her mother let her hands fall to her side. Her foot caught on the rug on her way to the table, so she fell into her chair, rather than sat down. "I stood up to the Dark God." She chuckled to herself and kept repeating that she'd done it. "And did you see those demons about him?"

Adrastea gave one more shiver and closed the door against the darkness outside. She had seen no one but the Dark God. No wonder her mother was perceived as mad. But now that she thought of it, there could have been others. Her focus had been so completely on Mor-Lath she would not have noticed if the whole of Dom-al-gol had marched up behind him.

"I say," Lillybet continued, her recent fright making her speak much. "He is not nearly so bad as any demon. I... Stir up the fire, girl. I don't feel like facing the darkness tonight."

After closing the back door, Adrastea turned up the lamp and stirred the fire, to provide as much light as she could. She checked the candle holder on the mantle, but it was empty.

Lillybet continued to babble. "I, I think I understand a bit more." Lillybet sat down at the table. She folded her arms about her and put in some thought. Adrastea noticed her mother trembling. She fetched a shawl from the hook behind the door and draped it over her mother.

"He is deceptive, isn't he, daughter. When you first came here the other day, you were shaken but not scared out of your wits. I think your face was more injured than your courage. I wondered how a slip of a girl could show such courage in the face of the biggest demon of them all but now I understand."

Adrastea sat on the bench, close to Lillybet. "He couldn't come in, Mother. He tried but he couldn't do it."

"Another legacy of your father." She pulled the shawl tighter. "When he built this house, he built it in such a way that as long as either one of us lived in it, we would be protected from harm. And yes, the demons stay away. They can roam the house outside but can't come in." Then, in typical Lillybet fashion, she changed the subject. "Are you thirsty?"

Adrastea shook her head.

"Me neither. There's a bottle in... ah. Never mind. I'll fetch it." Lillybet returned with a bottle of something fruity and stronger than wine. "I only feel like this."

Adrastea recognized the bottle as one of Ari's. Her hand, where she had touched him, sent little pins and needles to her heart. A nervous disposition, the tiny voice of the healer in her heat murmured. Lactoverosa for the nerves would be best.

But for now, a bottle of Ari's best would do. She quickly drained her cup of milk and held it out for a drop.

The bottle held some pretty powerful stuff. Together they sipped the contents, Adrastea from her cup, Lilly straight from the bottle.

After her head settled into a nice buzz, Adrastea asked her mother, "Who was my father, really?"

Lilly drunkenly shrugged. "A priest," and refused to explain further, no matter how much Adrastea cajoled. Surely, he had to be more than some wandering priest, to be able to protect a house against the Dark God himself.

Once the bottle had emptied, they sat staring into the fire until Lillybet fell asleep on the bench, her head down on the table. Adrastea ended upon the rag rug before the fire, her mother's shawl draped around her.

Lillybet woke with a start the next morning as the sun from the eastern window fell across her face. Adrastea snored softly on the rug before the dying fire. Wasn't she supposed to go to Mira's last night?

A knock rang out on the back door, which sent her head pounding.

Adrastea didn't wake. How lucky.

"I'm coming..." Who would knock at the back door? She opened it and squinted against the morning light.

Ah, it was Natan. "I've come to claim Mikal as my apprentice."

"Marta's got him," Lilly said, her voice acid.

"I know. But you're still his mother. I must announce myself to his rightful parents. Come with me and we shall fetch your son."

Lilly spared half a glance at her sleeping daughter. She wouldn't wake any time soon. Besides, she was off to fetch her son. She closed the door gently and followed her brother, silently vowing to keep Mor-Lath's appearance last night a secret. If Natan knew, his concern would be for his niece, and not for his nephew, whose future was more important at the moment.

Natan led her not to the front of the inn, nor the back door but out to the stables, where guests could put up their animals and be overcharged for feed. Natan knocked on the open stable door.

Tam Innkeeper answered that call. Tam was not a tall man but stockily built. He had to be, to withstand the drain his wife put on him with her demands. It washed the color out of him, leaving his hair sandy, his skin pale, his hazel eyes looking dark in his stark face. He sported a stubble of beard which Marta normally made him shave whenever there were guests.

After a quick glance at the inn, he greeted the mayor. "Natan."

"Tam. Is Mikal here?"

"He is." He looked back into the stables and nodded. Tam glanced toward the inn.

Mikal emerged from a stall. Lilly sprang forward and hugged her son, much to his silent embarrassment.

Natan looked to the inn as well. "I trust you've taken care of Marta?"

Tam shrugged. "She knows but didn't know when. I didn't want a scene."

Lillybet, still hugging her son, gave a muffled, "Thank you, thank you."

Natan and Tam shook hands. "Thank you for being good to my nephew."

"You would have done the same for one of mine." Tam seemed a little wistful. "I wish you had." He gave the mayor a small smile. "Marta protested when she first had to take him. Then she protested when we had to give him up. There's no pleasing that woman."

Lillybet said, "It's her own fault if she can't handle change."

As they turned to leave, a horse galloped into the yard. Lilly pulled Mikal back into the barn, sheltering him as she went.

"Leave off! I won't be run over," Mikal protested. But Lillybet threw a hand over his mouth. "Shh! He does not bring good news."

Natan watched his sister Lillybet embrace her son. His heart ached. She'd yearned for her son for years and he, as Mayor, had had to side with what was best for Mikal, which didn't always benefit Lilly. Small wonder she'd never stuck a knife in his back. But Lillybet knew what he had to give up to be Mayor.

It wasn't until she demanded her own son as apprentice that Natan realized, albeit a few years too late, that he could rescue his nephew from the Innkeepers and make his sister happy. Marta would rant and rail because she loved lording it over Lillybet.

To be honest, Marta had treated him as well as she treated all her own children. Had she abused the lad, Mikal would have been taken away from her and then she'd have nothing to hold over Lilly.

Not the most ideal situation, he admitted in hindsight, but it could have been worse.

A lathered horse galloped into the yard. Lilly and Mikal retreated to the barn. Natan remained. Who was this who came so swiftly?

Tam ran to grab the bridle as the rider, tall and thin, hopped off.

"Good Innkeeper," the rider shouted, "I must see your Mayor."

Natan came up. "I be he." Then he recognized the rider as Sam Mayor's apprentice, from the town of Crossroads. "Ely! What's the matter?"

Tam walked the horse around the yard to cool her down. The sound of a horse had brought several of the Innkeeper brood to the back door, silent and curious. Natan glanced back to the barn. Lilly and Mikal were not visible.

Ely Mayorprentice opened a leather satchel to remove a letter. "Sam Mayor sends this to you. I am to take your reply back as soon as possible."

As Natan broke the seal on the letter, he looked to Tam.

Tam, walking the horse, shook his head at Natan. "She's gotta cool down. He can't ride back for a good half-hour."

Natan nodded. "Ely, get you into the inn. The good Innkeeper will give you a bite to eat and a drop to drink."

Tam nodded in agreement. "Your tab, Natan." Tam beckoned to one of his children to come take the horse.

Natan did not reply. He had unfolded the letter and read it, mouthing the words silently.

A stark frown distorted Natan's face as he finished the letter. "Tam!" he barked. "I need ink. I must reply to this letter."

Tam fetched his writing desk. Natan followed him through the back door of the Inn.

⚭

Lillybet watched clandestinely from the shadows of the barn. As soon as it was clear, she hurried Mikal away from the inn.

Mikal resisted the firm grasp his mother had on his arm. "Where are we going?"

She slowed but did not stop. "I wish I could take you home but... No. That's not good. Natan's is the safest place for you."

"Why? What's going on?"

She looked at her son. "I'm sure Natan will tell you. I have a feeling he might tell everyone."

Also, she wanted to keep him clean of any knowledge of Adrastea's dilemma. "Stay at Natan's and wait for him there. He is your master now. Just don't eat him out of house and home."

"Mother? What's going on?"

With a brief hug and a kiss on the cheek, she left him on the porch of Natan's home. "I'll check on you later. I love you, Mikal Mayorprentice!" She hurried off, leaving Mikal to rattle at locked doors.

As Lillybet hurried back up the hill to home, she came across an angry Ari and a contrite Mira. The priestess looked like she hadn't slept at all, with dark circles under her eyes and her skin far too pale for her complexion.

"Where the hell have you been?" Ari demanded. "You've left Adrastea all on her own!"

"She's safe as long as she stays in the house."

"The hell she is!" Ari swore. "Mor-Lath could come at any time and steal her away."

Lillybet's head raced with the adventures of the morning; she got her son back, and Natan had something exciting happening. She gave Ari a wicked smile. "No, he can't. I wouldn't let him into the house."

"That's not going to stop him."

Lillybet folded her arms, a smug expression on her face. "Oh, yes it did. He popped by last night. He, too, thought he could just come into my house, but I told him no. And he couldn't. He tried but he couldn't come in."

Mira drew herself up, startled. "What?"

"Joe's protections worked."

"What protections?" scoffed Ari, her arms tightening.

"Nothing can harm us while we're in the house!"

Mira looked at her skeptically. "Joe was a lot of things—"

"But Mor-Lath couldn't come in. Don't you see? We can keep my daughter safe."

"I don't know—" started Ari.

"Look, if you were so worried, why have you left her on her own now?" She planted her fists on her hips and looked sideways at the healer.

Ari swore, more at herself, than anything, something about common sense deserting her at the most inopportune moments. She dashed back up the hill, leaving the other two to their slower pace, debating over the best method of keeping Adrastea safe. Before they reached the house, Mikal came huffing up the hill. "Natan... Mayor..." he gasped, "council... now." He huffed in exhaustion and folded his skinny frame over to catch his breath, hands on his knees. "Natan's called an emergency council. Right now, at the Inn. Everyone has to come."

Ari pointed a finger at Lillybet. "You stay with Adrastea."

Mikal shook his head. "He said, everyone." Having caught his breath, he added, "I've got to tell others." And off he went.

An emergency council meant something drastic. Nobody wanted to be late. "I'm not staying home," Lillybet insisted, her voice tightening. Curiosity over Eli Mayorprentice's urgent message burned in her. Before the other two could draw her into an argument and possibly bully her into staying, she took off down the hill. Mikal had looked rattled. Through his mix of excitement and stress, she felt Natan's familiar brand of worry, bordering on ulcer-causing anxiety. If Lillybet could feel that through the Lines, something serious was going on.

Let Ari and Mira fret. Adrastea would be safe as long as she stayed inside the house.

Natan did not bother to wait for latecomers. Mothers brought young children, craftsmen their apprentices. As soon as enough local villagers arrived he began without preamble. He clutched Sam's letter in his hand. Ely stood behind Natan.

"Feown is under siege. Armed soldiers are traveling along the Great

Western Road. It looks like they're going to block the Great Western Pass."

This brought loud murmurs from people. Nobody had ever seen a war.

Natan waved the parchment. "This is a letter from Crossroads, asking for our help."

"We can't go fight!" someone called out. Lots of others agreed with him.

"Sam's not asking for soldiers. He's asking for refuge." Natan read from the letter. "'We ask that you provide a safe haven for our children and those who cannot defend themselves. There are a great many people who are fleeing Feown. Our town is no longer safe. Please help us.'" Natan looked up. "I will offer them protection. Any say nay?"

Ari slipped in. She gave Natan a worried look, then sought out Lillybet. He shoved that concern into the back of his head. If it was serious enough for him to worry about, Ari would tell him.

Where was Mira?

Marta, who leaned against the wall next to the kitchen door, folded her arms and glared at Natan but said nothing. Peter Smith stood up. "Natan, where will we put them?"

"That was what I wanted to ask you. These are friends. Family, even."

Tam, not sitting near his wife, stood up. "Depending on how many there are, there may be rooms available in the inn."

"And you are giving these rooms for free?"

Perplexity crossed Tam's face. "Free?"

Natan folded the letter between his fingers. "These are children. Refuge-seekers. They do not have coin to buy bread, much less afford what you charge for room."

Tam said nothing. He would look foolish before the people if he maintained he would charge for the room, no matter how discounted. Marta would tan his hide if he volunteered the rooms for free. "The haying isn't due for another several weeks. My loft above my stables is more empty than full. It will keep them sheltered and give them a place to sleep."

Peter, still standing, nodded. "My loft is also half-empty. I would give shelter, provided they behave themselves."

People started murmuring to one another over this sudden burst of generosity from the two men. Would two lofts be enough?

Natan's expression hadn't changed. "Then what, after the haying?"

"What? What does that have to do with it?" Peter asked.

"Another thing about refuge-seekers is that you don't know how long they'll stay. They could be here for two weeks, but they could be here for two months, or even two years. Haylofts are fine for two weeks, but I think this war will last longer than that. We need something permanent."

Lillybet leapt up. "Why can't we foster them?" she suggested. "Someone took care of my son when I couldn't. I'd be more than happy to take on someone else's children in need. My house is large enough for three or four." Lillybet sat down with a smug glance in Marta's direction.

Marta glared even harder before leaning to her neighbor to pour her own bitter poison in the neighbor's ear. Natan would have to have a word with her over that.

"Also a solution," agreed Natan.

Rop Storekeeper had an idea. "What about the abandoned cottages?" A generation ago severe illness carried away a significant number of Sacred Spring's population. The village never recovered, and several houses remained empty ever since.

Marlon Poulter shook his head. "No good. They're all but fallen over."

Rop Storekeeper suggested, "Why don't we repair the abandoned cottages?"

Jak Carpenter stood up. "It's stonework and adobe. It'd take too long."

Marta added her own opinion. "But what about your henhouses? Those cottages are in good repair." The Poulters, who owned sizeable flocks of fowls, had converted some of the better cottages into coops.

Marlon shook his head. "We'll never get them cleaned in time. And then, where will we put the birds?"

The crowd buzzed with argument.

Jak offered another suggestion. "We could build them houses of their own. "

"From scratch?" Rop scoffed. "That'd take even longer!"

Jak was not to be riled. "Not if you do it right. Nothing fancy, mind. Find somewhere, build small houses log-cabin style. They could live there, 'stead of our own places. Then, when they're gone, we use the little houses like sheds or barns or storage or extra houses or something like that."

As Jak outlined his plans, several villagers nodded. Sounded like a great plan, they murmured to one another.

Natan wasn't so won over. "Houses require wood. And time."

"I'm sure we can donate time," suggested Jak. "I am. Maybe Dade Sawyer can give us wood."

Marlon Poulter shook his head. He was young, but he was quick of mind. "Dade's not a Springer. He won't give us wood for free."

Ari sighed. "Oh, just chop the trees down ourselves! You know you can use green wood for a log cabin. Besides, it's only temporary."

Nobody disagreed with this.

Natan turned to Jak. "How long will it take?"

Jak considered for a moment. "Just me? One cabin, three weeks. With two other hands, three cabins, one week. More hands, five cabins."

"Agreed. Volunteers?"

Several men and a few women held up their hands.

Natan took note. "Now, where do we build these cabins?"

Sheelagh said, "Not in the village proper. They'd be too crude. You'd need proper houses here."

Marta spoke. "Why not put them up on the hill behind Lilly's place?"

For the first time in her life, Lilly agreed with Marta. "You'd have to clear the trees but then I guess they'd be used to build the cabins."

Natan looked at his sister. "You acceptable with this?"

She nodded. "Where else are they going to go? I agree with Marta. Putting the cabins anywhere else would inconvenience everyone, including the orphans. It's best they go there."

Natan accepted the offer. Together he and Jak Carpenter organized volunteers and made plans. And that's how a village should work, he thought.

Chapter 7

Adrastea had learned caution. When the knock came on the door, she called out, "Who is it?"

"Mira."

Adrastea relaxed. Her imagination had taken leave from her common sense, running about with implausible worries about what might have happened had he shown up again. The best answer was slam the door and refuse him entrance. She pushed away that insistent little feeling which urged her to throw open the door and fling herself into his arms. Ridiculous. He meant her no good.

She peeked outside. Mira stood on the porch, her small arms wrapped about her body. The priestess looked away from the porch, down the hill.

Adrastea leaned in the doorway. "Something on your mind?"

Mira turned around. "Natan's called a council. The news isn't good, so I thought we would get started on some important things."

Council? "What kind of news?"

"You'll hear soon enough." She touched the doorframe. "There are strong Lines here."

"My father's protections, I'm told. Did you know my father was once a priest?"

Mira continued to stroke the wood. "I am not in the habit of telling other people's secrets. This feels like your mother's work."

Her mother? "But she said it was his work."

"And hers. She may have helped him."

Adrastea straightened. "My mother can do things like this?" If her mother could do it, could she do it as well?

Mira's hand lingered. "I can't do things like this. As for what your father may have done, it was... it serves you now." Mira held out her hand. "We have more important things to do right now. Let us go to my place."

Adrastea hesitated, her hand on the lintel. "Is it safe?"

Mira weighed that question, giving it due consideration. Finally, she said, "Your protection is not so much a place," Mira touched the wall with reverence, "though a refuge like this can help when you're tired or vulnerable. Your protection is in your ability to say no. So yes, as long as you refuse Mor-Lath, you are safe."

Adrastea blinked. Surely it couldn't be that simple.

"Unless you plan on staying here forever, how about you come with me to my home and we shall continue your very necessary lessons?"

As they walked through Sacred Spring, the absence of people disconcerted Adrastea. How unusual for the village to be deserted in daytime. When they reached the crowded inn, Adrastea understood.

A few people stood on the Inn's porch, too late to secure a seat inside. Mira avoided the meeting and hastened Adrastea along. News from Crossroads, was the only explanation Mira gave. Nothing to do with them.

Adrastea looked back. An awful lot of people seemed rather interested in the news from Crossroads. Why not Mira?

⤬

Adrastea liked Mira's cottage. Unlike her mother's clapboard home, Mira's much-older two-room cottage was built of adobe bricks. Mira had covered its wooden floor with a homey rag rug. A table dominated the small kitchen and there was a cupboard with a benchtop. Mira's few possessions resided on shelves along the walls.

The cottage was small, always warm and easy to clean. Mira did not cook often. She spent her evenings in various homes, her Book and glass in tow, providing spiritual guidance in exchange for a good meal. Mira did, however, have a soft spot for a good cup of tea. Most of her crockery centered around tea. She lifted her kettle off its hook on the fireplace and filled it with water from her stone urn.

She swung the full kettle over the fire. "Sit down, Adrastea."

Adrastea settled onto a chair. Mira fetched her Book of the Light from its place of honor on the shelf. "I'm afraid we've neglected your education. We must rectify that." She didn't open the book but spoke frankly to

Adrastea. "I think I know why Mor-Lath is so interested in you. Your talents in the Deeper Power are stronger than we anticipated. You can influence the Lines. Unless checked, it can be a strong temptation to turn Dark."

A chill settled in Adrastea's stomach. "Mira, was my father a Dark priest?"

Mira settled a hand on the book. "No," she answered, sure and faithful. "We hope to keep you the same way." A frown creased Mira's brow. "Mor-Lath knows you have the talent, after you demonstrated it quite well last week."

"He said he wanted to marry me." Now that she thought about it, Adrastea wondered what she would have said, had he asked her to marry him. But he didn't ask. He had told her how things were going to be. Never took into account what her feelings might have been.

What were her feelings? Still, would have been nice if he had asked.

Mira shook her head. "Don't believe him. As the Light stands for truth and righteousness, the Dark is the opposite. He doesn't want to marry you. That's just a ploy. He'll tempt you, then he'll seduce you without benefit of matrimony. When you are no longer any use to him, he'll abandon you, your soul twisted, your heart broken, your reputation ruined. Any future marriage you might make will be doomed, for what husband would want a wife who has consorted with the Dark?"

The one spark Adrastea had for Mor-Lath was snuffed. "Is that all really true?"

The kettle whistled. Mira poured the boiling water into the teapot on the table. One cup she placed before Adrastea. The other she cradled in her hand. "What would the Dark God want with a wife? Why now, and why you?"

It was not as if Adrastea hadn't asked herself these questions before going to sleep at night. Hearing them from Mira's lips stung. "I just thought that... I don't know; there might have been something special about me."

"Special, yes. You can use the Deeper Power. But is it enough to become the consort of the Dark? There are some powerful priestesses in Feown. No doubt the Tredan priestesses are the same. I'd think he would much rather choose from his own followers. You're a country girl, Adrastea. And you walk in the Light."

"Oh." Adrastea felt crushed. "I thought I was somebody special."

Mira placed her cup on the table before pouring the steeped tea. "You are. 'Great gifts come with great responsibilities,'" she quoted. "That's from the Book of the Light. Your talent is greater than mine because of what you can do."

"And what can you do, Mira?"

"I can sense the lines of Deeper Power and can read them with a fair amount of accuracy."

"But you cannot use them?"

Mira smiled—a reaction that Adrastea didn't expect. "I don't have to. I am of the Light. The difference between the Light and the Dark is a matter of trust. Those who live in the Light live clean lives, treat their fellow man honestly and keep their hearts pure. They do not dwell on the past but live in the day and look forward to the future. They trust that the Light will know of their good intents and deeds and send angels to watch over them and to bless them with success. They don't need to manipulate the Deeper Power. Anyone can follow the Light.

"Ah but the Dark. Therein lies a different path. Instead of looking outwards, the Dark turns in towards oneself. It is selfish and blind. Instead of trusting in the wisdom of the Light, the Dark encourages a man to use the Lines to his own end. Selfishness in one person means pain for another."

Adrastea immediately thought of Marta.

Mira added a spoonful of honey and stirred her tea. She took a gentle sip. "We are all interconnected. If someone starts pulling the Lines without thought, then tension is created elsewhere, thus creating bad for all."

This gave Adrastea pause. Ever since she'd grasped the Lines at the barrel, she'd had a growing desire to pull them again.

She had acted without thinking. "But you tried to pull the Lines!"

"Yes, but only because I read Little Peter's future in them." Mira sipped her tea.

Is that why it took so long for Mira to attempt to save Peter? Was she weighing up the consequences of her actions?

Adrastea shook her head. Something was missing but what? "How do you read them?" She lifted her cup. A few small leaves swirled in the dark brew. She waited while they settled before sipping.

"Why, with your heart. As the Dark is selfish, the Light is adept about being aware of others. We think of others, not just ourselves. That's why those who follow the Light refrain from pulling on the Lines, except when necessary for the benefit of another. I could feel that Little Peter wasn't ready to die yet. But all the Lines that connected him to life were being blocked by the barrel. I knew the only way to save him was to destroy the barrel, thus unblocking his Lines."

Mira sipped more tea. "Trust can be a very hard path to follow. Yet that is the path to joy. You have some tough decisions to make, Adrastea. Be extra watchful about them, even the simple ones. Observe the Lines to see your effects. Mor-Lath may come to tempt your body but by your strength you shall see the Light shine in your very heart."

Adrastea swirled her cooling tea. She'd heard of the Light all her life but never really put serious thought in that She was a real personage. Mor-Lath's appearance shook that doubt. "Do you think the Light is watching over me?"

"I would think She does especially. She must be aware of your talents and also the temptations thrown in your path. The best thing that you can do is resist Mor-Lath and trust in Her."

Adrastea had one more question: "I've always wondered, Mira. We women are taught to call the Light She, but men are taught to call the Light He. Why is that?"

Mira paused, thinking.

"Mira?"

After more thought, she replied. "I... never really meditated on that aspect. I assumed it was a way of making our god more personal to the individual."

Adrastea ventured a rather brave supposition. "Could there be more than one God of the Light? Maybe two?"

"No. There is only the one God of the Light. On that, the Book is sure."

That evening Lillybet sat on her back porch, looking up into the fresh clearing. Volunteers had chopped down all the trees to make way for the refugees' cabins. It suited Lilly to see so much change come to the village. Change was good, as far as she was concerned. She listened to the song of change through the Lines. Creation liked change. Change rattled the staid and allowed for new ideas to come in. New ideas made people better.

Furthermore, anything that annoyed Marta had to be a good thing.

A hand descended on her shoulder as the Lines of Deeper Power sang a deep, resonant chord.

"Evening, my pretty," Mor-Lath whispered into her ear. "Nice to see you out and about." Lillybet jumped but Mor-Lath's grip was too strong on her shoulder. "We need to talk."

Lillybet's heart beat rapidly against her ribcage. Blood rushed in her ears.

This was not the suave, calm Mor-Lath that had greeted them on her porch last night. This was the god in his full glory, an aura of power surrounding him. Lillybet could hear, though she could not see, the mocking jeers of the demons who accompanied him. All her childhood nightmares had returned.

He grinned at her. "I've come to ask you for your daughter's hand."

Lillybet screamed. She tore away from his touch and fled inside, slamming the wooden door. So hard did she slam it, the doorlatch snapped off its nails and hung uselessly. She pushed the door closed. Her fingers fiddled with the latch arm, trying to replace it in the limiter. The last nail came loose, and the whole latch fell away. Lilly leaned against the door, hoping that she could hold it shut.

In the entire world, only the house was safe. Only here, could she be safe. Joe's protections had kept the demons at bay.

Lillybet's courage faltered. She had seen terrible horrors in her youth. Whenever she had been bullied or beaten, mocked and scorned, her heart twisted, jerking the Lines about her.

This had brought demons with their snaking claws and burning eyes. They were creatures that appeared as smoke or mist, the center of them comprised of moving images like thoughts. While they had heads, their faces were nebulous, nor did they have eyes as such. Instead, the bright sparks of their awareness served as what could have been a pair of eyes. When their thoughts turned to Lillybet, so did these sparks, to stare into the depths of her soul.

They never touched her and didn't need to. Their very presence sunk her heart into the nadir of depression and left their footprints of fear.

If only Mor-Lath would go away. He would take his demons with him. The Lines vibrated with their antagonism until they sung like a whole orchestra, thick and powerful. Lillybet knew as long as he was there, he would have countless demons at his command.

How long could she last?

She drew in a breath. "Go away. I have nothing to say to you."

"No," he replied. She heard his touch slide across the door. "I have plenty to say to you." He did not push it open. Even a mortal man, putting his full strength behind his push, would have been able to force that door open. Mor-Lath did not. He didn't sound wrathful, though the pull of his presence tugged at Lillybet's soul.

And the demons that flitted about him. Forget the Dark God. It was the demons she feared the most.

Their unholy shrieks were yearnings and lusts that could never be satisfied, for they lacked a mortal body.

They were why she was inside. If she were to go out, they would crawl out of the ether like giant grey wingless bugs to snap at her with sharp, jagged teeth. Those sparks-for-eyes glowed bright with the mockery of the life they once had. The sins which damned them to this eternal torment screeched through their very existence. They eagerly crept forward to partake in the only relief to their misery—making a mortal soul suffer.

Even now, they scrabbled at the door. They could not come through it but that did not make their attempts any less frightening.

She hadn't meant to whimper. "Go away," she whispered, more to the demons than to their god.

They didn't.

Lillybet's hand touched the place on the door where the latch had come apart. That's when she remembered the other door. Her gaze flew to the front door, still wide open in its attempt to draw through the afternoon breezes.

With a cry of horror, Lilly dashed to it.

The demons followed, flying up and over the small thatch-roofed house, to screech their yearnings and frustrations at that front door. She slammed this door in their faces. At least this latch remained intact. She dropped it securely in its limiter and placed her forehead against the solid wood.

Behind her, the back door swung open. Mor-Lath leaned against the jamb but did not cross the threshold. "I don't know why you're closing that door when I'm at this one."

A truth settled into her heart. "It's not you I fear, Dark God." Its veracity solidified as she spoke those words. No, he did not scare her.

Only the demons frightened her.

"Fascinating..." he murmured.

Her head remained on the door, her eyes closed. She felt the Lines gaping in the distance, as if they were making room for... an opening? As one, all the demons departed, drawn towards this opening, if one could call it that, or was it a hole? It sucked them down, drew them away, like stones into a well.

The hole closed once all the demons were gone.

Silence enveloped Lillybet's tiny home. So quiet.

She turned from the wooden door. This was her home, with its plain table, few chairs and her looms. The stuff of her craft, from winding skeins of yarn and spools of fine thread, to folded piles of cloth and the rag rug on the floor padded the corners of her home so it did not look so bare.

And there was the Dark God, standing ever-so-casually at her back door, as if waiting for an invitation to come in.

The Dark God. The father of demons, the master of human sin, the punisher of the evil and the guilty, who drew away their souls to Dom-al-gol, the House of Demons, to torment them after death.

It was him who let the demons roam the living world. He had permitted them to torment her every day of her life.

How dare he!

That torment had driven her to follow the Light, to heed every single one of Mira's lessons, to live by every good rule. If every mortal had even a taste of what she'd suffered regularly, they, too, would have been driven to live good and worthy lives.

Anger, borne of her frustration, welled in her heart. It spilled out to her limbs and blinded her eyes with rage.

All this was his fault. Every. Last. Bit. She needed something to throw at him, something hard.

Her gaze settled upon her table, still cluttered with dishes from her last meal. The ceramic cup. That would do nicely. Her feet carried her to the table, her hand was outstretched.

Her foot caught upon the rug and she tripped. Her hand slid past the cup and ran up along the knife on the cheeseboard. Her torso fell forward. The edge of the table knocked the wind out of her.

At first it felt like a scrape but then the laceration on her arm began to sting. Blood welled forth from the cut to spill down her skin. She lifted her arm to stare in fascination. The cut started at her wrist and ended deep near the inside of her elbow. Oh, it hurt. It really hurt. Stars appeared before her eyes.

"Lillybet?" Mor-Lath's voice had an edge of concern.

The Lines wrapped about her, coming from him. She flung up her good hand. "No!" So forceful was her cry, it came out as a hoarse croak. "Don't you touch me." She reached for a tea towel to press against her bleeding arm.

He remained in the doorway, his hands gripping the door frame. "I can heal you."

A bitter chuckle escaped her lips. "I don't think so." It would be just like the Dark God to do her a favor and then hold her to ransom over her daughter.

"If I don't heal you, you will die."

As she pressed the towel to the cut, her heartbeat pounded in her ears. "What? And owe you my life?" Lillybet loved Adrastea. She reminded her so much of Joe. And now she displayed talent. She could never betray her to the Dark God.

Mor-Lath remained in the doorway. He could not come in.

The towel did not stop the bleeding, no matter how hard she held it.

The house was safe. Lillybet looked to her arm, pressed close to her side. Her blood soaked through the towel and onto her skirt. Was he right? Would she die?

Her body shuddered with a sob. Here was Death, coming for her, just as she'd come for Joe. Death stood behind the Dark God, in her pale robe, her strange, absent eyes studying, waiting.

Death was what Lillybet called this personage. She always came when someone was about to die. Lillybet had seen her roam the village from time to time. She even confronted her to plead for Joe's life.

Not that Death had listened. As Joe let his last breath go, she bent close to him, took his soul, and disappeared. Lilly refused to believe Death took the soul for anyone else but the Light.

Joe was good. He had been strong and clever. He'd laid a protection over the house before he died. Used his own blood he did, and a drop of hers.

Her blood still seeped. She looked past the Dark God to Death. "I'm going to die, aren't I?"

Death shrugged. "Everyone dies, in the end." Her not-eyes flickered to Mor-Lath.

A stillness settled in Lillybet's chest. So that was it. Death had come for her.

She stumbled to the door and slumped to the floor, unable to close it.

Mor-Lath also crouched down. "Lillybet, please. Let me save you."

"No." If she lived, Adrastea would be in danger. But in her death, she could protect her daughter.

Lillybet peeled back the useless towel and let the last of her blood flow over the doorstop. There. That would protect her daughter. That would keep the house safe. As Lillybet had, Adrastea could flee here to be protected.

Her consciousness flickered in and out. She leaned against the doorjamb. "Why her?" she asked. "Why my Adrastea?"

He weighed her questions. "There is none better than she."

"Why...?" The word was almost impossible to utter.

"It's not too late," he urged. "I can still save you. If you die now, it will be a meaningless death."

Words fled her as the world grew dark. She shook her head, a last defiance of the Dark God.

This is how Lillybet Weaver died, for the love of her daughter.

⚬❦⚬

Mor-Lath watched the light go out of Lillybet's eyes. He sighed. Such a waste.

Death stood on the porch. Her head bowed in sorrow. Tears filled her eyes. Those eyes, there and not there, bothered Mor-Lath, with the way they saw into every soul, living or dead. "You did that deliberately. You conned her into her own death."

He reached through the doorway and stroked her still-warm skin. "She stood in my way."

Death crouched down and straightened the body. "Her death shall come back to haunt you. Such interference twists the web of Creation."

Mor-Lath looked at the pale woman before him. "You, of all people, should not lecture me on the web of Creation. I am trying to restore the balance, as you well know."

"Hmm. Balance, huh?"

"What is one death in the greater scheme of things?"

"Because this one death may deprive you of that which you seek." Death rearranged the folds of Lillybet's skirt, so it draped properly against the lifeless legs.

"Not if she doesn't find out. Stop playing with her mother."

Death looked over her shoulder at him. Oh, those eyes made his skin crawl. She collected Lilly's soul and weighed it. "This one goes to the Light. You cannot stop her now."

Mor-Lath shrugged. "Perhaps not. But it doesn't matter at the moment. She is dead. My path is cleared." If only Lillybet knew blood magic was only good as long as the heart that begot it still beat.

Death's not-eyes narrowed. She had no more to say to the God of the Dark. She vanished, there one moment and gone the next.

Mor-Lath looked at Lillybet lying at his feet. "Well," he said to himself. "Let us sow a bit more discord here."

He picked the body up. "Sorry, my lovely." He carried it inside, stepping over the threshold that once was forbidden to him.

Martine knew the family would be in for a bad day. Too much change had come too fast. After yesterday's meeting, everything had gone topsy-turvy. Her mother Marta went to bed in a bad mood and woke in a bad mood. Her father Tam, familiar with his wife of twenty-five years, knew this would happen. He had arranged to be out of the house and busy before Marta woke. Martine held the same opinion as her father. The earlier she finished her chores, the sooner she could take off.

She hoped to take the laundry downstairs before her mother stirred. She was too late.

Martine had the misfortune to come up the stairs at the same time her mother came out of the bedroom. She saw the skirt lying in the middle of the hallway the same time Marta did.

"Martine! Why did you leave that skirt there, you stupid girl?" Marta punched her on the arm. Martine, with years of practice, ducked enough to avoid most of the blow but took some of it so her thwarted mother would not see fit to deliver another one. The skirt must have fallen out of the basket. She scooped it up and hastened downstairs.

"You'd better take it down right now!" Marta shrieked after her. "Miss Hoity-Toity I-can-leave-my-clothes-anywhere. We're not rich, you know!"

Martine banged open the rear kitchen door that led out into the yard, and thus to the wash-house. As she crossed, she noticed the tell-tale swinging closed of the stable door. Most of her siblings would have taken refuge in the stables, hiding along with their father.

Those who were not fast enough to cross the yard ducked into the wash-house. As soon as they saw that it was Martine and not their mother, they relaxed.

The wash-house was a wooden outbuilding with only a few small windows to let in light. One end boasted a large copper tank for heating water. Along one wall stood several buckets for washing, with paddles for stirring and beating the laundry. Several of her siblings, including the younger ones, tended the loads of wet clothing.

In the dark steaminess of the wash-house, Martine held up the bundle. "Who left a skirt at the top of the stairs?" she demanded.

Nobody owned up. All the children knew better than to leave anything lying around. Marta was house-proud, and woe betided the child who disturbed her kingdom.

"Well, somebody did it!" Martine shook out the skirt in preparation for washing.

"Ew!" screeched Sally. "What's that?"

Martine looked at the skirt, then opened the door for a better look.

It was spattered with far too much blood to be a womanly accident.

Mira heard the rumble of covered wagons and the bellow of an ox as the refugees arrived at Sacred Spring.

Adrastea's tolerance for lessons yesterday ran short. Eventually, Mira took her to Ari, where they learned of Ely's letter and Natan's agreement. With such upheaval pending, they could not afford to leave Adrastea idle at Lillybet's house. So back to Ari she went, there to be kept too busy to consider any inappropriate suit.

Nobody expected the refugees to show up so early. Too early?

Mira, still reading Mor-Lath's book, paused and looked out the window. She had been reading a section on lie-detecting and discernment, finding it most fascinating. No doubt Natan would come looking for her if she did not go out to help him. Should he discover the book, Mira didn't know what he'd do. Probably react as Ari had.

Tam Innkeeper hastened out to greet them as the wagons stopped before the inn. The drivers unhitched the oxen to allow them to graze on the village green.

Natan and Tam had a brief discussion. Something about Marta and Martine having an argument. Marta hadn't been feeling good of late.

Mira moved closer to Tam, approaching him from behind as he succinctly spilled his woes to Natan. She held out her hand to hover just over Tam's back without actually touching him and closed her eyes. Tam's Lines were vivid at this point, no doubt due to the stress of the latest of mother/daughter altercations.

Before, Mira would have simply read the Lines and have been done with it. But after having read that book of Adrastea's, she questioned whether she could be able to do more than just read the Lines.

Mira withdrew her fingers. It was enough that she could sense a certain patience about Tam, and the stress of the disagreement. If only Mira knew what it had been about.

The refugees were mostly children. The only adults apart from the ox divers and Carles, their priest, were nursing mothers and a few elderly people. In all, there were forty souls to remain in Sacred Spring.

"My old friend!" Carles declared as he enveloped Mira in a hug. He wasn't too much taller than her and certainly no taller than Tam. He wore a simple blue cloak of good fabric over brown trousers and tunic. Religious robes were unsuitable for travel. The stains would never come out of the white fabric.

Natan and Tam helped the Crossroaders unload the meager possessions from the wagons—some of which looked like barrels of food, as well as trunks and baskets for belongings.

"Ely gave me your letter," Carles said after their greetings and inquiries after mutual friends. "I have a young journeywoman by name of Chloe you can have." He sighed as he looked at the unloaded children huddling on the porch, bewildered more than frightened at their sudden exodus. "If this were any other situation, I would have sent her along instead, but I had a feeling I should come and visit you."

Mira's heart froze, as if to keep her secrets inside. "Oh? Why?"

Carles looked into Mira's hazel eyes with his warm brown ones. "You don't look too well."

"I'm fine..." Mira said, with no idea about what else Carles may have seen.

"You look like you haven't slept."

"I haven't," she admitted. "I must admit I've had a bit of a..." she mused over a good word, "situation happen here." For a moment, she debated over whether or not she should confide Adrastea's secret. "Walk with me and I shall tell you."

Carles suggested, if time allowed, that they visit the Sacred Spring. He had not seen it for a couple of years.

As they wandered up the pathway towards the Spring, Mira chatted with Carles about her lack of an apprentice and how the village was pressuring her to get one. "But nobody here, really, has the talent."

"Absolutely nobody?"

Mira didn't answer.

"Ah, so you do have a candidate. What's wrong with her—or is it a him?"

"A her. I'd had my eye on her for a while now but she's too old to apprentice. Besides, even if she was young enough, the people of the village won't accept her. They think she's strange."

Carles nodded his pale head. "The talented often are. Who is she?"

"Lillybet Weaver."

"Ah," he replied, then a frown crossed his face. "I don't think I've met her."

"She's not one for being social." The steepness of the hill made her breathe harder.

"And her apprentices?"

Mira sighed. She slowed her ascent. "She's another one without apprentices but nobody seems to care. They don't mind getting their fabrics and such from other villages. Besides, nobody wishes to apprentice their children to her."

"Why?"

How best to put this? "Lilly has a bit of a reputation for being odd. She's had it ever since she was a child."

"It can't be too bad. Someone apprenticed her."

Mira shook her head and resumed her climb. "Nobody would take her, so she was apprenticed to her parents."

"They are dead, I assume."

Mira nodded. "And her husband as well." She began to huff.

Carles seemed to have the same problems with breathing—not too many foothills to be found in Crossroads. "Could we slow down?"

Mira took pity on him. They sat on the grass so he could catch his breath.

Their vista looked over the village, including Lilly's house and the new constructions. The rawness of the clearing, with its gashes of dirt among the brownish-green grasses of summer betrayed its newness. Lillybet's house seemed too bare without its cloak of trees to hide it from the world. To Mira, the whole village seemed over-exposed. Down the hill, still thankfully covered with quaking aspen and a stray cottonwood, sat the smithy, also looking bare without its giant water tank. Wagons and busy little people filled the normally quiet village green.

"Does she have children?" Carles asked.

"Her son Mikal is Natan's apprentice, so you'll be seeing more of him."

"Not a glimmer of talent in him?"

Mira shook her head. "None that I could see." She plucked one of the long stalks of yellow field grass and twisted it into a circle to plait it together. "And she has an adult daughter, Adrastea."

"Odd name, Adrastea. Where does it come from?"

"Her father. He was from Feown."

Carles nodded. He, too, began plucking grass and playing with it. "There something you're not telling me?"

The moment had come that Mira dreaded. "Promise you won't think ill of me?"

"How could I? I've known you too long."

She took a breath. "Adrastea didn't show talent until a fortnight ago. Until then, I had no idea she possessed it, though I should have suspected it. I knew Lilly had been touched by the Deeper Power, and Joe was talented. The Lines behaved strangely around her. I realized later her influence on the Lines could be felt by the others. That's why they didn't like her. She didn't feel right. I suspected Joe—her husband—had some talents in that area. He seemed to create his own luck."

"I don't think I met Joe. Who's his family?"

Mira shrugged. "Don't know. He came from far away, a pilgrim who chose to stay." She pointed to Lilly's house. "He built that for his bride."

Carles squinted. "Something's not right about that house."

Mira twisted the ends of her grass around until it made a bracelet-sized circle. Funny how circles worked. "Oh, that's probably Lilly's influence. Told you she felt a bit odd."

"Oh." Carles nodded pensively. "I should like to meet her." He reverted the subject. "Her daughter, um…"

"Adrastea."

"Adrastea. What happened?"

Mira explained the incident with young Peter climbing on the roof of the smithy, standing on the cover of the rain tank, which had worm rot—though nobody had known—and falling through. She explained all, through to when Adrastea demonstrated her talent."

Carles continued to study the well-built house on the hill. No smoke issued from the chimney—not an uncommon thing in the height of summer—and the hillside behind it sported what looked like several new small cabins, albeit without roofs. Yes, the Weaver home did seem rather odd. Perhaps it was the missing trees.

"How old is she?" Carles asked. "The daughter, I mean."

"Twenty-two. She's been Ari's journeywoman for several years now."

"Natan's Ari?"

Mira nodded.

"If you were truly desperate, would Ari release her to you?"

Mira looked away. "It's not as easy as that. She, being Lilly's daughter, would not be accepted by the villagers as their priestess. Anyhow, she is—um—how to put this?"

Carles waited while Mira sorted her thoughts. Mira drew in deep breaths, trying to calm herself. Ever since they met during her journeyhood, Carles had always been able to read her. What vibrations did she send along the Lines? Would he guess her secrets? Her stomach knotted up. "Let us say she is bespoken."

Carles scooted closer and brushed a strand of blond hair from his eyes. "As in betrothed?"

Mira wiped her chin as a child would wipe grease from his face. "Not exactly. She has a suitor but one who is entirely unsuitable for her. We are trying to discourage the match, but he is most insistent."

"And you fear she will elope?"

Mira fretted and twisted her grass bracelet. "Not exactly. He is most persuasive. While she can see the logic of not marrying him, he seems to have a way of seducing her heart."

"She's told you this much?"

"She doesn't need to. I can feel it... you know." She waved her hand to indicate Creation.

"He claims marriage is his goal but from what I know of him, he does not strike me as the kind of someone to offer honorable marriage." To close any further discussions Carles may wish to pursue, Mira concluded by saying, "So, yes, I have a situation. I would be glad to have Chloe if she is willing to come here until I can find an apprentice. Meanwhile, much of my time goes to protecting young Adrastea from the unhonorable intentions of her suitor."

"Does he have a name?"

Mira shrugged too casually. "It's not important." She rose. "Look." Natan and the ox masters came up the hill dragging Peter Smith's baggage-filled handcarts. "Our guests arrive. Say, didn't you want to meet Lillybet?"

Chapter 8

Mikal still felt like one of the Innkeepers' brood. So what if he was sitting on the Mayor's porch and not the Innkeepers? So what if he had a new tunic and new sleeping arrangements, with a room of his own? Natan didn't live far from the Inn; Mikal could see his old home from Natan's.

Natan had persuaded Tam to be generous towards the oxdrivers, even to the free feeding of the oxen for the hour they were here. He watched as the oxen pulled at the piles of hay and dipped their heads into the creek from the spring.

Bored, Mikal got up, skirted the village green and headed back behind the Inn. No doubt Tom would want to hear the rest of Mikal's news.

As Mikal made his way to the stables, he heard someone hiss at him from the wash house. It was his older foster-sister Martine, peeking out from behind the door. She held it mostly closed as if afraid of being spied upon. Mikal glanced up to the windows of the Inn. Nobody looked down, least of all Marta.

Martine beckoned once, then disappeared back inside. With an ease long practiced, Mikal changed his direction and headed to the building. Once inside the dank, dark building, he learned what she wanted of him.

"Take this skirt," she hissed, as she shoved a damp bundle into his arms. "Hide it somewhere Mom won't find it. I'll come get it later."

"Why?" Growing up with this brood also taught him caution.

"Don't ask now. Just do it. Promise you won't tell anybody."

"Why?" Then he noticed a large dark patch on the skirt. It looked as if she'd tried scrubbing the stain away, to no avail. Having grown up with several foster-sisters, he guessed the meaning of blood on a skirt. No wonder Martine wanted to hide it from Marta. If his foster mother found out Martine had ruined another skirt, poor Martine would have to wear her shame for the rest of the year, for she would not get a new skirt until after winter.

She scowled at him. Mikal gave in, departing with the skirt.

Since he wanted to make a good impression on his uncle but not lose the good will of Martine he dumped the skirt on the back porch of the Mayor's house and returned to his duties as mayorprentice, whatever those might be.

Brute labor, it turned out. No sooner had he sidled up to Natan than the Mayor spied him. "There you are. Help load up."

The oxdrivers had unloaded the contents of the wagons, setting the smaller boxes and bags in the dust of the road beside them. Several of Mikal's foster brothers had piled the possessions into the handcarts, with Peter and Tam directing the best way to load them. Mikal loaded the smaller items to the front, letting the bigger and stronger men handle the heavier trunks. Already two handcarts wended their way up the hill, with Tam Innkeeper leading them.

Natan consulted with the Crossroader adults while their children clumped together, their eyes looking about the village. They stood quietly and awaited their fate. He'd offered them a smile and a greeting, which they did not return. Were they all right?

With nobody to tell him otherwise, Mikal went with the handcarts up the hill. Maybe one of the Crossroaders would tell him what was wrong?

Mira and Carles hiked their way toward the clearing. Lillybet's house was in full view now. Behind it stood two log cabins, with three more in various stages of completion. Carles paused on the path down the hill. "I feel cold. How can you live with that?" He gestured towards Lillybet's house. "That's not right."

Mira looked to Lillybet's home. Whatever it was that Carles felt, she felt it too, an unnatural stillness along the Lines. Lilly's house always had soul but now...?

A few more steps brought them to the back of Lillybet's house. Washed wool draped the fence, drying in the sun. Carles wouldn't even approach the fence. "I'm not going there. Something is not right there."

Mira turned to him. "You don't have to. The houses on the hill belong to your people."

"No." His voice was low and cold. She'd never seen him still like this, frightened. "Nobody is living here until that place," he pointed to Lillybet's home, "is cleansed."

Mira hadn't been expecting that. "Cleansed? What? Why?"

The way Carles stared at her made her feel like a guilty child again. "Can you honestly not feel it?"

Her heart began to thump. "Lilly's always felt a little odd." What if Carles wasn't sensing Lillybet but her own guilt?

He shook his head so hard that wisps of light hair whipped around his face. "This isn't oddness. This is evil."

Mira looked away. "If it would make you feel better, we can cleanse the place. I'll have to find my smudge sticks."

"This needs more than smudging."

Mira's eyes shot up. "Oh, no. Lilly won't let you."

Carles came forward and took her hands. "No. Burning won't be necessary. But it will need a full kashering."

What would Lillybet say? She would be not easily convinced to let Carles kasher the whole house. Perhaps if she could convince Carles to let them do all the hard work of moving furniture, scrubbing and washing everything, then Lilly would be more willing to let them do it.

If it kept peace among them all, Mira would do something. "I'll see what I can arrange." She gave Carles a pointed look. "Don't say anything to anyone until we get this sorted out." Perhaps Lillybet would be generous enough to allow the neediest Crossroaders to share her home, small though it was. Certainly, wouldn't hurt to ask.

As Mira entered Lillybet's yard, she wasn't sure if the cold dread she felt in her stomach was the stress of having to impose on Lilly, her own guilt, or if she was jumping at the shadows of Carles' caution. It grew stronger as she stepped up on the porch and knocked at the door. "Lilly? It's me," she called out.

No answer. She knocked again, just in case Lilly was sleeping, or busy. If she knocked loud enough, perhaps she would hear...

Nothing.

Mira shook her head. That didn't make sense. Lilly wouldn't—

A cold feeling bloomed in the pit of her stomach. It wasn't fear or dread. It was similar to the feelings she got when she had opened Mor-Lath's book.

Her senses overwhelmed her. What she was feeling wasn't Lilly at all. There was no twisting of the Lines in unexpected paths that usually accompanied Lillybet's presence.

This was the cold dark dread of emptiness.

She screamed out Lilly's name as she threw her shoulder at the door. It flew open. The latch was broken. Had someone forced their way in? She fell into the empty common room. Where was Lilly? What were those brown stains on the floor?

Footsteps pounded on the path outside.

"Mira...?" Carles voice pushed in through her haze of panic.

There. On the floor, behind the table. Mira scrambled over to Lillybet.

Lilly lay on her back, an arm up and over her face as if defending herself. From her arm rose a knife, the ugly stamen of a blood-red flower. It was stuck in her arm.

Mira's gorge rose. "Lilly?" Horror sharpened Mira's vision. Few Lines emanated from Lillybet. There was no living soul there.

She couldn't stay any longer. Mira rushed outside to empty the contents of her stomach on the ground. As she retched, two thoughts flitted through her mind: who did this, and who was going to tell Adrastea?

⁂

Natan didn't know who would tell her. He certainly didn't want to do it. Nor did he want to tell Mikal, although that duty would have to fall to him. Ari. Yes, Ari would have to. After all, Ari was the Healer and Adrastea her journeyman.

He had fallen into a chair at the table, and there he remained. He could not scrub the image of his dead sister from his thoughts. His mind drifted over the pale, pale face, the dark blood soaked into that infernal rag rug of hers. The knife stuck up from her arm like an obscenity.

Ari had come. She had not given herself over to grief but stiffened her expression and left her heart outside. While Natan sat at the table the Healer removed the knife, settled the body and, with the help of Carles, moved her to the bedroom. She did nothing about the rug.

Who killed Lilly, he wondered. Who killed Lilly? It had to be murder. The door latch was broken, and here was Lilly, a knife stuck into her arm.

He did not turn when Ari laid a hand on his shoulder. "Natan?"

Natan lowered his arm. "Who killed Lilly?"

Ari didn't answer.

Natan heaved a sob for his dead sister. "Oh, Lillybet. I'm so sorry." His eyes stung and blurred. Until today, he had rarely spilt tears over his sister. Now they spilled out of his eyes in hot rivulets down his dusty face. He should have protected her. He leaned forward until he rested on his hands, and then his forehead to the table, his back bent with grief.

Natan cried and cried. He cried until he had no more tears, then he sobbed until even those dried up. Then there was nothing to do but stay there and let the cold numbness of Lillybet's absence sit like an empty room in his heart. The world continued on its way, but he didn't care. He could only wait until the pain erupted fresh once more and he cried again.

Ari laid a warm hand on his back, startling him. "Natan." When did she come in?

Eventually, he sat up. His head buzzed, and his vision greyed for a moment as he returned to the ugliness of the world. Sacred Spring was a small town. Sure, people had their spats from time to time but this? The buzzing in his head turned in to the buzzing of a few flies that had arrived to investigate the bounty of blood.

Still in the chair, he turned his face into Ari's stomach and hugged her tight. His tears were gone but his sorrow still burned. She held him until he had the strength to rise again.

Ari was so good. His heart fluttered with gratitude. She patted his shoulder and set an empty cup in front of him. He wrapped his hand about it.

Outside, the shadows had lengthened as the sun prepared itself for bed. Night would come and what would it bring?

Ari checked the fire. A few coals remained to be coaxed into something of a small blaze.

Ari put a few pieces of kindling on the fire. "I've brought some tea," Ari said.

"I think I need something stronger.

"Mmm," replied Ari, her tone judging him. "I think you'll prefer this 'tea'. It's lactoverosa."

"I thought you were supposed to smoke that."

"You can drink it too."

She said no more until the water boiled. Ari spooned dry tea directly into the cup and poured the water over. It didn't quite fill it up, but it would be enough. "Carles said he would come back once he settled his people. He's staying at Mira's place tonight. It's too late to go back to Crossroads now." Ari sat in the other chair and laid her slim hand over his large one. "Mira's shaken. Carles told me something of what happened here."

Natan nodded.

As the tea brewed, Ari ventured carefully. "Do we know what happened?"

Natan stared past her to the fire. "Who killed Lilly?" he asked.

Her gaze flickered to the rug. "Was it murder?"

"That looked like no accident."

Ari nudged his hand about the cup. He lifted it, sipped and made a face. "I didn't kill her. Not you, not Mira. Not Carles. Not Adrastea?" Her voice rose a little in the end.

Natan looked at her with a frown. "No. Not her." His eyes suggested another possibility.

Ari drew a sharp breath through her nose. "Surely not him. He wouldn't have a reason. And why would a god need a knife?"

"Does he need one? A reason, I mean." Or a knife.

Ari sighed. "I guess not. But it doesn't make sense. If he killed Lillybet, how would that win over Adrastea?"

For the first time since entering the cabin, Natan straightened up. The creased of sorrow that hunched his forehead smoothed out. "It wouldn't, would it?" Adrastea would completely turn away from Mor-Lath if she thought he was responsible.

Her eyes grew wide and she whispered hoarsely, "We can't tell her that!"

"Her mother's dead. We've got to tell her something. Why not tell her he killed her?"

"Natan, that's not honest!"

Natan broke. "Bloody hell, Ari!" he shouted as he slammed his fist into the table. "My sister's dead and you're worried about honesty?"

"Drink your tea." She wrapped her hands about his and lifted the cup to his lips. "What if he didn't kill her?"

He drank with a sour expression. "Who else could it be?"

Ari shook her head. "If we tell her that he killed Lilly, what happens if he comes along and refutes the claim?"

Natan rolled his eyes. "I thought that was obvious. We call him the liar he is."

Ari drew in a breath through her teeth. "I don't think that's a good idea. We shouldn't be making him angry."

"I don't bloody care!" Natan slumped in his chair. He gulped down his tea, dregs and all.

Ari sat silent for a few moments. "If it was murder, the real killer is still loose, still angry."

Natan stared into his cup. That tasted terrible, but a pleasant hum sang lullabies in the back of his head. He wanted more.

"How about," she suggested, "we wait and see what happens before we say anything to anybody?"

"Who knows about this?"

Ari thought for a moment. "Um, you, me, Carles and Mira of course... I think that's all. A few people—Crossroader, mainly—suspect something's happened. Carles said he would do some—how did he put it—um, 'creative truth-telling', whatever that means. Oh, and possibly Mikal."

"Oh, no."

Ari shrugged apologetically. "Carles had a bit of a talk with him, I believe. He didn't tell me what he told Mikal."

Natan had a few more tears left. As they spilled over, he said, "I will speak with him first thing tomorrow. I will also speak with Adrastea. They'll know their mother has died but..." his voice trailed off.

"Worry about that tomorrow." With a sigh, she looked back to the bedroom, where Lilly had been laid out. Natan's glance followed. He wished she had closed the door. "Go home, Natan. I'll sit vigil for now. Carles said he'd stop by later, in case we needed him. When he does, I'll come see you then. Meanwhile, I have some more things I must do tonight."

At first, Natan wanted to question her over whether or not she would do it alone. He couldn't ask Adrastea to see her mother like that. He thought back to the deaths of his own parents. They were older then, and their deaths came with warning. First his father in the epidemic, then his mother a few weeks later. Most people survived the illness that swept through but the old or the weak it hit especially hard.

At least they had time to say goodbye.

"Where is Adrastea?" Natan asked.

"With Mira. Carles is taking care of everyone else."

Natan stared into the dying flames of the fireplace. His head had trouble focusing as the lactoverosa took effect. "And Mikal?" Even though his nephew hadn't been that close to Lillybet, he was still her son.

"He's with them too, I think." Ari rose from the table. She added another log to the fire. "Natan, go home."

Natan rose obediently. He swayed a little "Oh, Ari. How am I going to sleep tonight?"

Ari shrugged. "Ask me tomorrow."

Natan didn't sleep at all, despite the draught Ari had given him. He sat alone on his back porch in the stillness of the evening looking into his neglected back garden. He was never much of a gardener. This porch faced south, not west towards the mountains. He didn't think he could bear to look towards Lillybet's house, even from this distance. Instead, he overlooked the Poulters' place. On those rare days when a southerly blew, he smelled their henhouses.

He settled down on the rough-hewn bench that served as his seat in the privacy of his back garden. He settled down for a good, proper worry. Night had fallen, plunging the countryside and the mountains into gloom. Above him, the sky appeared brighter, a navy blue spread of glittering stars. The canyon breezes rushed down from the pass, bringing the scent of smoke and pine trees. The breeze blew against him. Somewhere a neighbor's wind chimes tinkled softly.

There he sat while Ari did her duty and prepared the dead. He waited for her while she balmed the body and burned anything stained with blood. He hoped the smell wouldn't be too bad; at least the canyon breeze would blow the smell of smoke away from the refugees' homes.

An odd thought: had the builders remembered to dig latrines? Sanitation would be an issue, especially up on the hill like that. Natan sighed. Another worry to add to his growing list.

Natan shivered as the canyon breeze died and the temperature dropped. Instead of fetching a jacket or blanket, he pulled his arms into his tunic. He watched as the stars moved across the sky, not wondering about the time but waiting for Ari and dreading the morning.

Adrastea and Mikal waited at Mira's cottage until Ari and Natan came home. Uncle Natan's eyes were red and bloodshot. Ari's had bags under them. Natan enveloped Adrastea in a tight bear hug. "Oh, my dear girl!"

Mira and Carles sat silently as Natan imparted the news of Lillybet's death.

"How?" Adrastea cried. She and Mikal sat side by side on Mira's bench. Adrastea took Mikal's hand and squeezed it tightly. Mikal did not pull away.

Natan did not answer. He looked to Ari. She held his gaze before answering. "She bled out."

"From what?" Adrastea asked.

"Knife cut to the forearm."

Mikal bowed his head and said nothing. Adrastea burst out in fierce tears. Nobody, not even Ari, moved to comfort her while she wailed out her initial burst of grief.

Her mother—gone. But hadn't she spoken to her yesterday? Lillybet had told her so many, many things. Stories of her father, her grandparents and more. Things Adrastea never knew. Now she would never know the rest.

Natan took what was left of his family up the hill to Lillybet's home. The shutters were closed, and the curtains drawn. The house was dark but for the light from the open door.

Ari had done a good job. She'd washed the body well and had dressed Lillybet up in one of her best dresses—a winter one, with a high neck and long sleeves to hide the wound. She even dressed Lillybet's brown hair, brushing it until it shone. But nothing she could do could disguise the pallor of Lilly's exsanguinated face, nor could she completely disguise the faint coppery smell of blood.

Her mother looked so, so pale, and so empty. Lillybet's soul had gone.

She took her mother's hand. It was cold. She dropped it immediately. Then, picking it up again, she held it, noting how it didn't respond. Behind her, Natan and Ari stood in the doorway. Mikal leaned back against them, as if trying, unknowingly, to push past them and escape.

"She didn't die naturally, did she?" Mikal asked.

Natan put a hand on Mikal's shoulder. "No. She didn't." Mikal turned away from the body.

Adrastea gazed upon what was left of her mother. A few flies buzzed about. She shooed them away when they got too close. Then, gently, she laid the stiff hand back on Lillybet's chest.

She drew in a dry, shuddery sob. As much as she tried, she couldn't will the tears to stay back. Her vision blurred. Her eyes stung before the tears spilled across her cheeks. Her black scar didn't hurt any more. As she wiped the tears away with the back of her hand, she couldn't even feel the mark. Her skin was as smooth as it had ever been.

"Was she killed?" Had it been an accident, Ari would have said so. But since everyone was treating this all hush-hush, that meant there was a secret to be kept. And what sort of secret could be kept about a death except for a murder? There were far too many secrets here for her comfort.

"We don't know," Natan replied.

Adrastea turned an accusing glare at him. "Why not?" she demanded.

Mikal drew in a sob of his own, then, with a strength nobody would have expected of him, he pushed his way through Natan and Ari and ran down the hill.

Natan and Ari exchanged a single glance. Natan turned and followed his apprentice at a more leisurely pace.

Ari folded her arms and pursed her mouth.

Adrastea felt guilty. She hadn't meant to speak so harshly. She hung her head but did not apologize.

The long night showed in the dark circles under Ari's eyes. "We suspect it was someone who had access to the Inn."

Adrastea stiffened. "How so?"

Ari went to Lillybet, lifted the hem of the dead woman's skirt and brought out a knife. "This is what we found."

Adrastea saw the word "INN" scratched into the handle of the knife. The Innkeepers were in the habit of marking all their goods. "Did one of them do it?"

Ari shook her head. "We don't know. It could have been anyone. It could have been an accident."

Adrastea's heart tightened. "So, we won't find her killer? Is that it? And who goes around killing people?"

With a gentle hand, Ari replaced the knife and lowered the hem. "When he is ready, I will give the knife to Natan and let him sort it out. We don't know what happened. I only wish we had a Constable here, so he didn't have to do it. Maybe Carles can send one when he returns to Crossroads."

"What happens now?" Adrastea remembered her father's funeral, her hand on the torch.

Ari dropped her hands. "Tomorrow eve, the pyre. After that? I don't know."

Adrastea turned away. "Who else knows?"

"I don't know. Not many."

Adrastea sniffed. "What are we going to tell the village?"

Ari came forth and with hands on the young woman's shoulders, drew Adrastea away. "Let Natan and Mira worry about that. For now, you and I must go gather wood."

Chapter 9

Natan sighed as he left Lillybet's house. This was not the way he wanted Mikal's new apprenticeship to start.

Mikal wasn't that hard to find. He'd fled straight to the Mayor's house. Those few villagers who were out and about were more than helpful in pointing the path of his flight, and Natan caught up with him he turned the corner of the house. There was his apprentice, fishing out a bundle of clothing from under the bench on the back porch.

Mikal froze when he saw his uncle. "I know who killed my mother!" His adolescent voice cracked.

What? Natan glanced both ways to ensure they were not being observed. "Turn around and walk slowly back into the house."

Only when the door was securely shut and the curtains safely drawn did Mikal reveal his bundle. He shook out the skirt, which cracked and wouldn't fully unfurl, as it had dried in its crumpled-up state. On the skirt, all over, were large brown stains. That was an awful lot of blood.

Natan stared in horror at them. "Where did you get this?"

Mikal broke. A tear ran down his face. "Martine gave it to me. She told me to hide it where Ma, I mean, Marta, couldn't find it."

Natan turned away in thought. His hand sought the chair at the table. He sat down, for he didn't know if his legs would support him. "Not Martine," he murmured to himself. To Mikal, he said, "Did she say why it had to be hidden?"

Mikal shook his head. "Martine was supposed to wash it. She couldn't get the stains out. I think it scared her."

Natan said, "Speak of this to no one. We shall ask Martine about it later."

Mikal nodded mutely. Natan rose, pondering on what the bloody skirt could mean. Why did Martine want to hide it? There were far too many unanswered questions.

As Natan prepared for his sister's funeral, his new apprentice was as good as his word. He hung close to Natan during the rest of the day. Had his apprentice been anyone else but Mikal, Natan would have sent him to spread the news of Lillybet's death. Instead, Natan laid aside Natan Mayor and let himself be Uncle Natan, the only familial pillar of strength the lad had left.

A Mayor would have ensured the news spread, accurate and true. A brother only wanted to grieve.

Natan didn't feel like going to them. If they cared about her, they'd come ask.

He wanted them to come ask. He wanted them to come to him. He wanted them to prove that Lillybet mattered in the village. To him, to send someone around to remind them because they had forgotten betrayed his sister. Let them ask. Let them come to him.

Later that evening he and Ari, Mikal and Adrastea piled wood in the village commons. Ari came along and Natan was glad of her presence. They chose a spot close to where the wagons had stood yesterday, not far from the Inn or Natan's home.

After all the grief the villagers gave his sister throughout her life, she deserved to be the center of attention. Ain't nobody going to forget Lillybet Weaver. They might have relegated her to the fringe of society but Natan was bound and determined to make them notice her in the last moment of her existence.

From time to time, villagers came to stare.

Too few offered direct condolences. Carles handed the family food during one trip back to the village with his cartload of wood while Mira kept vigil at the house. "I never knew her. Still, I am sorry for your loss."

Kyfa Spinster, the one person in the village could have been counted Lillybet's friend, stood on the edge of the green, among the trees that grew in the lee of the hill. She cried for the rest of the afternoon.

Otherwise, everyone left the family to themselves. Most villagers were up the hill helping build cabins for the Crossroaders.

The hard work of cutting, loading and moving brush wood from the cabin offcuts kept the pain of sorrow away. When Mikal showed signs of stopping, it was Adrastea who whispered sharply in his ear. Later in the afternoon when they paused for a drink of water, these siblings who hadn't spent much time together, embraced each other tightly. Natan's heart ached. Other than him, they only had each other left. That was a lonely feeling. He looked to Ari, who worked alongside them to build the pyre sufficiently high. His heart ached. He vowed he'd do better by her.

As the sun drew closer to the horizon, Jak Carpenter stopped by. He'd put in a full day's work on the cabins. He brought a handcart full of scraps for the pyre. "I'm sorry for your loss," he began without preamble. "I heard rumors of bad news."

"Who told you?" Natan demanded with a weary voice.

"I saw for myself. I'm sorry." He wilted. "There was a fire and smoke from the chimney. I thought Lilly was home." He sighed in a breath as if tired. "I needed something from her, so I went and knocked on the door. When I heard no answer, I poked my head in." He laid a bony hand on Natan's shoulder. "Ari did a good job."

Natan's heart sank in the fading light. "Who have you told?"

Jak shook his head, the silvery white wisps of hair floating softly around his head. "No one. I thought it better that way. You know how the Springers are."

Natan nodded before returning to work. Gossip took root all too easily in the hearts of the villagers. "You're right." Jak raised a hand, thought better of it, then lowered it and turned away. Before he departed completely he inquired, "If you're planning on keeping this a secret, you're going about it the wrong way."

Natan stopped for a moment. "Who said anything about a secret?"

Adrastea laid one last log on the pyre that stood as high as Mikal's waist. She let her hand linger over her mother's final resting place. "I wish we had more time," she sighed.

Night fell. Darkness surrounded the village. Above her, stars emerged, one at a time into the navy sky.

There were a few smaller logs left but Adrastea couldn't be bothered adding them to the pile. Her grief had worked itself out. Her arms and legs burned from the work.

Natan stretched his back, groaning from the pain of his day's work. "That's enough," he declared.

Mikal sighed and sat down on a spare log, more than happy to stop working. Even his fidgety hands settled on his chest.

Ari leaned on Natan, drooping like a discarded shirt. "I'm so tired." She draped her hands on his shoulder and let her head fall on his massive chest.

Natan patted her. "Let's go."

Adrastea grabbed Mikal's hand; he let her take it. They followed their uncle up the hill to Lillybet's house for the death vigil.

The house lay silent and dark—most uninviting. In contrast, the rough cabins on the hill behind the house showed signs of life. Fires glowed outside the doors. The sounds of children afraid to go to bed in a strange place filtered down through the darkness. It might be some time before the Crossroaders settled into their new life.

Natan led his family into the dark house. The fire had burned to coals. Ari stirred the fire to bring more warmth to a house whose coldness had nothing to do with the temperature. From the coals she lit a taper, then lit a lamp she had sitting on the mantle. Its glow filled the house and shone upon the cold body on the table.

Natan looked upon his sister. Ari had done a good job. Lillybet lay ever so peaceful.

Mikal held back at the door. "I don't want to go in there," he whispered. "I've never seen a dead body before."

Natan didn't bother to plead with Mikal. "If you will not come in, you can sleep on the porch."

"Can't I go back to—"

"No!" Natan pointed a beefy finger at his apprentice. "Your mother fought long and hard to have you returned. She suffered much in your absence and she didn't get a chance to enjoy your company. You will gift her with your presence to honor her in death." He stood back out of the doorway. "It is warmer inside."

"It's safer too," Adrastea blurted.

The other three looked at her. "What do you mean?" Ari asked.

Adrastea blushed. It was her mother's secret. But did it matter, now that her mother was dead, who knew?

Adrastea took a breath as she considered her next words. "My father... he placed a protection on the house. As long as we're inside, nothing bad can happen."

Ari shook her head, skepticism in her eyes.

"But it does work!" Adrastea insisted, stepping forward.

Ari waved her back down. "We don't doubt you but..." she left her sentence unfinished, her gaze falling on Lillybet.

Adrastea looked to her mother. Finally, she uttered, "He couldn't have done it. He couldn't enter the house."

"You don't know that," Ari replied.

"I do. I saw it." Her hand stroked the doorframe.

"He who?" Mikal asked.

"Besides," Adrastea blurted, ignoring her brother, "I don't think it was him."

"Him who?" Mikal insisted, although he remained outside the door. "Somebody killed my mother. I want to know who."

Adrastea tilted her head. Was her mother murdered? With her hand still on the wood, the idea that she'd been murdered didn't feel correct. She drew in a breath and concentrated on the Lines. Tragedy, yes. But no violence.

The house had been protected at the time. If the Dark God himself couldn't enter, how could any mortal with ill intent do so?

Natan looked at his apprentice. "It could have been anyone. I say we hold on the matter until after the funeral. I think the truth will out then." His firm look at the others put the subject to rest.

Ari set the lamp at Lillybet's head. Its light spread around her in a circle. The Light had not protected her in life. Would light watch over her in death?

Adrastea pulled the two chairs toward the fire. As she sat, her chair creaked dangerously. She wondered if she should offer to make tea or something. Even if nobody felt like eating or drinking, maybe the scent would drive away the smell of death. Her mother's body had begun to settle. The smell, while not strong, let its subtle presence be known.

For the rest of the evening, they didn't speak much. Natan finally convinced Mikal that it was better inside, though he kept his distance from the body on the table. Ari sent Adrastea to pull blankets from the linen press in the bedroom for them all. They'd stay there that night.

Adrastea closed her eyes. She felt her mother's presence in the quilts.

Lillybet had woven that fabric. She felt the keen loss of her mother, not just in her death but also of the years Adrastea spent in apprenticeship with Ari and not living with her mother. In the past few days Adrastea had learned more about her mother than she had in the past ten years. Her mother was more than the "Mad Lilly" the villagers thought she was. She'd had talent. She could have been a priestess or maybe something greater.

When she returned with the blankets, she had made up her mind.

"I would like to stay here for a while," she announced. "I mean, for the next week or so. Maybe longer.

Ari looked far too tired for reason. "I need you in the village."

Natan took the blankets from Adrastea and doled them out. "How about we discuss it tomorrow? Or the next day?"

"I'm staying here until then. I need to know more about my mother."

Ari wrapped her blanket around her and claimed the choicest spot in front of the fire. "Fine," she said, before turning her back to the rest of the room.

Natan joined her on the floor and Mikal curled up with the two adults between him and the corpse.

Adrastea watched them settle, then chose a place at their feet. This was supposed to be a death vigil but since Lillybet was quite dead and not going anywhere, there was little reason to stay awake and watch. Since nobody had gotten much sleep the past few days, slumber caught them as soon as their heads touched the floor.

A drastea stirred, her back aching from the hard wooden floor. She'd slept late.

The voice of hunger and the need for the outhouse sounded louder than the call of slumber. Ari had woken and had stirred up the fire.

Lillybet had little food left in the larder. There were stores in the loft above, if one could get to them through her weaving supplies. Adrastea breached a barrel of wheat. Soon she had a porridge boiling. Ari found the honey while Natan folded away the blankets, save one to drape over Lillybet's body, perhaps to hide it from the curious eyes that would be coming this way as well as to ward off flies.

The family had guarded her through the night. Now, according to custom, the mourners of the village were to come by. They would pay their respects and leave a food offering for the family, to see them through the sorrow of the week.

Ari opened the doors and windows. The curious drifted down for a look. At first it was the refugee children who came by, hands empty. They didn't know anything about Lillybet's status in the village, nor did they care. They were looking more for something to do rather than pay respects. A few of the more elderly came, perhaps to seek a moment's relief in shade? The nursing mothers came too but only as far as the porch. Not being from the village, they brought no offerings and gave few words of comfort. Nobody had shown up yet from Sacred Spring.

"I don't know what's worse—strangers with no food or the villagers with no respect." Adrastea muttered. Her sleep hadn't been as restful as she wished. She felt out of sorts. She sat in a chair by her mother's head but not too close, for her mother had a decidedly stronger odor about her. She wanted to cry but had run out of tears.

Ari didn't have to be there, but she remained. She went out on the porch. Adrastea could hear her chatting in a low voice with the various people who came by.

At Lillybet's side Natan straddled a chair. He laid his chin to rest on his hand as they lay folded across the back. Mikal lolled around, clearly uncomfortable with being there. He roamed the perimeter of the house, poking at the items on a shelf, easing open a cupboard door to peer inside, leaning his head against a wall.

Over and over Adrastea pondered the mystery of her mother's death. How did it happen? Was it murder, or had it been an accident?

She watched her uncle as well. Every once in a while, he'd reach forth and trace the curve of Lillybet's arm. Ari had folded Lillybet's hands across her chest. She looked not so much peaceful, as gone. Even Natan, who appeared tired and old this morning, had more spark of life in him.

"I wish we knew what had happened," she murmured.

Natan did not lift his head but did look at her with his hazel eyes. "There will be time enough for that tomorrow. For today, forget everything and simply mourn."

drastea watched the sun drop behind the mountains. Her mother's last day had come to an end.

Natan carried the shrouded body down the hill. Ari, Adrastea and Mikal followed. The refugees also followed but at a distance. Lillybet was not one of theirs.

The whole village turned out for Lillybet's funeral. Peter and Sheelagh, Marlon and Amarice Poulter, Jon Tanner, Jak Carpenter and more, including Tam Innkeeper with his children. Marta was conspicuous by her absence (not that Adrastea missed her). Nobody spoke, nobody offered condolences. Adrastea didn't know why they bothered showing up now and not earlier at the vigil. They should have turned up to the vigil, if not in grief, at least in hopes of a wake with food. Not that there had been any—only Mira's scant offering of soup.

Mira waited at the pyre, a torch in hand. Carles had returned to Crossroads with the oxdrivers. He had his own flock to tend. Mira must have prepared the pyre, for there was a splashing of coal oil over the green wood, to help it catch quicker.

Natan laid the body of his sister on the pyre. He gave her covered forehead one last kiss before returning to the comforting arms of Ari. Adrastea came forward and placed her hand on her mother's forehead. "Goodbye, mother. I wish I knew you better."

Mikal had no goodbyes.

Mira bent her head and whispered, instead of calling out, the funeral rites. "I comment your spirit to the Light," she said, the only words loud enough for Adrastea to hear.

Adrastea nodded, for she was sure that was where the dead woman had gone. For all her quirks, Lillybet was not an evil woman. Much evil had been done to her, but she had not stooped so low as to resort to the ways of her tormentors. Only now did Adrastea realize just how noble her mother had been.

Now she was with her beloved Joe. Adrastea felt a pang in her heart. Her mother had loved so deeply. Adrastea wanted to love as her mother had.

Mira gave the torch to Natan, who held it parallel to the ground. Adrastea and Mikal wrapped their hands around the torch. Together, as a family, they guided it to the pyre and thrust it into the tinder stacked within until the flames caught.

Slowly, fire licked the logs of the pyre. The sun had set, and twilight had fled, leaving only the flare of the fire and the occasional lamp held by a villager to light the village green.

Natan turned back to Ari. Adrastea watched as the big man collapsed in sorrow upon the shoulder of the woman he should have called wife. He could never offer her marriage, yet she offered him comfort.

Mikal had left her as well. He had drifted into the safety of his foster brothers and sisters, who gathered around him to keep him safe.

As the fire built momentum, Adrastea stood there, her back to the rest of the green, standing apart from the others. She watched the mortal remains of her mother be consumed by the fire. Her mother's body would return to the ashes and dust of the earth, to become something new again. Her soul was, no doubt, resting in the comfort of the Light.

Never had Adrastea felt so alone. The feeling of abandonment filled her and spilled out her eyes. She wrapped her arms around herself. She wished she had a blanket, a shawl, anything to comfort her.

A firm, sure hand descended to her shoulder. A warm cloak of the blackest, softest material wrapped around her as Mor-Lath pulled her in close to him. He rested his head on her shoulder as he murmured in her ear, "Adrastea, I'm so sorry."

Adrastea did not question his presence, nor did she pause to wonder if anyone else saw him. Overwhelming sorrow rushed through her like a flood, tearing down the walls she had built to protect her heart the past few days. She spun around in his embrace, pressed her face to his chest and sobbed.

He held her close and let her cry out her sorrow, saying nothing. When her surge of crying had dwindled to a trickle of hiccups, he tilted her face up to wipe away her tears with his thumbs. "Grief is but a moment in mortality and will pass eventually."

"How did she die?"

"An accident. She tripped on that rug of hers, fell across the table and slit her arm open with the knife."

Of course. It made sense. "But the knife was from the Inn." What was her mother doing with one of Marta's knives?

An apologetic smile twitched at his lips. "She'd taken it a long time ago, probably to spite Marta."

The flames, now raised to a roar, illuminated his face with dancing shadows. She couldn't fathom his eyes, but she didn't care. He stroked her cheek once more before bending down to place a gentle kiss on her lips.

But Adrastea wanted more. Her lips sought his and he replied, deepening the kiss to stir her soul and leave her yearning. To her reluctance, he pulled back. "You don't want that now." With firm hands he turned her around to watch the flames consume her mother.

He held her there for the rest of the night, his arms wrapped securely around her waist. She let him hold her. She needed to be held, even if by the Dark God himself.

One by one the other mourners drifted off, their curiosity sated into boredom. Adrastea did not see Ari take Natan home, but she did catch Mikal's eye before his siblings whisked him away to his former bed.

Adrastea stayed until dawn, when sheer exhaustion and the emotional drain left her barely able to walk. It was then Mor-Lath carried her to Lillybet's doorstep—Adrastea's doorstep now—and set her down.

"Good night," he said, despite the encroaching daybreak. Behind him the pale pillar of smoke still rose from Lillybet's pyre. It would burn for hours yet. "Go to sleep. A new day dawns and for the living, life must go on." He stroked her face again and Adrastea, too tired to think straight, flung herself into the comfort of his arms. He embraced her closely one last time, gave her another kiss and stepped back.

Before Adrastea could protest his leaving, he was gone, nothing but a faint swirl of air where he used to be.

The emptiness of her heart consumed her until exhaustion overtook her in sleep.

Chapter 10

Ari sat at Natan's table, close to his tiny stove. In her hands she held the knife with "INN" scratched into the wooden handle. Her head ached, and she craved a drink.

She had held Natan in her arms until he cried himself to sleep, his worry box too small for this trouble. Now she waited for him to wake up before the afternoon passed too far. The funeral was over. While he mourned, the sun would rise, move across the sky, and sink behind the mountain to rise again the next morning. The villagers would wake, eat their breakfasts and go about their day. Just because one life stopped, it didn't mean the rest of them wouldn't go on.

Natan would have to be their Mayor.

Ari had already searched Natan's house for a drop of strong stuff. She found none. Her heart warred with the need to go fetch a drink from her stillroom and the need to be there when Natan awoke.

Natan did not like to see Ari drink. Ari did not want to tell Natan she drank because of him. He was Mayor. A Mayor only served the village. He could not serve family as well. If he ever had to choose between her and the village, he always chose the village, as a good Mayor should. When that happened, the loneliness of it emptied her heart.

She drank to forget, if only for a little while.

As she turned the knife in her hands, she wanted to fling it far away, forget about the horrors of the past two days and snuggle up with Natan. She wanted to keep him there in bed and never let him go out into the fickle world again.

But would he forgive her for making him abandon his beloved sister, even in death?

So, she waited out here with business for the Mayor. The bedroom was for Natan her lover, and not the man everyone called Mayor.

He came out, half-dressed and puffy-eyed. Ari did not say anything but pushed a fresh cup of tea in his direction.

"Lactoverosa?" he asked, his voice husky with yesterday's grief.

She shook her head. "Green with chamomile. And honey."

He accepted the cup with both hands and gulped it. He studied the empty cup. He replaced it carefully on the table. "Tell me about the knife."

Ari lifted it up, balancing it, dull side down, on her fingers. "This is the knife that killed your sister."

A shuddery breath shook Natan. "An Innkeeper blade."

Ari nodded. "Surely nobody would be stupid enough to use their own knife."

Natan sighed and glanced at his back door. "Only if they weren't thinking at the time."

Ari set it down. "You going to ask questions?"

"Only way get answers."

Ari did not envy him his job today.

⁂

The pyre smoldered on the village commons, nearly a pile of ash. The morning breezes sent its acrid smell across the village. Natan ignored it as he made his way to the Inn, the bundled skirt under his arm.

In the empty common room, Natan rang the bell on the wall next to the door. Tom came running.

"Morning, Mayor," he said with a bob of his head. "Fancy some breakfast, then?"

Natan laid his bundle on the nearest table. "No. I need to speak with Martine. Is she busy?"

Tom didn't ask the Mayor's motives. He dashed into the kitchens to fetch his sister.

Martine emerged, wiping her hands on her apron. She wore her bodice without a shirt and a skirt with no petticoat. She wasn't expecting visitors. "How can I help you, Mayor?"

Tom followed her out, curious. A stern glance from Natan sent him wordlessly back into the kitchen. This was none of his business. If Martine wanted to tell him later, she could. It would be her choice.

Once they were alone, Natan unfurled the bloody skirt. In a low, private voice, he said, "Explain this to me."

Martine wilted. "I don't know." She glanced nervously towards the kitchen door.

"Mikal said you gave it to him and told him to hide it. Why?"

Martine looked near tears. "I panicked. Mom found a bundle in the hallway, thought it was mine and told me to take it to the laundry." She folded her hands into fists and pressed them against her chest. "It's not even my skirt."

"Do you know whose it is?"

Martine shook her head. She avoided his gaze.

Natan took a breath. He wasn't getting anywhere. "When did you first see this skirt?"

"Yesterday, the morning of the refugees."

"Did you see the blood then?"

"I didn't see it until the laundry."

"Was it still fresh?"

Martine gave him a blank look.

Natan rephrased the question. "Was it still damp?"

She nodded. "That's why I panicked. I didn't know what to do with it."

Mikal slunk into the common room, his clothes still wrinkled from last night. "Ah," said Natan. "My apprentice makes his appearance. Make yourself useful, lad, and go fetch Mira."

Mikal had the same haunted look as Martine. "But what if I can't find her?"

"What makes you think you won't find her? Go, boy!"

Mikal went.

Natan folded the skirt and placed it on the table.

"Tom," Natan called out. There was a scuttle behind the door where the Mayor knew Tom was eavesdropping. Tom burst through the door as if he'd run clear from the table.

"Yes, Mayor?"

"Fetch your mother."

Tom dropped his gaze. "Ah," he said, toeing the floor.

"What?"

"She's asleep," he confessed.

That would explain the sloppy appearance of her children. Martine and Mikal would never have gotten away with slovenliness if Marta was awake.

But it was the afternoon. "Has she been asleep all day?"

"She's pregnant again." Tom's wrinkled nose showed he did not think much of his mother when she was pregnant. "Please, Mayor. It's best we let her sleep."

"Can I go now?" Martine asked. Natan had forgotten about her.

Natan shook his head. "No." He turned his attention back to Tom. "I'm afraid this cannot wait." He laid the knife on the skirt. "Do you know anything about this?"

Martine slapped both hands over her mouth and gave a squeak. Tom stared at the items, then shook his head. "Please," he muttered. "Come back later."

Natan shook his head. "Council's tomorrow. I want enough time to sort this out before then. I'll wait patiently until Mira gets here then I am waking up your mother."

"Don't bother," came a tired voice from the kitchen door. Marta stood there, sleep-wrinkled and her hair in a tangled mass. She wrinkled her nose as if the smell of the common room nauseated her. "I'm already awake. I could hear your booming voice across the inn." She eased herself into the room. "You never could keep quiet, could you, Natan?"

Martine and Tom slunk out, keeping just outside their mother's reach, leaving the Mayor alone with her.

He wasn't going to rise to the taunt. "Oh, I'm very good at keeping quiet. It's just that you never hear me when I am and so never remember." He looked her up and down once. "I hear you're pregnant."

She shrugged and hitched up her short sleeve. Her bodice had been loosened but not undone entirely, and like her daughter, wore a skirt with no petticoat so that it drooped listlessly from her hips to the floor. No doubt if she stood in the sunshine, Natan would see far more of Marta than he ever wished to. "'Bout a couple of months or so along. And no," she replied to his usual question, "Ari doesn't know. I don't see any reason to bother her." She returned his scrutinizing gaze, her eyes lingering on the skirt and knife on the table as well. "I take it you're not here to discuss my good news."

He gestured to the skirt. "Know anything about this skirt?"

She glanced at it and looked back to Natan. "No."

"This skirt was found in your house."

Marta shrugged. "Lots of skirts in a house full of girls."

He unfolded it to show the blood. The knife he held up. "This knife—your knife—was found in Lillybet." He gestured towards the skirt. "Is that her blood?"

That got her attention. She frowned at the skirt, pursing her lips as if trying to remember something. "I didn't do it, if you're accusing me," she said in a low voice. Her frown deepened. "Is that what you think I am? A murderer?"

Natan stood his ground, his features hardening. "At this point, I don't know what to think."

Mira arrived with Mikal trailing behind her. "I believe I'm needed?"

Natan narrowed his eyes at Marta before addressing Mira. "Tell me what you feel about her." He jerked his thumb at the Innkeeper.

Mira gave him a blank look. "What do you mean?"

"The Lines!" he spat. "The Lines of Power must say something. Can you tell me what it is?"

"Natan," Mira chided. "I cannot command the Lines. It's not as if I can read them like a book..."

"Mira!" Natan snapped, his temper wearing thin. "Here is a bloodied skirt found on the premises of the Inn. There is an Innkeeper's knife, found buried in my sister's body. I need some answers."

Mira paused and considered something. "Well, perhaps I can try something."

She bit her lip and hesitated a moment before stretching out a hand to Marta. Marta folded her arms and did not resist when Mira touched her.

Mira laid her hand on Marta's face and muttered, "Give your secrets to me..."

Marta drew in a quick breath and her eyes grew wide. She plucked weakly at Mira's hand as if to take it away from her face.

Mira bent her head down and began to tremble. Then, as if burned, she snatched her hand away and stumbled back, bumping into the table behind her. "Oh, Marta. I'm so sorry."

Marta's eyes filled with tears and before Natan could stop her, she slapped the priestess across the face.

"Hey!" Natan roared as he snatched Marta by the shoulders. "What did you do that for?"

Mira, dabbing tenderly at her bleeding lip, laid a hand on Natan's angry arm. "No, Natan. It's all right. That was my fault. I... um... listened too hard." To the innkeeper she said, "Marta, I'm sorry."

Marta suddenly burst out crying. Then she fled back through the kitchen, heedless of the eavesdroppers she hit with the door.

Natan helped Mira off the table. He patted himself down, realizing he did not have a handkerchief upon his person. "What happened there?"

Mira sat down and dabbed at her split lip with the hem of her skirt. "I learned some new things this week in my studies. Ways of listening... closer, one could say." She shrugged. "I guess I don't know my own strength." She continued to dab at her lip and study the spots of blood. "We're all extra sensitive since Lilly... Her death was, um, more powerful than expected." She tongued the split gingerly. "I didn't know it at the time, but I felt her death that afternoon. It was as if the tension on the Lines of Power was suddenly released. Death doesn't usually feel like that, but this is Lilly. Nothing was ever predictable with her."

Mira rose, still very introspective of the hem of her skirt.

Natan laid a heavy hand on her shoulder. "Mira, did Marta do it? Did she kill my sister?"

Mira considered the question, then slowly shook her head. "Marta despised Lilly. Didn't know how much until now," she muttered to herself. Then she looked at Natan with sad eyes. "There was bad blood between them but not Lilly's blood. Marta had nothing to do with Lilly's death."

Natan gathered up the skirt and the knife, wadding them and hugging the bundle tightly to his chest. "How did the skirt get to the Inn?"

Mira shrugged. "To frame Marta?"

Natan sighed and wilted. That made sense. There were a few people whom Marta annoyed. But would anyone in the village go so far as to kill Lillybet and frame Marta for it?

"I don't like mysteries," Natan said.

"Mysteries are but secrets as held by others. And secrets can be found out." With that, Mira gave Natan a knowing look.

Natan shuddered. Something about Mira didn't feel right.

That afternoon, all that was left of Lillybet's funeral pyre was ash. Adrastea held her hand over the pile hoping for heat.

The ashes were cold.

Natan and Mikal approached with spades and buckets. This final job also belonged to family. By tradition, they would scatter the ashes into the stream, letting the sacred water carry the mortal remains away.

As they swept away the last remains of the pyre, Adrastea approached her uncle Natan. "I think my mother's death was an accident."

Natan sighed. Adrastea watched Uncle Natan put aside the grief of a brother for the mantle of a Mayor. How lucky he was to be able to do that. Adrastea wished she could fill in the empty hole left by her mother. He motioned her away from Mikal. "I have evidence that says otherwise."

Adrastea didn't know what to say about that. "Do you have someone in mind?"

He did not reply at first. "I have much to think about," he said, when she pressed him for an answer. "If it was an accident, there are still unanswered questions."

"What are you going to say tonight, at Council?"

"Only what is necessary." And that was the end of the conversation.

∽◉≈◉∽

The dead may be dead but the living went on living. Adrastea wished the whole of the world could stop for a while to let her wallow in grief. Even Ari had not let her stop. She kept Adrastea busy catching up on neglected stillwork until evening came and they could attend Council.

Ari carried the lantern to the Inn. Adrastea followed, her footsteps slower. As they mounted the porch, Mikal detached himself from a group of youths loitering about. He pulled Adrastea to the side. "Can I talk with you?"

Adrastea looked at Ari. The healer nodded and continued to the inn.

Mikal's gaze darted about. "I don't think you should be here."

This surprised Adrastea. "Why not?"

He looked over to the group of youths. Martine was there, and Tom, and others from the village. They clustered together, watching cautiously. Did they know what Mikal was saying to her? "There's been a few rumors going around. Some of them concern you."

Adrastea put her hands on her hips. She wasn't going to be bullied as her mother was. She was going to stand up for herself, even if it meant she'd have to beat every one of them into submission.

Mikal grimaced and pulled at his collar. "Thing is... who was that man with you the other night?"

Adrastea froze. "What?" she uttered, faintly.

Mikal looked over to the group. In the falling darkness, they watched him. Martine lifted her chin. He swallowed. "Me and Tom and a few others saw you at the pyre with a man. A stranger. Who is he?"

Adrastea's heart beat rapidly. She had never stopped to consider that anyone would have seen the God of the Dark the other night. Her grief had overwhelmed her common sense. Surely, he couldn't be so foolish as to be so careless. "I don't know who you're talking about."

Martine stepped forward. "Well, he seemed to know who you were!" The others nodded in agreement. "Who is he? We don't like strangers around here."

Adrastea didn't answer. Martine coughed. Fear ran along the Lines so thick Adrastea couldn't help but feel it.

Mikal drew himself up. "We've talked it over. Since there are lots of strange things going on, the others would appreciate it if you kept your distance from them until we figure things out."

Adrastea couldn't believe her ears. She looked about her. "You're shunning me?" It was Lillybet all over again.

Mikal shuffled his feet. "No. Just playing it safe."

"Safe from what?" Anger rose in her heart. "I can't believe you're doing this." She stepped towards Mikal. The whole circle startled back, then gathered closer to him in solidarity.

Mikal held up both hands. "Just go. It's better this way."

She stiffened. "I don't see how!" She folded her arms. "Anyhow, I am going into Council. Unlike the lot of you," she shook her finger at them, "I can do that."

Ari arrived at Council in time to get a comfortable seat at one of the tables. Council meetings could go on for hours. They were more bearable in comfort.

Then Amarice Poulter came in. Ari knew Amarice's secret, one that could not be kept from the rest of the village for much longer. Ari sighed and rose, offering her chair.

"Oh, I couldn't," Amarice replied, waving the offer away with her hand.

But Ari was not putting up with that nonsense. She leaned in close and whispered, "You know I know."

Ari placed her hand on Amarice's shoulder and looked into her pale eyes. "Please," she said. "Come see me later."

Amarice jerked her shoulder out from under Ari's grasp. "I'm fine." She did however, accept the chair.

Marlon Poulter, Ari's handsome dark-haired nephew, came up and put his arm around his wife's shoulders. He did not deserve the grief that would come to him before the year was out, if Ari was not allowed to help. Even though she dressed loosely, Amarice hadn't been able to hide her condition from Ari for several months now.

"Please, Amarice," Ari whispered again. "I may be able to save you."

Amarice turned her face away.

Ari appealed to her nephew. "Marlon, please."

He looked away, unable to meet her eyes. "Not now, Aunt Ari."

Ari saw Mira beckon her over. Mira had secured a chair at the table nearest the kitchen door. Behind her was room on a bench. Alas, it was not as comfortable as the chair she'd relinquished but it was better than standing.

When Ari sat down, she was closer to Natan than she was before. Her new seat gave her a splendid profile view of him.

"Is it my imagination," Mira leaned over and murmured, "or is this the greatest number of people we've ever seen at a Council meeting?"

Ari scanned the room. Besides the Springers, many of the outdwelling farmers had come in as well. More were arriving, so many more, that there were not seats for them all. Some had to content themselves with standing. "This is more than I can recall." The noise of their conversations filled the room.

"Do you think Lillybet's death has something to do with it?"

Mira shrugged. "Maybe. And the refugees and the coming war. There have been rumors flying around. Some of them may be true."

Ari leaned closer. "Oh? What?"

Susan Farmer, a comfortable, not-yet-middle-aged woman, poked Ari's skinny back. "Ari! Sit back. I can't see!"

Ari turned and frowned in annoyance. "Council hasn't started yet!"

"I know. I just want to see who's putting their name on the slate."

Ari looked over to the Mayor's table. A few people gathered around, chatting. Were they there to make their mark and have their say, as was the right of any villager?

Adrastea slipped in, looking rather flustered. Still, she had a defiant spark in her eye. Uh oh. Something had happened outside. Ari waved her over. Adrastea made her careful way through the crowd.

Mira scooted her chair closer to Ari. "Speaking of rumors, is..." Mira glanced towards Amarice. "Is she pregnant?"

Ari snorted. "Who told you that?"

"You did."

"I did not!"

"You offered her your seat. You wouldn't have done that just to be nice."

Ari dropped her indignation. "Oh." If Mira noticed, would anyone else? She quickly changed the subject. "So... rumors, what have you heard?"

"I know Marta did not kill Lillybet..."

Ari sat bolt up and declared, louder than she meant to, "She what?"

"Shh!" Mira waved her down. A few of the closer villagers looked their way before turning back to their own conversations.

Adrastea made it through the crowd. She sank down on the bench between Ari and Susan Farmer. "Honestly!" she gasped. "Uncle Natan needs to have a word with Mikal."

"Oh?" Ari responded. Natan rose. The murmurings of the room quieted. "Tell me later."

Natan Mayor rapped three times on the table. Ari thought he looked splendid in his mayoral robes, even though they were a little too big for him. "I welcome you all to our weekly council," he announced.

Natan consulted his slate. "There are only seven names on the slate, yet many of you inquired as to whether or not I would be addressing you all. I have a feeling many of you have something on your minds. If you wish to discuss it, I call for one last chance to put your mark here." He held up the slate, but nobody came forth. "Anyone?"

Nobody moved.

"So be it. The first name... is..."

Natan stared at the slate as incredulity twisted his brow.

"Bugger!" he cursed loudly, dropping the slate as if hot. His eyes shot up and he looked around.

"Do go on, Mayor," drawled a masculine voice. Ari felt a ripple through her heart that left her cold. Something about that voice. "What is the name at the top of the list?"

Everyone turned to the speaker. Sitting in the middle of the Inn, his booted feet propped up on the table, was a man dressed all in black. When did he show up? Ari felt she should know him but couldn't place his face. He was handsome, though, with dark brown hair, burning green eyes and well-balanced features. He looked familiar.

Adrastea squeezed Ari's hand. She slipped off the bench and snuck out the kitchen door before anyone noticed.

Ari's heart dropped. It couldn't be, she told herself. He wouldn't come here, would he?

Mor-Lath.

Mira slid from her chair to the Mayor's table and consulted the slate. Softly, she slipped it out of sight under the table. With the slate tucked behind her back, she crept back to her chair.

Natan's eyes narrowed. "What the hell do you want?"

The man stood. "What the hell indeed." He walked forward, his arms out, palms outstretched as if to show he carried no weapons of any kind. If he was who he truly claimed to be, he wouldn't need weapons.

He spoke as he approached Natan's table. "Is it not considered proper to announce betrothals publicly in weekly council?"

At this, the whispers started again, fiercely but the man in black merely glanced from side to side and they subsided. Not that all stopped, for Ari saw those behind him continued to whisper directly into neighbor's ears, their clandestine efforts useless as he in all likelihood heard them all.

"You're not from our village," Natan declared. Ari's heart cheered as Natan took a stand.

"But my betrothed is."

"She's not your betrothed."

"She accepted my token of betrothal."

"You did not give her a choice!"

It took Ari a moment to realize that the black scar on Adrastea's face was the token. She briefly marveled at Natan's quick wit. Then again, was it wise to stand up to the Dark God?

The Dark God sighed. "Perhaps not but ultimately, it will be her choice." He folded his arms. "I have been nothing but honest with her. It is the only way to begin a successful marriage."

"There will be no marriage if I have any say about it." Natan's jaw tightened.

Mor-Lath shrugged. "You don't. Only her word matters."

"As her only surviving relative, I think I do have a say."

Mor-Lath shook his head. "No, you don't." He strode forward the last few steps to reach the table, waving his arms. "Oh, you can exclaim and bluster all you want but it doesn't matter." He reached the table and leaned over it towards the mayor. He was not as tall as Natan but seemed to tower over him nonetheless. "Only her heart and her hand matter, a hand freely given."

"I will see to it that she will never give her hand to you."

The Dark God turned from Natan, a satisfied smirk on his face. "Oh, we shall see." He wandered back to his seat, a seat that suddenly had all the room it needed around it, as everyone scooted back from this stranger.

Before he took his seat, he turned once more to Natan. "Oh, sorry to hear about your sister, dear chap. I really wish I knew what to say."

Natan's face started to purple. "You know something, don't you?"

The Dark God settled down into his chair and propped his feet back up on the table. "Who am I to reveal the sins of others? All I can say is that your sister's death was an accident. However, there is someone here in this room who would have you believe otherwise." He glanced around meaningfully.

Neighbor turned to neighbor and a low rumble of discussion filled the air. Ari clutched her hands. Susan Farmer leaned over to Ari and murmured, "Did someone kill Lillybet? Is that what he's saying?"

Ari turned to her in surprise. She had no idea what to say to Susan.

"My business is done," he declared. "Please, Mayor, do continue. I know there are several here who want to have their say." He rose. "Have a pleasant evening. I shall see you again."

He was there one moment and gone the next, much Ari's astonishment. How did he do that?

So much for an orderly Council.

Chapter 11

Adrastea sat at Ari's kitchen table, a coal oil lamp the only light provided. She gazed distantly at the stove across the room through a haze of smoke from the pipe she held in her hand. Her chin lay cupped in her other hand. She'd only lit her second bowl when Ari and Mira arrived.

The first thing Ari said when she came home was, "Bugger!" She slammed the door. Then she opened it, so she could slam it again. "Bugger!"

Adrastea glanced at Ari for a moment after the expletive, then went back to puffing.

Mira had a hand over her mouth as if she feared what might come out.

Ari had plenty of curse words to share. "Bugger, bugger, bugger!" She thumped her head against the door. She followed this with a whimper.

Mira looked at Adrastea. "What are you smoking?"

"Lactoverosa." Adrastea puffed some more, nigh oblivious to the fretting of her mistress.

"Why?"

"When he showed up, I thought, 'that's it. It's happening all over again.'"

Mira sat down. "What is?"

Adrastea drew another deep breath. "I'm my mother. Already the villagers are shunning me."

"That's not true."

Adrastea shook her head. "I'm sorry I ran away. When he showed up, I knew I couldn't stay. Now that the villagers know—"

"They know nothing," Ari spat. She pushed away from the door and plunked down opposite Adrastea.

"Well," amended Mira. "They know someone wants your hand in marriage, and Natan's opposed to it. Come to think of it, nobody knows his name. He never gave it."

"But they know he wants to marry me." Her forehead sank into her hands. "Oh, Light. Mikal was right."

"Mikal?"

"He said the villagers wanted nothing more to do with me."

"Why?"

"He and the others saw me and Mor-Lath at the pyre the other night and—"

Ari cried out, "What?"

"Now," Mira interjected. "Let's not start screaming here. We've got some things we need to sort." She scooted her chair closer. "Now, first things first; is that any good?" she gestured to the clay pipe.

Adrastea shrugged and deeply drew another puff.

"Of course, it is," Ari snapped. She beckoned for the pipe.

Adrastea handed it over. As Ari drew in a rapid, greedy drag, Adrastea slowly blew her smoke out, the tendrils curling about her head.

"I don't know where to begin," Mira said, waving away smoke.

Ari gestured sharply at Adrastea with the pipe. "I want to hear what you were doing with Mor-Lath. I thought we agreed you were to avoid him."

Adrastea laid her head down on the table, her chin on her hands. "You were busy with Uncle Natan. Mikal had Tom and everybody. And I was left there all by myself." That abandonment, even unintentional, stung. "But he was there. When nobody else was, he was there for me. He told me how sorry he was, and he held me until morning."

Neither woman said anything to this for a long while. Ari continued to drag on the pipe, sharing with Adrastea. When all the lactoverosa had burned up, Ari wordlessly handed the pipe to Adrastea and tapped the empty bowl.

While Adrastea refilled the pipe, Mira confronted Ari. "I didn't know you smoked. And you've got Adrastea doing it as well?"

Ari merely raised an eyebrow at her. "Healers must know everything about the herbs they use—their effects, their potencies, their application. You wouldn't want me to recommend something to you that I hadn't tried first. Besides, you don't tell me all your secrets; why should I tell you mine?"

"I don't have any secrets," Mira said in a small voice.

Adrastea lit a twist of paper from the stove. She touched this to the contents of the pipe, puffing it with skill until the herb took. She drew a few more puffs then presented the pipe to Ari.

Ari also puffed, then offered it to Mira, who refused. "Suit yourself," the healer replied.

As Adrastea settled down, she asked about Council. "I'm sorry I ran. I couldn't face the village, not after what Mikal said."

Ari shook her head. "I don't know what we're going to do with you, girl. Your lover is most persistent."

Adrastea clenched her hands together. "I don't want to be shunned like my mother!"

"I don't want you shunned either." Mira held out her hand, palm up. When Adrastea didn't take it, Mira wagged her hand in insistence. Reluctantly, Adrastea took the proffered hand.

"Now listen here," Mira explained. "This has to be Mor-Lath's doing. He wants to stir us up. He wants the village against you. He wants..." Mira stopped, then turned her head aside in thought. She bit her lip and squeezed Adrastea's hand.

Her eyes brightened in epiphany. "He wants you willingly." She looked up at Adrastea. "He wants you to come to him willingly. That's why he's doing this. That's why he told us someone had framed Lilly's death as a murder. He wants to divide us and alienate us! By turning the village against you and each other, he's hoping to isolate you, and thus convince you to plight your troth."

"Plight my what?"

"He wants you to agree to be his wife." Mira released Adrastea's hand and returned to her thoughts. "There must be something important about him marrying you. What is it? If he just wanted you, he could have taken you that first day but no, he's got to convince you to go to him willingly. I must say," she said as she regarded Adrastea. "He's half-convinced you already."

Adrastea snorted. "So, all I've got to do is say "no" and that's that?"

"Well," quipped Ari. "That's one plan foiled."

Mira gave Ari an impatient look. "It's not that easy. He's playing the villagers like a fiddle." Mira tilted her head back. Her lips move as if she whispered a prayer to the ceiling. "How could we have been so stupid? He's set us up rather well."

Mira dropped her gaze back to Adrastea. "I'm wondering if it would be better if you left Sacred Spring."

This startled Adrastea. "What? Leave? Where would I go?"

"Carles would be willing to take you in. The Light knows we've got plenty of his people here."

Ari exhaled. "But who would protect her?"

Mira sighed. "That's the sticking point, isn't it?" Then a light dawned in her eyes. "It's not so much protecting her from Mor-Lath but protecting her from herself."

"What?" Ari exclaimed. Adrastea gave Mira a puzzled look. She took the pipe from Ari's surprised fingers and took a quick drag.

"For whatever reason Mor-Lath wants you, it requires that you go willingly. He's already started his attack. He seeks to woo you and tempt you. He probably knows your weakness and is getting you through that." Mira searched for an example. "The comfort at the funeral."

Adrastea pointed at the scar on her face. "And what about this? It hurt when he gave it to me."

Mira hadn't an answer for that.

Ari spoke. "You still haven't told us... um..."Ari had lost her train of thought. "Oh, dear."

Mira sighed. "Ari, it goes much further than a few rumors and a tarnished reputation. Mor-Lath wants our Adrastea for something." She looked the young woman up and down. "Your talent must be stronger than we thought, if he's after you.

"He's probably willing to move the whole of Creation to get you. This isn't a matter of protecting the village, or even the world but it is a battle between Light and Dark. Suddenly, we don't matter anymore." She gestured to herself and Ari.

"I think we matter very much," Ari retorted.

Mira ignored her. "Adrastea, you must be strong and resist him, even if it means all our deaths."

"Hey now!" Ari protested. "I'm not ready to die!" She took the pipe back from Adrastea.

In a small voice, Adrastea said, "I'm not ready for you to die either."

Mira waved her small hand at the smoke. "And would you give in to him to prevent our deaths, even if it meant that your giving in could mean the deaths of thousands? Because that's how important it is."

Tears streamed down Adrastea's face. "I don't want anyone to die." Her voice caught in her throat.

"I think it's too late for that." No matter how gently Mira said it, her words still stung.

Ari passed the pipe to Adrastea, who took a half-hearted puff. Ari had to pluck it back from Adrastea's numb fingers before it slipped to the table.

"Please, Adrastea," Mira begged. "Be strong. He's going to attempt to seduce you through your most vulnerable spot—your heart. You've never had enough love in your life, and for that I'm sorry. Your mother did her best but perhaps it wasn't sufficient. Mor-Lath seeks to seduce you through offering you the love you never had. But realize this: he is the God of the Dark. He is Evil personified. His way brings hatred and bitterness. You will never gain love from him, not in a thousand years." She jabbed her finger on the table to emphasize each word. "Do not let him fool you!"

Adrastea simply nodded, more stunned than acquiescent.

"Meanwhile," Mira continued. "I think it best we have you lay low and avoid the rest of the village for the next little while."

And so, Mira departed after they all agreed that they would sleep on it and come up with a solution on the morrow. Before she left, Mira had Adrastea make a promise that she would come for instruction in the Deeper Power. "Tomorrow afternoon. I feel it may be your only hope in resisting the Dark God."

After Mira left, Adrastea and Ari had a good, long talk about the events of the night.

Adrastea tapped her finger along the pipe, now cold. "I'm sorry about what happened at the pyre. I wasn't thinking."

Ari patted her hand. "Grief and reason never share the same table. I'm sorry I failed to think about your grief." She lifted her teacup, found it empty. She picked up the teapot. It, too, was empty. She scowled at the bottle and nudged it away. "I know all about needing the wrong man."

Adrastea's head dropped into her hands. "Why did he have to show up tonight, in front of everyone? Why'd he say we are betrothed? Now everyone will think I've said yes."

Ari conceded this point. "Between the children and the adults, there will be a great deal of curiosity about this suitor of yours. They will want to know his name."

"What do we tell them?"

Ari shrugged. She tapped out the ashes from the pipe directly onto the table. "I am tired and cannot think of such things tonight. Perhaps we should let Natan solve this problem."

Adrastea let Ari shuffle her off to bed. She gave Ari a few wistful glances as she headed up to the loft with a taper.

The candlelight cast a soft glow over the place Adrastea called her bedroom. Her modest bed called to her. She put the taper on the sill of the window and sat down to undress for bed. She faced the candlelight to unlace her bodice. Once that was free, she dropped it to the floor and reached back to untie the laces of her skirt.

Something prickled along her neck.

"Good evening, my dear."

Adrastea gasped and turned around. Mor-Lath stood behind her, a little too close for her comfort. He stood in the tallest part of the loft, so his head grazed the apex of the roof. He was not fully dressed either, with no cloak or coat and his black shirt laces were loosened as if he were readying for bed as well. Surely, he wasn't expecting...? She shoved that thought out of her head.

"Go away." She moved away from his too-close presence. The back of her legs hit the bed, forcing her to sit down.

He came forward, straddling her legs, his knees pressing either side on the straw tick. Adrastea scooted back against the wall.

"Is my betrothed so eager for me that she wants me in her bed so soon?" He stroked her unscarred cheek and then brushed back a wisp of her hair.

Why did he have to mention that? A warm thrill lit through her. She pushed it away. "What do you want?" Her heart beat fast and she feared he could feel it.

He leaned closer until she could feel the warmth of him near her cheek. "Oh, how like a maiden she blushes."

Adrastea closed her eyes and turned her face aside. Would he seduce her now in her own bed? Would he be so bold, even with Ari so close by? But when he did nothing she risked a glance.

He still knelt straddling her but the look on his face was more bemused than lustful. "Oh, please," he said, sitting up. He grabbed her by the front of her blouse and pulled her off the bed, setting her on her feet. "If I wished to frighten you, I have more terrifying methods than innuendo. And if I wished to seduce you, I would long ago have played your Lines like a harp, making you throb with desire." His gaze studied her throat, her exposed décolletage. "You would have been begging me to take you, even if we were in the middle of the village common, so great would have been your lust."

He snorted in disappointment. "Really, my bride. I think we are past playing these childish games. I mean to marry you. I mean to have you willingly. And I'm not going to lie to you as one of these petty little village youths would. I would have your good will with both eyes open. I'm not going to 'woo you with promises of love,' as your little Mira would put it. I'm going to woo you with the truth."

Mor-Lath hadn't relinquished his grip on her blouse but leaned forward to whisper in her ear. "If only you knew your true potential. You are capable of great power."

A thrill of excitement vibrated through the line on her face. "Tonight, I'm going to show you what that means." He drew back. "But first, we must have a talk about this insipid little act of yours. I was hoping my bride would have had more courage in her heart. Nobody is going to take you seriously if you whimper and defer as you seem so fond of doing. Get some backbone, woman."

That stung. As insult fueled her anger, she drew in a deep breath. "ARI!" she screamed.

But instead of startling the Dark God, he smiled. "That's my girl."

"Adrastea?!" came Ari's shrill reply.

"Ari!" Her voice became more panicked for she didn't know what Mor-Lath meant to do with her.

He pulled her to him and wrapped his arms around her just as Ari's head poked above the top of the ladder. She stopped short at the sight of Mor-Lath.

"Adrastea!" she called as she scrambled into the loft.

He gave her a wicked grin and winked at her, before both he and Adrastea disappeared.

Chapter 12

In darkness, Adrastea's bare feet touched down on cold stone. She wasn't expecting that. The chill made her step back in surprise. She felt a moment of vertigo. The power required to pull them from the loft to… wherever it was they were, had been tremendous. She felt it coursing through their bodies, far more powerful than any herb she had smoked, any wine she had drunk, perhaps even the forbidden stirrings of her loins. The line on her face vibrated with it.

A breeze, not as cool as the stone, ruffled her hair. So, they were outside. The scents and sounds had changed as well. She could hear the wind keening with a higher whine than normal. It took her a moment to realize she couldn't hear the rustling of trees. Her eyes adjusted to the darkness. Adrastea looked down to find herself high on a parapet, overlooking a thousand points of blurry light below. They flickered but not like stars. Adrastea squinted. Were they distant fires? There were so many of them. The voices of men drifted up with the smoke. And food. The scent of cooking wafted upwards.

As she looked up, she saw stars. They told her she gazed north. To the west were a few low hills, their outlines a darkness against the navy blue of the heavens. "Where are we?" she breathed.

Mor-Lath laid her hands on the wall of the parapet. "We are standing on the city walls of Feown."

Feown. As she turned around, she saw the parapet was like a road, two paces wide, stretching from guard tower to guard tower, hundreds of meters away. She crossed to the other wall and gazed out over the great city of Feown. So many buildings crowded together with no room between them for a cat. Lines of streetlamps showed where the many roads twisted and turned. Farther on, taller buildings stood. Toward the middle of the city rose several tall towers, dark against the night sky.

Ari had spoken of the time she spent in this capital city. The crowds of people, the markets, the university. She had been a journeyman here. Adrastea loved Ari's stories of Feown, but Ari only told them when they were alone, and never around Uncle Natan.

Adrastea had always wanted to go to Feown. But to actually be here?

The lights were dimmer on the city side, muted even. The smell was worse, of sickness and decay, of unwashed human bodies and despair. This was not as she'd imagined it.

"What happened?" she moaned. Cities were supposed to be glorious with bustling marketplaces and everything. But this?

"This is the siege of Feown. They've been cut off by the army over there." He guided her back to the side with the flickering fires. "It has been only a fortnight, yet Feown was caught unprepared. They don't have enough food to last them much longer. Their storehouses, by some ill luck, were torched. Already they butcher the animals. If stubbornness outlasts their common sense, they may start butchering each other."

"That's terrible," she exclaimed. Her eyes narrowed. "I'll bet you're reveling in all this!"

He shrugged. "No. I didn't start this war."

"Oh, really?" She folded her arms tightly.

"It is the evil in men's hearts that start these wars."

"But you're the God of the Dark," she mocked, waving her hand in embellishment. "You're the one who tempts men to evil."

He spread his hands as if not at fault. "Surprisingly, no."

"But all dark souls belong to you."

"Yes, eventually." He looked over the wall to the numerous fires of the besieging army. "I do not cause evil. I end evil. After they have been judged, the souls weighed down with sin come to me. I deal with them."

Adrastea clutched her hands to her chest. She knew guilty souls went to Dom-al-gol, the home of demons and good souls ascended to the Light. But she had never given any thought to what happened to them after that.

She approached the wall and stared down at the besieging army below. "It is your job to stop evil? Put a stop to all this. You can stop this war."

Silence fell between them. He laid a gentle hand on her shoulder. "I can't. Not alone."

She turned towards him. Was he being honest with her? The

darkness was too much for her to see his features clearly. "Aren't you an all-powerful god?"

"A god, yes. But all-powerful? If I was all-powerful, what need would I have of you?"

This had her thinking. She had displayed talent. That had drawn him. He had proposed marriage. She'd assumed— "Are you saying you do not love me?" she replied in a soft voice.

He took her hand and pressed it to his chest. She felt his heart beat. "You speak to me of love." The mocking tone was back. "Could it be you love me?"

She pulled back her hand. "No," she said, too hastily.

He grabbed her before she could think of stepping away, pulling her into the all-too-familiar embrace, her back settled against his chest, his arms about her waist. "Just think, my dear," he murmured into her ear. "Together we would have the power to stop this war, you and I. Be my bride and end all this."

She hesitated, then answered. "I can't."

"What? Be my bride or end this?"

After a moment of consideration, "Either."

"You truly don't know your own strength, do you?" He held her hands out, his fingers entwined in hers. "All life is connected through the Lines of the Deeper Power. We are connected to the land, to the fires that burn, to Creation and to each other. It pulls at us, seduces us, for we are part of it all."

All those Lines he spoke of appeared under her fingers, a faint, shimmery web. "Feel the Lines of Power that binds everything. Through them we can control Creation."

Energy ran through them. The world connected to her, who in turn was connected to Mor-Lath. The crux of the power resided in him, far more than she ever thought existed. The power threatened to overwhelm her, for it flowed through her as well.

He was right; it was seductive. It felt like it did that day nearly two weeks ago when she freed young Peter from the barrel, only infinitely more powerful.

"Each one of these Lines connects to another human being—those down there on the plain. Can you feel the essence of their lives?"

She could. They sang to her in different tunes, each one unique and all blending in one great symphony. She stroked the strings to make the sound louder. It sang not in her ears but in her heart. It thrummed through her vitals. It excited her.

"Now," his voice was low and ragged in her ear. "Grasp those strings and pull. Think of all the lives on the end of them. Lift them up and away from here and the siege will be over."

Adrastea wasn't listening to his voice but the resonance of his connection to the Deeper Power through her. She pulled his arms in to wrap about herself. She could hear the sweetness of the Deeper Power singing within him.

She wanted it. She had never wanted anything so much in her life.

"Adrastea..."

Instead of grasping the Lines like he had instructed, she buried herself in the sound of its sweetness, the chorus of all those lives. The loudest one of all was Mor-Lath himself. The chorus built until it overwhelmed her, and she pressed herself against him as if to indulge in more, for more she wanted.

Mor-Lath stumbled back under the force of her passion. He untangled his hands from hers and retreated. His departure left a gnawing, empty hole in her. Adrastea, desperate, pursued him.

His back hit the wall as she pushed up against him. Together, they slid to the floor She seized his Lines and pulled them to her.

He cut her off, sending the Deeper Power away from her unslakeable thirst. Her body shuddered as she grasped one last taste of the sweetness of Power before it evaporated, leaving behind a stillness. No matter how much she grasped for them, the Lines eluded her.

She sat astride Mor-Lath's lap, her head against his shoulder as her face dripped sweat. Her hands gripped his unlaced shirt as if trying to will more of that sweetness from his very skin. Her breaths came in ragged gasps.

Mor-Lath drew a deep breath, a bit winded though not as much as she. "No, no," he chided. "Not like that." He pushed her away when she tried to draw closer to him again. His will battled hers and won. "The whole world must have felt that." He stood up to keep her at arm's distance.

Guilt rushed in the empty space her passion left behind. Her face flushed in embarrassment. She had not meant to lose control like that. Who knew the Deeper Power could feel so sweet? "You tricked me," she accused.

Mor-Lath's fists clenched. He drew a deep breath and turned from her. Would he hit her? Or worse; would he seduce her, despite his declarations? He looked over his shoulder at her. The force of his glare poured over her, for there was still a connection of Lines between them. She sensed his frustration and… something else through those Lines—a whisper of the harmony that still sang to her soul. "You did not listen."

"You lied to me." A cold emptiness replaced the warmth. "This was just another trick to seduce me and it almost worked."

He pushed his hands through his hair. "It didn't work at all. The siege would have ended if you hadn't decided to sate your lusts first."

"Liar!" She threw her arms out wide to indicate the fires far below. "I'm starting to think this is just another one of your tricks. If I did as you asked, would I have had a guarantee that my actions would have ended the siege? I don't think so." She paced as she ranted. "You would not have kept your word. After all, you don't care about a single soul down there!" She pointed at the fires.

Mor-Lath drew himself to his full height. Adrastea could feel the coldness of his frustration through the line on her face. She put a hand to her cheek.

"Oh, but I do," he replied in a low voice. "I do. I care about every single soul that lives. It is you who does not care." He went to the parapet and gazed out over the army below. "If you think you are so wise, so be it. Let the deaths of every Feowan be on your head."

M ira heard desperate voices outside her cottage. Slamming Mor-Lath's book closed, she secreted it to a hidden shelf under her table. How many times had other priestesses hidden things there? Certainly, no secret as bad as hers.

Natan didn't even bother to knock but burst in, a sobbing Ari in his arms. Mira sat at her table, smoothing out her tablecloth. She sent an automatic prayer to the Light that she would not be discovered with the Book. Her conscience burned even more; the Light wouldn't help her cover her guilt. She promised herself she would talk to Natan about her sins. Just not tonight.

He sat Ari gently down on the bench in front of the fire then joined her, rocking her sobbing body against his.

Mira sat on Ari's other side. "What happened?"

"Mor-Lath took Adrastea," Ari cried.

"Oh no." A wave of dizziness washed through her head.

"He took her right before my very eyes," Ari howled. "Just smirked at me, then disappeared." Then Ari's story took an unexpected turn. "It was my fault. She called out to me. I came running but I couldn't stop him. I couldn't stop him." And she dissolved into utter misery.

Natan and Mira exchanged worried glances over Ari's bowed head. They let her cry while Natan held her.

Mira half-rose to fetch something strong to calm Ari. Then she remembered the lactoverosa the Healer had indulged in earlier. Perhaps it wasn't wise to combine the two. She sank back down, then rose again at the thought of tea. Nothing soothed the soul better than a cup of tea, even in the face of failure.

For that's how Mira felt. She was the Priestess of the Light for the village. Despite her lack of talent and lack of knowledge, she should have at least had the presence of wisdom to look ahead for something like this. Instead, she'd been indulging in illicit knowledge, things for which she knew her fellow priests, even her good friend Carles, would condemn.

"It's none of our fault." She didn't voice what must have been on everyone's mind: would they get their Adrastea back? She stared into the fire. At her feet next to the fireplace was the hob she found outside Ari's door. "Oh, this is yours," she said, nudging the hob with her foot. "I found it out by your garden. I meant to return it." Her heart twisted again at this half-truth. Mira pressed her knuckles to her lips.

Ari sniffed.

A log popped and collapsed in the fire. "So, that's it then?" Ari asked, and she didn't mean the hob. "You think she's gone for good?"

"Ari! Don't say that!" Natan wailed. "She can't have gone just like that. He spent all this time wooing and saying he'll have her willingly, then he steals her from under our noses without any warning? It doesn't make sense."

"He could have been lying," Mira ventured. "He is known to do that."

Natan shook his head. "But why say all that? Why take all this time and declare his intentions? Why didn't he just take her in the first place?"

She conceded his point. He, being a god, must have had a reason for doing what he did. "All right, then. What if she said yes?" Mira asked.

Ari pushed up from Natan's embrace. "No. No. Not our Adrastea. She wouldn't have left like that. Not without a goodbye." The last she said to Natan.

He took her back in his arms. "Maybe he didn't give her a chance this time." His embraced tightened. First his sister gone, then his niece. Mira couldn't imagine what he was feeling.

Mira pushed herself to standing. "Look. If she's gone, she's gone, and we'll have failed. But if she's coming back, we need to come up with a plan to protect her. Obviously, Ari's not going to be enough. No offence, Ari."

Ari only sniffed.

"I think the best option is if she lives with me." Mira didn't mean to make the offer until after she'd spoken the words.

A worried frown crossed Ari's face. "Clearly Mor-Lath grew tired of his game and has claimed his bride. We have no idea if she's coming back, ever."

Mira sighed. "If she doesn't, then that is that. Then again…"

Natan's grip tightened on Ari. "What makes you so sure she'll return, Mira?"

Mira considered her words before delivering them. "We have not been able to accurately predict Mor-Lath's reasons or intentions. We're assuming that just because it seems she's gone, doesn't mean that's what has happened." As she said this, she felt a bit stupid. Natan and Ari stared at her incredulously.

"That doesn't make any sense," Ari replied.

Mira turned to the fire so they couldn't see her worried expression. Why was she so certain Adrastea would return? "I feel it best we remain optimistic. Assume she will return and plan for that." Her gaze fell upon the too-smooth table cloth. "Mor-Lath hasn't been subtle in announcing his intentions. His appearance to Adrastea was rather dramatic, to go by her description. Then he declared his intentions in Council. Quite the show. He can't help but play to an audience. For some reason, I have a feeling he won't take her away unless there is some melodrama to be had first."

Ari gave another sniff and wiped at her nose with her cuff. "So, say he does bring her back. Then what?"

"Well, she comes and lives with me."

"But I need her," Ari blurted. "There's too much to do."

Mira had a suggestion for Ari as to what she could do with herself but chose to keep it for the time being. She felt hot and impatient. Ari and Natan seemed to be unusually obtuse. That annoyed her. And how could Ari give up on Adrastea like that?

Natan looked around Mira's little cottage. "There's not much room here for the both of you. You'd get on each other's nerves."

The priestess wasn't finished. "I thought it best if we lived in Lillybet's house."

"But Lilly died there," said Ari.

"True. But didn't Adrastea say there was a protection over the house?"

Ari wrinkled her nose. "I don't know if she'll stay there. She tends to get bored if you don't give her enough to do."

Mira allowed a small smile to twist her lips. "Ah," she said, wagging her finger at them. "That's where we can keep our Adrastea out of trouble. I promised Carles I would look after his people until he could return next week."

Natan looked surprised. Mira shot him a quick apologetic glance; she'd forgotten to tell him what Carles asked of her. Perhaps she was being obtuse as well, assuming he knew everything? "Adrastea can come with me. She can tend to the physical needs of the people while I tend to their spiritual needs. And she can learn practical priestcraft by observation."

"I need my journeyman." Ari's voice sounded lost.

"You need another apprentice. Someone you can teach and boss around. I hear Marta's got some suitable daughters. Light knows she keeps trying to foist them on me."

"I don't think so."

"Well, start looking. I know we're not a big village. Maybe some fresh blood from Crossroads..."

She left this thought for Ari to consider.

"Now," she said to Natan, "it's late and there's nothing we can do tonight. If she's gone, she's gone. If she comes back, it'll be a new day and another chance."

A wave of tiredness washed over Mira. "Let's get some sleep."

"I can't sleep," Ari said. "I can't be alone right now."

Natan simply put his arm around her shoulder. Ari leaned into it.

Mira said, "take her home and convince her to sleep. Then you and I," she gave him a meaningful look, "can talk tomorrow when we go have a look at Lillybet's house."

Natan nodded.

Adrastea sat at Ari's table, a half-finished pint of brandy holding far more interest for her. The mostly-empty bottle sat on the bare tabletop next to the taper she had lit to keep herself company. Brandy would ask no questions. She had no answers.

She did not look up when Natan and Ari came home.

When they came stumbling through the door, they froze when they saw her. "Adrastea. You're all right," Ari cried.

Adrastea gave them a baleful look. It didn't stop Ari from knocking her off the bench in a hug.

"We were so worried!" Ari's voice was muffled as she pressed Adrastea tightly to her. Natan enveloped them all in a strong embrace.

But Adrastea was not in the mood for all the loving attention. She shoved her way free from the hug and disentangled her limbs from Ari's grasp. "Look," she said. "I just want to go to bed." She lifted the taper from the table and picked up the bottle by its neck.

Natan and Ari clung to each other. "But Adrastea," Ari whimpered. "We thought we'd never see you again."

Adrastea didn't look back. She climbed up the ladder, bottle and taper in the same hand, the other hand for balance. How odd it felt, after having had the Power of Creation flow through her, to simply climb a ladder.

"What happened?" Natan murmured. He followed her up into the low loft. He had to stoop to fit in. Adrastea didn't stop him. Ari followed, her worry strong enough to sing through the Lines.

Adrastea had always known when Ari was worried. Now she understood better how the Lines worked. It was as if Ari's worry looped more and more Lines about her.

Adrastea knelt by the open window. The canyon breeze blew in, a little colder than Adrastea liked but at least it didn't have that acrid smell that Feown had. Her taper fluttered.

Natan asked, "What did he do to you?"

"Nothing," she muttered. It had been a failure, whatever he had tried to accomplish.

Ari knelt beside her. She reached out a hand. Adrastea pushed it gently away. "Please, what hap—" Ari started.

Adrastea turned to her. "Nothing. Really," she blurted, hoping an answer would make Ari go away. "He thought he could tempt me with power. I stood up to him and told him no. And that's all." She turned back to the window. Was that what happened?

Ari continued to fret. "He wasn't angry, was he? He didn't hit you or..."

Adrastea shook her head. "No, he wasn't angry. He was..." she sighed. "Disappointed, I guess." She laid an arm on the windowsill and let her chin sink down onto it.

Wisps of pine-scented wind ruffled her hair. "Now, I'm really tired and would like to go to sleep." She felt the haze in her head from the brandy, not quite enough to make her stop caring. She had disappointed him. To her surprise, that hurt.

Ari tried one more time. She laid a hand on her journeyman's shoulder. "Adrastea, please—"

Adrastea stood up and flopped onto her bed. She pulled the blankets tightly around her. They would get no more answers from her tonight.

Natan murmured something quiet in Ari's ear. Adrastea didn't know what he said but it was enough to make Ari retreat. Soon, Adrastea was alone. She didn't want to be alone, but company was worse.

Natan stayed up later than he should have, discussing Adrastea with Ari. The girl might have returned but that hadn't stopped his Ari from worrying.

She fretted and paced in her bedroom. "You don't think he..."

"I don't know what to think," he had replied. "Even if he had, there's nothing we can do about it tonight. Focus on being glad Adrastea's back." If he had been home in his bed, he would have tucked this worry away in his box, to deal with the next morning. But Ari could not let go until he wrested the worry from her.

It wasn't until he undressed her and pushed her into bed, that she conceded there was nothing more she could do. Still, it was quite some time before sleep won the battle. Her worry had made her toss and turn all night.

Thus, sleep teased them until morning.

Natan rose with the dawn, as he did every day. For a moment he wondered what he was doing in Ari's bed. The woman he loved most in the world slumbered on beside him. He couldn't help but disturb her as he climbed out of bed. She woke, bleary, the worry still across her face.

While Ari stirred the kitchen fire and made tea, Natan poked his head above the top of the ladder to see his niece still dozing away, a hand tucked up beneath her cheek. He looked at her, this young woman who was the closest he'd ever had to a daughter. There were traces of her mother about her but mostly she took after her father, all dark hair and coppery skin. So very Feowan.

Before he descended, Natan rested a chin on the top rung. What did Mor-Lath want with Adrastea? Surely, she couldn't be that talented with the Deeper Power. It might run in the family, but he didn't have it, nor did his parents. His grandparents he couldn't remember that well. Then again, old Aunt Crozie had it. And Lillybet had her quirks. There had to be something else.

He let her sleep. After descending the ladder, he kissed a tired Ari as she sat at the table with her cup of tea. "I'll fetch Mira," he said.

Natan left by the front door, not caring if anyone saw him. They knew better than to comment on Natan the man's whereabouts during the night.

The end of the summer drew nigh, though the ripe scent of autumn had not yet come. A few of the quaking aspen in the mountains sported more and more golden leaves. Heat still shimmered across the plains to the east, although the sun had not risen far from the horizon. It seemed unfair that the weather could be so lovely when such a heavy burden lay on his family.

Mira didn't answer when Natan knocked on her door, so he let himself in.

He found her asleep face-down on the table, her head resting on a large book. He shook her gently. "Mira?"

She startled awake and sent the book sliding. Her moment of panic wasn't enough to send it clean off the table, but it teetered on the edge. She grabbed it and scooted it towards her lap. Was she blushing?

"Oh, Natan! You scared me." She straightened up, gingerly rubbing her neck. "Oh, I really should stop doing that."

"Falling asleep on a book? Start reading in bed, then."

Mira nodded as she yawned. She gently rotated her head the other way and sat back but not before she covered the book with her skirts.

"Natan," she said without preamble. "We need to talk."

"Later, Mira. Adrastea's back."

Mira straightened. "She is?"

Natan shared what little of the tale there was. Mira listened as if searching for clues. "So, he did... nothing?"

"That's her story."

Mira mused over this, her thoughts a mystery to him. "Why did he return her?"

"She said no."

She didn't reply to this but Natan could see her wheels turning.

"You got any breakfast?" he inquired. "I came straight over." Mira waved a hand vaguely towards the pantry. Natan found bread and jam. The teapot was empty and the kettle dry. That was quickly remedied.

"I've done something I'm not proud of." Mira fumbled under the tablecloth.

Natan looked around for a plate. "Oh?"

"When you asked me to read Marta, I did a little bit more than I should have. I didn't just read the Lines. I delved into her. I tried to see inside her head, to see if I could find any thoughts about Lillybet."

Natan froze, his hands full of food. "Can you do that?" A little battle broke out inside him. Knowing what someone else was thinking fascinated and horrified him at the same time.

Mira nodded. "It's not exactly of the Light."

He sat down. "You never told me you could do this."

A grimace crossed her face. "I... I didn't know I could either until recently. I didn't think I'd have the talent."

All the breath escaped Mira. She crumpled face-down onto the table and draped her arms over her head. "I'm so sorry, Natan. I should never have done it." She sat back up. "People's personal thoughts should remain their own. Yes, they can affect the Lines and their luck but to delve in like that... What I did was truly terrible."

Natan placed a full plate on the table. "So... what does this mean, then?"

"Apologize to Marta, penance for myself... and hope I haven't done any more damage than I already have."

Natan pushed the plate before Mira. Perhaps some breakfast would be welcome? He found he made better decisions on a full stomach.

Mira scooted the plate closer to herself. "You know what? I've been thinking. What if it was Mor-Lath who killed Lillybet? What if it wasn't an accident like he said?"

"Oh?" Natan's eyebrows shot up. "What makes you say that?"

Mira spread some jam on a chunk of bread with a knife. "To create chaos, of course. Of all the people who could protect Adrastea from him, it would be family. Who is closer to you in your family than your mother?"

He considered this rather clever turn. Mor-Lath truly needed Adrastea's good will. He'd lose it if Adrastea found out he'd killed her mother. "We've got to tell her."

"No!" Mira's hand shot out to his. "Not without proof."

So, what if they told Adrastea? If she believed them in the beginning, what would happen the next time she encountered Mor-Lath? She'd accuse him. She might scream or cry at him; she certainly wouldn't be calm. And then the Dark God would sweet talk her out of her conviction. 'I need you, Adrastea,' he might say. 'I would not be so foolish as to do that,' he would lie. 'Someone else in the village did it. They don't like you. They don't want you. Leave them and come with me.'

Mira voiced his thoughts: "No matter what we'd say, he'd twist our words to make us look like we were liars. Then Adrastea would not trust us and there goes her support base."

Natan nodded. "You know, if it wasn't so evil, I could like the brilliance of such a plot."

"Natan!" gasped Mira. She blushed.

"And that little trick of his at Council, accusing one of us of framing her murder... that was another ploy, wasn't it?" He accepted the knife for jam from her. "He wants to unsettle the whole village and isolate Adrastea."

Mira nodded. "And if last night's meeting was any indication, I'll bet everyone went home and thought long and hard over whom of their neighbors they were going to accuse later."

"Well, at least let's tell them it was a ploy." He took a bite of bread after he smeared it with jam.

Mira opened her mouth but didn't reply. She seemed to sink down again. "No," she said, after a moment of mulling. "I don't think that's a good idea either."

"What? Why?"

"Think about it. Say we tell everyone that he lied last night, even if we don't tell them who he is. If they don't believe us, you and I are going to lose a great deal of credibility. Now if they believe us, they may stop accusing each other to band together to wonder about the identity of Adrastea's suitor. If the village comes to suspect who he is, they'll kill Adrastea as a witch."

Natan stopped chewing and put down his bread. "Surely we'd do something before it got that far?"

"They are frightened people, Natan. Lillybet died. Someone interfered with her to make it look like murder and blamed it on one of us."

"We've never had a murder here before." Murder's for other places, a storytale specter brought in by travelers and traders to swap at the inn for a beer and some company. Natan kept the records for Sacred Spring. His predecessors never mentioned murder.

"Her death has brought some seriously bad luck to the village."

Natan stared at the plate. Mira's accusation stung. "Lillybet's not the cause of it."

"But Adrastea is. Not directly, not willingly but I believe all this is happening because of her. Do you know what the saddest thing is? I have no idea how it's going to end."

Natan sniffed. "He's really got us tied over a barrel, doesn't he?"

"Yes."

Natan's head filled with worries. How does one defend against that?

Chapter 13

Natan left his personal self back at Ari's. He hoped he'd return soon to pick it up. He took his Mayoral self out into Sacred Spring. Maybe today something completely unrelated to Mor-Lath would happen. He welcomed a simple, uncomplicated village squabble.

As he approached his modest home, an opportunity presented itself.

Marta, plump of hip and full-skirted, faced off against Sheelagh, muscular and clad in very manly leather trousers. Sheelagh barred Marta's way into the smithy. Marta wasn't taking no for an answer.

Natan sighed. Trust Marta to be the one to start a fight and Sheelagh to finish it. This was the Sacred Spring he knew. It was almost comforting.

Sheelagh saw him. "Mayor," she called.

Marta turned, her fists on her hips. "Tell her she can't do this."

A familiar sinking feeling runneled through his stomach. Yep. Back to normal.

"What now?" At least he'd had breakfast before dealing with this.

Marta spoke first, as she always had to. "She's refusing to complete promised work."

Sheelagh folded her brawny arms. "I'm refusing to have anything more to do with her."

"We had an agreement," Marta shrilled at her.

"I don't care!" shrilled Sheelagh. "I know what I know. I will have nothing to do with you."

Marta drew a sharp breath. "If you can't keep your end of the bloody bargain, I'll have to—"

Natan interrupted. "What bargain?"

Marta took a swing at Sheelagh. Natan wasn't expecting that. The plump innkeeper's fist merely glanced off Sheelagh's chin.

Sheelagh returned the favor. Unlike Marta's limp-wristed tap,

Sheelagh put the full strength of her powerful smithy arm behind it.

The crack of her fist meeting Marta's jaw echoed loudly.

Marta spun about before falling face-first into the dust.

Natan exclaimed out loud. Normally the fisticuffs didn't come until after the yelling.

She sat up with murder in her eyes, wiped a wet smear of dust and blood from her mouth. She pointed a sharp finger at Sheelagh. "You bitch!"

Natan placed himself between the two women. Otherwise, both would continue the brawl and Marta would come out second best. Natan held out his hands to keep them both at bay. "Neither one of you have answered my question."

A new voice spoke. "Natan?"

He looked around. Mira stood there, Adrastea behind her. His niece clutched a large bag to her chest as if it were armor.

Sheelagh made a move toward Marta, her braided hair coming loose into wisps around her head, her chest heaving. Natan caught her. She pointed to Marta, who had been left to stand up on her own. "She killed Adrastea's mother. She's the only one who could have done it."

Natan's hands froze on Sheelagh's arms. How did she learn this? Did the whole village know?

"What?" squeaked Adrastea. Her bag fell from her arms. She drew in a ragged breath. Quickly, Mira took a hold of her.

Sheelagh struggled against Natan. She could probably arm wrestle every man in that village and beat most of them. She certainly gave Natan a good challenge. "Oh, yeah. She was bitter after Lillybet got her son back. I don't care what that man said. She went up there and killed her. That's why I will have nothing more to do with her."

Mira clutched Adrastea's arm. "You don't have any proof."

"Oh, bloody hell," cursed Natan. "Marta didn't kill Lillybet."

"The hell she did." Sheelagh pulled herself free from Natan but did not go after Marta. "Nobody else in the village could have done something like that. Only her!"

"Bitch!" Marta hurled herself at Sheelagh, sending them both to the ground. She pummeled Sheelagh about the head with her fists.

"Lilly's death was an accident." Natan hauled the Innkeeper off the Smith. He was glad he'd left Natan the man at home. Natan the man would have easily let Marta be the scapegoat for his grief.

Sheelagh picked herself off of the ground and checked out the scrape on her bare elbow. Brown dust coated the back of her breeches and her black bodice, as well as the bare skin of her shoulders. "Then she made it look like a murder," Sheelagh muttered. "I know she did. I know it's her. It has to be. Only she'd do something like this."

Sheelagh consulted her elbow again with a hiss of pain. Adrastea hastened to the quenching barrel, dipped the hem of her skirt in, and used that to dab at Sheelagh's wounds. Despite everything that had happened, Adrastea was still a healer. Natan clung to that hope.

Marta, who could never stay silent, shouted, "I didn't do it!"

Tam Innkeeper came running from the Inn. He took charge of his wife from Natan.

Natan murmured low, "Take her in and keep her away from everyone." He looked at Marta's lip, which was starting to swell and turn purple. "You may wish to put something cold on that." That's what Ari would have said. Nothing like giving someone something to do to direct their focus and keep idle hands busy.

With a promise he'd come talk with them later, Natan watched the Innkeepers retreat. This was no mere disagreement. This bordered on civil war.

Mira shepherded Sheelagh to a bench by the smithy door. "We don't have proof."

Sheelagh stared at the priestess, her eyes wide in disbelief. "What more do you need? We know how much she hated Lillybet." She hissed as Adrastea dabbed at her elbow. "Gently!"

Mira stood in the doorway, her hands folded tightly before her. "She was nowhere near Lilly that night."

"You don't know that! And what about last night?" Sheelagh's eyes drifted over to Adrastea. Adrastea averted her gaze to the wound she dabbed. "We all know someone at Council was responsible."

Natan sighed. "But Marta wasn't there. Remember, I'd banned her for two weeks." Natan wouldn't even let her in her own inn. "If what M— that man said last night was true, then Marta can't be the killer." Then again, he could have lied.

Ah, now there was a distinct possibility. After all, this was the God of the Dark. He was never up to any good.

"That man," Sheelagh echoed. She looked to Adrastea. "He's your betrothed, isn't he?"

Adrastea hunched her shoulders and patted the wound dry. "No," she replied, her voice faint. "We're not getting married."

"Not if we can help it," Mira said.

Sheelagh forgot her scrapes. "What's his name? Who's his family? Is he from Crossroads?"

"Does it matter?" Mira said. "He'll be gone soon, and we'll see no more of him."

"Who is he?" Sheelagh asked, addressing Adrastea directly.

Adrastea pressed a hand to her mouth. She backed away. "He's nobody."

Before anyone could say anything else, she fled up the hill and, hopefully, towards the sacred spring.

"Adrastea," Mira called after her. She and Natan exchanged looks before Mira followed his niece.

Sheelagh looked up at him, her face perplexed. "What I say?"

Natan sighed. He scrubbed his hands through his hair and deliberately changed the subject. "I recommend you leave Marta alone. Unless you have proof, I would ask that you refrain from voicing accusations of her or anyone else."

Sheelagh turned her shoulder to him. "Until you can prove she didn't do it, I think it best I not deal with her at all. And you can tell her that."

In the end, he made her promise she would not speak of this, or anything that happened that day to anyone else until the matter was sorted.

Before he left, he noticed Adrastea's bag on the ground. Knowing his niece, she would not be back any time soon from wherever it was she'd run off to. He picked it up, trudged up the hill and left it on the porch of Lillybet's home.

The hike up the hill was harder than Mira remembered. She had come up with Carles the other day but that had been a pleasant walk. She hadn't noticed the hill so much. Before that, it had been a long time. Too long. Mira added another twinge to her growing pile of guilt. As priestess, she should visit here regularly, even if pilgrims had stopped coming.

Sweat broke out on her brow. Her lungs burned as she made it to the spring. Mira breathed a sigh of relief when she saw Adrastea safe and sound.

Adrastea sat by the water, staring into its inky depths. "I'm sorry," she mumbled as the priestess drew near. "I panicked. I didn't know what to say. We promised to keep it a secret, and..."

"It's all right. We took care of it." Mira joined her on the ground. Even in the late of summer the grass next to the spring was still green and cool, when the rest on the hills had turned golden. In a month, the trees would turn as well, and winter would soon be upon them. "We never expected Mor-Lath to show up like that. I guess we need a cover story."

"Like Marta's?" she said in bitterness.

Mira looked at her. "What? Oh, the... um. Yeah." She reached out a hand to Adrastea. "Please listen. Marta did not kill your mother."

Adrastea turned away. "You don't know that."

Mira sighed. "I know that for sure. I'm the priestess. I have... I can read the Lines of Deeper Power. They say Marta's innocent. Whoever did this tried to make Marta take the blame."

Adrastea turned back to Mira, her eyes blazing. "Well, if you can tell Marta's innocent, you can tell who's guilty!"

That stung. Mira drew back. "And what would you do if we found the guilty party?"

"I'd..." she drew in a sharp breath. "I'd want to..."

"Kill him?"

"Well, hurt him, at least." She drew in a shuddery breath. Adrastea fell into Mira's arms in a fit of crying.

Mira held her for the next long while as Adrastea cried out her sorrow over her mother. It was best to let her have her cry. Later she would try to temper this darkness that rose in the young woman.

A cold thought chilled her heart. What if this darkness was what Mor-Lath wanted?

⁓❦⁓

Natan left Adrastea's bag on Lillybet's back porch. He paused to study the new extensions to his village. Her home was not as isolated as it once was. Behind it stood all the rough cabins they'd thrown up for the refugees. 'Little Crossroads', some of them called it. It was not a comfortable, homely place.

Despondency hung in the air as he stepped into the circle of rough cabins. A few Crossroaders tended fires, giving them the occasional bored poke but for the most part, everyone sat around. It wasn't the joyful time-wasting of an apprentice with a rare free afternoon but a dull marking of time, as the days blended into one another. Nothing to do, nothing to look forward to.

A woman with an infant sat on a log in front of a cabin. She watched him, baby to breast, as he inspected Little Crossroads. "You're Mayor, aren't you?" She had that maternal portliness about her that came with maternal experience. Her skin looked sallow and her eyes looked as dark as her hair and about as limp.

"I am," he replied.

"Do you know when Carles Priest is coming back?"

"In less than a week."

The woman sighed. Her arms let the baby sag. The baby scrabbled with its fingers at the pale breast. The woman hitched it back up. "I don't know if we're going to last that long. This isn't our home. The children are restless. Kahni's going to have her baby soon and we didn't bring a healer."

Natan looked around. "Isn't Adrastea here?"

"Who?"

Where was she and Mira? "I've sent one of our healers to come and help you, as well as our priestess. They'll live there," he pointed to Adrastea's house. "They can help you until…"

"Until what?"

Natan shrugged. "Until you go home, I guess."

The woman with the baby sniffed and looked elsewhere.

Natan wasn't sure what to say to someone who didn't want to talk much. His benediction: "Let me know if there's anything you need."

Well, that was another worry to add to the box tonight.

He spied Mira and Adrastea letting themselves in through the back gate of Lilly's garden. He hurried after them, calling Mira's name. "I've been waiting for you," he said with some relief. "Could you have a look at the Crossroaders? I'm concerned."

Adrastea looked a little washed-out, like she'd been crying. He didn't blame her. Nevertheless, she nodded.

He watched them head to Little Crossroads to address the various ills, physical and spiritual. Perhaps a bit of service would help take their minds off their own problems.

Natan found a seat on a log next to a cabin. He leaned back against the rough wall. The nursing mother who spoke to him earlier came over and sat down next to him with a huff. She still nursed a child, having swapped him to the other breast.

"My name is Laika," she said, brushing a stray lock of straggly hair out of her dark eyes. "I'm sorry I was so short earlier. You must understand our difficulties."

He nodded. "It must be hard having to leave your home."

Laika pondered for a moment, shifting the baby. "I think it's the shock of having to leave suddenly but in a day or two it will be the boredom and lack of routine that will cause us the most trouble."

Natan looked again at the nursing infant. He was dressed in a different color. "Is that another child?"

Laika nodded. "It's Carey's. All this talk of war has been drying everyone up but me. I always have lots of milk."

"And where's your baby?"

Laika looked about. "Oh... she's around somewhere. Should be asleep by now, I'd think." She squinted at the group of women gathered around Adrastea. "Your healer's rather young."

"We have two. The other one had something else to attend to."

Laika continued to squint. "That one know her business with babies?"

Natan shrugged. "She's helped birth a few."

Laika nodded. "I have a woman's complaint I'd like to see her about." Laika turned her gaze to Natan. "You're very good."

"I am?"

"You want us to believe you're going to do something, but I know you couldn't be bothered with people not your own."

Natan sat up a bit straighter. He didn't like it when people guessed his thoughts. "Carles is coming back soon."

"But not to take us home."

Natan didn't have an answer for that. "I am leaving Adrastea here with you. The healer," he clarified when he saw Laika's confused expression. "Since we've two, I can easily spare one for you."

Laika only hmphed at this. "But not your priestess."

"Actually," confessed Natan. "Her too."

"And what will you do without her?"

"You won't need her the whole time. She can minister to us all. But she will live with Adrastea for your convenience."

"How very generous of you."

He wasn't sure if she was genuine or sarcastic. Natan rose. "I must leave you. I do have some matters to attend to." He strode away.

"Mayor?" she called after him. "Thank you." Sounded like she meant it.

Chapter 14

Sheelagh was true to her word; she kept away from Marta and said nothing about their spat. She had her honor to maintain.

Instead, she applied herself to work outside the Smithy. If she wasn't home, she wouldn't have to deal with any of the Innkeeper brats who might have been sent by their mother in her place.

The Poulters had a broken lock on one of their henhouses. They had converted an abandoned cottage to house their birds. Its heavy stone walls kept out foxes, whereas the doors kept out other chicken thieves.

As she replaced the lock, she listened and nodded to Amarice, who seemed rather talkative that morning.

"I think it odd," said Amarice, who toyed with her hands underneath her apron, "that our Adrastea has been betrothed to a complete stranger and nobody in the village has been introduced to him."

Sheelagh wiped a stray bit of down from where it tickled her nose. "Natan seems to know who he is."

"Natan doesn't like him very much. Nor Ari."

"Nor Mira," added Sheelagh, though she did not elaborate further. Adrastea certainly did not wish to speak of him. Who was he?

One side of the lock had been made too big for the hole in the wooden door. It wouldn't go through. "Gimmie that file there. No, the round one." Sheelagh pointed to the tools in her work bag.

Amarice grunted as she stooped down to pick it out. Holding it gingerly, she handed it to the smith.

"Ta." Sheelagh worked the lock out. A goose, too curious for Sheelagh's comfort, came over to investigate. She hissed at it to move but it was Amarice who had to shoo it away.

"Anyhow, I heard that Lillybet didn't want him to marry Adrastea."

Sheelagh stared up at the blonde woman. "You don't think he killed her to get her out of the way?"

Amarice shrugged and looked away. "Some say Marta killed her."

Sheelagh nodded but said nothing. Her promise to Natan might have prevented her from saying anything but it did not cover listening to others when they expressed their opinions or from agreeing when they matched her own.

A few more rasps of the file finished the hole. She worked in the shaft of the lock and placed the back before pounding in the rivets to hold it all together.

Amarice shifted from foot to foot. "Marta is the most likely person, don't you believe, Sheelagh?"

Sheelagh shrugged. "Marta never did like Lillybet. Day and Night, those two. Keeping to themselves, yet meeting only when their paths cross." Lilly had the right idea. Sheelagh wished she'd thought of it earlier.

She brushed the dry goose droppings from her knees. "The rest of your locks okay?" She looked out to the other converted cottages beyond the first henhouse. "I could check them if you wish."

Amarice looked over the stone walls to the other houses. "No, they're fine."

"You know, I could fit locks to your house as well. Whoever it was, someone had it out for Lilly. Or Marta. And, well, you know, with the baby and all—"

Amarice's pretty features drew into a scowl. "What baby?" she denied.

Sheelagh sighed. "It's not something you can hide forever. How far along are you? Seven months?"

Amarice covered her face with her hands before tears ran down her face. "How did you know?"

Sheelagh smiled gently. She moved to put an arm around plump Amarice, but the shorter woman slid away from the connection. Her smile faded. She dropped her hand. "I've been talking to your belly for the past ten minutes." She'd had her suspicions for a while now but wasn't sure until today. "What does Ari say?"

"Ari says I'm fine!" Amarice's voice rose in pitch. "And never you mind what Ari says."

Sheelagh had already had enough arguments for the day. She had no wish for another one. However, she did leave Amarice with one last thought: "There's no guarantee you'll die like your mother." As she left, she heard Amarice dissolve into tears.

Ah. Maybe that wasn't the best thing to say.

Awful lot of strange happening lately. Perhaps home was the best place to be.

◦◦◦

When Natan returned to his house in the late afternoon, he didn't recognize the place. The house was spotless. Mikal had opened the windows and let the breeze blow out the stale smell of bachelorhood. He'd cleaned the table and polished it well. He'd scrubbed the cooking pots and the floor and somehow, found a place for everything.

Not used to having an apprentice, yesterday he'd given Mikal vague instructions to straighten the house and do something about the garden. Between the Council and Adrastea and everything, he confessed he'd forgotten about him.

Mikal, lounging in a chair with his feet up on the table, jumped up and began to swipe at the table with a rag.

"Easy there, boy. I'm not your—" he almost said your mother. "Just sit back down."

Mikal did so but did not relax like he had before.

Natan poked his head out the back door to find that Mikal had gotten to the garden as well. Of course he had, after having been abandoned for twenty-four hours. He had piled the long weeds in a far corner of the garden where the stack reached above the wall separating the properties.

Natan whistled in approval. "You've been busy, boy."

Mikal cleared his throat. "I, um, cleared out the loft. I hope you don't mind."

"What? Why?"

Mikal hesitated. "I— I thought that's where I'm supposed to sleep."

Natan scratched his head to cover his embarrassment. He had forgotten that he had to house the boy. "Well, yeah. But you can only get to it from outside."

"I don't mind," Mikal replied hastily.

"You sure you don't want to sleep down here?" Come to think of it, where had he slept last night?

"Quite sure."

"You won't be cold?"

Mikal shook his head. "I found an old bedstead up there. It's not big and I'll need to get a new tick, but I put it close to the chimney, so I'll be fine."

Natan nodded his approval. "Now, how about dinner?"

Mikal froze. "Oh... I'm sorry..." He began to bustle about, opening the nearly-empty pantry and starting to set plates out on the table.

Natan caught him by the shoulders. "Easy there, boy. I don't expect you to make dinner. I thought we'd go impose on Ari tonight. Adrastea's off with Mira, so I think she'd be rather lonely." Or rather, he felt unprepared. "Look. I'm sorry about last night."

Mikal blinked at him. "Why? What happened?"

"I didn't mean to leave you by yourself."

He gave Natan a half-shrug. "I don't mind. It was kind of nice to spend some time on my own. Oh." He blushed. "I ate the last of your bread."

"That's all right. I'll get more tomorrow." Yep, definitely time to go to Ari's. "You have a jacket, lad?"

He did. Had brought all his possessions over from the Innkeepers, not that he had much. At least Tam and Marta had kept him clothed.

As Mikal fetched it, Natan pondered over how much to tell his nephew. By the time he'd returned, Natan thought it best to keep his secrets for now.

Ari wasn't expecting them but she welcomed them anyhow. She admitted to Natan that yes, it was quiet and lonely without her journeyman. "Do come in, and I'll see what I can do to stretch dinner."

Natan sniffed the air. "What are we having?"

"Chicken."

"Really?" Mikal piped, his eyes lighting up. Ari figured that he wouldn't have had chicken too often at the Innkeepers. If they had, best he got was a wing or so. Ari grew up with a few brothers—nowhere near as many as Mikal had as fosters—and she still had to fight them for every scrap.

"Really," she said. "Marlon brought one by today, thinking I'd want it. 'No particular reason,' he said, which means there is something. 'Don't bother dropping by to say thanks,' he said."

"Really?" Natan replied. The tone of his voice told her he'd came up with the same conclusion she had reached earlier—Amarice was pregnant after all.

"Tomorrow," she assured him, "I'll pop by."

Mikal, ever the efficient one, had pulled out two extra plates before Ari or Natan could ask.

Ari watched the innkeeper diligence then sighed her own resignation. "I guess I should go pick more vegetables from the garden."

"Oh," said Natan and Mikal at the same time, sounding equally disappointed.

"Well, how else am I going to stretch dinner?"

"More potatoes?" Mikal suggested.

"Not unless you want to wait an hour."

That let out his steam. She watched hunger force him to resign to a side of fresh peas.

Dinner couldn't come soon enough for them all. With Natan's quick murmur of thanks to the Light, they all dug in.

A knock, furious and quick, came at Ari's door. She felt the bottom drop out of her evening. She looked at Natan across the table. They both sighed. Mikal didn't pause in shoveling food in his mouth.

"Ari! Please come! Mom's been hurt!" the caller shouted.

"That's Martine!" said Mikal.

As one, they all rose from the table, abandoning their supper.

Natan opened the door to Martine. Ari grabbed her healer's bag and swirled her cloak over her shoulders.

Martine bounced up and down in anxiety. "Kyfa attacked Mom in the Inn. Rop's there but she's been hurt. She's covered in blood!"

"Where is she now?" Ari demanded.

Martine pointed. "The common room."

Natan ushered her in. "Tell me what happened."

Ari fled out the door, cloak streaming behind her in the warm evening air, leaving Natan and Mikal to get the rest of the story from Martine.

Ari found Marta sitting in a chair in the common room, with Rop Storekeeper, her eldest son, holding a bloody rag to her head. Marta waved a hand weakly at Rop as if to shoo him away but otherwise sat still. A few of the children stood around uselessly.

"Marta?" Ari inquired. "You okay?"

Marta let out a small groan. Her eyes were screwed up tight and she held up her blood-smeared hand as if trying to shush the room. Marta was conscious but clearly in a bit of pain. That wasn't a bad sign.

Meanwhile, the crying of the younger children wasn't helping matters any. Tom didn't cry but his white face betrayed his anxiety.

"Tom," she ordered, "I assume there's boiling water in the kitchen?"

Tom stared at her for a moment, slack-jawed. "Uh, I don't know."

"Well, go find out. If there isn't any, make some."

She pointed to a younger girl. "You, Salle."

"I'm Ada." She sniffed and wiped her nose with the cuff of her sleeve.

"Well, whichever one you are, go help your brother. He's going to need some more fuel. And take that one with you." She indicated the youngest, a three-year old who stood there blubbering, the fat tears rolling down her face. Chances were, she didn't know why she was crying.

They left as dismissed and Ari turned to Marta. "What happened?" she asked as she wrapped her cloak around Marta's shoulders.

Rop answered. "Kyfa came in here, shouted something about Mom killing Lillybet and then struck her."

Ari took over the compress on Marta's head. She lifted it to inspect a nasty gash across the scalp, a parting between the matted hair a good handspan wide. A fall of blood stained the front of Marta's bodice but no more flowed from the staunched wound.

Tom poked his head through the kitchen door. "Water's ready. What do I do with it?"

Ari poked gently at the wound. It seeped a little. "Bring a kettleful and a teapot. Also, two cups." Tom's head popped back through the door after a brief nod.

Marta wasn't saying much. Ari replaced the bloody rag. She tilted Marta's chin up to look into her eyes. They seemed a bit glazed from shock but otherwise, seemed fine, reacting to the change in light. "Marta? How do you feel?"

"Mmm."

"I've got to have a look. It might hurt a bit."

Marta didn't reply. She let her gaze wander off.

To Rop, Ari said, "Keep pressure on that compress and make sure she stays warm. Her body's not going to react well to this."

Ari wiped her hands on the edge of her cloak as Tom came through the door with both a kettle and a teapot of water. "Just put them there on the table, Tom. Oh, and I'll need a wash bowl.

She measured one kind of tea into the teapot and poured the boiling water over. While it steeped she tried to get the whole story. "So, Kyfa came in here and struck Marta with what?"

Rop pointed to a chair lying on the floor, some meters away. Ari hadn't noticed it before. "I don't know the whole story, really. Martine says they were cleaning up the tables when Kyfa came in. She started screaming at Mom then picked up a chair and swung it at her head."

"Kyfa, hmmm?" Kyfa was Baran and Ariah Shepherd's youngest daughter, one of three who, in the off-seasons after shearing, tended dye gardens and dyed wool, flax and other fibers for the village. Kyfa wasn't much older than Adrastea. Her older sister Jira was Rop's wife. Kyfa, like much of the village, tended to keep her distance when Marta's temper disintegrated. Kyfa had a fondness for Lillybet. She was the closest Lilly had, outside the family circle, to a friend.

Marta liked order. For her, there was one way of doing things—the right way. And if things weren't done her one right way, it was wrong. As long as everything was in order, Marta was fine. But when chaos threated, her fuse shortened. She became unbearable to live with. Ari wondered why Tam put up with it as he did. She wasn't this bad as a child, although she did tend to run to her bossy side. Things didn't get really bad until after she was married...

"Marta?" Ari asked. "Are you pregnant?"

"What?" declared Rop. "Oh, no, Mom. Not again."

This got Marta's attention. "Not your business, Rop. And none of yours, Ari."

Tom returned with the wash bowl, two cups and clean rags. Ari ordered him to leave and take his sisters with him.

Now to deal with Marta. "After today, I think it is my business. We've got to protect you if you're carrying a baby."

"You could have protected her before," Rop snapped.

"We didn't know she was going to be attacked," Ari snapped back. "Things like these aren't supposed to happen here."

"You should have known something like this would happen when that man accused my mother of murder."

"Mor-Lath never said anything about your mother." Then Ari realized what she had said. She caught her bottom lip in her teeth, then turned around to busy herself with her tools. "That wound needs stitching," she said in haste, as soon as she could think of something to say. "That's a pretty bad gash." She lifted the teapot and splashed tea into a cup. "Drink this, Marta. It will help with the pain."

Rop stared at her. Ari wished his eyes would go somewhere else. "Mor-Lath?" he said, his voice incredulous. "His name is Mor-Lath?"

Ari paused, a pair of tweezers in her hand. "I didn't say that," she replied stiffly.

"You did."

Marta muttered. "Stupid name. What mother in their right mind would name her son Mor-Lath? I chose decent names for my children."

Ari let out her breath. She turned from Rop's surprised gaze and set out the rest of her tools. She took the compress from Marta's head. "It is an unfortunate name. His family probably isn't strong in the Light. You can see why we are against the match." To Marta, she said, "This is going to hurt."

Marta stiffened, her hands clenching around the cup of tea. Ari picked at the dried blood around the wound. "I'm going to have to trim the hair. Your head needs serious stitching."

"Who is he?" Marta muttered, not so much to make conversation but to distract herself from the pain; that's what Ari would have done. "Where is he from? Who's his family? I've never seen him here before. Where's he staying? Certainly not here. I don't like the sound of him."

Ari did not answer as she trimmed the blood-encrusted hair away from the gash. It seemed worse once the hair was gone. Marta was lucky. Her brain didn't seem to be affected; her eyes looked normal, but she shivered. "I'm cold," Marta complained.

"Keep the cloak around you and drink more tea."

"Perhaps something stronger?" Rop suggested.

Ari shook her head. "No. The tea is best for now."

Marta obediently finished her tea. Ari poured some more. She waited until Marta's shaking ceased before stitching.

"What do we know about this Mor-Lath fellow? His clothes seemed very fine. Is he from Feown?"

Ari shrugged. "I don't think so." She threaded one of her curved needles with a piece of sinew.

"Is he a lord?"

"Yes."

Rop pulled a chair over and sat next to his mother. He wrapped an arm around her shoulders. "What does he want with our Adrastea?"

"Nothing good. Now, this will sting." Ari matched up the two edges of the wound. She stuck her curved needle in.

Marta hissed and jumped. "Bugger, Ari! That hurts!"

Ari put a firm hand on the back of Marta's head and stood close to her, bracing the head against her chest. "Nothing I can do about that." Marta squeaked in protest, but Ari's bracing kept her from jerking her head away She stitched and knotted and asked for her scissors. "I don't know what he wants. Nothing good. What lord would come out here to woo a village maid?"

"Maybe he knew Joe?" Rop suggested.

"I doubt it," replied Ari. "Joe was from Feown."

In the end, it only took three stitches. Ari wrapped Marta's head with strips of the rags. "Luck is with you. Your hair will grow over the scar and nobody will notice."

"I'll notice," Marta muttered. She had drained the contents of the teapot, including the dregs. Her focus wavered somewhat.

"Where's Tam?" Ari asked Rop.

"After Kyfa ran, he went to have some words with Baran and Ariah."

"Oh, is Baran in?" As a shepherd, Baran spent more time out in the fields with his sheep rather than in town. Some say he preferred the company of the silent sheep to the incessant gossiping of his wife.

"Probably not."

Ari nodded. She inspected Marta's eyes again. "It's all right for your mother to go to bed if she wants. Best she go to sleep before she starts complaining of pain." She removed her cloak from Marta's shoulders. "Get your own blanket and stay warm," she said to Marta.

"Thank you, Ari," said Rop.

Marta, now under the full effects of the tea, waved her hand in a vague manner. Best Rop get her upstairs before she fell asleep in the common room.

Ari nodded. "If you see Tam soon, please, please, please ask him to speak to Natan before he does anything rash or stupid. There's been enough foolishness in this village for now. We don't need any more." Ari regarded Marta for a moment. "Marta, I think it may be in your best interests if you left the village for a little while."

"You want to get rid of me?" she mumbled.

"I want to protect you. Kyfa's not the first person to suspect you. I don't think you did it—"

"I didn't. Light's honor."

"But others may not be so rational. For your own safety, it may be best you leave until this matter is cleared up. Do you have somewhere you can go? Maybe Mutch and Millie's place?"

Rop put his arm around his mother. "We'll think about it."

"Don't take too long. I can stitch up wounds. I can't heal death."

Natan woke to a knock on his door. "This is getting ridiculous," he muttered. He slipped out of bed and wrapped a robe around him for warmth. He had only just dropped off to sleep after banishing his worries to a wooden box beside his bed.

He jerked open his front door. He startled Tam Innkeeper, who dropped his box lantern. He caught it before it clattered on the porch.

"This had better be good," growled Natan. He'd already put several worries regarding the Innkeepers into his box. Ari had been over earlier to add to the pile. Looks like Tam was going to add some more.

Tam began to back away. "Perhaps I should have waited until morning."

"Damn right."

"Oh. Well, since you're awake..."

Natan sighed and folded his arms. "What is it?"

"Rop said you wanted to see me before I did anything foolish."

"So now you're going to go do something foolish?"

"No," the Innkeeper replied hastily. "I just wanted to tell you when I spoke with Ariah, she told me Kyfa hadn't come home tonight." His words came rushing out. "I will leave this matter in your hands, but you've got to do something, Mayor. I will not stand by while my family gets attacked."

Natan stood there, squinting against the pale light Tam brought to light his way. "Fine, as you wish. Now, are you going to get the hell off my porch?"

Tam stepped off the porch but did not continue down the gravel walkway. "Rop also told me what Ari said. She said—"

"Yeah, she told me too. So what?"

Tam hesitated. "Um, I was just saying that Marta will be leaving Sacred Spring for her own safety. It's best for all."

Ari had mentioned the possibility. "I agree. Anything else?"

"No. Oh, yes. We're leaving tomorrow; there's cousins of ours up Sawyers' way who'll have to take her but I'm coming back. Someone's got to run the Inn."

"Fine. Go away." Natan shut the door. He returned to his bedroom and sank his bulk on the bed. Before he returned to sleep, he took his little wooden box and whispered, "Find Kyfa tomorrow, get whole story. Marta to be leaving. Hallelujah."

Chapter 15

Natan woke early because Mikal woke early. His apprentice walked around with heavy feet. Mikal clattered down the outside ladder, which just happened to be on the wall that Natan's bedhead rested against. He splashed his ablutions in the back porch bucket he filled yesterday. He stomped into the kitchen to start breakfast.

Was he always this noisy, or was he celebrating the fact he didn't have to tiptoe about the Inn anymore?

Breakfast. Cornmeal mush, most likely. It was all Natan had in the house at the moment. He hadn't leaned over the back wall to beg some eggs from the Butchers lately. He rolled over as soon as the smell of cooking reached his nostrils.

Natan pulled on a clean pair of pants and a fresh shirt before padding out along the wooden floor to the kitchen. Have to love an apprentice who could cook.

"Morning," Mikal said, too chipper for Natan's liking. "Breakfast's not ready. There's no milk."

"That's fine," Natan yawned. He was grateful for a breakfast he didn't have to make.

"Uncle Natan? Is Ma— Marta leaving today?"

Natan woke up. "What?"

Mikal turned back to the small stove and stirred the pot. There was an awful lot of porridge in that pot. Mikal was not used to cooking for only two. "It's just that... I wanted to say goodbye first."

"Now, how did— you listened. Didn't you?"

Mikal didn't deny it.

"Fair enough," Natan conceded. "I guess I can't stop you from eavesdropping. But I can stop you from talking to others about our business. You're a Mayorprentice now. The first thing you need to learn is that while everyone's business is our business, it's not anyone else's business what our business is." Did that make any sense? "Keep your mouth shut, boy. People will respect you more if you are reliable about keeping secrets."

Mikal served up a bowl of cornmeal mush, lump-free and glazed with honey. As Natan dabbed his finger at the golden sweetness, he thanked the Light at least there was some of that left. Sacred Spring had no beekeepers any more. All honey had to be traded from Crossroads or beyond. Perhaps he should convince Ari to take up beekeeping—just a small hive, naturally. It'd be good for her garden.

The boy settled opposite Natan at the table with a bowl of his own. He shoveled great spoonfuls into his adolescent mouth. Halfway through breakfast he asked, "What are we doing today?"

"We?" Natan paused to muse. "I guess it is we, now." Natan drew in a breath through his nose and mentally emptied out his wooden box of worries. "Let's see... Marta's going for a visit."

"Where?"

Natan shrugged. "Don't know. And you don't know either, if anyone asks, even when you do."

Mikal wrinkled his nose but didn't comment.

"We need to sort out a matter with the Shepherds." He didn't elucidate, and Mikal didn't ask.

He did ask about, "The refugees? We need to do anything about them?"

Natan considered. "Maybe. Carles Priest is coming in a few days' time to remind them they haven't been deserted. Maybe we'll find out then."

"Oh. All right." Mikal finished his breakfast, well ahead of Natan. He helped himself to seconds. Natan wasn't going to stop him. If Mikal didn't eat all that mush today, there was a good chance Natan would have to eat it later. Mush was good for breakfast but Natan drew the line when it came to other meals. He preferred something hot and meaty.

"And what are we to do about Adrastea?"

Natan stopped eating, his spoon paused half-way to his mouth. "The less said about that, the better."

"I need to know, Uncle Natan. She is my sister. People've been saying things."

"What sort of things?"

"Well, they wonder who he is. Who is he?"

For one brief moment, Natan debated over whether he should tell

Mikal the truth.

No. It was too soon. "He's an outsider."

"My real father was an outsider."

"Your real father proved his worth."

"Well, maybe this man can."

"No, he can't. That's the problem."

Mikal poked at his mush. "Maybe you haven't given him a chance."

Natan brainstormed quickly about how he could quench this discussion without raising Mikal's curiosity any further. "We know he doesn't mean well by our Adrastea."

"Why? What's he planning on doing?"

"We don't know." This was Mor-Lath. His reputation preceded him. So far, he was living up to that reputation. Death, distrust, the destruction of families. He was doing a very good job of spreading chaos about the village.

Natan wondered for a moment: what if Mor-Lath had come to Sacred Spring, had used a different name, won our trust, then had taken our Adrastea away? We'd give her willingly, maybe even gladly, happy that there was someone who wanted Mad Lilly's daughter to wife.

He looked up at Mikal. "He refuses to tell us. And that makes us suspicious."

And yet Mor-Lath had been so honest about so many other things. It was uncharacteristic of someone reputed to be the Dark One. That he had power? Clearly demonstrated. That he didn't fear anyone in Sacred Spring? That too was obvious. He made his identity clear to Adrastea and his reason for his interest in her to everyone.

But he never shared his identity with the others. Natan had seen his name magically scrawled on the slate but never heard the Dark One's own name from his lips. Why was that? He wondered if he had found a weakness. He'd have to ask Mira later.

Mikal begged, "At least tell me his name."

Natan wrinkled his nose in thought as he regarded his apprentice. Oh, how curiosity must be burning in him now. "Call him Master M for now."

"M?"

"Yeah. Mystery, he is. Do you know," he told his apprentice matter-of-factly, "not once has he ever told me his name?"

As Natan and Mikal walked through the village, they caught sight of Marta through one of the upper windows of the Inn; she had not left yet.

"So, she's really going?" Mikal said, his voice sounding small. "She didn't do it. Kill my mother, that is."

Natan put an arm around his new apprentice. "You and I know that, but we haven't had time to convince everyone else. Despite your mother's reputation, there were people in the village who liked her. And because of your foster mother's reputation, there are those who don't like Marta. This is a perfectly good excuse to "get one back on her," guilt or no guilt. Until we can convince everyone of her innocence, or find who's really at fault, it's best for her safety and that of the new baby that she leave."

Mikal echoed the words 'new baby'. He rolled his eyes.

Their first call was to be the Shepherds house to inquire after Kyfa. Mikal wanted to know the nature of this business. Natan refused to tell him. "You will discover that when you need to know."

The Shepherds town house sat at the opposite end of the village, on the other side of the commons, nestled next to the foothill. The trees that grew on the foothill separated the Shepherds home from Lillybet's. They provided adequate shade in the afternoon. Natan sometimes wished his Mayoral predecessors had had the same presence of vision as the early Shepherds and built his home there.

They never made it across the green. A galloping horse approached them in front of the Smithy. It passed them but wheeled around and stopped. Mikal made a grab for the bridle so the rider could dismount.

"Natan!" the rider called. His big bass voice boomed across the village green.

Natan stared at the dust-drenched rider. "Sam?" Natan shouted in surprise.

Sam Mayor of Crossroads had no riding coat, nor any hat. He looked as if he had jumped on the first available horse and fled. Crossroads was a good several hours, even on a fast horse. Mikal walked the lathered horse around to cool it down, staying close enough to hear the conversation of the two men.

Sam didn't bother to brush the dust off before enveloping the larger man in a hug. He was shorter than Natan, though not by much, and of a slimmer build. The dust in his hair made it seem lighter than Natan remembered it. There could have been some grey in there too. Natan hadn't seen Sam in over a year but he remembered the warm hazel eyes of his peer.

"What are you doing here?" Natan exclaimed. For Sam Mayor to come personally... "Oh, no. Don't tell me something's happened—"

Sam took in a big breath. "Feown has fallen. The Cithran army has breached its walls and the city is taken."

Feown, that great City of the Plain, that hub of commerce on a river reputed to be wider than Crossroads was big, had fallen to the Cithrans.

Natan had never been there. Ari had. Feown was the center of existence. Its influence touched even modest Sacred Spring, with occasional pilgrims or, every few years or so, an overzealous tax collector. While Crossroads sometimes put out a modest news sheet, the great newspapers were Feowan, not that there had been any of those for months. Most of the luxury goods like tea or cotton or coal oil came from its ports.

"We're fine for now but I come to ask a really big favor of you."

Fear wrapped tendrils around Natan's heart. Whatever Sam wanted, it must have been pretty big, for him to come in person on a lathered, spent horse. "Ask."

"With the fall of Feown," said Sam, "there's been an influx of refugees and worse. There've been... incidents." He put a hand on Natan's shoulder. "There are rumors that bands of Cithran soldiers are spreading out, burning villages, to quell any potential uprisings. I know this is a lot to ask but," he hesitated, "can you give us sanctuary?"

"What? The whole town?"

"Half."

"That's a lot of people. You're five times the size of us!"

"And you're half of what you used to be. What about all those empty homes?"

"Uninhabitable, what few remain standing."

Sam's grip tightened on Natan's shoulder. "Hay lofts, outbuildings, anywhere."

"We had to build shelters for what few we took in already."

"We'll build more." Sam was begging now. He put both hands to Natan's shoulders. "Please. The stories we've heard have been confirmed by those who have survived to run. War is here, Natan."

"Do you really think they'll get this far? There's no promise they'll destroy Crossroads."

Sam gave Natan a shake. "Yes, there is. They plan on capturing the Great Western Pass. Crossroads is but another country village to them. They're not going to care. Please, Natan. I'm sending craftsmen with their tools. They'll help you repair the cottages, if you let them live and work here. They'll be productive."

Natan considered this. Should war come, that would be an end to trade. If the craftsmen lived and produced here, then perhaps Sacred Spring would not suffer as much. Foodwise, they were self-sufficient. But would they have enough to feed more than twice their size? And winter was coming soon.

"I might take them in, under my conditions. First, they must bring your entire food storage to here. Second, you send the harvest machines. If they get destroyed in this war you foresee, I don't want to have us reaping by hand. Third, they build or repair their own homes but only where we designate."

Worry puckered Sam's face. He let his hands drop. "That's asking much."

Natan folded his arms. "Those are my terms. I think they are reasonable. We save the food you have. We preserve a way to get more food, should this war pass. The dignity of your people is preserved through their self-sufficiency. I will sweeten the bargain. I will allow you to have my home as your own."

"I won't be coming."

"What? Why not?"

Sam drew in a breath. "I told you only half would be coming. The rest of us will be staying behind to defend the village. I'm sending the women, all the apprentices and all the craftsmen too old to fight. I'll agree to half the food and all the harvest machines. But I will need to rely on you to help them with houses."

"We'll help with the houses, but I want three quarters the food. That will leave enough for your men to eat. If you need more, you can always send a wagonmaster."

"I may not be able to spare a wagonmaster."

"If you can't spare anyone to come fetch food, then I'd say you're having problems worse than empty stomachs."

In the end an agreement was made, and the two mayors shook on it.

"There's a bit of cornmeal mush left for breakfast," Natan offered. Sam accepted gratefully.

Natan told Mikal to hobble the horse in his back garden, "but don't let him drink too much yet. After that, go fetch everyone in the village and tell them to gather to the Inn. We've got another Council."

❧

Emergency Council? Mira fretted. Of course, the whole village came. What could Natan have to say that he'd call another emergency Council so soon? Mira inhaled deeply as Natan Mayor shared the news, Sam Mayor at his side.

"Feown is at war." No welcome, no preamble. Just straight up.

Silence fell across the room. Mira shook her head. "So that's it? War is coming here?"

"Not yet," replied Sam. "But soon. No one expected Feown to fall this fast."

A chair scraped and fell over backwards. Adrastea dashed past Mira, pushing her way out the door, her curly dark hair streaming behind her. Was she going to be sick?

The windows were open, so all could hear as she shrieked out her anger. "You bastard!"

As one, everyone flew to the windows, Ari and Mira fought through the people to reach her.

Outside, Adrastea collapsed to her knees in the dust. Sobs wracked her body. Mira said nothing but knelt down next to her. Everyone's attention felt heavy on her back. She wished they'd go away. No chance, though. She did not look forward to all the awkward questions they would ask later.

Ari fell down beside her, draping her brown cloak over the sobbing figure.

Adrastea heaved great sobs and rivulets of tears ran down her face. Mira simply held her while she raged out whatever it was that tore her heart. The priestess glanced back to the inn. Everyone gathered at the doorway and windows. They whispered back and forth, worry, concern, and even fear making the Lines thick between them.

"Back in," Natan said to the others. "We have business to discuss." He shooed everyone into the common room.

Soon Mira, Ari and Adrastea were alone in the road. She waited until

Adrastea felt the need to speak.

"I could have done something," Adrastea confessed. "I could have saved them all."

"Who?" Ari asked.

"Feown."

"How? You are only one woman."

"The other day, when— when he— He offered me a choice. I thought he was tempting me. So, I didn't take it. And now look what's happened."

Mira drew in a breath. Of course, this was Mor-Lath's doing. He caused Feown to fall, all for the sake of Adrastea. She rejected his temptation of power, so he showed her the consequences of her choice, thus submersing her in guilt. What an evil, evil bastard.

Ari sat back on her heels, a fist pressed to her lips.

"It is not your fault," Mira replied, maybe a little more forcefully than she meant to. "He's manipulating you. He wants to put you in a place where you don't have a choice, where your actions become the wrong ones. It is not your fault that Feown fell. Oh, I'm sure he wants you to believe that. Don't give in! Feown would have fallen even if you had never been given the choice."

Adrastea wouldn't listen. She wrapped her arms about herself and rocked back and forth, keening in a low voice. Mira wondered what sort of power he tempted her with that would lead her to think she could have saved an entire city.

Ari rose and dashed back into the Inn.

"You are a mortal, Adrastea. You are not responsible for these choices."

"But I could have saved them."

No, you couldn't, would have been a useless argument. "And if you did, then what?"

Adrastea swiped a piece of hair from her face, where it was stuck in the dampness. She wiped her nose with her cuff. "They would have lived."

"And what about you?"

This gave Adrastea pause. "What about me?" she eventually said.

"I don't think you know what would have been involved in stopping Feown falling. Whatever you could have done would have disrupted the balance. Were you to convince an entire army to pack up their swords and go home?"

Adrastea didn't answer.

Mira couldn't emphasize it enough: "Mor-Lath is evil. He is not just the rotten apple that spoils the barrel but the worm infestation that destroys the entire harvest. He is the Dark God. All this is his doing. I don't care how sweetly he speaks to you. He means no good. He will drag your soul down to eternal torment. I don't know what gifts the Light has given you, but they must be pretty powerful indeed if Mor-Lath himself seeks to turn you."

Ari returned, a glass of water in her hands. "Here, drink this."

Adrastea took it and gulped it down. She handed back an empty glass.

"More?" Ari asked.

Adrastea shook her head. She wiped her face with the hem of her skirt and drew in a raggedy breath. "I never thought of it like that. He doesn't really want to marry me, does he? He's just saying that to turn me, isn't he?"

Of that, Mira was sure. She'd read Mor-Lath's book. It was no book on scripture but a grimoire, possibly his own personal writings for his priestesses' eyes only.

Then Mira knew what Mor-Lath had in store for Adrastea. He wanted to make her a Dark priestess, a witch to turn people from the Light and towards their own selfishness. She'd heard of the Dark priestesses who had completely converted Avelia, the kingdom to the south. They could also be found among the Tredan peoples, who lived on the other side of the mountains.

Now he sought a greater foothold here and he was starting with Adrastea.

Mira's contrition over her ill use of Marta had steeled herself against the lure of the book. Sure, she had read more than half of it again already. She made a promise to herself and to the Light that she would not use any further Dark tricks.

Mira nodded. "You didn't really think his intentions were honorable?"

Adrastea didn't answer, didn't meet Mira's eyes.

Only now did Mira put her arms around Adrastea. Ari laid a hand on her head. "I'm sorry, child," Mira said. "He's shattered all your dreams, hasn't he? He promised you something you've always wanted but he has no intention of keeping that promise." Adrastea's hand stole up to the cheek where Mor-Lath had left his mark. "He used you something fierce, all to turn your soul." She reached out and tilted Adrastea's chin up, so she could look into her eyes. "Know that you are a child of the Light, and the value of your soul must be very great. Protect that soul. If you weren't up to the task, then the Light would not have put this great burden upon you. You are strong, you know. Rise to that strength and stand against the Dark One."

Fresh tears soaked her face and dripped onto the bare skin above her laced bodice. She nodded and enveloped Mira in a tight hug.

Mira let herself be hugged, even though she found it hard to breathe. The dampness of Adrastea's freshet of tears made the linen of her blouse prickle uncomfortably. Her feet threatened to fall asleep, so gently she pushed Adrastea back.

Ari took back her cloak. "It's nearly noon and you are probably hungry. Go get something to eat."

Mira took her up the hill to the house that Joe built. Mira couldn't feel it, but she believed the protection he gave the house was still there. It would protect Adrastea.

Finally, the girl understood what was happening. Finally, she saw Mor-Lath for who he was. When next they met, he would find a young woman of steel, Mira vowed. Her heart was broken, its bitter edges sharp enough to cut through his meaningless lies. Adrastea would see with clear eyes if Mira had anything to do with it. But did it have to take such a painful road to open them?

The next day, Mira watched the wagon train of refugees arrive from Crossroads. From Lillybet's house she saw the plume of dust a good half-hour before the wagons pulled into the village green. So much going on. Would she'd have enough energy to deal with the influx of people and still be there for Adrastea?

Natan had briefed her earlier on the Council's decision. The Crossroaders would stay.

She shared with him what happened between herself and Adrastea.

"I hope you don't mind," she said to him in that conversation, "but I think it would be best if I let Carles know about the situation. After all, if his people are to live here, he needs to know what's going on."

Natan had his doubts but agreed in the end. "Only Carles. And only because I agree that Adrastea needs a few more priests on her side."

So, Mira watched wagon after wagon arrive in the village green. She kept her eyes open for that familiar honey-blond head of Carles Priest.

Unlike the first batch of refugees, these came better-prepared. They had clothes, furniture, possessions, tools and more. Men and women unloaded boxes from the wagons while the wagonmasters watered their oxen, still hitched, from big leather buckets. The Innkeeper children kept busy fetching and filling these buckets. Then the wagons turned and headed back to Crossroads.

The Crossroaders had brought one of the great big harvest machines, the kind that was drawn by oxen or horses through the fields at harvest time. They had large cart wheels connected to a contraption of scytheblades. It could harvest the grain and leave it lying in the rows for gathering.

"Mira!" Carles called as he came around one of the newly-arrived wagons. He had bags under his eyes and his blonde hair hung limp against his head, but he had a genuine smile for Mira.

She greeted him with a hug. "I was hoping you'd come back today."

Carles released Mira and looked at Adrastea. He held out his hand. "Afternoon to you…?"

She took his hand. "Adrastea Healer." No doubt both of them meant for it to be a brief encounter but a moment after they grasped hands, their casual handshake slowed, and they paused, not relinquishing their grasp.

Mira felt the vibrations through the Lines as Adrastea's and Carles' eyes met. They gave each other measure. Would there be trouble? Adrastea frowned as if she wasn't sure of Carles. He studied her with more curiosity rather than caution. What was going through his mind?

Mira felt left out.

"I'm pleased to meet you," Carles eventually said. "I hear you are assisting Mira in administering to our people."

Adrastea gave Mira quick glance as if to question how he knew that. Mira did not return any meaningful glances.

As Mira looked away, her gaze fell on a tall, slim woman with cool blonde hair. She came toward Carles and waited patiently at his side. She folded her hands in front of her plain brown homespun travel clothes. Her blue eyes sized up Mira and Adrastea.

Mira felt a twinge of guilt, almost as if this cold young woman could see into her heart. Mira was still priestess here. For a moment, she wondered if she should reach out her feelings and take measure of the young woman, rather than wait for an impression along the Lines of the Deeper Power. It was an easy matter for her mind to slide along the Lines, toward the young woman. She felt a certain cautiousness. It was as if there was a wall up between them. She didn't know if she could push through the wall. She didn't dare, for she didn't want this priestess—it was obvious by now who she was—to get the wrong idea about her.

Carles noticed the young woman at his elbow. "Mira, this is my apprentice, well, former apprentice, now that she's a journeywoman. This is Chloe Priestess. Chloe, this is Mira Priestess of Sacred Spring."

The wall collapsed. Mira pulled her thoughts back in surprise. Mira knew all about her, from Carles' letters but never had the opportunity to meet her.

So, this was Chloe, whom Carles offered to send to Mira. She and Carles had only discussed the possibility of him sending an older apprentice, not a full journeyman.

Once Mira had been introduced to her, Chloe warmed up. Mira sensed a cautiousness at her core.

"I'm pleased to meet you," she said as she shook Mira's hand. "We are most grateful for your generosity."

"Glad we could help," Mira replied. Chloe seemed a solid woman, if maybe a little on the cool side. Probably a little lacking in humor.

Chloe hadn't spared more than a glance for Adrastea. Normally, Mira would take this an insult. For some reason, she wanted Chloe not to take any notice of Adrastea. As soon as she acknowledged this to herself, a great flood of relief flowed through her. She hadn't released Chloe's hand. Chloe seemed too polite to pull it back.

She found herself clasping Chloe's hand in both of hers. "I'm glad you're here," she said. Then her relief faded. If Chloe remained, she would have to be told about Adrastea. What would she say about that?

Giving Chloe her hand back, Mira turned to Carles. "I have some things I must discuss with you. I meant to speak with you before, but recent events have me at a disadvantage." She glanced at Adrastea, who was studying the wagons. Chloe surveyed the village. No doubt she must be curious about the place that was to be her home for the next long whenever.

"Tell me, Carles," Mira continued. "Will you be staying long?"

"A few days. Then we'll be heading back. Chloe and I can't leave Crossroads for long."

"Oh." This surprised her. "Chloe's not staying?"

Chloe's attention turned to the conversation at the mention of her name. Adrastea had taken a step closer to Mira but was studying the wagons. She wasn't paying attention to the conversation at all, or so it seemed.

"I'm afraid she can't stay at this point," Carles said. "I will explain later. Meanwhile, what arrangements have been made for the night?"

"You can have my cottage for the duration of your stay." Mira offered. "Adrastea and I have been living in her mother's house up on the hill, so we can be close to the refugees."

Mira remembered Mor-Lath's book. As much as she trusted Carles, she didn't want him to know about it. "I'll remove a few of my personal belongings and the cottage is yours."

"You're generous, old friend."

"I don't know about that. The loft hasn't been used for an apprentice since... ooh, me. I've been using it for storage. It may need to be cleaned out. Or, we could move the truckle bed down. We'll see."

Chloe spoke up. "Why don't I come and live with you for a few days, Mira. It would be best if I was near the Crossroaders too."

Mira didn't know what to say. She wasn't ready to have a stranger possibly witness something untoward happen around Adrastea. "Um," she said, to give herself some time to think. "I have a better idea. How about you stay in my place. Carles can come up to Lillybet's?"

Chloe looked doubtful.

Mira bit her lip. "Did Carles explain my situation? I mean, about not having an apprentice?"

Chloe nodded once.

"If you agree to come be the priestess here, then my home would become your home. Also, living in town would give you an opportunity to meet our villagers, get to know them. They will become your people one day."

"I don't know," Chloe said. "I really think—"

"No," interrupted Carles, studying Mira. "Perhaps she's right. You take the cottage. I can sleep on the floor in the other house."

Chloe didn't look too happy about the prospect but she deferred to her former master.

"Lighten your heart, Chloe," Carles said, giving her a one-armed hug. "Sacred Spring's not such a bad place. "Sometimes she is too serious," he said to Mira.

Chloe sniffed at this and retreated to the wagons, presumably to fetch her belongings.

Adrastea inched a bit closer to Mira. Her hand touched the priestess' arm. She was still looking at the wagons.

"Adrastea? What's wrong?"

"Don't know," the young woman replied, still looking at the wagons.

So why did Mira have an eerie feeling? Adrastea seemed to radiate... something. Irritation and what else? For a moment, Mira wavered between keeping the secret and telling Carles.

Carles was an experienced priest. His talent was stronger than Mira's. He dealt with a larger congregation. He'd always been a calm, reasonable man. Mira trusted him as much as she trusted Natan.

With Chloe gone, Mira led Adrastea and Carles to her cottage, not too far from the Inn. As soon as they were out of earshot of the others, Mira said to Adrastea, "I'm going to tell him about you."

Adrastea stopped. "What? You can't." She shot a nervous glance at Carles and looked him up and down as if she was afraid he'd bite.

Mira turned to face her. "He's got to know."

Carles had turned to her as well. His eyes burned, and his fingers fidgeted with curiosity. "I thought you had a secret, Mira," he said with some lightness.

Adrastea looked at him with worry then back to Mira. "Does he have to know?"

Mira nodded slowly. "His people are in danger too, you know."

"Please," Carles said as his expression drew serious. "Tell me."

Adrastea wilted. "Please don't think bad of me."

Now Carles looked worried. "Mira?"

Mira drew them away from the crowd of people and towards the isolation of her cottage. "What I am about to tell you is a heavy secret. Natan knows, of course, and Ari knows. Lillybet knew but no one else. I'm sure you'll see why we have to keep this a secret. Please, Carles."

"I'm listening."

"He'll have to vow," insisted Adrastea."

But Carles shook his head. "I cannot do that," he told her. "If this means danger to my people, I may need to warn them—whatever this is."

"But," protested Adrastea, "they like me."

Mira had to concede that. Adrastea had, surprisingly, dealt well with the refugees. They never knew her mother. She had been judged for herself.

Her skill in healing helped with that. The people had been grateful for her relieving their ailments. But unless the Dark God gave up... "He can't not know." It wasn't that Mira needed Adrastea's permission, but she did want to keep the girl's good will. "It will be better if he knows."

To Carles, she said, "Please don't judge her harshly. It's not her fault."

And then she told him. "Adrastea is being courted by Mor-Lath, God of the Dark. He wants her as his bride."

Chapter 16

What?!" Carles shouted. Adrastea covered her face in her hands and turned away. People over by the Inn looked their way.

Mira flung her arms around the two and hurried them around her cottage, away from others' eyes.

"Mira Priestess," Carles said as she hurried them along. "You can't be serious!"

"I'm dead serious."

Once they were out of the sight of others, Adrastea sank down on Mira's porch. "I didn't ask for this," she said in a quiet voice. She clenched her fists between her knees.

Carles paced back and forth. "When did this start?"

"A few weeks ago," said Mira.

"How?"

Mira told the tale of the rain barrel incident and Adrastea's display of talent. "I didn't know she had such skill." She reconsidered her words. "Well, that's not true. I did know something."

"Mira," he said, "you are full of secrets today."

Mira didn't look at him. Instead, she gazed into the past, dredging up the events of more than twenty years ago. "When Adrastea was born, I had a vision. Sure, I'd felt the influence of the Deeper Power, but I'd never expected a full vision like that."

"You never told me that." Carles folded his arms and leaned closer to the priestess.

Mira shrugged. "I am not a prophet, nor a seer. I wasn't sure what it was I was seeing. Besides when you grew up, Adrastea, I never felt anything different about you. I thought it was just me being tired that night. It was rather late when you were born."

"So, what did you see?" Naturally, Adrastea wanted to know. Carles also leaned forward.

"I saw a vision of you a woman grown. You stood on a hill. I think it was Sacred Spring Hill. It was night time, so I couldn't tell. There were people in pain coming up the hill. You stretched forth your hands and they were healed."

"Could this have been by the Deeper Power?" Carles asked.

Mira shrugged. "It could be. At the time, I didn't think so. I know Joe had talent; I could feel it. Lillybet did too. I should have known but..." Mira shrugged. "As a child, Adrastea didn't display any talent whatsoever. Then Joe died, and Lilly went odd.

"Anyhow, it wasn't long before Adrastea was to be apprenticed. Since I couldn't sense any talent, I eventually took the dream as figurative. Ari always thought it figurative, so we agreed to apprentice Adrastea to her."

"What?" Adrastea declared. "Ari knew too?"

"Was that the whole vision?" Carles prompted.

Mira shook her head. "No. Then I saw Mor-Lath. I knew who he was in the vision. He appeared on the hill with Adrastea. Then more people started coming up the hill, all in pain. Adrastea stretched forth her hands and healed them. And that's it."

Carles sat down, not too far from Adrastea. "So, Creation had her pegged from the beginning."

"Creation?" spat Mira. "This can't be Creation's doing."

Carles tilted his head. "It could be. Mor-Lath learned about the vision. He could have misinterpreted it."

"A god misinterpret?"

Carles shrugged. "Could happen."

Mira shook her head. "No. At the end of the vision, Mor-Lath wrapped his arms around Adrastea and said, 'Mine.' That's not something anyone, much less a god, would misinterpret."

"I see your point."

"Did he?" squeaked Adrastea. "Say that, I mean?" She sniffed and put her hand up to her nose.

Mira didn't answer her question. "I never expected to take it literally."

"I can see why," Carles remarked. "No one expects the Dark God to stop by."

Adrastea whimpered. She drew her knees up to her chest. She folded her arms across them. She looked so small like that. Mira put her arm around Adrastea's shoulder.

"Wait a minute," continued Carles, as he stood up. "You're saying that— that Mor-Lath himself has shown up? Here? At Sacred Spring?" He began to shake. He paced again. "You're saying a god has been here?"

Mira nodded. "I have seen him myself."

Carles had to sit down again. He dropped where he stood onto the graveled pathway. "The Dark God... here?" His hand covered his mouth.

Mira nodded. "The day Adrastea displayed her talent was the day he showed up. He waited until she was alone, then declared his intentions to marry her."

"Marriage," he exclaimed. "Who'd have thought?"

Mira shrugged. "One does not associate marriage with Mor-Lath. Marriage is of the Light. What we haven't figured out yet is what he wants with Adrastea. She's got talent, that's true. But there's got to be something else. There are plenty of others in the world with more talent than she."

Carles shrugged. "Maybe you're looking at this too deeply. It could very well be that he sees her only as a plaything. I know many a mortal man would promise a woman the world to get in her good graces, so he can get into her bed."

Adrastea's head shot up at this. "I am not a trollop!"

Carles held out his hands. "I didn't mean to imply you were. I'm just saying that we don't know what Mor-Lath wants. I mean, why marriage? What advantage could marriage give him? You're mortal. You will die, at most, in fifty years. For a god, that's but a moment in time." Carles ran a hand over his stubble as he considered the situation. "No, I agree with Mira. I don't think marriage is his intent."

"He's sure persistent about it," Adrastea put her chin on her arms.

Carles studied her. "That scar," he asked, rising to his feet. "Where did you get it?"

"Mor-Lath."

Mira explained. "It's his betrothal mark. Said he wanted to make sure everyone knew she belonged to him."

Carles shook his head. "I don't sense any Darkness in you, Adrastea. Sorrow, yes. But I don't sense any bad vibrations in your Lines.

"We are all born good," he said as he sat down next to her. "It is only our choices that lead us to turn to the Dark."

"I know," Adrastea sighed.

Mira had preached that often enough to her as a child. One early interpretation of the vision had been that Mor-Lath was figurative and that Adrastea would end up being a wicked child. But as Mira had shown love, patience and tolerance with her, as did Ari and Natan, Adrastea grew up confident and good. Thus, she dismissed the vision, thinking she'd thwarted the dark future she thought the Light had warned her about.

How wrong she had been.

"May I touch it?" Carles asked.

Adrastea shrugged, which was probably the closes he'd get for permission. Mira had never thought to ask to touch it.

Carles reached out and stroked a finger along the line, gently, smoothly, slowly. "Oh, yes. Oh, wow." He drew his finger away and rubbed it against his thumb as if feeling some residue that may have come away. He reached out for it again but didn't actually touch her skin. "How unusual. It's almost as if... Mira, feel that."

Mira turned Adrastea's face towards her. Adrastea allowed her to do so without resistance. Mira reached out a finger but hesitated before touching the line. Then she stroked it with her finger.

A power and influence sang to her through the scar. It was as if there was a piece of Mor-Lath there, under her skin.

Mira quickly withdrew her finger and curled her hand into a fist. She pressed it tightly against her lips as if to kiss away the memory of that touch, like one would kiss away the pain of a child's scraped elbow.

"I think he means business," Carles surmised.

"Is there anything we can do?" Mira asked.

The priest didn't answer. "How many times has he been here?"

Mira counted. "Four, no five times, I believe." Adrastea didn't correct her, so this must have been right.

"All in a few weeks?"

Mira nodded.

"You said Natan and Ari knew. They've witnessed this?"

Mira started to answer, then said, "Oh, dear. Everyone knows," she confessed. "First he appeared to Adrastea alone. Then Lillybet saw him and Ari saw him..." A knot of anxiety formed in her stomach. "Then everyone saw him. He came to our weekly council and announced his intentions towards Adrastea."

"Bugger me," he swore. "I thought you said only Natan and Ari knew."

"His true identity, yes. He never announced his name at the meeting only his intention. Everyone's been gossiping about who he is and what he wants with our Adrastea. Some say he's a lordling from Feown. Others say... I don't know. Lillybet's death has shaken us all."

Carles asked, "Could the two events be related?"

Mira didn't want to think about that. On the other hand, if Mor-Lath did kill Lillybet, that would be another point in his disfavor. "Perhaps. We have no proof, though. But Lilly's death is tearing the village apart. People are accusing each other."

An idea crossed her mind. "Maybe he did kill her, to divide the village. After all, in his little Council visit, he did tell us that someone in that room was trying to deceive us about Lillybet. He was there, so it could have been him." Mira nodded. "Yes, I think you're right, Carles. But what? Did he really think that Adrastea would never find out?"

Adrastea's head dropped to her knees. Her body shuddered. Grief so strong Mira could feel it rolled along the Lines.

"We've got to stop him," Mira said. "But I don't know how."

Carles nodded his agreement. "I've brought you a surprise, Mira. I've brought my entire collection of books—for safekeeping, of course," he clarified. "I'll be taking them back when this war nonsense is over.

"I've collected quite a few treasures from the trade caravans that come through Crossroads. Some of them are, shall we say, of dubious origin but they may hold a clue as to why Mor-Lath is so interested in your Adrastea, or better yet, how we can dissuade him. There's got to be a reason why he's here. Find that out, and we'll find out how to fight him."

Mira nodded. "I'll just go pack a few personal items, then we can move your books to Lilly's house and get to work."

Mira's one box and Carles' several boxes were loaded onto a handcart for the journey up the hill. As she packed, she wrapped Mor-Lath's book and his cloak in a dirty sheet—no one would think to touch someone's dirty laundry—and stashed them in the bottom of the box.

Mira hadn't had a chance to look too closely at the others from Crossroads. She recognized Ely Mayorprentice, who had come in Sam's stead. He saw to the settling of the Crossroaders. Rop storekeeper spoke with Ely as barrels and boxes and bundles of goods were carried into the storehouse. Rop's wife Jira inventoried the goods before they entered the store. Rop kept record on a slate.

Many of the Crossroaders had made the journey up the hill. As Carles and Mira pulled the handcart through the village, Mira saw Jak Carpenter with several Crossroader women as they inspected some of the more uninhabitable cottages. Adrastea stood behind the cart, giving the occasional push as the situation warranted it.

"How long do you think you are staying?" she asked Carles. "The Crossroaders, I mean."

Carles shook his head. "I don't know. Sam is organizing a defense of Crossroads. They're building a wall around the town square at the expense of a few buildings. It'll be somewhat defensible. One thing's for sure; Crossroads will not survive as we know it. We'll have changed forever. If—when we survive this war, we'll be building a wall around the town—one much bigger than the stockade we've got now."

"Why don't you do that now?"

Carles smiled. "You've never built a wall before, I see. It'd take too long. We need defense now."

The hill grew steeper. Their conversation lulled. Mira pulled while Carles and Adrastea pushed.

"Why must books be so heavy?" Adrastea complained.

"It's the weight of all the knowledge," he replied.

They rested at Lillybet's before unpacking. Adrastea stared at the sheer number of books Carles had brought. There had to be nearly a hundred! "How could you possibly have time to read them all?"

Carles smiled. "Trust me, you make time. These are only the ones I did have time to read. You wouldn't believe the amount of books that come through Crossroads now. It's all about fashion."

"Fashion? What does that have to do with it?" Adrastea let a pile of books thump onto the table.

"Do you know why books used to be so expensive? It's because nobody would import them. The Nobility in Feown thought it unfashionable to be seen reading books, so they didn't buy them. If they didn't buy them, then they didn't get imported. They grew rare because of the whims of fashion. So, if you wanted a book, you had to pay extra for it." He ran his finger along their spines. "Recently, books have come back in fashion. Suddenly, it seems that everyone who's anyone has a library. Problem is, they don't care what's in the books.

"So, when the booksellers came through Crossroads, I'd go through their collections and bought whatever was of interest to me."

Mira stared at him, jaw open. "How long has this been happening?"

"Oh, a few years now."

"A few years?!" She gave his chest a thump. "Why didn't you tell me, Carles?"

Carles took Mira's hands. "I'm sorry. I didn't think about you. Sometimes, in the day-to-day routines of our lives, we forget there are other places outside of Crossroads."

Mira had to concede his point. Until Mor-Lath came, her world was little more than Sacred Spring.

While they had been talking, Adrastea had been looking through the books. She'd open one and look at a page or two before putting it down and picking up another. Adrastea never did like reading. She'd balked as a child when Mira had tried to teach her, so she had left Adrastea's literacy up to Ari. Maybe that hadn't been the wisest move.

"If you'd like," Carles said to Adrastea, "I'll keep my eyes open for some physicks. I hear there have been some amazing advances in medicine."

Adrastea shrugged. "Ari may be interested."

After they unpacked the books and squared them away on the various shelves that Lillybet once kept her weaving shuttles, Carles suggested they visit the refugees.

⌒❦⌒

Mikal went up the hill with the first group of Crossroaders. Natan's orders: visit the refugees and help them get started on more homes. The Mayor stayed behind to sort out the business of the wagon trains.

When they started at the bottom of the hill, Mikal had counted two handcarts and eleven men. When they reached the top of the hill, there were twelve men. He counted again to make sure. Yep, twelve men. He sighed. Natan had said it was important to know who was about you. It didn't help that he'd not yet made the acquaintance of the Crossroaders. Still, he could have sworn they started out with eleven men.

Everyone helped unload the carts in the area of the cabins. Two men started back down with the handcarts. The rest went to visit with the refugees.

All but one. The twelfth man sat on a log bench in the shade of a cabin. He stretched out his booted feet and tilted his country straw hat over his eyes. Was he going to take a nap?

Natan said to be observant. Mikal thought he'd go learn more about this man who'd joined them somewhere on the hill. Without invitation, he sat on the log next to the man. "Good afternoon."

The man knocked his hat up from his eyes and looked at Mikal. Mikal knew him.

"You're Master M," he exclaimed. "I didn't know you were from Crossroads."

Master M settled back and pulled the hat back over his eyes. "I don't expect you to know much about me, Mikal Mayorprentice."

"You have the advantage of me."

Master M chuckled. "I tend to have the advantage of lots of people."

Mikal would not be daunted. "You know my name, but I don't know yours. What is your name?"

"You do get to the heart of the matter, don't you?"

Mikal shrugged. "It's my job." But when Master M didn't volunteer anything further, Mikal pressed the matter. "If you are to marry my sister—"

"That rather depends on her."

"—then I really ought to know your name."

Master M sat up straighter. "Promise you won't laugh?"

"I promise." He crossed his heart.

Master M chuckled. "Mor-Lath."

Mikal didn't buy it. "You're jesting me."

"I could be."

"No. Really. What is your name?"

Master M sighed and settled back. "Master M will do for now. You are full of questions, so I'll thank you to seek your answers elsewhere."

But Mikal didn't want to let go. "Does my sister find you this infuriating?"

Master M plucked a piece of grass that had not yet been trampled. "I imagine she finds me more so. She is not too happy with me at the moment." He chewed on his piece of grass. "Women are like the weather.

First hot, then cold, then hot again. And then cold. Never very predictable."

Mikal nodded. Marta was like that, as were many village women. Martine had started to show signs. Mikal had no doubt that his sister wasn't any different. "So why would you want to marry her?"

"I like her."

"Finally, a straight answer."

Master M chuckled. "Wouldn't we all like more of those?"

One of the Crossroaders approached the pair. He addressed Master M, "Goodman, we could use your help clearing these trees."

Master M nodded and rose. "You could ask your sister about me. As I am currently not in her good graces you will most likely receive the edge of her temper, rather than a straight answer. Tread carefully, Mayorprentice."

⁂

"**B**race yourself, Master Wainwright." Adrastea levered the dislocated arm a little higher, then applied force to get it back in its socket. Master Wainwright bellowed in pain. His companions held him still.

Adrastea stood up and put her fists on her hips. "All better but you won't be working again soon."

One of his companions playfully punched him in his good arm. "Lucky you, Okie."

Okie Wainwright grimaced in pain. He kicked his friend in return. "Doesn't mean I can't boss you around."

Adrastea placed his arm in a makeshift sling. As she tied the elbow knot, she caught another glimpse of someone she had been seeing around all day—Mor-Lath. Had he been lingering long enough to catch her eye? He'd been pulling his fair share of work, with tree chopping and log-lifting as if he was another villager. Interesting. He blended in well, being dressed in the same brown pants and tunic as all the others, including one of their common straw hats.

She studied him. What was his game?

He must have felt her gaze. After assisting another Crossroader, he grinned at her before disappearing into the crowd.

Adrastea shook her head. Nobody had thought to question the stranger in their midst, the Springers thinking he was a Crossroader, and the Crossroaders thinking he belonged to Sacred Spring.

Adrastea didn't know whether to cry or scream. Seeing Mor-Lath so casually accepted by the others infuriated her. Didn't they know what a monster he was? He had caused the death of hundreds and the fall of a city. Now the Cithran army controlled the river. They were coming for the Great Western Pass next.

It was all his fault. She'd be damned before she'd let him pin this on her.

Adrastea found Mira with Carles, who administered to his flock. They shared a conversation with a Crossroader in some shade. Carles sat next to him on a log bench, chatting and laughing. Mira stood nearby, mostly listening.

Adrastea came up to her, made her apologies to Carles and pulled Mira aside. "He's here." She didn't need to explain who 'he' was. "I think he's been following me all day."

"Oh, glory!" Mira muttered. "What does he want?"

Adrastea folded her arms tightly. "I'm not talking to him if that's what he wants."

Mira gave her a sly smile. "You're a woman. It's your prerogative to give him the silent treatment."

Adrastea wasn't sure what prerogative meant but she knew all about the silent treatment.

"Mistress Healer!" one of the Crossroader apprentices came running. "We need your help!"

Adrastea sighed. "It never stops." She grabbed Mira by the hand and followed the tow-headed lad, skin and bones, this adolescent boy. "There are far too many accidents today," she told the priestess. "Ari's tending a broken leg. I've had two dislocations, three smashed feet, a crushed hand, numerous scrapes and bruises and one nasty bump on the head. At least I haven't had to stitch any cuts."

"Don't say that," Mira cautioned. "Don't want you causing more bad luck."

"I blame Mor-Lath," Adrastea replied flippantly.

Mira jerked on Adrastea's hand as a warning. "Careful what you say."

The apprentice brought them to a small knot of people. "Here, Mistress Smith," he said as he pushed through. "I've brought the healer." He dropped next to the woman lying on the ground.

"What happened?" Adrastea asked as she knelt down next to her.

Mistress Smith was a stocky woman dressed in leggings and a tunic, her bare arms looked as strong as any man's. In that, she resembled

Sheelagh Smith, even to the blonde hair. She lay on her back, propped up by her elbows. "I twisted my ankle. More bad luck, than anything."

Mira gave Adrastea a pointed look.

"I twisted it on a rock as I was carrying a plank," Mistress Smith explained. "Really, it's not that bad."

Adrastea eased the boot off and examined the foot. She gently rotated it. "Does that hurt?" Mistress Smith hissed and nodded. She examined it until she was sure that it was only a sprained ankle. Adrastea opened her bag and removed a scroll of bandage. She'll have to get more of those soon.

With tender care she wrapped the foot tightly. "Now, we need to get you to the Spring. If you soak your foot in its cold waters, then keep it lifted up, it should be right and well tomorrow." To the apprentice, she said, "You. Go fetch two people to help her to the Spring."

While Mira knelt down next to Mistress Smith to commiserate how rotten bad luck could be, Adrastea closed her bag and rose to her feet. As she slung her back over her shoulder, she felt a hand on her back.

"Such skill," Mor-Lath murmured in her ear.

Adrastea gasped, flinched away from his touch. Before she could think she whirled on him and slapped him across the face with a resounding crack.

Everyone around Mistress Smith looked up at the pair. Mira jumped to her feet.

"Go away!" Adrastea shrilled.

He smiled at her, teasingly. "Ooh, the woman has passion in her blood."

"What are you doing here?" Her slap had not knocked the expression off his face.

He spread his hands. "Same as everyone else."

"Well, you can just rack off, because I don't want to talk to you." She wanted to turn her back to him but didn't dare. He might snuggle up to her again.

"Someone has been pouring poison in your ear. I simply wish to set the facts straight." He stepped towards Adrastea.

Mira reached out and shoved him. "She doesn't want to talk to you!"

The smile faded from Mor-Lath's face. He towered over Mira. "I will have words with you later, Priestess. Do not think to interfere in my business."

Mira drew in a sharp breath. "She doesn't want anything to do with you."

He gave her a mock expression of pain, laying his hand over what wasn't a broken heart. "How can you say that? I have nothing but the most honorable intentions towards her?"

"Just give up and go away. She's never going to give in." Mira looked almost comical as she stood up to the Dark Lord. Adrastea had the oddest thought. Would Carles have found this funny?

An indulgent smile spread across his face. "Give in? Oh no, no, no. It's not giving in. Giving in makes it sound so... so tawdry."

As a blush suffused her cheeks, Adrastea glanced over at the Crossroaders. They sat motionless, watching the exchange. Did they have any idea who they were looking at? Since the first refugees arrived, Adrastea had developed a good relationship with them. They liked her and greeted her by name. What would they think of her now?

"It is marriage," Mor-Lath said, "and nothing less that I will settle for."

"And who would stand to hear your vows?" Mira sneered. "It certainly won't be me."

"There are other priests," Mor-Lath sneered. "Do not think you are so indispensable."

The apprentice had returned with two strong men. Great. More audience.

"It doesn't matter," Adrastea spat. "I'm not marrying you! Not after what you did."

One of Mistress Smith's companions leaned over and whispered in her ear. Mistress Smith shrugged and whispered back. Adrastea's blush grew even hotter. She would never forgive him if he ruined her reputation.

"Whatever it is you think I did, I can assure you I didn't do it."

"Liar!"

Mira moved herself between Adrastea and Mor-Lath. "Leave," she ordered him.

Mor-Lath only snorted. "Back down, Priestess. You've done enough harm for one day." He held up his hand. Mira took a stumbled step back, then another. Her eyes grew wide in apprehension. Her knees buckled beneath her. The two men meant for Mistress Smith caught her and held her upright. "I will speak with my betrothed without your interference," he told her.

With that, he scooped Adrastea into his arms and strode away with her.

Chapter 17

His actions surprised Adrastea. "Put me down, you son of a bitch!" "Be kind about my mother. She did her best." But he did comply. He didn't let her go completely but wrapped his arm around her waist, making it almost impossible for her to strike him again. It was like this he marched her up the hill, through the trees and away from everyone else. He didn't stop until they reached a grove of quaking aspen. Their leaves fluttered in the sunlight, sprinkling dappled spots across the grass that grew beneath them.

It was here he turned her to face him. "First of all, let us get one thing straight. I did not cause the fall of Feown."

Adrastea sneered at him.

He closed his eyes and took a deep breath. For one moment, Adrastea thought he might to strike her. After all, she was defying a god. But he didn't. He opened his green eyes, his expression most serious. "Listen to me as I tell you the truth. I have no control over the Cithran army."

"You could have made them go away!"

Now Mor-Lath looked worried. He released her. He took off his common straw hat and ran a hand through his hair. "No, I couldn't. You and I could have together but alone?" He shook his head. "Not without causing some serious damage to Creation. Not even I would go that far. I needed you to help stop that war the best way possible. But you refused."

Adrastea shook her finger at him. "Don't you dare blame this on me!"

"And don't you continue to think I'm doing nothing but making your life miserable. You bring that on yourself." He held his hands out to her. "Don't you understand what I'm offering you? Are you really that country bumpkin that you can't see what your own potential is?"

Adrastea felt unsure. What was he saying? Some of her bluster went out of her. "What does potential have to do with it?"

He didn't answer her but only closed his eyes and sighed. "There is so much you don't know. If only you had kept my Book, you would know."

Adrastea blushed. Of course, he knew she'd lost it. Did he know where it was? In all the excitement with the refugees and the evacuation of Crossroads, she'd forgotten that the book had gone missing.

"Do not worry about the Book, for I can get you another. But you need to stop fighting me."

She shook her head. "You're the God of the Dark. I should be fighting you with every essence of my being. You're the Evil One, the Master Liar, the Warmongerer, the—"

He waved his hand dismissively. "Yes, yes, I've heard all my slanderous titles before. No need to repeat them. But you could give me one I've never had before: Husband."

Did he have to be so persistent? "No."

"I won't beg but I will continue to plead my case."

"No."

"Adrastea—"

"I said no."

He sighed again and sat down on the grass. "Is it because I'm the Dark God? Is that all?"

Is that all? What more could it be? She stared down at him in disbelief. "You think I can forget something like that?"

"Right now, it's all you see. Can't you see past that to the man?"

"You're not a man, you're a god."

"And you're a foolish country girl who's turning down an offer thousands of other women would jump at."

"Well, go offer it to them." She wrapped her arms about her.

He shook his head and looked up at her. "I don't want any of them." He patted the grass beside him. "Won't you at least sit?"

"No."

"Please?"

That one word turned her head. She had never expected him to use it. It quite surprised her when he did. He reached out to her. She unfolded her hands but did not take his proffered one.

Instead, he snatched her hand as quick as lighting and pulled her to the ground. He'd cheated. The Deeper Power undermined her footing. "Oh," she gasped as she plunked onto the grass. She shoved him away. She did not stand back up but kept her distance, hugging her knees to her chest.

"If I was a mortal man, would that have made a difference?"

"You never will be. Why should I bother speculating?"

"Light forbid you might like me un-omnipotent."

Whatever that meant. He was trying to seduce her again, to sweet-talk her out of her determination. Mira had warned her of this. As long as she stayed strong, she would succeed.

"If I were a mortal man, you would not be so stubborn. You'd be happy to get the attention. Deep down you were afraid that you would never marry. You're the daughter of Mad Lillybet. Any man who knew your mother would fear that you would turn out the same. Never mind that you are more like your father. Although you appear to lack his sense of humor.

"You fear to leave Sacred Spring but only because you know nothing else. How would you know if some other village would accept you or would they find out your guilty little secret? Better the devil you know, eh?" He grinned at his own joke.

Adrastea turned away from him. "That's not funny."

"You wouldn't have said that if you hadn't seen the humor in it in the first place.

"How about this one: A woman approaches the village healer with a quandary. 'I've borne too many children,' the woman says, 'and I don't want more. What can I do?' The healer tells her to sleep with her feet in a ten-gallon bucket. Several months later, the woman returns, pregnant. 'It did not work,' she complains. 'Did you sleep with your feet in a ten-gallon bucket?' the healer asks. 'No,' confesses the woman. 'We didn't have a ten-gallon bucket, so I used two five-gallon buckets.'"

Wait. Did he tell her a joke? That was cheating. Adrastea jammed a knuckle into her mouth to keep herself from laughing. He would say anything to get into her good graces. She turned from him and inhaled several times to get a hold of herself.

"My answer is still no." Adrastea focused on thoughts of Mira. Mira was right. She could not, should not, trust the Dark God.

He scooted closer to her but did not touch her. She turned her shoulder to him. "Have you never wondered why I have offered you marriage?"

Adrastea looked up in surprise. No, she never had. All she had thought about was whether or not his offer of marriage was genuine. That she doubted very much. But if it was, there had to be a reason behind it. "I don't want to know. How do I know you wouldn't be lying?"

He sighed. "I see my reputation works against me." He stood.

Feeling vulnerable, she, too, leapt to her feet and faced him. He was full of tricks, this one. She could not let her guard down.

He thrust his hands into his pockets. "It seems that anything I say will be doubted. So here is my quandary. The only way I can prove my sincerity in marrying you is to kneel before the priest and make my vow. But until you're certain that I intend to do this, you're not having a bar of it."

She clung to her doubts. Words were meaningless, she told herself.

He wasn't going to give up so easily. "Have you never wondered why the Light hasn't come to defend you?" He watched her for a moment. A smile spread across his face. "Ah," he said, pointing a finger at her. "You never have."

She raised a hand to her cheek for it suddenly felt hot. She turned away from him again.

Then a new thought occurred to her. Why didn't she just walk away from him? By remaining she gave him permission to continue this.

She stepped forward. She would not remain here and keep saying no for her presence was saying yes. No wonder he wasn't taking her seriously.

But Mor-Lath matched her pace for pace. "That's right. The Light knows your destiny lies with me. Else why haven't They done anything?"

"I don't expect Them to." Them? "The Light doesn't involve Herself in the simple affairs of mortals."

"Yes, She does."

"She trusts me enough to stand up to you. She knows I will succeed."

"Or She doesn't care?"

"That's not true." Adrastea clambered through the trees and scrub brush until she came to the Sacred Spring path.

"Isn't it? Come with me to the village. I can prove it to you."

"It'll be a trick, and therefore worthless."

He ran both hands through his hair. "Will you at least give me a chance?"

"No."

He moved faster than she thought possible. He caught her around the waist then hefted her over his shoulder. "If only you were a little less stubborn, you would find me a reasonable person."

Her head swam as she felt him draw upon the Deeper Power, again, stronger than she expected. A craving erupted in her. She fought it.

She felt a disorienting shift, like when he'd taken her to Feown. She clutched at his shirt. Where were they going?

They hadn't travelled far. He set her down on the road in front of the Poulters. Dizzy, she clung to him to keep from falling.

"Look there," Mor-Lath said, pointing. "See Amarice Poulter, as she feeds her flock?"

Amarice scattered grain while a carpet of red chickens bobbed and pecked around her skirt hem. She called to them, oblivious of being watched. Lines wrapped about her, as if embracing her belly.

Then Mor-Lath passed his hand before Adrastea's eyes. When next she looked again, she gasped. Amarice was surrounded by the brightest beings she had ever seen, their glory rivaling the overhead sun. They were luminous creatures with long white hair, or perhaps they were veils. They wore flowing robes, which floated around them as if on a soft breeze. When they saw Mor-Lath and Adrastea, they gathered closely around Amarice, standing firm guard.

"These are angels, messengers of Light. They guard Amarice and her unborn child. While I might try to get past them now, they would be able to resist me until the Light Themselves came to her aid. I can't even get close enough to tell whether it's a boy or a girl.

"She is untouchable, whereas you, my dear..." he slid his arms about her waist and pulled her close.

A familiar yearning flowed through her as the Lines of Deeper Power enveloped her. Adrastea pushed against his chest. He smiled indulgently at her struggles then let her go. "Where are your angel champions, Betrothed of the Dark?"

Adrastea backed away. A pit had opened in her stomach. She was a child of the Light. Yet if what Mor-Lath showed her was true, why wasn't the Light defending her as well? She shook her head. "No. This is another trick." She waved her hand at the angels around Amarice. "That's an illusion." Amarice turned and went into the house. The angels followed her, though some stood guard outside.

Mor-Lath frowned. "If you can't believe the truth seen with your own eyes, maybe you will believe the truth of your own hands."

He snagged her by one and dragged her up the lane to one of the abandoned cottages. There, Jak Carpenter and about five others consulted about how best to restore the cottage. They had stacked fallen adobe bricks, cleared out the floor of the cottage and inspected what remained. Mor-Lath and Adrastea stood at the perimeter of the yard. Mor-Lath pointed at the Crossroader man on a ladder leaning against the chimney. "See Master Mason? In a few moments he shall fall."

"No," Adrastea said. "You stop this!"

"It's not my doing. What happens next is all at the hands of mortals."

Adrastea pulled her hand from his and dashed through the gate. "Master Mason! Be careful!"

Everyone looked to Adrastea in surprise, including Master Mason. His grip slipped. Adrastea watched in horror as his body tumbled off the ladder. When he landed his leg slammed against a fallen stone. She heard the pop of a broken leg.

"Oh, dear Light!" She ran forward. She pushed through the workers to Master Mason's side. She checked his eyes as Ari had taught her. They looked glazed but otherwise seemed okay, reacting to the sunlight. Instinctively, she reached for her cloak, but it was not around her shoulders. It was healer practice to wrap the injured and keep them warm. Something like a cloak or blanket was pressed into her hand. She spread it over Master Mason, leaving the broken leg uncovered.

She examined it. The impact on the stone had not shattered it but it was surely broken. Blood soaked his clothing and stained the stone beneath it. Where the leg had struck the rock, his skin had been torn.

"We need to move him back," Adrastea commanded. "Drag him backwards by the shoulders."

Jak Carpenter and one other Crossroader leapt to her command. They dragged him back with Adrastea guiding the leg off the rock to prevent further damage. Master Mason cried out in pain whenever his leg moved.

Upon request, someone handed her a small knife. She cut away the bloodstained trousers. While the broken bone distorted the line of his leg, at least it hadn't broken the skin.

"I've got to set the bone," she said. "It's going to hurt."

Master Mason nodded. Someone gave him a rag on which to bite down. Jak and the other man held Master Mason firmly under Adrastea's instructions. One of the others held down his uninjured leg. They nodded their readiness to Adrastea.

She pulled with all her might. Of all the limbs, a broken thighbone was the hardest to set.

Master Mason screamed through his muffle while Adrastea realigned the bones. Her luck must have held for she got it right the first time. For having set a bone this large only once before in her life, she felt relieved to have had such good success.

Master Mason's screamed settled into muffled sobs. He rolled over onto his tummy as instructed.

Adrastea inspected the wound on his leg. The skin had been torn back. The muscle underneath had also been torn. "I'm going to need my bag for this."

Mor-Lath kneeled down beside her. "You could do it without your toys."

Adrastea scowled at him. "I'll need to clean it out or it will fester. Then I'll have to stitch it up."

He laid a hand on her shoulder. "You have talent. You can sense the Lines that connect all. I would show you a better way but send a man for your bag if you wish."

Adrastea did so. "Master Carpenter, my bag is up in the refugees' camp. Please, bring it." Jak sped off to do her bidding.

Mor-Lath sat back on his haunches. "Now, we can sit here while this good man suffers in pain or I can show you how to heal. Properly."

Adrastea did her best to ignore him. She gave the wound a cursory glance but didn't see any obvious foreign material. She replaced the skin and pressed against it to stop the bleeding.

"There is dirt in there," Mor-Lath observed.

He let the Deeper Power flow into her, startling her. It was like stepping from a dark house out into the sunshine. The brilliance of it filled her mind and sang a sweet song to her heart. She saw the Lines, a great relief as they connected everything to everything else, none of those wispy out-of-the-corner-of-her-eye gossamer threads.

Then she saw what he was talking about. Like different-colored specks, the dirt showed up under the skin. They didn't belong there but belonged to the earth. She also saw how the body was supposed to be connected and how it was disrupted. It reminded her of her mother's weaving. Before being apprenticed to Ari, she had spent several years of her childhood watching her mother work the threads. She had even owned a small hand-loom of her own, making clumsy little placemats or washcloths.

"Pull the Lines and clean the wound," he instructed. "Command the dirt to leave."

The Lines of the minute specks of dirt were so fine. She touched them, then wound them about her fingertip before lifting them away.

Out came every last speck.

"That was easy," she admitted, even easier than pulling apart the rain barrel.

Mor-Lath watched over her shoulder. "That's because you are restoring the earth to the earth."

"Now, the injury. See how the Lines are supposed to connect the flesh together? Tell them to rejoin."

It took more concentration. She commanded the Lines to return as they were before. They obliged, more than happy to join up as they should have been. Not only the muscle but the bone as well. In return, she felt what she could only call waves of gratitude flow back along the Lines. Then they faded, as her assistance wasn't needed any more.

Loneliness filled her without the touch of the Lines of another human body. She wanted to reach out and stroke them again. Mor-Lath pulled back her hand. "Your work is finished, Healer." He lifted her up from the ground and gave Master Mason room to rise.

Adrastea's patient stood up. By all logic, he should not have been able to. He looked at his leg, tested it by touching his foot to the ground, then putting weight on it. Everyone stood back and watched as a man who, not less than five minutes ago had a broken leg, walked around the yard.

"It's a miracle," one of them breathed. They all turned to Adrastea, their expressions stark.

Their stares made her uncomfortable. Guilty, even. She wrapped her arms around her and turned away. She looked past Mor-Lath's shoulder to beyond the village.

With gentle hands, he tilted her chin, so she looked at him. "The Light has given you a great talent, Adrastea. It's about time you learned to use it."

"So why do I feel like I've violated something?"

He shrugged. "That is for you to tell me." He glanced over her shoulder. "But later. I see your uncle approaching. He never has any good words for me."

Natan hurried down the road towards them. Jak must have told him about what had happened.

She felt, rather than saw, Mor-Lath leave. Adrastea wished she could just vanish like that too. She had no idea of how she would explain this to her uncle.

⁓ ⁕ ⁓

Natan had no idea Mor-Lath had roamed the village that day until after he arrived up at the cabins. After hearing about 'that man who was so familiar with the young healer' from the Crossroaders and Jak confirming the identity as Adrastea's suitor, he worried even more.

Where was Adrastea?

It wasn't until a Crossroader came dashing back for Adrastea's bag, that he learned her whereabouts.

He followed. His steps only hastening when he recognized his niece and the man standing too close to her near one of the old houses.

Mor-Lath had disappeared by the time Natan showed up, but his influence remained.

The Crossroaders buzzed about, discussing some 'miracle'. Some were in awe, others were dubious.

But nobody knew the whole story.

It took him speaking with Master Mason himself, a man who had retired to a quiet corner with a mug of tea in his trembling hands, to hear about what Adrastea had done for him.

A healing—a full, complete and scarless healing.

Adrastea had retreated to Lillybet's house and had locked the doors. He found Mira on the porch trying to convince her to let her in.

Adrastea had refused.

He shoved Mira aside. "Let me try."

He rapped sharply on the door. "In the name of the Mayor, open up."

Only then did Adrastea admit him alone.

"What happened?" he asked as she barred the door behind him.

"I don't want to talk about it."

All right, a different tact. "Was this Mor-Lath's doing?"

She didn't answer him. She turned from him and pressed the back of her hand to her mouth.

"They say you healed a broken leg. Can... Can you do that? I mean, I didn't know that was possible."

She shrugged.

"Did he do this for you?"

Her gaze looked sideways at him. She shook her head.

"So it was you?"

She turned her face away.

Natan scrubbed his hands through his hair. "Give me something. Was it your idea, or his?"

Only then, did Adrastea give in. "His. Said I had Light-given talent. Told me I didn't need my 'toys'. Told me how to do it." She fell silent.

Natan waited. Sometimes silence could prod someone into speaking again. He waited until she squirmed.

She caved. "It wasn't like I could say no, could I?"

Ah, the rock and the hard place. Natan knew that place too well. "You could have."

"And let Master Mason suffer? I'm a healer, Uncle Natan." She paced the room. "And—and now I've been shown this other way, a better way, of— of fixing people." She stared at her hands. "I..."

So that was his game. "You see what he's doing?"

"I see exactly what he's doing. I've set it down in no uncertain terms that I have no interest in his interest in me. No is a pretty powerful word."

"So is what you did for Master Mason."

Natan wanted to help her. He truly did. But he couldn't help her, not really. It was one thing to say you'll say no but quite another to have to be stuck in that kind of decision. Light knew he'd had to make several of those as Mayor.

He had nothing to offer her by way of advice. Feeling he failed as a Mayor and an uncle, he left her to her solitude.

He spent the rest of the afternoon piecing the story the together from the words of a fretful Mira, a surprised Carles and several bemused Crossroaders.

The Crossroaders seemed rather amused at 'the healer's suitor', even regaling the mayor with tales of her slapping him and his carrying her off over his shoulder. Their comments suggested that a wedding sooner rather than later might be on the cards.

That was the last thing he needed.

By evening, Adrastea still had not come out. Eventually he persuaded her to let the others in for the night. Adrastea coldly excused herself and locked the bedroom door behind her.

He, Mira and Carles sat at the table in Lillybet's house that evening to discuss the matter. Surely Adrastea would hear every word they said.

Let her. There were others in the village, both Springers and Crossroaders, who would feel the influence of Mor-Lath's presence. This was bigger than a single woman.

Mira appeared to be the most shaken of them all. Her hands trembled around her teacup. "I tried to stop him. I stood up to him and willed him to stop. He pushed me aside like a paper doll. He told me to stand down and mind my own business, then my legs gave out underneath me." Tears filled her eyes. "I was helpless. How do we fight a god?" She turned to Carles.

He shrugged. "I'm concerned about my townsmen. They genuinely like him, even though they don't know who he is. He's certainly charmed them. They're full of stories of his help and his camaraderie. To hear them speak, you couldn't see anything wrong with him.

"Adrastea, on the other hand..."

Mira opened her mouth but Carles put up his hand. "I know. Mor-Lath was there but nobody saw him doing anything except whisper in her ear. It was Adrastea who did the healing."

Natan mulled this over. "So, nobody thought that he was urging her on?"

Carles slumped. "We haven't had a word out of Master Mason all afternoon. The only other Crossroader to have anything coherent to say about it simply believes that 'Master M' was simply giving the healer encouragement, like he has everyone else. He has been making himself useful all day, I'm told. Everyone likes him.

"If I didn't know better—if I didn't see him with my own eyes—I would say you were mad to dissuade a man like him."

"So, you felt it, didn't you?" Mira insisted. "You felt his power?"

Carles nodded. "That I did."

For the first time, Natan admitted near-defeat. "How do we fight against him? We're powerless to stand up to him when he wishes to have a word with our Adrastea. He's got my people fighting each other over Lillybet's death. Now all your people are wholeheartedly supporting him."

Carles steepled his fingers and tapped them against his lips. "It seems Adrastea is the key to this all. He wants her willingly but why? Find that out, and we may find the key to defeating him." He leaned in over the table. The others leaned in close. "We could kill Adrastea," he whispered.

Natan even leapt to his feet. "NO! We can't do that! Are you mad?"

"How badly do you want to be rid of him? Remove his reason for being here and he is gone."

Mira frowned. "Cure the disease by killing the patient?"

Natan winced. "I thought the whole idea was to save her."

"It may be the only way to save her soul."

"Not by—" he whispered the last part, "—killing her."

Carles only nodded. He sat back in his chair. "So, you admit it's not simply a case of saving your village but the case of saving one person. In the end, not one of us matters, only her."

Mira's eyes narrowed. "You didn't mean what you just said, about..." she cleared her throat. "You know. Did you?"

Carles returned her gaze calmly. "I was only thinking of the worst things that could happen."

"The worst thing that could happen is that he takes her away." Mira slapped the table hard.

Carles cocked an eyebrow at her. "So, her death would be preferable?"

Natan, who was still standing, folded his arms. "What are you getting at, Priest?"

Carles held out his hands in a peace offering. "I'm just saying you haven't explored all options yet. You love her too much to give her over. And you love her too much to grant her an alternate mercy."

"You know," said Mira in a soft voice. "There is the possibility he wouldn't let us kill her. If he wants her that much, he will see that her life is spared."

"Or," Carles said, drawling the word out while his thought finished coalescing. "It could be that he is merely toying with you. He's teasing you, disrupting you and pushing you to see how far you can go, all for his own amusement. And wouldn't it be dandy if he managed to get you to kill an innocent woman?"

Natan sank to his chair. "How do we know what he is up to?"

Mira sniffed. "Light only knows."

Carles mused this over. "Yes, the Light does. We could always ask Him."

'Safe' was a rather vague term when applied to Adrastea. She admitted, with great reluctance, that Mor-Lath could show up anywhere, any time. It didn't matter what she said or not, he always got his way.

Mira refused to leave Adrastea on her own, even at Lillybet's house—not that her presence had helped much that afternoon. Meanwhile, Carles told the priestess that it was rather pointless to attempt to come between the God of the Dark and his object. If he hadn't carried her off by now, he probably wasn't going to do it tomorrow.

Adrastea preferred to be left to her own thoughts. She refused to speak to anyone for the rest of the evening.

That night she laid awake in bed. Let Mira and Uncle Natan and the others think what they want about today's encounter. It wasn't so much what Mor-Lath said to her but rather what she had done on her own.

All her life she had learned that the Deeper Power was what bound Creation together. She had been led to think that their lives were guided by the Light. The Deeper Power was Her hand in Creation. Mortals were supposed to get on with the living of their lives, keep in Her good graces and leave all the miracle-making to Her and Her angels.

But Adrastea could not deny the power that flowed through her hands that day. Some would say 'miracle,' but others might say 'witch'. They drowned witches in stories. Did they do that in real life? Adrastea had heard the chilling tales of witches who were subject to baptism in the Sacred Spring to cleanse them of their evil. Sometimes they weren't let up out of the water, if their evil was bad enough.

They might have been mere stories, but stories had to come from somewhere.

The next morning Carles persuaded Mira to leave Adrastea. He had suggested a day of fasting and meditation for answers. "As long as she stays here in Lillybet's, she should be safe from him."

"Won't protect me from anyone else," Adrastea muttered. Mira had given her a bowl of porridge for breakfast. It was thin and watery. Mira's cooking skills left much to be desired.

Mira touched Adrastea's hand. "We're going to be gone all day. Are you sure you'll be all right?"

Adrastea shrugged. "Ari told me to prepare the garden out back." Busywork but necessary, if the Crossroaders were going to stay for a long time. There was just time to establish perennials before autumn set in.

Mira withdrew her hand. Adrastea sighed, relieved to be left alone. She didn't feel like explaining what had happened today. She was curious about Mira and Carles' plans. "So, what does one do for fasting and meditation?"

"It's a purification ritual. Fasting clears the body while meditation clears the mind. It leaves the priest more susceptible to reading the Lines of Deeper Power and receiving inspiration. Prophets use it all the time." She slipped outside to fetch water from the rain barrel.

Adrastea looked at her breakfast. Only she had a bowl. She'd presumed they'd eaten earlier. Now she realized they'd not eaten at all. They'd had only water. "I thought prophecy just happened."

Carles carried the glasses to the dishpan. "Sometimes it does but when one isn't forthcoming, then you've got to go find it."

"So, you're looking for a prophecy about me?"

He paused for a moment. "Well, not exactly. We're looking more for a why than a what. We already know what."

"So, what are you looking for?"

"Purpose. Certain events pull on the Deeper Power. The more sensitive a soul, the more they can sense. When interpreted properly, it makes for prophecy."

Adrastea toyed with her food. "And what happens if it's misinterpreted?"

He sat back down at the table. "A comedy of errors at best. Tragedy at worst. For you, we're hoping to find out Mor-Lath's purpose. It is hard to fight what we do not know."

◦◦◦◦◦◦◦◦◦

This second day of solitude grated on Adrastea. Once Mira and Carles left, she found the house uncomfortably empty. She tried reading some of Carles' books but found them incredibly dull. Sitting and reading wasn't her thing. Took too long to figure out the words.

As she flipped through yet another boring tome on priestcraft, her left foot jiggled. Her fingers tapped and finally, her attention wandered out the window. The garden called to her, that poor, neglected garden of her mother's. Soon she found herself outside in the warm morning sun, pulling up tall weeds. Certainly better than reading.

Mor-Lath leaned over the stone wall. "Need some help?" He wore common clothes again. While they fit his body perfectly, they seemed out of place on him, in her opinion. He should have been wearing fine clothes— lord's clothes. Or nothing at all. She pushed that thought away.

He looked quite handsome when dressed in fine clothes. But today, he seemed just like any other man.

Adrastea looked up and scowled at him. "No."

"There is an easier way of doing that."

She gave him a look then went back to yanking a prickly weed. It was uncomfortable to grab yet came up with little effort. She tossed it onto the pile. She knelt down to work on some of the others. They were tougher, with deep taproots.

Nothing was harder to get up than grass, smooth, seemingly innocent but with deep, complex root systems that brought up great clumps of dirt.

She yanked hard until a bundle of grass came up. She slammed its base against the ground to knock off the dirt, hitting it harder than necessary.

"If you did it the other way, you'd have more time for other things."

A straggle of hair came loose, and she blew it from her face. "What other way?" And what other things? It wasn't as if she had anything better to do. If not this garden, then some other chore awaited her.

He waved his hand and all the weeds came up.

Adrastea looked about her at the weeds lying on the ground. She put her fists on her hips and declared, "I'd rather do it myself!"

Mor-Lath shrugged. "So be it." He waved his hand again. The weeds jumped back into the ground, even the ones she'd already pulled.

Adrastea sniffed and continued to yank out weeds her way. She pulled at them angrily. After giving Mor-Lath one look of defiance, she took out her anger on the weeds.

"Come on," he cajoled. "It's not that hard. They would obey your merest whim. Reach out with your thoughts and command them."

She paused in her tugging of a particularly stubborn clump of grass. "I don't think my soul is worth a garden of weeds."

"Whatever." He didn't wave his hand this time, but the weeds yanked out of the ground again. "Ari's coming. Now you'll have plenty of time to listen to her woes."

He disappeared as quickly as he came, before Ari huffed around the corner, hessian bags of established plants in her hands.

"You're awake," she said. "Garden looks great. You've been busy. Now come with me to my garden. I've got more herbs for you."

Chapter 18

Down in the village, Adrastea shuddered at the uncommon silence. Only a horse-drawn cart stood in front of the inn, its head down to crop at the grass.

She and Ari walked through the village, watching three of the elder Innkeeper children, Marak, Martine and Tom, loading things into the back of the cart.

Tam brought Marta out of the Inn. Adrastea stopped, startled. There were beings of Light and Darkness around Marta. The angels, like the ones Mor-Lath showed her, stood sentinel around her. Around that protective line there circled dark spidery creatures. Demons, Adrastea guessed. Every once in a while, a demon would lurch itself at an angel. The two would wrestle until the angel drove the demon away.

Adrastea blinked, and she couldn't see them anymore. Then she blinked again, and she could. She blinked a few more times to be sure that it was truly her own control that allowed her to see the ethereal plane. That was a useful gift. She felt a grudging gratitude to Mor-Lath. "Ari, is Marta pregnant?"

Ari stopped. "Yes. How did you know?"

"Telltale signs."

Ari looked perplexed. "Your eyesight is rather good today. Normally you can't see the other side of the green."

Tam helped Marta down the step of the porch and to the cart. Marta limped. Her head was still bandaged.

"What happened there?"

Ari grunted. "Their story: Marta tripped and fell. True story: She and Ariah got into a fight about Kyfa, who attacked Marta the other day. Marta came out second best both times."

"So she's leaving?"

"She's leaving because Natan told her to, for the sake of peace in the village. Marta may not have killed your mother but unless we prove that to everyone, there will be people who think so."

Ari put her hand on Adrastea's shoulder. "You want my honest opinion? I'm thinking Mor-Lath killed your mother to sow discord among us."

"It would be easy to blame him, wouldn't it?"

Ari stepped back. "You defending him?"

Adrastea blushed. "I didn't mean it like that. It's just that..." She wanted to wilt. "He said..."

"You know you can't trust anything he says."

Adrastea wrapped her arms around herself.

Ari frowned. "Why? What has he been saying?"

"Oh, nothing about this. I'm just thinking about what he said at the council. Everyone was so ready to believe him, but they wouldn't believe one of their own, even if it is Marta."

Ari thought about that. "His influence, do you think?"

Adrastea nodded. She got to thinking. Generally, Mor-Lath was well-meaning towards her. He didn't yell or bully and he made himself downright likeable at times. It had to be a trick, this good nature of his. It had to be only a matter of time before he showed his true colors.

"Come," said Ari. "Tam wishes a word."

They approached the Innkeeper, who had helped his wife to her seat on the cart. He beckoned to them. He grasped hands with Ari and nodded to Adrastea. "It'll be best if we don't tell you where we're going."

Ari nodded. "Take care. Did you wish me to write a letter to the healer, whoever they are?"

Tam shook his head. "I think we'll be all right. I'm coming back but Marak's staying with Marta. She's seen enough birthings to know what to do."

"Will the Inn be fine while you're gone?"

"Rop's keeping an eye on the place. Natan knows what's going on. Hey!" He shouted to his children as they dropped bundle in the dust! "You be careful!" Tam hurried to help them.

Ari followed to continue her conversation.

Adrastea should have followed Ari.

"This is your fault," Marta hissed to Adrastea from the top of the cart. "You and that lover of yours. If he hadn't said what he'd said, then none of this would happen."

Adrastea's jaw dropped. She hadn't been expecting this.

Marta wasn't done with her poison. "I swear he's in league with the Dark One himself. You're no better than your witch mother. I heard what you did yesterday. Don't think you've got me fooled. Soon everyone will know you for what you are. I don't care what the Crossroaders think. I know what you are."

Adrastea shrunk back. The demons circling Marta howled with glee, then went back to teasing the stoic angels. Were these demons always around Marta?

Adrastea beat a hasty retreat to Ari, who had made her final goodbyes to Tam. "How long do you think she'll stay away?"

"Not long enough."

They watched the cart turn onto the road that headed towards the small pass. Up the canyon was the woodcutters' village. Beyond that, nothing until the mountain meadows and the shepherd villages.

"Good riddance," stated Adrastea, sotto voce. Ari nodded in agreement. As they turned to Ari's house, Adrastea attempted to resurrect the conversation. "You know Amarice's pregnant?"

"Mm hmm. Everybody should know by now. She's been quite obvious for the past week or so."

"How far along?"

"Eight months at least, from what I can see. Her skirts and aprons couldn't hide it forever. She really popped out."

"And nobody noticed until now?"

"No. Amarice's naturally ample figure can hide a pregnancy until the last few months or so. She tried to keep it a secret, afraid she'd be forced to get rid of it. One can't hide that sort of thing forever."

That shook Adrastea. "Why? Why the deception?"

"Because her mother died giving birth to her and her grandmother died giving birth to her mother."

Adrastea had forgotten. "And she thinks she'll die?"

Ari nodded. By now, they'd reached Ari's cottage. As they followed the path to the back, Ari studied her garden. "Her grandmother died of plague soon after giving birth. Her mother died because she wasn't big enough to give birth."

"But shouldn't Amarice have died as well?"

Adrastea knelt down next to some rosemary. "Yes, but Mirah had heard of a new way of pulling babies out. She used spoons and managed to get Amarice out before it was too late."

"Do you think you could do the same?"

"I saw it done in Feown. Even got me a pair of funny spoon forceps, just in case I ever needed them. Haven't needed to until now. Springers birthe easy." Ari pulled some scissors out of her pocket and snipped off several sprigs of rosemary. "I'll set these for you and you can grow a hedge or something." She roamed around the garden looking for other transplant candidates.

"So, if Amarice is this far gone in her pregnancy, why is she keeping it a secret now?"

"Fear and ignorance. I shall talk to her this week and see if I can examine her. We may be able to get her going early. A small baby might fit through fine.

"Now, how about some onions?"

Adrastea made stew that morning by throwing whatever vegetables she could find into a pot and left it on the hearth. It could sit there for hours, even days, ready to eat, for who knew when Mira and Carles would get back? She missed cooking on Ari's stove and wondered if there was a way for her to get her own. Maybe Peter and Sheelagh could make her one—just a small one?

Mira and Carles came home well after dark, tired but elated.

"Mmm," purred Carles as soon as the scent of cooking filled his nostrils. "Dinner."

Adrastea rose from her place at the table. She had been trying to read one of the books again. This particular volume was all about faith and letting go and trusting the Light. It wasn't helping. Sitting around and doing nothing didn't strike her as the best way of standing up to Mor-Lath.

"I didn't have time for bread today," she confessed. Ari had kept her busy all afternoon planting.

"Garden looks good," Mira sunk down onto a bench at the table. "I'm starved."

"Well, sun's down. We can eat." Carles ladled stew into the bowls

Adrastea had provided. He slid one bowl across the table to Mira and then sat down with the second. Adrastea had already eaten, her empty bowl still on the table.

She watched the priests, their enthusiasm palpable. "Well?" Adrastea asked. "What happened? Did you learn anything?"

Mira and Carles didn't answer at first, so busy were they shoveling food into their mouths.

"Curiosity will be the end of me if you don't tell me what happened," Adrastea gasped.

Carles swallowed. "It was amazing! We fasted and meditated. Mira fell asleep in the afternoon." Mira only hmphed. "And then, as the sun was about to set, we both received the same vision."

"I've never seen anything like it," Mira added. "Suddenly the hillside was covered with heavenly beings. And in the midst of them was a woman who gave birth while two men supported her upright."

Carles added, "After she gave birth, she and the two men melted away."

Mira's countenance glowed with a happiness Adrastea hadn't seen in her for a long time. "And her child stood up strong, with long blonde hair. All the angels rejoiced. Oh, she was beautiful!"

Carles nodded, his mouth full of stew. He and Mira glanced at each other. Mira took a quick spoonful of her supper.

"And?" asked Adrastea.

They looked at each other and something unspoken passed between them. "And that was it," concluded Carles. "We both saw the same thing."

Mira reached across the table and patted Adrastea's hand. "I'm sorry. There was nothing about you. Believe me, we asked. We asked about your destiny. We meditated upon it. And, well, nothing."

"Oh," replied Adrastea. She pulled her hand away from Mira's and sat back in her chair. She had been hoping that they would have seen something—anything—about her. "Maybe I was the woman who gave birth?"

Both priest and priestess shook their heads. Carles sighed. "It was not you. That much was clear."

Mira offered an apology. "The woman was blonde like her daughter."

"Was it Amarice?"

"No."

Adrastea fell back against her chair. "Well, that was useless."

"No," said Carles. "Just unexplained. There has to be a reason why we saw it. The Light wouldn't have sent it to us without a reason, especially at this time." They looked at each other again. Adrastea was sure they weren't telling her everything.

"I'm leaving tomorrow," Carles said. "We'll continue as we have been. Wait to see what hand the Light has dealt us. I need to get back to my home and defend it."

Mira's countenance fell. "What time are you leaving?"

Carles rose and put his bowl in the dishpan. "First light tomorrow." He pulled the spare straw tick down from the loft and prepared a bed before the fire. "It's been a long day. I hope you don't mind if I turn in early." He yawned.

Mira yawned too. "That was hard work." She retreated to the bedroom, leaving Adrastea to bank the fire.

"G'night," Carles mumbled before he rolled over. "Be strong."

Adrastea headed off to the bedroom. Mira was already tucked up into the big bed, but she had the thoughtfulness to pull out the trundle bed for Adrastea. "Mira? Please tell me more about the vision."

But Mira had fallen fast asleep.

Finally, Ari convinced Amarice to consent to examination. As the healers walked down the lane towards the Poulters' home, Adrastea saw sentinels of angels in the yard. They were so thick that if she let her mind drift fully to the ethereal plane, she would not have been able to see the house. As they passed through there, the angels whispered to her, "All is quiet here." They reached out with their slender hands to stroke her hair and shoulders as she passed.

Amarice let them in and closed the door tightly. She planted her plump back against it. "I don't want anyone to know," she explained in her high-pitched voice.

Ari folded her arms. "Everyone already does. Nobody will make you give up the baby."

Amarice shook her head. "You don't understand. I really want this baby. I must have this baby."

The healer sat her down at the table. "And you can. There are things

I can do that will ensure the baby will be born alive."

Amarice gave this some thought before consenting to Ari's ministrations. Ari looked in Amarice's eyes and checked her skin and thumped on her large belly—all standard practice.

Adrastea gazed around the Poulters' sizeable cottage. This main room was divided in half, with the larger half being this kitchen, complete with stove. The smaller half was a storage room. As it faced north, it would remain cooler in the summer. Another door led to the bedroom. Above that was a loft with plenty of room to stand upright.

"Into the bedroom," the healer ordered. Adrastea followed, bringing the coal oil lamp. Marlon and Amarice's bedroom was a comfortable affair, with a bed larger than Lilly's. Plastered and whitewashed walls, a fine double-bureau and white linen curtains at the window lent a comfortable air about the place. Adrastea cleared a space on the bureau of Amarice's hairbrush and knick-knacks and set down the lantern.

Ari had Amarice strip to her shift and lay on the bed. She pressed on Amarice's belly. "Are you sure you're only seven months? You look more like the latter half of eight."

"I thought I counted right." Amarice took in a breath. "I feel dizzy."

Ari helped her upright. "You're too big for seven months. You've got to be more. When was your last cycle?"

Amarice tried to remember. "Autumn feast, I think. A week or so before."

Ari ticked off the months and seasons on her fingers. "Goodness and Light, woman! You're nearly due, if that's true."

Amarice shrugged her pudgy shoulders. "I've never been regular."

Adrastea looked at Amarice's discarded petticoats. She had taken to wearing several this summer. Now Adrastea could see why she was able to hide such a late pregnancy for so long. Amarice had sewn several petticoats ruffles to a single layer. The single layer covered her belly and the multiple layers hung below, thus giving the illusion of wearing many petticoats. Now that she thought about it, every time she saw Amarice, she had held a basket or a bag in front of her belly. And if she didn't have anything to hide behind, she popped her hands under her full apron. Adrastea had to hand it to her; that was rather clever on Amarice's part.

She helped Amarice back into her clothes, for couldn't dress herself without aid.

"I'll figure out exactly how far along you are," Ari said. "If it's safe enough, there are ways of bringing babies early. If it is small enough, you can give birth and possibly survive."

Amarice fell on Ari in an embrace. She blubbered hard, the surprising outburst bringing a freshet of tears. Ari jumped, stared over Amarice's shoulders in surprise, then belatedly put her arms about the distressed mother. Adrastea excused herself back out to the kitchen. She didn't feel like witnessing the scene.

The kitchen wasn't as empty as it was before. Angels drifted in through the walls. They all wanted to touch Adrastea. "Be well," they whispered to her. "Be strong. Be true."

Adrastea didn't answer. What does one say to angels? She plunked herself down on one of Amarice's chairs and cupped her chin in her hand.

"Listen to the truth and obey," an angel told her. "Destiny awaits you as the Light would have it."

Adrastea straightened. "I'm listening."

"Act when the time is right."

"But when?" she asked. "And how?" What did the Light expect her to do?

The angels did not answer.

A week passed, and Adrastea saw nothing of Mor-Lath during that time. Life in Sacred Spring settled down. The Crossroaders were happier, now that their homes and the company had improved. They held their own council, run by Chloe Priestess.

Adrastea wanted to attend one of their councils. She figured it would be good to see how they ran things. Chloe informed her that this meeting was, "for Crossroaders only," and dismissed Adrastea without further thought. Since then, Chloe had few words to spare for Adrastea.

"Let her be," Mira advised Adrastea when she voiced her complaints. "Let the Crossroaders have their priestess." If Mira objected to Chloe, she never shared it with Adrastea.

"They would have done better to send some healers." They would have been far more personable than Chloe, Adrastea was sure of it.

"I believe they will require all their healers at Crossroads."

So, Adrastea was "it" for the Crossroaders, tending to their ills. This put her in the path of Chloe. She saw her all the time at the camp becoming known as "Little Crossroads". Thankfully, she had little occasion to speak with her. Mira consulted with her from time to time. Otherwise, Chloe kept to herself.

Trade between the two communities opened up, not only of goods but of skill. Adrastea gave Dara Weaver access to her mother's loom. Dara was happy to sit at the loom all day and weave simple fabrics. It wasn't the same as her mother's colorful shawls. Probably wouldn't bring as much money, either. Dara was dark-haired like Adrastea's mother had been, but she had a plump bottom that took up most of the loom bench. When she sat down at the loom, Dara forgot all but the cloth before her. When she wasn't weaving, she was a most talkative woman. Not much of a listener, though, to Adrastea's relief.

Every few days Ely Mayorprentice arrived with letters. Natan, Mira and Chloe received letters every time and a few others—those who could read—got occasional ones.

Natan saved his to be read out at dinner that evening. Ari had invited them all—Mira, Chloe and Adrastea—to Natan's house for supper. Natan thought it politic to add Chloe to the group. Adrastea did not think this fair. If Chloe couldn't be bothered to include any Springers at a Crossroader council meeting, why should Chloe be invited here?

"Because, prickle," Natan told his niece, "she will not always be a Crossroader."

Adrastea folded her arms. "Oh. Does Chloe know this?"

Natan rubbed his hands together. "I hope not. I want to see the expression on her face when she finds out."

Natan had borrowed two extra chairs from Ari. They crowded around his small table. Natan sat at the head, with Ari and Chloe on either side of him. Mikal sat on the other side of Chloe, and Adrastea with Ari. Mira sat at the foot so she could conduct pre-dinner worship.

Adrastea had caught the tail end of Chloe and Mira's earlier conversation about the lack of a chapel in Sacred Spring. Chloe thought it necessary, while Mira preferred this more private ministration. What Adrastea knew, and Chloe didn't was that Mira liked the side-effect of a meal, whereas if she ministered in a chapel, who'd feed her? She wasn't much of a cook.

Adrastea's stomach rumbled. The scent of roast tantalized her. Uncle Natan must really want to impress Chloe.

Mira unpacked a candle and a glass. Inwardly, Adrastea groaned. Devotion before degustation? She was starving. Couldn't they have done it after, like Mira usually did?

As the sun had set, Ari lit the candle. Not as good as sunlight but it would do. Mira poured water into the glass.

She lifted the glass so she could see the candle through the water. "As the light shines through this water, let the Light shine through me."

She offered the glass to Chloe. Chloe looked startled. "That's it?"

The glass in Mira's hand wavered. Then she held it firm.

It was Natan who explained. "We take care of the important things first. When we have empty consciences and full bellies, then we listen to the rest."

Chloe weighed these words. "With your permission, Mayor, I'd like to do a full Offering next time."

Natan bowed his head, conceding. "Your house, your dinner, your Offering. We'd be honored."

Chloe's lips parted but nothing came out. Mira lifted the glass towards the priestess. Chloe recovered herself, took the glass and sipped. She looked again to Mira.

"You can tell me now, or later." Thoughts and confessions were traditional after the sipping.

Chloe handed back the glass. "I'll confess later. Dinner seems to be the important part of your meetings. We wouldn't want to miss that." Adrastea couldn't miss the wry tone of her voice. Why did Uncle Natan want her to stay?

Mira did not meet Chloe's gaze. Her face betrayed nothing. The Lines, however, strengthened so much Adrastea felt Mira's embarrassment as if it were her own.

What was wrong with their devotions to the Light? So, what if Mira didn't do the full Offering every time?

Natan and Ari sipped without a pause. Adrastea held the glass in her hands. She wasn't feeling too kindly toward Chloe. This was not the best attitude for devotion. She pressed the glass to her lips but did not drink. Then she passed it to Mikal. He took a quick gulp and returned the glass to Mira.

Mira murmured a brief prayer, so low Adrastea could barely hear it.

Only Mikal's fetching of the food broke the tension in the room.

He had made a splendid meal from a joint of meat and some roasted root vegetables. "I got them out of the garden," he boasted as he served.

"What?" Ari exclaimed, examining the potato on her plate, "Natan's patch?"

"Yeah." Mikal spooned some onto Chloe's plate. She kept her hands folded in her lap and said nothing.

"But I let that go fallow this year," Natan replied, he also eyeing off the vegetables.

"Potatoes are funny," Mikal replied. "Unless you get every single one, there's a good chance they'll come up the next year."

"And the carrots?"

Ari answered that one. "If you let your garden go, like you did, some things will reseed themselves."

Mikal had no problems with the vegetables. He shoveled them into his mouth as if they were the most wonderful thing on earth.

One bite had Adrastea agreeing with him. They were delicious potatoes and Mikal had done a good job with them. She allowed herself a small guilty thought: for the first time, she didn't feel bad that their mother was dead. It would kill her to learn that Mikal's time among the Innkeepers had boded him well.

They ate while Natan read Sam's letter aloud.

"'The battlements are up," was Sam's news, "and we've repelled five attacks already. One nearly got through. They attacked at night when most of us were asleep. We're going to have to hold more night watches. The other attack was from a small band of Cithran soldiers. We think they were on a raid, because they had no discipline. As we were getting low on gunpowder, we took them out with slings.

"'One good thing about these raids. If we kill all the attackers, we claim the goods on their bodies. Some of them have extra rifles and sometimes enough shot and gunpowder to load them. Without enough gunpowder, the rifles are useless.'"

There were some rifles in Sacred Spring, tools, more than weapons, like how Marlon Poulter owned one, as did Baran Shepherd. Natan had one as well, not that he ever had the need to load and fire it. For the most part, the weapons most of the villagers owned were slings and the occasional bow and arrow, mostly for hunting. There was little need for killing people here. Looked like that would that change in the future.

He continued with Sam's letter. "The raiding parties seem to think we have supplies here. I'm glad you talked me into moving most of them to

Sacred Spring. They will be most surprised should they manage to break in. I hope you continue to remain safe. Please remember us in your devotions. Your Friend, Sam Mayor.'" Natan sat back and shoved a roast carrot into his mouth. "Thank the Light we're safe here," he said as he chewed.

"You can't be sure of that," Chloe said, her voice low and smooth. When Chloe ate, she'd lift her fork, take a bite, put her fork down, fold her hands in her lap and chew. As a result, her plate was more than half-full when everyone else was nearly done with seconds. "Feown is so far away, yet the war touches us here."

"We're out of the way," Natan returned. "From what reports we get, it sounds like the army is moving westerly toward the Great Western Pass. They have no reason to turn south and come here."

"We have the supplies," Chloe replied.

"They don't know that."

A slight frown creased Chloe's forehead. "There is a road leading here from Crossroads. It stands to reason that sooner or later someone is going to explore along that road. They will discover us. They will see a hastily-erected village of mostly women and children. We're marked as easy targets."

Mikal, who had been eating before the food ran out, listened carefully. "We could raise battlements like Crossroads."

Natan took a swallow from his tankard. "Harvest is soon upon us. I don't know if we'll have the time or the manpower."

"Doesn't mean we can't get started. Master M says that if you work on something little by little, eventually it'll get done."

Natan's fork clattered to his plate, sending bits of gravy spattering across the table. Everyone paused and looked at him. Chloe, who continued to chew, looked around at the suddenly quiet people at the table. "Who's Master M?" she asked after swallowing.

"When the hell were you speaking with him?" Natan blurted out in anger at his apprentice.

Mikal shrank. "He's— he's all over the village. He'll stop and talk with me from time to time." He looked to Adrastea. "Says he's keeping an eye on you."

Chloe turned to Adrastea and repeated her question. "Who is he?"

Mira answered, a little too hastily. "He's nobody. A foreigner. He came to the village one day and declared his intention to pay court to our Adrastea. Can't take no for an answer."

Chloe gave Adrastea a disapproving look. Whether it was of 'Master M' or his suit, or perhaps even Adrastea's rejection of his suit, she did not know.

Chloe continued her questions. "Has he a profession? Who's his family?"

Natan spat, "He has no profession and we don't care who his family is." He pointed a finger at Mikal. "I forbid you from speaking with him. He's bad news and I don't want you to have anything to do with him."

Mikal slunk down in his chair, two bright spots burning on his cheeks. One did not argue with Uncle Natan.

But Natan was not finished. "And later you will tell me every single thing that he's told you. You will forget nothing. Now eat your supper."

They spent the rest of the meal in silence. Any attempt by Ari to start a conversation about the weather died quickly.

And thus, was a damper put on the evening.

As Mikal cleared away the plates and everyone moved away from the table, Adrastea watched Chloe. The wheels were turning in Chloe's head, of that she was certain. The butterflies turned in Adrastea's stomach. What was the Crossroader priestess thinking?

⊙⃛

The mention of Mor-Lath killed any good feeling there had been at the meal. After, Natan shuffled them all out the door without an offer of tea to round off the meal. Chloe protested at the lack of devotion.

Adrastea promised herself she would get Mikal on his own and threaten him with bodily harm until he confessed what Mor-Lath had said to him. If Mor-Lath was speaking with Mikal, who else was he speaking to?

The four women stood outside Natan's front gate. Only Ari had thought to bring a lantern. She lifted it high, illuminating them all. Mira hitched up her bag that held her Book of the Light, the glass and a few other things.

The moon gave just enough light to keep the village from utter darkness. Chloe grabbed Ari and Adrastea's arms. "Who is Master M?" she asked. Adrastea heard steel behind her smooth voice.

"Does it matter?" Adrastea said.

"Yes, I think it does. You haven't told me anything about him. If you don't like him, there must be a reason. That reason seems to be good enough for the Mayor. I must know."

Adrastea jerked her arm away from Chloe's grasp. She put her hands on her hips and faced off the taller woman. "Do you want to know? Really and truly?"

Mira cleared her throat loudly. Ari warned, "Adrastea…"

Mira slid in front of her. Behind her back, she waved a cautionary finger at Adrastea. "Mo— Master M consorts with Darkness. He may be all smooth words and charming smiles, but don't you be fooled. He's been the source of much trouble here. The reason behind Marta's leaving was because of him. And we have reason to believe he may have been involved in a death that happened some weeks ago."

Chloe blinked and looked away, but she hadn't released her hold on Ari. "And when you confront him with it, what does he say?"

Mira folded her arms. "He refuses to give us a straight answer."

Chloe didn't say anything at first. Because Ari's lantern was behind Chloe's head, her face was cast in shadow. "And you are sure," Chloe said finally, "that he consorts with Darkness?"

"Very sure. He told us himself. At least on that point he has been honest."

Chloe's arms tightened. Her shoulders hunched. "A Dark priest comes among you. And you don't drive him out of town?"

The three women from Sacred Springs shuffled uncomfortably." He is a hard man to drive off," Ari offered by way of explanation.

"Yes," added Mira. "He keeps coming back and we're not sure how to get rid of him."

Chloe sounded impatient. "Then lock him up. If he won't go then he can surely stay at the Mayor's pleasure. Just don't let him come to expect breakfast. And if he causes further trouble, don't forget you have the Sacred Spring. Baptize him and cleanse him of his evil."

Ari brightened. "How long does he have to be held under? Ten minutes? Twenty? Can I do it?"

Mira laid a hand on the healer, thus silencing her. "I think we'll keep your suggestions in mind," Mira said. "If you see him, turn and run the other way."

Ari took Chloe firmly by the arm. "Here. I'll walk you home. You never know who you'll meet in the dark."

Chloe did her best to resist Ari, but the healer's superior strength won. Off they went, taking the lantern with them.

Mira and Adrastea made their way up the hill to Lillybet's house in darkness.

The moon cast enough light to let them see their path. The dust of the road had been churned by the constant coming-and-going of the Crossroaders handcarts. It muffled their footsteps.

"Did you have to tell her all that?" Adrastea insisted of Mira.

"I had to tell her something. Carles told me she had this funny way of looking at everything in only black and white and to tell her as little as possible until she needed to know. Thanks to Mikal, now she knows about Master M. So, we told her what she needed to know, nothing more." Mira sighed "At least she'll be more cautious about him."

"She suggested we baptize him."

Mira let out a small sound. In the darkness, Adrastea couldn't tell if it was a laugh. "We'd have to leave him under water for three hundred years before he was cleansed of his evil. Even then, I'm afraid it will have washed so much of him away there wouldn't be anything left."

Mira reached out a hand to Adrastea's arm. "The situation is getting worse, not better. He is coming out into the open, in front of people. I think he's trying to bring further pressure to bear. But whatever happens, you must not give in." Mira's fingernails dug in to her. "It is better to die in the Light than give in to the Dark."

Adrastea felt another arm drape over her shoulder, startling her. A dark shape came between her and Mira, cradling them both. The priestess let out a little squeak of fear. Her bag fell from her shoulder, landing in the dust with the distinctive sound of breaking glass.

"Evening, ladies," said Mor-Lath. "It's an awfully dark night for you two to be out wandering on your own. You never know who you'll run into."

Mira struggled to get away, but Mor-Lath's grip must have been strong. "Let me go." Her voice rose an octave.

He released her. She backed away until she stumbled into the bushes.

Adrastea didn't struggle. His arm felt so familiar across her shoulders.

"Oh, come now!" he chided. "Let me at least walk you home." With a flick of his finger, a gentle ball of light appeared before them, much like a lantern. It lit the fresh dirt road beneath their feet and the brush and grass. It floated in the air before them with no visible means of support.

Mira snatched her bag from the dust. "We don't want you here," she ranted. "Let her go and leave."

"That's not very nice," he purred. He slid behind Adrastea, wrapping his arms about her waist. Slowly he ran his hands up her bodice. When they reached her breasts, she squeaked in embarrassment and swatted them away. "You stop that." Adrastea retreated from him.

He put a hand over his heart. "You wound me again."

"You don't fool us," Mira spat, clutching her bag to her chest. "We see through you. We know what you're truly like, and we'll not tolerate one bit of you here."

Mor-Lath snorted derision at them, his face growing darker despite the soft glow that floated between them. "No, you don't know." He took a few steps closer. The ball followed him like a puppy. "Do you want to see what I'm truly like?" He drew upon the Deeper Power. The line on Adrastea's face came alive with it. "Keep your place, Priestess, or I shall show you all you don't want to see and more."

Adrastea looked at Mira. The priestess had wariness but not fear, in her eyes.

Then Adrastea knew. When it came to marriage, Mor-Lath was asking. Not demanding but asking. He kept on asking. He could have taken her against her will. Adrastea knew for sure that was well within his power. But he didn't. He asked and waited for the answer he wanted.

And Mira, poor weak-talented, short-statured Mira stood up to him every time. She did not waver, she did not back down. She stood her ground and defied him.

The action itself was easy. The courage behind it? That was the hard part.

Mira's example bolstered her own courage. She would say no and no and no until he gave up and went away. If he thought he could convert her to the Dark, to make her one of his priestesses, he had another think coming.

"Ha!" cried Adrastea as she pulled her own courage to her. "I don't see why you bother." Mira put a hand to her arm. Adrastea found it comforting and it gave her strength. "I'm not going to fall for your games anymore." She put her hand on Mira's, to draw strength from the priestess.

He studied her as she kept her defiant stance. "So be it. No more games."

If Adrastea thought he'd called upon the Deeper Power before, she had no idea just how little he'd tapped. He spread his arms and it was as if Creation itself flowed into him, filling him, overwhelming her. The line on her cheek vibrated until she couldn't tell where it ended, and she began. She put a hand to her face. How sweet the Power sang to her.

And it was like a chorus, a thousand strong, its siren song shaking her resolve.

The god in his full glory stood before them. Adrastea's knees quivered. Her very flesh wanted to flow to him.

Mira's grip on her arm grew painful. Adrastea felt the raw terror flowing from her. In front, the feeling of power grew, as pairs of little bright eyes manifested behind Mor-Lath. One by one, demons appeared, their dark bodies absorbing the light of the floating orb. More eyes lit up behind him, like wind rippling through wheat. Soon hundreds, if not thousands of demons surrounded them, the center of them being Mor-Lath. He stood there in all his awful glory and Adrastea swayed under the influence. The demons did not shriek or mock like they had around Marta but watched the women silently. Their yearnings for mortality, a craving through the Lines, plucked at her as if she could assuage it.

She felt the pull of Power and also of something else. Desire built within her—so familiar. Mor-Lath stepped towards her and reached out his hand. He stroked her cheek, sending ripples of his essence through her.

She took a step forward, but Mira pulled her back. "Don't," she chattered. "It's a trick."

He leaned forward and whispered into her ear. "You know me for what I am, yet you still yearn for me."

"No," Adrastea whispered back. "It's just another of your tricks."

"You crave Power."

"Not when you're absent."

He touched her face and let the Power flow through her. She gasped and lacked the strength to pull away. "Tell me how much you want it," he urged.

Speech fled her. Oh, it tasted sweet, this Power. It thrilled her body and begged to be used. Some tiny, ignored voice inside her told her to resist.

Her knees felt weak. She twined her arms about his neck and her mouth sought his. Oh, his kisses were sweet. The Deeper Power vibrated throughout her body until the voice of reason in the back of her head was silenced. She wanted to press her skin against him and pull as much as she could from him. He gave her all the Power she wanted and more until her head fairly buzzed with it. She clung to him hungrily and protested when his head pulled back. "You can have all this and more," he tempted her. "So much more. Marry me..."

A second voice sounded in her ear. "Fight back, Adrastea!" She wanted the voice to go away and let her revel in the sweetness that coursed through her body. A hand fell on her shoulders, pulling her back. "He's tricking you!"

It was as if a bucket of cold water poured over her.

Mira was right; he was tricking her again. She had come so close to saying yes. She pushed away from him with both hands and felt the Power drain away. It was almost painful, and she wished for it back. She stumbled into Mira's waiting arms. Mira pushed her upright and held her firm, a pillar of support. Adrastea sobbed. The sudden withdrawal of Power combined with the sting of betrayal made her heart ache.

Mor-Lath stepped forward, his hand outreached. "Adrastea, please..." It sounded like begging. "I need you."

She leaned toward him.

Adrastea felt something cold press against her neck. "Forgive me," Mira whispered in her ear as she drew a sharp slice down her throat.

A warmth flowed onto her cool skin. A stinging pain shot through her neck.

Through the line on her face an adrenal flash of panic blossomed.

Mira's body was torn from her, to fly through the air. It landed, quite inelegantly, in the dust. Something glittered as it shot from her lifeless hand. A shard of glass. Adrastea's vision darkened. Everything went numb as she fell forward.

Strong arms caught her. "Adrastea," a panicked voice said to her from the other end of the tunnel. "Stay with me."

She felt a gentle hand on her throat. The stinging went away, the numbness departed, and her vision returned.

In the dust, Mor-Lath cradled her. Had she fallen? His hand rested on her forehead. "Give yourself a moment for the blood to return."

Her bodice felt damp against her chest. She plucked at it. Her hand was red.

A flood of relief flowed over her. Mor-Lath's?

She looked up at him. Worry creased his forehead. Behind him the little glowing ball waited.

Mira?

Adrastea pushed herself up.

Mira had not moved. Adrastea struggled free from Mor-Lath and crawled through the rocks and dirt to Mira's side.

It was not her healer's skills but the Lines of Deeper Power that revealed the truth.

Mira was dead, killed by Mor-Lath's hand.

Adrastea's hatred bloomed. Rage filled her. The Deeper Power blossomed within her. She grasped it, drawing upon as much as she could. As she stood up, she let it fuel her anger. "You killed her."

Mor-Lath held up a finger and took a step back. "She killed you first."

"You didn't have to kill her!" She advanced on him.

He took another backwards step. "I would do anything I need to, for you, Adrastea."

A red curtain fell across her eyes. She called all the Power within her and threw it at the god. She felt it strike Mor-Lath, knocking him into the dust. All that was in her, she poured out onto him. If she could have pounded him into the earth she would have. She struck at him over and over until the power was all gone.

When the last of it left her hands, she fled, her feet guiding her on a path her eyes couldn't see. Fury roared in her ears. If Mor-Lath knew what was good for him, he'd not come after her.

ↄ◉ଛ◉ↄ

Chapter 19

Mor-Lath lay imbedded in the dust of the road, several rocks pressing painfully into his back. A good thing his betrothed hadn't realized her full strength yet. Rage blurred her focus, much to his relief.

"This time, you've gone too far, Mor-Lath." Death watched Adrastea flee into the darkness.

"Perhaps," he admitted, dusting the country dirt from his clothes.

"She won't forgive you for this."

He didn't say anything but tightened his grip on Mira's surprised soul. "You've been quite a handful of trouble," he told the dead priestess.

Even in death, she stood up to him. "I will always oppose you, Dark One."

"You surprise me." He had not expected Mira's choice to sacrifice Adrastea's life to save her soul. "Few people can do that."

"Better dead in the Light, than living in Darkness." The fear that had dogged her in life had disappeared. "You cannot harm me now." Oh, her defiance was endless.

"Oh, really?" he taunted her.

"Give me the soul, Mor-Lath." Death held out her hand.

He didn't relinquish it.

"It won't do you any good. In the end, her good deeds outweigh her bad ones."

Mor-Lath stared at Death. "She tried to kill my bride."

"She is not your bride yet."

"She will be."

Death gave a demanding shake of her hand. "Give me the soul. She is destined for the Light."

He shrugged and let Mira go. "She can't interfere now."

Death pursed her lips as she claimed the soul. "The Priestess, no. But you reft her before her time. The Light is not pleased about this."

"Oh, the Light is never pleased over what I do," he snarled. "They'd see me destroyed, if it wasn't for what I do for Them. Why should I care what They think?"

Death cradled Mira's soul, comforting it after its rather sudden transference from mortality to eternity. A small smile played on her lips. "Because for every stupid thing you do, because of your pride, or your selfishness, it tips the Balance against you. And now that you've irreparably offended your Bride, I can't wait to see the consequences. She'll never be yours now. It's all over."

"It is not over until I am dead."

⁂

Bastard," Adrastea chanted as she fled up the hill, "bastard, bastard, bastard!" Her anger and rage had settled to a cold thirst for... she wasn't sure yet, but she would figure it out. And Mor-Lath would feel the brunt of it.

Bugger that he was a god and bugger that he might not be able to be hurt by mortal means. She knew what he wanted, and she had full power over denying him that.

Her flight slowed but she huffed determinedly on, up to the Spring, up where the air was clear and up to where Mira had so recently communed with the Light. It was not right he was allowed to kill people at his whim.

He had to have killed her mother, too. It was far too convenient for Lillybet's death to be an 'accident'. The bastard would pay for that as well. For every person he killed, she would make him pay. Even if it took her the rest of her life, she would find a way to make him suffer.

Something else bothered her as well; she could still taste him on her lips. Her face burned with more than exertion. She wanted to curl up and scrub the influence of him from under her skin. His essence still thrummed within her traitorous body.

It wasn't her thoughts, she told herself. It was purely his influence. It had to be. No woman in her right mind would willingly choose him, knowing what she knew about him.

If only she had a dull knife and three weeks, possibly four, oh, what she would do to him.

No way in Creation would she agree to marry him now. The passions were a trick. As long as she kept one thought to herself, it would be, "Say no." She repeated it to herself. Say no, say no, say no.

What did he want from her?

By the pale moonlight, she found the marshy edges of the Sacred Spring. She dipped her hands into the cold, cold water, splashing it over her burning face. She pulled off her clothes and stepped in, gasping in shock as the cold water stung her legs. Naked and not caring, she washed herself. If she scrubbed hard enough, maybe his influence would go away.

She could not have felt more violated. That was a seduction. The worst part of it was that she wanted it—begged for it. She embraced him. She kissed him. She would have done anything he said, if only it meant more Power. But it had been all his doing. She had been a foolish, foolish girl for letting his passion take her by surprise. He knew she was unprepared. That had been her mistake. She had betrayed herself.

"Well, no more!" she shrieked out to the moon that watched her with a lazy eye, never winking, never seeing, reflecting only the light of the sun and having none of its own.

Her body shivered. She wrapped her arms around herself. "Light," she prayed. "What am I to do?"

"Well, you can get out of the Spring, you daft girl. You're contaminating the water."

Adrastea whirled around, ashamed at her nakedness. She hadn't seen the gentle light approach. Now it showed her secrets bare.

An ancient woman in brown rags set down the lantern and the bucket she carried. She picked up Adrastea's clothing. Her gnarled hands shook and her voice wavered as well. "Come here and we'll help you dress."

Adrastea stepped from the spring and shook the excess water from her limbs. The faintest stirring of breezes and guilt caused goose pimples to rise on her flesh.

"Barmy, she is," the old woman muttered as she tossed Adrastea's skirt to her and shook out the underthings. "Dry yourself with that, then get dressed in the rest."

Adrastea complied. She felt a bit better once mostly clothed. She shook her skirt to help it dry before she put it on.

The old woman picked up her bucket. She peered into the spring and hmphed to herself. "Look at what she's done," she cackled. "We'll have to wait until that clears before we get some water."

Adrastea kept her distance but moved over to peer into the inky darkness of the Spring.

"Ah," the old woman said, cocking a wink and a smile at her. "You see it too, don't you?"

Adrastea turned her face away and sniffed.

"We can see there is much evil on you, lass." The woman came closer. Adrastea could smell the strong scent of lavender oil and peppermint. At least she didn't stink of filth. "How can someone be so covered in filth, yet have such a bright soul?"

That gave Adrastea pause. "I... what?"

"Oh, you're a daughter of the Light, no doubt there. Powerful one too," she said, after giving Adrastea a sniff. "But what forces have you been tangling with, girl? You're no priestess, Adrastea."

Adrastea wrapped her arms around herself. "You have the advantage of me, old woman."

The woman snorted. "We knew of your father. You look a lot like him. At least you don't feel like your mother."

"My mother is dead." Her heart ached. "Thank you for bringing up painful memories.

"Sorry to hear that," the woman replied. It sounded like she meant it.

"Who the Light are you?"

The old woman hunkered down next to the Spring. "I was called Crozie, once."

That took Adrastea's breath away. "What? The Crozie? Th— the priestess before Mira? That Crozie?"

The old woman nodded.

Adrastea let out a sigh. She didn't feel so bitter, now. "But Mira said you were dead."

"No, just gone. We had our reasons, so don't bother asking." She looked up from her scrying of the water. "How is Mira?"

The pain of loss hit Adrastea hard. "She's dead!"

"Hm. Lot of that going around."

Adrastea flung herself on the grass in grief. Crozie let her cry it out. The old woman scooped up her bucket of water. "So, how'd she die?"

Adrastea raised her head. "Murdered."

"When this happen?"

"Tonight." How could this old woman be so uncaring?

Crozie had picked up her lantern but she put it back down. "Tonight? How'd it happen?"

Adrastea laid her head down. "It doesn't matter," she told the grass.

Crozie came over and sat down next to her, placing the lantern near her head. "We think it does. You can't lie to us, girl, not without us knowing." She huffed and settled herself in a comfortable sitting position, close enough to touch, yet not touching. "Tell me: did Mira walk in the Light?"

Adrastea sat up and wiped her face dry. "Oh, yes. She was a good priestess."

"Oh, good. She wasn't very talented. We feared she'd turn to the Dark."

Adrastea hugged her knees to her chest. Really? That wasn't the Mira she knew. "No. Quite the opposite." Adrastea took a breath and chose to confide in this strange old woman who, by all accounts, should have been dead. "She died defending me against the Dark."

But instead of agreeing at Mira's heroics, Crozie snorted. "Foolish girl. She should have known better than to go up against a Dark priest."

"Oh? Why?"

Crozie threw her palsied hands into the air as if illustrating a story. "Oh, they know all sorts of nasty tricks. Twisting truths, bending Creation... things of that ilk. But there's ways around that."

"How do you fight against something like that?"

Crozie smiled and tapped the side of her nose. "Easiest way? Kill them."

"What?" Adrastea nearly leapt to her feet. "You're jesting me."

Crozie laughed. "No. Killing them's one of the kindest things you can do."

"But killing another person is against the Light."

"Salvation hurts them more." She scooted closer to Adrastea. Adrastea wasn't sure this was such a good idea. "See, the Spring has divine properties. The Light once walked here and when Her feet touched the earth, this Spring came forth. So, what you do is bring the Dark priest up here and dunk him in. That washes away the evil tainting his soul."

"Then he's redeemed?"

"Nah. With the burden of Evil gone, it's safe to kill them, knowing their soul will go to the Light."

Adrastea stared at her in horror.

Crozie stared back, her wavery eyes glittering in the lamplight. "I jest about that last part. We've never killed any Dark priests after baptism, but it sure hurts them while the evil is being washed away."

She couldn't believe her ears. "You've done this? How many times?"

"Just the once. Should have heard him scream." And Crozie chuckled at the memory.

Adrastea shuddered. This was a priestess of the Light? "But what does it do to them?"

"Told you. Washes away the evil. Granted, it leaves them a bit addled. But when you've seen what they did to your people, you don't care. You got someone who needs a baptism?"

Adrastea mused this over. "Oh, yes. Say, this wouldn't work if I carried a vial of Spring water around with me?"

"Alas, no. It's not the water itself that is blessed but the ground from whence it flows. Stand here and not even Mor-Lath himself can touch you here."

She brightened. "Really?" She wiped at her running nose.

Crozie gave her a narrow look. "We sense you've got more to tell us."

Adrastea folded her arms on her knees and laid her chin on top of them. "Promise you won't think bad of me if I do?" Not that Crozie had any high moral ground to stand on, with her callous dunking of Dark priests.

"You're a good person at heart. Tell me."

She did. "Mor-Lath, God of the Dark, wants to marry me." Adrastea let the whole tale come tumbling out, from her first encounter to why she now sat by the Sacred Spring.

"Bloody hell, girl," shrieked Crozie. "What are you going to do?"

"I don't know," Adrastea confessed. "How do I fight him?"

"To be honest? I don't know." Crozie groaned and stood. "Sorry. Our old bones aren't what they once were." She picked up her lantern and her bucket and trudged back to the forest. The light of the lantern wavered about, making the shadows of trees dance.

Adrastea scrambled after her. "Please, Crozie Priestess. Tell me how to fight him. I don't want to marry him now."

Crozie stopped and straightened up. "'Now'? You saying you wanted to marry him at one time?"

Adrastea shut her mouth.

"And why don't you?" Crozie continued. "Go off and have fat babies.

It's the end of an Era, the prophecies say, when the world turns itself upside down and you can't tell the men from the women and the birds don't know which way to fly and thousands drop dead in an instant. Might as well get some loving out of it before the hourglass turns."

"I don't love him."

"Does he love you?"

"Of course not." Adrastea followed her as far as the forest edge. "Please, tell me what to do."

Crozie turned. "We already told you what to do. Go off and have a son or two and leave us alone. Nobody can find us because we don't want to be found."

Adrastea started to follow but Crozie held up her lantern, barring her way. "Better stay here tonight, girl. If the Dark One's after you, you won't last long away from the confines of the Spring." She put down her bucket and lantern and pulled off what looked like several ragged shawls. "Take these and leave them by the Spring in the morning. Summer's nearly over and it is a tad cold at night."

Then Crozie left, to become a bobbing werelight in the forest before disappearing completely.

Adrastea found a thick clump of grass near the Spring. It was here she curled up. Yet, despite the shawls, the coldness of the ground seeped through. It wasn't until the warmth of the rising sun fell upon her, that she was finally able to sleep.

Mikal Mayorprentice had quite a list of chores. First thing in the morning, before he got his breakfast, he headed up the hill on Natan's orders to check on Little Crossroads. On his way up, he found Jak Carpenter, kneeling by something on the ground. "Jak?" he called out across the path. Something in his stomach told him he didn't want to approach.

Jak raised his head, tears streaming down his wrinkled old face. Next to him, in the dust, lay Mira. She was too still and her face too pale. Jak had folded her hands neatly across her chest and had pillowed her head with his jacket. Like his mother, Mikal knew that she was not sleeping. There was no soul in that body. "Fetch Natan, will you lad?" Jak asked.

Mikal didn't need to be told twice.

"Uncle Natan!" Mikal shouted as soon as he burst through the Mayor's door. "Mira's dead!"

At first, Natan didn't say anything, his pen poised over his journal. He set it down carefully, quietly. "Where?"

"Up on the hill, towards Adrastea's house."

Natan pressed his knuckles to his mouth and frowned. "And where's Adrastea?"

Mikal shook his head. He knew nothing of her whereabouts.

"Bugger," Natan muttered as he slammed his journal shut, forgetting about the wet ink. "I pray he didn't." To Mikal he issued another order. "Go fetch Ari and Mi— uh, Chloe. Tell Ari but don't tell Chloe why. Meet us on the hill."

Mikal nodded once and headed off to finish his task. As he ran through the village, he realized Natan wasn't excluding him. He had implied he come along. Mikal felt important. Maybe he'd find out what Natan was talking about.

Who would kill Mira?

Natan seemed to know more about Mira's death than one would suppose.

As Chloe intimidated him, Mikal headed to Ari's house first. He found her pulling weeds. "Ari! Natan needs you up on the hill. Mira's dead."

Ari ceased cursing at the weeds. She stood up. "What?" Her forehead wrinkled in a funny way. "You could have said it kinder," she recommended before breaking out into noisy sobs. Then she sank down in the dirt and cried hard.

Mikal squirmed. He didn't mean to say it like he did; he hated to see her cry like this. He excused himself. "I've got to get Chloe. Natan told me not to tell her why. I'll uh, be back soon." He lit out as quickly as he could.

He knocked at Chloe's door, When she opened it, she looked rumpled and grumpy as if he'd woken her up.

"What?" she grunted.

He took a step back. "Natan bids you come. But we've gotta get Ari first."

"Couldn't you have fetched her first without me?"

"I did." He stubbed a toe in the dirt. "We'll have to go help her."

Chloe rolled her eyes. "Give me half an hour."

"Natan says right now."

Chloe glared at him, but Mikal wouldn't let her intimidate him. "Believe me," he explained. "You'll want to see this."

"Oh, some gay surprise, I suppose?"

Mikal felt he'd outworn his welcome. He backed down the path to the front gate. "Surprise, yes. Gay? Only if you've got strange tastes." He turned out through the gate. "Be there or the Mayor won't be pleased with you."

"Be where?" she called after him.

"Just head up the hill!" he called.

Ari, her face red and damp, met him on the road. He led her to where Natan knelt by Mira's body. Jak Carpenter sat in the dust, silent and mournful. Natan had Mira's head in his lap. The tears ran down his face. He smoothed the dark hair back and examined the few silver threads there.

When Natan saw Ari, he released Mira's head and held his arms to Ari. They hugged each other in their grief.

Natan, over Ari's shoulder, said to Mikal, "Go up to Lilly's and get a shroud." Then he returned to his sorrow.

Mikal nodded, swallowing the lump in his throat. He liked Mira. She'd never called him by the wrong name, like so many others did with the Innkeeper brood. She'd spoken kindly to him. While she never singled him out for any particular attention, he knew that to her, he wasn't just another kid.

His eyes blurred. Jak put a hand on his shoulder. "You stay here, lad. I'll get the shroud."

Mikal nodded. He sat next to Mira. A body didn't look the same after death, did it? A part of it was gone.

"He did this, didn't he?" Ari said eventually.

Natan looked in her face. His look affirmed the answer. Mikal felt left in the dark. He who?

They clung to each other tighter and cried harder. Ari muttered something about Adrastea.

So, Adrastea knew something, did she? Mikal gave Mira one last pat and stood. He'll go ask her and he won't take anything but a straight answer.

He met Jak coming down with a sheet for a shroud. Mikal inquired, "What did Adrastea say?"

Jak shook his head. "She wasn't there. Mistress Weaver gave this to me."

Where could she be? Mikal went to Adrastea's house. Maybe she had been in the outhouse or something. He checked the newly planted garden, then went inside the house.

Mistress Weaver didn't acknowledge his presence until he greeted her and inquired after his sister.

"No, I haven't seen her," Mistress Weaver said, as her hands slowed their work. "She may be up in Little Crossroads."

He checked there but nobody had seen her. "We'll keep an eye out for her," one of them said. "Let her know you're looking for her."

He went to the village, though he thought she wouldn't be there. If she had been there, she would have been with Ari, most likely.

He returned to Mira's body. Ari had already wrapped the diminutive priestess.

Natan carried Mira's body down the path, followed by Ari, Jak and Mikal. They took her to Natan's house.

Mikal ran on to Ari's house, in case Adrastea had shown up there.

No sister.

Then he saw a washed and neatly-dressed Chloe step out of her cottage. "Took your sweet time," he chastised her. "The Mayor wasn't asking for a social visit."

Chloe frowned at Mikal.

"Anyhow," he continued. "They're now at Natan's house. You'd better hurry up. I don't think he's going to be too happy with you." Then he skipped off before she could ask for a further explanation. He headed toward the inn in case his sister might have stopped to talk to Martine. A long shot but he was running out of ideas.

His foster siblings hadn't seen her for quite some time.

Adrastea had to be somewhere. But where could she be? "Blast it, Adrastea. Where are you?" he muttered aloud as he stalked away from the Inn.

Master M caught his arm. "Slow down, lad. She's up at the Spring."

Mikal jumped. Master M wasn't there a moment ago. "Bloody Light," he cursed, then put his fingers to his mouth. "Oh, sorry." Marta would have slapped him for his blasphemy, but Master M didn't flinch.

"She's not too happy with me," Master M continued, "so kindly don't mention you've run into me here. And please don't take anything she says as gospel. Angry women are like that."

Mikal nodded and headed up towards the Spring. There she was, just as Master M said she would be. He found her fast asleep in a clump of grass. She smelled strongly of lavender. He gave her a shake. "Adrastea. Wake up."

She startled and sat up, nearly punching Mikal in the chest. "Light! Don't do that!" Then she groaned and put her hand to her head. "What the hell do you want?"

"Natan wants you. Mira's dead."

Unlike the others, she did not react but kept rubbing her aching head. "I know. I was there when it happened."

"Bloody Light! Why didn't you go get anyone?"

"I was too angry."

A cold stone of fear sank to the bottom of Mikal's stomach. "Light," he whispered. "You didn't kill her, did you?"

"No, I bloody well didn't," she shouted. "Mor-Lath did, and I'll never forgive him for it. He killed our mother too, did you know?"

Mikal gaped at her. What was his sister saying? Had she gone mad, the way their mother Lillybet had?

Adrastea leapt to her feet and paced angrily. "He's been nothing but trouble since he showed up, the bastard!" She catalogued all the prolonged and painful things she planned on doing to him when she caught him.

A cold pit formed in his belly. "What? You mean Master M?" Mikal could only shake his head. "He can't have. He's too nice."

Adrastea paused. "The hell he is. It's just an act. He'll say and do anything, but I'll not marry him. And you can bloody well tell him that. You'd best not speak to him again if you value your soul." Then she started muttering to herself, using several very unpleasant words.

Mikal waited until she ran out of ways to punish her suitor. "I think you'd best see Natan. He and Ari think you've— um..." He wasn't sure himself what they thought but whatever it was, it concerned them gravely.

"Oh, Light." Adrastea threw her hands in the air. "They must think I've gone with him." She grasped his shoulders. "Please tell them I'm all right but I can't leave the Spring. And could you bring me some food? I'm starving. Oh, and a few blankets."

"What? Why?"

Her grip tightened on his arms. He squirmed. "He can't get me here, see?"

"He already knows you're here. He told me how to find you."

"What?" Her voice increased several decibels. "The bastard!"

To his relief, she released him. "You really don't know who he is, do you?"

Mikal shook his head.

"He's the bloody God of the Dark." And she folded her arms, waiting for his reaction.

He stared at her, waiting for the rest of the explanation but that was it. "He what?" Then it sunk in. "Wait a minute! You saying...?"

She slowly nodded.

"Bloody hell. You're jesting me."

"Now you know why Natan told you to stay away from him."

"Wait. You're serious? Master M is really Mor-Lath? The Mor-Lath?"

Her face confirmed that he was.

"But... why?" he asked. "What does he want?"

Adrastea's anger evaporated, leaving weariness behind. "Please don't ask me that. Just let Natan know I'm all right but I can't leave the Spring. It's the only safe place for me right now.

"But, what's to stop him from coming here?" He meant Mor-Lath.

She gave him a tired smile. "It's holy ground. He can't tread here."

"But you can't live here forever."

Adrastea dropped her head into her shaking hands. "I'm hungry. I can't think much beyond breakfast. Just— just do this, will you?"

He nodded. He looked to the trees beyond the meadow. "He wouldn't kill me too, would he?"

Adrastea opened her mouth then shut it. Best not to say what was on her mind. "I think he likes you." Then she waved him away before returning to her grass nest. "Just deliver my message to Uncle Natan. He can come see me here if he wishes."

Chapter 20

As he headed back, Mikal pondered over what his sister had told him. Mikal never put much store into Mira's parables at the dinner table. And what about the stories told by guests around the Inn's fireplace? How could one tell the tales from the truth? Master M claimed his name was Mor-Lath but for him to be the actual god? It was too fantastic.

Master M—Mor-Lath—had had nothing but kind words for Mikal. When Uncle Natan forbade him from speaking to him again, Mikal couldn't understand why.

Unless Uncle Natan knew something.

Could Master M have killed Mira? Mikal couldn't see why he would want to. He had thought Natan had let him in to the adult business surrounding Master M. But if what Adrastea said was true, there were still many, many untold things.

If Natan didn't want him talking to Master M, he could have at least explained specifics. Mikal knew too much now. He had to be told everything.

What about Chloe? Mira had kept the priestess in the dark. Now that Mira was dead, how much did Chloe know?

Mikal quickened his step. If Chloe was to be told, it would be now. If he hurried, he might learn something new.

Natan sat on the edge of his porch with a mug of tea and an apple. His eyes were puffy from crying. Mikal joined him, his eyes glancing to the closed door. "What's going on in there?"

Natan shrugged and sipped his tea. "They're washing the body. Best we clean her up a bit before we took her home."

Mikal pulled his legs to his chest and hugged them. "Will there be a wake?"

Natan swallowed a bite of apple. "I suppose so. Lots of people liked Mira."

"But will they bring food? She's got no family."

"She's got us."

"That doesn't mean anything," Mikal muttered. "They didn't bring food for Lilly—and we were family."

"I think this will be different."

"It shouldn't have been." The words were more for himself than Uncle Natan.

His uncle put an arm around the boy and hugged him. "I'd like to say it'll be all right, but I don't know that." He sunk down. "Or maybe now it will be, now that he's gone."

"Who's gone?"

"Your Master M."

Mikal didn't understand. "Why would he be gone?"

"Well, he got what he came for."

"Which is?"

Natan looked at his nephew and apprentice. "Master M was Mor-Lath, God of the Dark."

If he was expecting Mikal to be surprised at this news, he must have been disappointed.

"I already knew that. Adrastea told me."

Natan sat up straight, pulling his arm off Mikal. "When did you learn that?"

"This morning." Oh, the message. "She's up at the Spring."

Natan coughed and spluttered.

"She told me she's not coming down because of him. She really hates him now, doesn't she? But I can't blame her if all what you've said is true…"

As soon as Natan recovered from his coughing he was off like a shot.

"She wanted you to bring her some breakfast!" Mikal called after him.

Apparently, Natan didn't hear him. Mikal stood up, muttered something about wanting breakfast himself, and stepped inside the house.

He saw the two women washing the bare body of Mira. Mikal shaded his eyes. "Oh, I'm so sorry." He made to back out, but Ari said, "No, it's all right."

Chloe lifted the shroud and covered the body. Mikal came inside and closed the door. "Just wanted some breakfast," he excused himself. The women had laid the body out on the breakfast table. "Oh, blight," Mikal whined. "That's where we eat."

Ari sniffed and squeezed out the water from a rag into a bowl.

"Didn't you eat this morning?" the new Priestess wondered.

"No." Mikal regarded her, then looked to Ari. "Anyhow, it's not for me." He jerked a thumb at the door. "Natan's off on some business. If I tell you, you'll run off too." Mikal pilfered the pantry.

Ari dropped her rag. "Mikal..." she said in way of warning.

"Promise you won't run off?"

Chloe put her hands on her hips. "What are you talking about?"

Mikal put food into a gunny sack and slung it across his shoulders. "Oh, and I'll need some blankets." He headed towards the bedroom and returned with a quilt from the press.

Ari grabbed his arm. "Will you please explain?"

Mikal pulled free. "Just this: she's all right." No way was he telling her more until he got more information. He slipped out the door and walked slower than normal.

He heard the door open like he knew it would. "Mikal Prentice, where is she?" Ari called. She came after him.

Mikal, already at the gate, turned, gave her a cheeky grin and said, "Gotta go!" Then he lit off down the street, turning right, not left, at the smithy. He hoped he could outrun the Healer. Easily outpacing her, he doubled back behind the smithy then took off up the hill towards the Spring.

He found Natan and Adrastea sitting next to the Spring, having a deep conversation. They ceased as soon as he approached. Breathlessly, he dropped the bag and blankets at their feet. He pointed a finger at Adrastea. "You owe me one favor."

Natan frowned when he saw the offering. "You can't stay here for the rest of your life," he told her.

"I can't get to the house from here," she countered. "And that won't be much better than a jail."

"A house is more comfortable than an open meadow," Mikal quipped.

Natan scowled at his apprentice. "Mikal," he warned.

He gave his uncle his best innocent look. "What?"

Natan rubbed his forehead with his hands. "I am not equipped to deal with this right now." He stood up. "Stay here if you wish, Adrastea. I've a funeral to arrange."

He started down the hill. Mikal followed, glancing back at his sister. She leaned forward and drew the bag to her, mouthing "Thank you" to him. He grinned and hurried after the Mayor.

Adrastea owed him a favor now. Maybe it could be repaid in information if he was unable to glean more from the others.

⁂

A ri brushed Mira's hair. Her best friend looked so peaceful in death. Chloe watched nearby, having straightened up Natan's home for want of something better to do. Occasionally her lips would twitch but she wouldn't say anything. What was going through that head of hers? Ari plucked out a few more of Mira's silver hairs so she wouldn't look so old. She smoothed a few of her own back.

"Chloe, could you do me a favor and fetch some clean clothes for Mira?"

Chloe sprang to her feet. "Gladly." And she left as quickly as she could.

Only then would Ari let herself cry again. She dropped into a chair and lowered her head to the table next to Mira's. Whose death was next? How long would this go on—until Adrastea gave in or they all were dead? She feared the latter, for this murder would alienate Adrastea from Mor-Lath forever.

If she understood Mikal's cryptic message, Adrastea was alive and safe—if safe had any meaning at all. There had to be a way of stopping the Dark God. But how does one stop a god? The easiest way would be to sacrifice Adrastea to him. Then maybe he'd go away and leave the rest of them alone. But to what sort of life would that damn Adrastea? It all came down to the question of why he wanted her. He needed her willing; that was for sure. To thwart him, all she had to do was say no.

But at what price?

What price could one put on a young woman's life? Mira's for sure and possibly Lillybet's lives had been sacrificed. Who else? Would Ari be next?

Ari wasn't that keen on dying. She glanced sideways at Mira's profile. "Was your death worth the price?" Would hers be? She wasn't eager to find out.

Why did they have to die? Why would any more die, should it come to that? More deaths weren't going to convince Adrastea unless he wanted to threaten her. If that was so, why not just threaten to kill everyone in the first place?

It didn't make sense. Ari wanted a drink. No doubt Natan had something stashed somewhere. No. Ari would wait until tonight when she could drink as much as she wanted, and nobody would say anything.

Harvest was coming. She'd have to make beer soon.

Natan and Mikal returned, closing the door gently behind them.

Ari raised her head. "Well?"

Natan said, "Adrastea's all right."

Ari collapsed back to the table. "Oh, thank the Light!"

Natan sat down at the table. Mikal moved to sit down as well but Natan beckoned to him. "Head upstairs and fetch us a nice bottle of something, will you lad?"

Mikal, his bottom halfway to a chair, made a face and rolled his eyes. But he acquiesced to his master's wishes faster than Ari expected.

"Well?" she said, eagerly leaning towards Natan as soon as Mikal was out of earshot. "Did you learn what happened?"

"Not really," he confessed. "She's become a very closed-mouth young woman since he showed up. There's a few secrets there."

Ari gasped. "You don't think they've..." she looked askance and cleared her throat.

"I don't want to think about that." He cleared his own throat and leaned closer. "What I did get is that Mira did something to displease Mor-Lath." When Ari started to ask what, he held up his hand. "She didn't tell me, and I didn't press but he killed Mira." He scooted his chair even closer. "But hark to this: she says when she was up at the Spring she encountered Crozie!"

"Crozie's dead."

Natan shook his head. "No, she went missing. Not the same thing. We never found a body."

"We've never found her alive either. Surely if she's living up in the woods we would have come across her sooner or later."

"I don't know." Natan held up a finger. "But I do know this: ghosts and angels don't fetch water."

Ari swallowed. It would have been a great help if Crozie had been alive. Mira had never been half the Priestess Crozie had been. Crozie was clever and her tongue was quick. But after her beloved sister died, Crozie withdrew. She disappeared, leaving a fully-trained yet woefully-undertalented Mira in her place.

"Adrastea said, that Crozie said, that as long as she stood at the Spring, Mor-Lath couldn't touch her."

"And she believed this?"

Natan sat back. "What? Don't you believe it's true?"

Ari wasn't sure. "Well, we haven't had a baptism in a long time. Nobody comes to the Spring any more. I thought the stories of healings and purgings were true but..." She'd heard stories of how the waters of the Spring had powerful properties, to cure madness and heal the sick and raise the nearly-dead. She shook her head. "I don't hold store in that any more. I'm having a hard time believing in the Light at the moment. If the Dark God can show up here and do the things he's done, then where is the Light? Why isn't She here setting things to right?"

Natan sighed. He didn't know either, apparently.

Ari grasped his hands. "Mira and Carles had a fast before he left. Carles told me they had a vision but neither one told me what it was. You don't think it had anything to do with Adrastea, do you? Do you think that's why Mor-Lath killed Mira? Mira learned something, and he didn't want Adrastea to know?"

But Natan shook his head. "Mira had plenty of time to tell Adrastea what she saw. The death had to be about something else." Natan swallowed. "I'm thirsty. Where's that boy?"

Natan looked around, then slowly lifted his head to the ceiling. "Get down here, boy," he shouted. "Eavesdropping's bad form."

There was a guilty scramble. Mikal returned from the attic. He slunk red-faced into the kitchen from the back door and drew the cork of the bottle. Ari sighed that he'd only brought one.

"You might as well sit and listen here, Mikal. You know the rules; promise you won't share this with anybody."

"Yes sir," he mumbled and drew up his own chair. He did pour three glasses though.

"So, do we leave her up there?" Natan asked, nodding his head towards the Spring.

Ari finished her glass and poured another one. She toasted Mira wordlessly and drained her drink. When she'd had a good swallow, she regarded her empty glass. "There's a saying I remember Crozie quoting when we were young: 'The Light goes to bed at sunset.'"

"Meaning?"

"I think she's safe enough in the village by daylight but had better be somewhere safe come dark."

⁓⦿ֆᘐ⤳

Chloe headed up to the house Mira had shared with Adrastea Healer. Nobody answered her knock, so she let herself into the dark interior.

Mira's box was in the bedroom. Chloe resisted the temptation to look through Adrastea's belongings, but Mira's were fair game. Most likely all would come to her as now-rightful Priestess of Sacred Spring. For a moment she marveled at Master Carles' insight in sending her. She had balked when he told her it would be permanent. This village was in desperate need of reform.

Did he know Mira would die so soon?

Her heart ached at the loss of a fellow priestess. She may have been weak and sloppy with her devotions, but she had been their priestess.

Mira's clothes were folded neatly on top of her precious five books—old, worn and well-read. Chloe looked through them. Nothing spectacular. She set them aside and looked through the bed linen. Most of it was serviceable, albeit worn. As she dug through to the bottom, her fingers felt something quite unlike the homespun feeling of the sheets—something soft and fine.

After lifting out the sheets, she found a parcel wrapped in the finest black fabric she had ever seen. It didn't seem right, this fine cloth amid the beige country homespun.

When she unwrapped the parcel, she found a book as black as the cloak, with a cover of fine leather and tooled in fancy scrollwork. Unlike the others, this book did not bear the marks of frequent use. Nor did it have a title.

Hastily she put it back. Something about this book was not right. If books were such a treasure, Chloe surmised, then what was this one doing buried away?

Put it away and forget about it, was her first thought. It was Mira's business and none of her own. Put it away and never look at it again.

Her fingers itched to open the cover of the book, if only to see the title.

There was no title, but her eyes caught the signature of a dedication: Mor-Lath.

"Light!" she cursed before she slammed the cover. Chloe leapt to her feet and backed away, bumping into the doorframe. She fought against her first desire to flee, and her second, more intellectual desire, to read the dedication. She took a few deep breaths, smoothed her skirt and her hair. Grasping the cover of the book with the edge of a sheet, like one would use a cloth on a hot pot, she lifted it again and read the elegant inscription.

She saw the words 'Adrastea', 'betrothed' and 'Mor-Lath' before the cover slipped from her numb fingers.

Chloe sat on the floor with a thump. "Light preserve us," she said aloud. Adrastea was a Dark Priestess! And what about Mira? Was she in this as well? The book was clearly Adrastea's, but it was in Mira's press. Did Mira find it and hide it away? Is that why she died?

Did Adrastea kill her?

Or were they both in this together?

A cold pit settled in Chloe's stomach. So, this was the secret everyone was trying to keep from her. They were protecting two of their own. The Light did not suffer witches to live.

She heard a noise outside and scrambled to standing. Hastily, she shoved the book and the cloak and all the linens back into the press, then went to listen by the bedroom door.

Nothing. She peeked out into the common room, before venturing out. False alarm. She returned to the bedroom and folded everything neatly, hesitating over the book. Should she put it back? Should she burn it? Burning it would be the best thing to do. She replaced the cloak in the box. She put the sheets and the clothes back best she could remember, keeping aside a selection of the nicest for Mira's body.

The fire was banked from last night. Chloe uncovered the coals and shoved the book in as far as she could. She laid bits of kindling on top and waited for them to alight. Once the fire burned brightly, she gathered Mira's clothes.

She left, after checking that no one watched the house. Dark Priestesses meant trouble.

As she returned to the Mayor's house, she mulled over the best way to approach the situation. From what little she knew, Adrastea had disappeared after she had killed Mira. Was she gone for good or would she return? If she returned, then what?

By the time she returned to the Mayor's house she was no closer to an answer. Until she knew more of what was happening here in this strange little village, she would keep her opinions to herself.

As she raised her hand to knock on the door, she listened first. Her intent was not to eavesdrop but to ensure she wasn't interrupting something.

"'The Light goes to bed at sunset,'" she heard Ari say.

"Meaning?" asked Natan.

"I think she's safe enough in the village by daylight but had better be somewhere safe come dark."

She who? Chloe knocked on the door. She stepped in without invitation. "Here are Mira's clothes. I chose the best ones."

Ari, Natan and his apprentice sat in a circle of chairs near Mira's head. They all held cups. Toasting the dead? "Do you want me to arrange the funeral?"

Natan and Ari straightened up but did not leave their chairs. "You are priestess now," Natan said. "Gathering wood may be more difficult, because of all the house building and extra people of late but I'm sure we can find enough for a pyre. Use Mikal to spread the news; that's what he's there for."

Mikal set his cup on the floor, there was too much dead Mira on the table to fit anything else. Chloe sighed at the thought of him doing important work. He wasn't that old—early teens—but old enough to carry messages reliably.

Chloe wished Carles was here. Despite his light attitude towards life, he could judge a situation more accurately than anyone else she knew. As soon as Fly came through next she would send a letter to Carles asking for advice. Surely, he knew about Adrastea. If he didn't, he ought to.

"Well?" said Natan. "Hop to it, boy. You don't need to tell them how she died. When they ask, tell them she suffered a fall on the hill. Laying-in will be at her cottage. You and I will be there, as will Chloe."

Mikal gave the Mayor a sour look. "Do I have to tell them all that?"

Natan fixed him with a firm look. "Mikal..."

"All right, all right. I'm going." He flung himself out of the chair and headed out the door.

Chloe took the chair the apprentice recently vacated. She chose the method of her attack. "So, when were you going to tell me about Adrastea?"

Natan and Ari exchanged glances. "What do you know?" Natan

asked. He was going to play this game carefully.

Chloe didn't blame him. The girl was his niece and the journeyman of his not-so-secret lover. Was nothing in this village honest? "I know of her connection and involvement with the Dark God."

To her surprise, both Natan and Ari relaxed. "Ah, that," he said. "Tricky business, dealing with gods, especially that one."

"I know she is your niece but why do you tolerate such things in your village? Does your constable know?"

Natan leaned back and scrubbed his hand through his hair. "As to that last thing, we have no constable," he admitted with some reluctance. "We're just not big enough for one. If there is trouble, I'm the one who sorts things out."

"I see your conflict of interest." Her eyes flickered to Mira's body. "I trust she knew?"

Natan nodded. "She knew. I knew, and Ari knew, as well as Mikal and Lillybet, my sister. Nobody else knows. I think it best we keep it that way. Oh, wait," he amended. "Carles knows."

Chloe stared at him. Carles knew? He knew and didn't tell her? He all but signed her name to the village book and couldn't tell her this one Very Important Thing? "Does he know everything?"

"I believe so. Mira did tell him a fair bit. But he's a smart chap. He won't be spreading any rumors."

Chloe sat back, stunned. Of course, he wouldn't be saying anything. None of them would, if they wanted to prevent riots. Still, as long as Adrastea lived in the village, the potential for violence was present. "You will have to get rid of her."

"What?" Ari, who had been sitting quiet with a cup in her hand and staring at Chloe the whole time, protested. "We're trying to protect her, not get rid of her."

Chloe drew up her backbone. This was no time to be weak, even though she did not like confrontation; it was distasteful to her that two adults could not see reasonably eye-to-eye. Why did she always have to deal with the irrational people? There were far too many of them in the world for her taste. "If she's already made her deal with the Dark, then I don't think there's much you can do for her."

"But she hasn't." Ari jumped to her feet.

"Sit down, Ari," Natan said in a weary but patient voice.

Ari sat back down but she had a new light in her eyes. "You don't know the whole story." She laughed at Chloe in a mocking way.

This offended Chloe. She sat stock upright. "I do not appreciate being laughed at in my ignorance."

Natan, apparently, had had enough as well. "Ari, shut up and get Mira dressed." He rose to his feet. "I'll take Chloe. We'll go prepare the cottage for the Laying-in."

Chloe followed the Mayor out of the house, leaving Ari to tend the body of her friend, alone in her grief.

Outside in the streets, Natan explained a few things to Chloe. "First of all, Adrastea isn't a Dark Priestess. Until a few weeks ago, we didn't know she had any talent at all to speak of." He explained the incident of the Smiths' rain barrel. "Not that I'm surprised she displayed any talent. I think my sister was somewhat sensitive to the Deeper Power and her husband Joe hid the fact that he had talent. It seems to run in the family, though not so strong any more. My parents didn't have any talent that I knew of but my aunt Crozie was the Priestess of this village before Mira."

Chloe didn't buy this story of sudden talent. "Maybe she had it all along but didn't want anyone to know, because she was afraid they would find out what she was."

"Oh, believe me, no one—not even she—knew until that day. It wasn't until she displayed her talent in the Deeper Power that trouble started."

Then Chloe listened in growing horror as Natan spilled out the story. "Mor-Lath, God of the Dark himself shows up and declares her to be his betrothed." He explained all, leaving no detail out of the battle between mortal maiden and Dark God. "So, that's pretty much it. He wants her as his wife. She keeps saying no and he's raising the stakes."

"Oh, glory!" Chloe gasped, her hands covering her mouth. "He killed Mira?"

Natan sighed. "Yes. Adrastea's hiding up at the Sacred Spring until we know what to do with her. She wasn't too clear about what happened. Apparently, Mira did something to provoke Mor-Lath and he did away with her."

Oh glory, Chloe thought. Not that she expected any different from the Dark One. No wonder everyone was so careful about the secret.

They reached Mira's cottage. While she had been living there, she still considered it Mira's cottage. Chloe didn't feel right about putting her personal touch on someone else's home. Maybe it was in the hope she could talk Carles into letting her return to Crossroads.

Well, it was hers now. She would have to make changes... if she chose to stay in this village. Not that that was likely, if she was given the choice. But if she went, the Springers would have no representative of the Light to guide them.

Chloe did not feel adequate to battle the Dark God himself. She let Natan in to the cottage.

While it would pain Natan and Ari greatly, she could see only one solution to the problem. "I'm sorry I must tell you this, Natan but the only way to be rid of the Dark God forever is to be rid of Adrastea."

"I would appreciate it if nobody tries to kill my betrothed again," came a new voice. Both Chloe and Natan spun around to find Mor-Lath, dressed in common villager clothing, standing between them and the door. "I am rather fond of her."

Chloe's thoughts left her. Never, in her lifetime, had she ever expected to see an angel or a demon, never mind a god. Especially not this god. She stumbled back against a chair. She pushed past the obstacle until her back came to rest against the opposite wall of the cabin. Her breath caught in her throat. Maybe he wouldn't notice her.

Natan seemed to have had more practice in dealing with him. "Nobody said anything about killing Adrastea."

Mor-Lath stood there with folded arms and a dark expression that Chloe knew better than to cross. "Mira tried. Would have succeeded, had I not brought my betrothed back from the edge of death. She paid the price for defying a god."

Natan would not be cowed. "Mira's a priestess of the Light. Of course, she's going to stand up to you. We've told you. Adrastea's told you. She doesn't want to marry you. No means no."

The Dark God regarded him. Oh, what thoughts were tumbling through his head? "We'll see." And he was gone before Chloe could draw a second breath, a faint swirl of air marking where he once stood.

"Bugger me," Natan vented as soon as Mor-Lath left.

"What the—?" Chloe started, daring to breathe again. "That was the Dark God!"

"Well-observed."

Natan, now in a temper, paced the cabin, kicking a wooden bucket by the door. Chloe thought it most prudent to remain by the wall. "Bugger, bugger, bugger," he continued to curse. "That mongrel defiler of virgin goats." Chloe did not reprimand his vulgarity. "That snake-sucker, that..."

Chloe let him curse out his frustration while she tried to ponder a course of action. What would Carles do? He would look for the missing puzzle piece. Then the solution would present itself.

"What does he want with Adrastea?"

"How the hell should I know?"

"Find out that and it should be an easy matter to solve the problem."

"Don't you think we haven't thought of that? We don't know what he wants. All we know is he wants marriage and he needs her willing."

That was a surprise. He needed her willing. "Well, killing Mira is not a good way of winning her over." Something was still missing. "No, there's got to be more than that. What had Adrastea got that nobody else has?"

Natan slowed his pacing to think. "Talent?"

Chloe gave a small snort. "I've got talent."

"Can you heal broken legs?"

A touch of envy tugged at Chloe's heart. "I heard about that. Everyone wouldn't be so impressed if they knew that directly interfering in the Deeper Power is a Dark art."

"I'm sure Adrastea didn't know that."

"If she doesn't, she should. Where is the girl?"

"She's up at the Sacred Spring. No safer place for her in the village than there."

Chloe weighed this up. "You have no other circles of protection? I thought Mira would have placed some here."

"Ah." Natan sat down at the table. "Lillybet's house is protected," he started.

"It is?" Chloe didn't expect that.

"Someone set a protection on it long ago. It seems to have worked so far."

Chloe questioned the veracity of this. She didn't sense any kind of protection when she was there. "Who did it?"

He didn't answer her question. Instead, he rose to his feet. "I don't know much about circles of protection. Could..." he hesitated, as if he knew the gravity of what he was asking, "Could you cast one around the village?"

"What? The whole village?" He wasn't jesting when he said he didn't know anything about circles of protection. They required giving up one's own lifeblood for the sake of the Light—the bigger the circle, the more blood was required. "That would take a tremendous amount of blood. It'd take weeks to circumnavigate the village, and by the time I made it all the... no.

I cannot. Nobody could, not alone."

"Oh." He rose. "That limits our choices, doesn't it?"

"Here, yes." She folded her hands before her. "But there are other places in the world that have strong circles of power. A Temple of the Light, perhaps. Maybe we could find refuge for her in one of those."

"Where's the closet one?"

"Feown."

Natan shook his head. "Feown is a fallen city. There is no guarantee you'd make it safely."

"Adrastea would, apparently. She seems to have the Dark One's own protection."

"I doubt it would extend so far as to seeing her safely delivered into the hands of his enemies."

Chloe sighed. "Perhaps we should speak of this later," she suggested. Clearly, he was too irrational at this point to see reason.

Natan snorted. He opened the door. "We'll bring Mira down soon. See the table is ready.

Chloe inclined her head and shut the door behind Natan.

Chapter 21

O h, Light bless you, baby brother." Adrastea cried when Mikal plunked another bag of food and blankets on the grass before her that evening.

He squirmed under her spontaneous hug. "I can't stay. Uncle Natan needs me."

"I understand." Although she could have used the company.

He left, glancing back once as he hurried back to the village.

Mikal had included enough food for two meals. Adrastea portioned it out to last for three. She devoured her allotted portion to the last crumb and sated her thirst from the Spring. Then she curled up in the warm quilt and settled back into the grass to sleep. While it was relaxing, the meal had woken her up and sleep eluded her.

Perhaps she should have asked for something to do—spinning, mending, even a book to read. Waiting out the rest of her life on a hilltop looked to be rather dull. She fought her own wandering thoughts for she did not wish to dwell on the thought of Mira.

Should she be angry that Mira slit her throat or sorrowful because of how things turned out? Did Mira believe the only way to save Sacred Spring was to kill her?

In the end, was that the only way?

"Oh, there you are," Mor-Lath said. He stood beyond the meadow in the grove of trees. He leaned against one casually. "You foolish woman. Why don't you go home and get some sleep? You've got a funeral coming up later."

At the sound of his voice she leapt to her feet. But he didn't come closer. "Hmph," she snorted and sat back down, turning her back to him. Not only did she want to insult him, but she didn't want him to see her tears. He was right about home. It was just as safe there as it was here, thanks to her father's protections over the house. But she wasn't going to let him know he was right.

"Have it your way," he said, his voice uncaring. "I've got better things to do today than watch you go spare from boredom." When she didn't reply, he took a different tack. "You should hear what they're saying in the village about Mira."

She turned around and glared at him but that only seemed to humor him. "You're a mongrel."

He shrugged. "I haven't kept any secrets from you. Truth is the best basis for a good marriage."

"I'm not marrying you." Where was a rock to throw when she needed one?

"You wouldn't say that if you could see into the future."

That surprised her. "You can see into the future?"

He spread his arms. "I'm a god."

"You killed my mother and Mira."

He straightened. "I didn't kill your mother."

"You did kill Mira."

"She killed you first."

Adrastea resisted stroking her neck. His healing had been so complete there was no scar. Too bad he couldn't heal the emotional ones. "No way in hell I'll ever marry you now."

He chuckled. "Oh, you will, when you learn that there are things stronger than hate."

She folded her arms tightly about her. "I will not love you."

A coy smile played across his lips. He turned to leave. "Also," he said, before he passed too deeply into the trees, "I've got other things I need to focus on. You're not the only concern on my mind." He walked away from her.

She settled down to keep vigil just in case he lurked or came back. If only there was a way of keeping track of him while he was gone.

A thought occurred to her—perhaps there was. She raised a finger to her face but didn't touch the skin. She held it over the black line on her face. She remembered when Carles had stroked it and she felt the resonance beneath her skin. Had that been Mor-Lath's presence? Every time he was near, she felt it in that scar.

She took a risk and stroked it once. It sang to her inside and she felt a very faint echo far, far away. Then she berated herself. She probably alerted him. Wrapped in the quilt, she waited for him to show up again, but he didn't. After the longest time and no Mor-Lath, she held her hand over the line.

There was that echo, still, far away.

She wondered...

She dropped her hand to her skin, coming in contact with the line. The echo was there, still distant. With her hand in place, she ventured to the edge of the meadow.

Nothing changed.

She stepped into the trees.

Still nothing. As far as she could tell, she was alone.

Time for boldness. Adrastea ventured into the forest further, her steps moving quickly.

Without incident or encountering another person, she made it to her mother's house. She ran through the back garden gate, up the pathway and onto the porch, expecting Mor-Lath to pop out and say, "Ha, I tricked you." But he didn't.

She made it through the door. As she slammed it behind her, someone jumped up from behind the table. It was Chloe Priestess. Chloe let out a yelp of surprise. She lifted the fire poker in her hand in defense. Her hands trembled.

Adrastea screamed. "What are you doing here?" Her heart pounded hard.

Chloe lowered the fire poker and resumed poking at the fire. She kept her eye on Adrastea. "I— I think you had better explain this," Chloe said, pointing to something on the hearth. Her voice wavered.

Adrastea gave her a puzzled look. She came around the table, cautiously, in case whatever it was that Chloe was referring to might jump up and harm her.

It was a book, covered in ash.

Chloe didn't ask anything. She leaned on the poker as if it were a walking stick, waiting for Adrastea's answer. Adrastea hated that. Why was Chloe treating her like a naughty child?

"I don't know," she spat back.

"Don't you?" She flipped open the cover to show the inscription. "Has your name in it."

Her name... A cold dread filled her. Adrastea stepped forward.

"To Adrastea," it said, in a most elegant script. "A betrothal gift for you, Mor-Lath." By the Light, it was the book Mor-Lath had given her, Ari attempted to burn, then what went missing when Adrastea tried to hide it again.

She felt faint. "Where did you find this?" she whispered.

"You don't know? Mira had it. It was in the bottom of her chest."

Mira had it the whole time?

"This book is evil," Chloe said, keeping a close eye on Adrastea. Adrastea didn't care. She knelt down and reached out to touch the book, but Chloe slapped her hand away with the poker, harder than necessary.

"Ow." Adrastea lifted the offended hand to her mouth. "What did you do that for?"

"Don't touch the book." She clutched her hands about the poker to keep them still.

"But—" She was going to say it was hers, but did she really want it?

"Did you know that this book won't burn?"

Adrastea shook her hand then inspected it for bruising. "Yes. We tried burning it the first night we got it. Then it disappeared, I wondered if it had fallen into the wrong hands." She sat back with relief. "Thank goodness Mira had it."

Chloe let the tip of the poker fall to the floor. "What did you do when you discovered it missing?"

"Panicked." Adrastea probed gently at her injured hand. "Look, I've got to get some nicotina for this." She stepped towards the bedroom door, but Chloe started as well, possibly to block her.

"Why don't you just heal it yourself?"

Adrastea stepped away from Chloe and put her hand behind her back. "Why?"

"I hear you have a talent for healing."

"Maybe." Her eyes narrowed.

"I know you healed Master Mason's leg."

Adrastea looked away. "That just happened. I wasn't thinking at the time." Adrastea took another step backwards.

"Perhaps you should think more."

Adrastea's nerved prickled. "I don't understand what you want."

Chloe readjusted her grip on the poker. "You're a Dark Priestess." A shuddery breath rolled through her. "The Dark God himself favors you. The others may try to hide it, to deny it but I know what you are."

"I'm no such thing."

Chloe only glanced at the book, but Adrastea caught her meaning. "Wait. You can't condemn me because of a book. I haven't even had a chance to read it yet."

"So, you meant to read it, then?"

Adrastea opened her mouth. She had to force the words out. "No. Not much of a reader, really." That poker made her nervous. Mira had no problems slitting her throat. And Mira loved her.

Chloe studied her. The intensity of her gaze made Adrastea squirm. Was she or wasn't she going to attack? If Adrastea had been faced with an enemy in the same position, she might have swung that poker by now.

What would Mor-Lath have done in her position? He would have sweet-talked his way out of it if he cared and ignored Chloe if he didn't. But Adrastea couldn't afford to ignore an enemy with a fire poker and a faith. She didn't have all of Creation at her beck and call, to defend her against a superior enemy.

"You're my enemy, aren't you?" she said. Words were her only defense here. Anything she did with the Deeper Power would condemn her. She didn't know if she had sufficient command over Creation to fight cold iron or a woman who thought right was on her side. "It doesn't matter who I am. You've already condemned me."

Chloe considered her further. She didn't let go of the poker, but she relaxed her grip on it. "You truly believe yourself to be innocent, don't you?"

"I am innocent."

Chloe leaned on the poker again. "Do you know that use of the Deeper Power for your own ends is a sin?"

Adrastea didn't answer. She felt trapped. If she made any move to leave, she was certain Chloe would attack her. Anything she said, Chloe would twist it. She couldn't win. "What do you want?" she asked the Priestess.

"For the good of the village, you must leave Sacred Spring."

This surprised Adrastea. "But I can't leave. I live here."

"As long as you stay, people will die. If you care, you will protect them and leave."

"And if I don't care?" she spat, then regretted her words.

"Then why are you here?"

Adrastea couldn't win. Nothing mattered to Chloe but how right she was. Adrastea's dislike turned into loathing. "Get out of my house. You don't belong here."

"Why? You plan on killing me too?"

Adrastea folded her arms. "If I planned on killing you, I would have done it by now."

Chloe didn't reply. What was going on in that little head of hers?

She didn't wait for an answer from the Priestess. "What are you doing here anyhow? This is my house."

"I came for Mira's things."

"You can't have them."

"They are technically mine now."

"Not the books."

"No," Chloe conceded. "Those are Carles' but I'll be taking them with me, for you will have no need for them. Not much of a reader, I recall."

Adrastea wished she had taken the chance to read them when they were available to her. "You can't take them all right now. And once you leave, I'm not letting you back in."

Chloe replaced the poker by the fireplace. "No matter. Natan will support me in this." She turned to the door and left without a final parting shot.

When she was gone and well out of earshot, Adrastea screamed at the door. If she had a rock, she would have thrown it.

In an act of defiance, she scooped Mor-Lath's book off the floor. If she was going to be condemned, it might as well be for something she's done. She spent the rest of the day reading it, interrupted only by upwellings of grief and sorrow for Mira. Her anger at Chloe kept her grief at bay, mostly.

⁂

Ari brushed Mira's hair so she looked nice. She smoothed out a wrinkle in Mira's skirt and made sure her hands rested together. One could only do so much to make a dead body look good.

Now they were back in Mira's cottage, they did their best to tidy the place for visitors. She and Natan had shoved Mira's table against the far wall. They draped it with the sheets from Mira's bed for Chloe had returned empty-handed from her second foray to Lillybet's home.

Chloe didn't say much except to let Natan know that Adrastea was back in the house.

"Really?" he exclaimed. He sped off to have a talk with her, leaving Ari to finish laying out Mira.

What a relief to think about Adrastea instead of Mira at the moment. Her heart went out to her journeyman. What could the girl be going through?

Chloe sat by Mira's fireplace. There was no fire lit, for one would not be needed. "Where are we going to put the food?" Mira only had the one table.

"Jak Carpenter's house is next door. Borrow a table from him."

"You're also next door."

"True but Jak can help you carry a table."

Chloe sniffed and left, the door shutting harder than necessary.

"Leave the door open," Ari called after her. Chloe re-opened the door she had closed.

Ari fussed over Mira until she felt it was truly useless. Chloe was a poor choice to replace Mira. Perhaps they would have been better off without a Priestess. She didn't see how Chloe was going to help them against Mor-Lath.

A timid knock came on the doorframe. Ari looked up and found Kyfa Shepherd.

"Kyfa! What are you doing here?" Ari hadn't seen her since before she attacked Marta.

"I— I had to come before everyone else did. Mother didn't want me to come but I had to. I'm so sorry."

In her arms she carried two loaves of bread. "I baked these yesterday. Mother won't be happy I swiped them." She looked around for a table on which to lay them, but it hadn't arrived yet. Ari gestured to the cupboard where Mira had prepared her meals.

Kyfa laid down the bread as if they were sleeping children. "I can't stay long," she said. "I'm leaving."

"No, please. Stay and chat for a moment. I haven't seen you since..." Ari didn't mean to bring the attack up.

"No, I mean, I'm leaving Sacred Spring. I can't stay here anymore."

"But where will you go? There's a war..."

Kyfa twisted her fingers together. "I know but I've really messed things up here."

Ari wasn't sure she should be listening to Kyfa's confession, but Chloe wouldn't do.

Kyfa continued. "I know Marta's gone and all, but she'll come back. And when she does, she'll come after me. I..." she shook her head. "I can't be here." She turned back to the bread. "I can't live with my mother any more. She makes everything sound so bad."

Resting a hand on one of the loaves, Kyfa explained, "This one is for Lillybet. I wanted to go to her Laying-in, but my mother wouldn't let me. She said I had no reason to."

Tears flowed down her cheeks. "Lillybet was my friend. I spun the best thread for her and she'd give me the best shawls. Then when I went to Crossroads, I'd sell them and we'd split the money. Nobody knew but us. I don't care how crazy she was." Her voice dwindled. "She always had nice things to say to me. She never asked what my mother had said."

Ari could sympathize with Kyfa. She, too, had felt the sharpness of Ariah Shepherd's gossiping tongue from time to time.

"Please, Ari. Don't tell anyone I'm leaving."

"When are you going?"

"It's best you don't know. I've got to go." She gave the Healer a kiss on the cheek. "Bye, Ari." She ran out the door before Ari could say another word.

Kyfa was not prepared for a world beyond Sacred Spring, especially a world filled with war. There was a good chance she would suffer more there than if she had remained behind. Ari vowed to catch up with Kyfa later. Perhaps she could talk her out of her foolishness. No doubt Lillybet would have.

Ultimately, this was Mor-Lath's fault. Was he going to ruin everyone's lives? Ari swallowed, her mouth too dry.

From her front door, Adrastea watched the village prepare for Mira's funeral. If she squinted, she could make out the growing pyre.

Natan dropped by. He joined her on the porch and watched the busy little villagers below in the village. "You can see everything, now that the trees are gone."

"Mmm." From this distance the village was blurry.

He put a paw of a hand on her shoulder. "I'm sorry you have to stay here. It's safer."

She shrugged. He was right. Didn't make it any easier.

"You need anything?"

Adrastea shrugged. "Food. Company."

"Food, I can do something about. As for company..." He had no answers. "I'm sorry."

Her uncle stood up and became the Mayor. "We'll figure this out." He had the whole village to consider and couldn't remain to comfort Adrastea.

As the sun set, both Sacred Springers and Little Crossroaders paid Mira their final respects. Adrastea, all alone, leaned against her doorjamb and watched the whole village gather. She wanted to go. She desperately wanted to say goodbye.

"Go, then," said Mor-Lath, appearing on the porch next to her.

Startled, Adrastea yelped. She scooted backwards through the door, slamming it shut.

Why did he have to do that? He could, at least, give some warning. She put her hand to her cheek. Yes, his presence was very near. Really, she should pay more attention to that line.

The door swung open, but Mor-Lath didn't enter. He couldn't, she reminded herself.

"Nothing is stopping you from going to the funeral. It's not like you have to be a prisoner in your own home."

"I'm not listening to you." She slammed the door again.

He let her fume for a moment then swung the door open. "Do not think you are so safe in there."

"Bugger off." She tried to slam the door a third time. He caught the swinging door and slowly pushed it open. He placed one foot over the threshold, then another and quite ably walked into her house.

"No..." She backed away. "You're not supposed to be able... No. Get out of here." Her insides wished to melt. Her knees grew weak and she wanted to collapse to the floor. Was no place safe?

He approached her. "The protection over your house dissolved with the death of your mother. It would only last as long as either your father or your mother lived."

Adrastea let out a sob. "So that's why you killed her?" She glanced to the back door. Could she make it if she made a dash for it? The only other door was the bedroom door. No way she would permit him in there.

"I didn't kill her. She tripped on this damned rug of hers." With a flick of his fingers, the rag rug flung itself out of the way, to bunch up against the wall. "There are several things we must clarify." He held up a finger. "First, there is nowhere you can go that I cannot find you. Second, I think I shall have to keep a closer eye on you. Third, you will—"

"I refuse your conditions," she snapped. "You are not in a position to tell me what to do and we are not making a barter."

He smiled at her fieriness. "I am very much in a position to barter. Isn't a marriage contract little more than a bargaining agreement?"

"I'm not marrying you." Her voice rose in pitch and she balled her fists. "I don't care how many people you kill. I'm not marrying you."

"Ah but you do care how many I kill. You care so much for the paltry few that have died so far. I guess two or twenty don't really matter to you, or even two thousand. How many Feowans have died so far?"

Rage filled her at having her words twisted so. She pummeled him with her fists. He caught them before she could do any damage, pinning them against her shoulders. His grip rendered her efforts useless.

"I'm not going to hurt you," he assured her.

"Tell that to Mira." She struggled to get free.

"You ready to listen to reason?"

"Bugger reason!" Her hands may have been trapped but her knee was free.

Before she could put it to good use, he closed in, pressing her body against the wall with his. "You think too slowly and too loudly."

"Let me go!" Her body had a different opinion. It wanted to melt into him, to draw every last ounce of sweetness from his skin, his soul.

"No." His hands glided over her fists and down her arms. Once freed, her fingers opened, to spread across his chest.

She pushed but he was stronger than she. Physical force alone would not free her. Adrastea let the fight drain out of her. She would have to take a different approach. "I hate you," she said, low and bitter.

"Better than indifference."

Adrastea turned her face away from him. That only made him laugh. "You can't fool me." He whispered into her ear. "I know the passion that burns beneath your skin."

She felt that far-too-familiar thrill course through her body. He was doing it again; he was trying to seduce her. "Stop that."

"Stop what?"

"I won't give in."

"How about giving out?" An amused smile played across his lips.

Adrastea gasped. "No."

"Good," he murmured. "I love a woman with stamina."

Tears coursed down her face. Couldn't she win just once?

He watched her then released her. "What is it you want from me?" He cast his eyes heavenward. Exasperation?

Her hand, the one Chloe bruised, throbbed in pain as soon as he released it. It served to irritate her further. "I want you to go away." She cradled her hand. Between him and Chloe, she would be black and blue.

"I can't do that," he replied. She didn't expect him to agree.

She snorted her doubt and examined her hand. The mark of the poker lay there, purple and straight. She should have used the nicotina when she had the chance.

"Give me that," he said, not unkindly. He held out his hand for hers.

"No." She hid her hand like a child guarding illicit candy.

He ignored her protests and pulled her hand out. He stroked the bruise once. It faded along with the pain. "Now, I think we should come to some sort of agreement. You have me at a disadvantage, in that you know what I want but you haven't made any counter-offer."

Was he mad? Adrastea stared at him in disbelief. "I told you, I'm not marrying you."

"So you say but I know better."

"Light, Mor-Lath. I will not marry you!"

"Not under current conditions, no." He folded his arms. "What would it take to get your consent? What do you want?"

She balled her fists but knew better than to dare strike him again. He might not be so willing to heal any subsequent bruising. "Give me my mother back. And Mira as well," she demanded. "Bring them back to life."

Doubt crossed his face. "Ah, well, as to that... I'm afraid it doesn't work that way."

This twisted the anger in her belly. "Oh really?" she scoffed. "What happened to the all-powerful God of the Dark?"

His face wrinkled in concern. He drew in a breath as if to speak but thought better of it. "Adrastea—"

"I thought you had the Deeper Power at your command." Then she realized what she had discovered. "Wait," she gasped. "You aren't all-powerful. You can't do everything. Light," she crowed. "You're weaker than I thought."

He tightened his folded arms and his expression grew dark. "It's not weakness. It's... incompleteness. If I could do everything, what would I want with you?"

Then all her anger cleared, leaving a cold pit of realization in her belly. "Are you saying that if..." could she even utter what her mind only now put together? "If I marry you, it'll complete you? And then you will be all-powerful?"

"Finally, she figures it out." He let his breath out in relief. He backed off and gave her space.

An idea occurred to her. "So, if I marry you, you would have the power to bring back my mother and Mira?"

The hardness came back into his face. "What is your preoccupation with resurrection? We will visit with their souls every day, if you wish."

He made it sound so casual. "We could do that?"

"Yes. They're dead. Not gone." He scrubbed his hands through his hair. "You really have no idea what death is, do you?"

"I do so. It's where people... well, die." That sounded stupid and a flush rose to her cheeks. So much for appearing clever.

"Death is the release from the anguish and pain of mortal life. You go ask any angel if they want to go back to a mortal body. Their answer will be a resounding No."

"I don't believe you."

"I thought not." He grasped her hand and pulled her away from the wall. "How about we go ask an angel? There are far more than necessary here in the village. I'm sure one of them would be willing to talk to you."

She resisted. "Why should I?"

"Because you refuse to believe anything that comes out of my mouth." He, being stronger, pulled her through the door. "Come, my little Darklet. Let us seek wisdom from the Light." He whisked them away In that disconcerting godlike way of his to stand in the street outside Mira's home, where a few villagers approached, bearing food offering for the dead.

Adrastea froze for she did not want anyone to see her with Mor-Lath. What if the villagers knew that he was Mira's killer? Their wrath would also fall upon her for bringing him here, albeit not deliberately.

"Relax." Mor-Lath draped an arm about her waist. "Nobody can see us. We stand on a different plane." He pointed. "See there?" He pointed to the awkward form of Amarice. Angels of brightness surrounded her in undulating sentries. A few of the Innkeeper children sat outside Mira's home with lanterns on poles. Their lights paled in comparison to the glory of the angels.

As Amarice passed, the celestial beings would reach out graceful hands to stroke her face. "These are the angels that guard pregnant women." He pushed her forward. "Go. Go and ask them."

She turned back, suddenly shy. "But what do I say?"

"Whatever you want. Believe me, they'll forgive you if you say something stupid. Ask your question." He clasped his hands behind his back and waited.

Adrastea approached the angels, who smiled when she drew near.

"Greetings, Daughter of the Light." They reached out to stroke her hair and face.

Her first impulse was to hug them. When she reached out a hand, she discovered that it passed right through; they could touch her, but she couldn't touch them."

"I... I have a question." The angels with their graceful limbs and flowing robes slowed enough for Adrastea to observe them closely. Their nearly human faces, framed by exquisite white hair, were far more beautiful than any mortal she knew. Their eyes shined with pure love.

She selected the one closest to her. "Were you once mortal?"

The angel smiled beatifically. "Of course. We all were once mortal." The angel's voice was dulcet and smooth. Adrastea felt a pang of disappointment when the angel did not explain further.

"Would you go back to mortality if you could?"

The angel's expression took on a look of pity. "Poor, sweet Daughter of the Light. Your path is not an easy one."

"You didn't answer my question."

"I would not return to mortality, should that ever be my choice."

"But why not?"

The angel spread her arms and basked in the love of her god. "Imagine an existence free of pain, of sorrow, of anger, of misery. That is the life of an angel. Why return to the trial of mortality when the Light has rewarded me for my good deeds on earth?" The angel stroked Adrastea's face once more. "Granted there are advantages to mortality that I can no longer taste. I have done my time and I do not miss them. My reward is to continue in the love of the Light forever." The angel leaned in closer. "Joy can still be yours," she whispered to Adrastea. "But only if you choose correctly."

Mor-Lath shooed the angel away as one would a pesky fly. "Yeah,

yeah. You've said enough. She believes you. Now go back to your little sentry."

The angel and her companions drew themselves up, rank and file. "We are beyond your domain, Dark One."

"Whatever," he said, drawing Adrastea away.

She could not help but look back at the beautiful angels. They resumed their eternal vigilance over a life yet to be. Before her heart could yearn for their company once more, Mor-Lath took her back home. The coal-oil lamp she left on the table still burned. The fire had reduced to coals.

He released her. She felt empty, alone. He threw a small log onto the fire and encouraged the flames.

As it was the end of summer, the nights held an edge of chill. Adrastea remembered how cold last night had been. The comfort of a warm fire called to her.

If only Mor-Lath would leave.

He did not look like leaving anytime soon. He'd scooted a chair closer to the fire and had even kicked off his boots.

"Go away," she ordered him.

"No."

"You can't stay here."

"Actually, I will be staying here. After our little disagreement last night, I realized I'd been rather careless when it comes to you. From now on I shall be paying very close attention to you. If you even think of running to the sanctuary of Sacred Spring, I will know, and I will stop you."

Adrastea folded her arms stubbornly. "And I can stop you."

He sat up straight in his chair and turned around to face her. "Oh, really?" he said, with mocking humor dancing in his eyes. "I'd like to see you try."

"All right then," she said, smugly. "Go ahead. Ask me to marry you."

He stopped, apparently surprised at this unexpected tack. He chose to humor her. "Will you marry me?"

"No."

He rolled his eyes.

"See, as long as I say no, I defy you."

"Oh, you clever little minx," he said in a mocking tone. "Some day you and I will be in a position where you will find it to your benefit to say yes."

"I don't see how."

He shrugged and settled back down in his chair. He leaned back so he could place his feet before the fire. "I'm sure I'll think of something. Or you could save me the trouble and agree tonight. I hear there's a new priestess in the village. We can exchange our vows before the moon rises."

"Bastard," she muttered.

"If my parents were alive, I'd take you to meet them." He rose from his chair. "I can tell from your state of your temper that you haven't had dinner yet. Please allow me to demonstrate my skill in the kitchen."

It was Adrastea's turn to be surprised. "You can cook?"

Mor-Lath started to rummage in the under-stocked pantry. "I have many talents. I perform them all with a great level of skill." His glance back was full of innuendo. Adrastea chose to ignore it. No way in Creation she would let him seduce her again. She chanted in her mind, "Just say no, just say no," over and over.

"Now, as to this marriage thing, it is all a matter of finding what is a reasonable bride-price. I see threatening you isn't the best tactic. Perhaps that is where I erred. But then, I am the master of Darkness and am not known for my charity."

He found something useful in the pantry but tsked over the other scanty contents. "We shall have to restock tomorrow if you do not wish to starve."

Adrastea, her curiosity finally outweighing her anger, sat down at the table and watched Mor-Lath. He was right; she was hungry. If she was to battle the Dark God, it would be best done on a full stomach.

"Now." He filled a small pot with water and set it among the coals. "I see I shall have to proceed with more finesse."

Adrastea's emotional strength left her. She slowly shook her head. "Light burn you," she murmured. "You killed Mira..." The pain of loss overwhelmed her. Death may be all well and good for those to whom it happened but for everyone else left behind, it stung fiercely. She did not fight the tears that coursed down her cheeks.

He placed a gentle hand on her head, saying nothing. It rested there a moment. He returned to his cooking. Through her tears she watched him make dinner.

She missed her mother. She missed all the times they should have had but didn't. She cried for the secrets she'd barely learned, and for the ones she'd never know.

She cried for Mira, whose funeral she was missing. She put her head to the table and gave herself over to grief.

At the very least, he could have said he was sorry. But that would have implied he wouldn't do it again.

Adrastea had a feeling his killing wasn't over.

It wasn't until he placed a plate in front of her that she lifted her head.

He sat down opposite her at the table. "Now, don't be stubborn. Go ahead and eat. You don't have to marry me tonight if you don't want. But you do need to eat."

Adrastea looked down. There was no meat in the house, but he managed to make something that smelled delicious. It was mostly vegetables in a spicy sauce, topped with a biscuit that had baked in the pot. He had a plate of his own. He took a bite to show nothing was wrong with it. She'd never thought of him needing to eat.

"What?" he asked, when she hadn't touched her food.

She blushed. She had just been thinking on how they hadn't said grace. Was it improper to thank the Light for a meal prepared by the Dark? She offered a silent prayer to the Light and hoped he wouldn't notice. No doubt he'd mock her for her piety.

Carefully, she lifted a spoonful to her lips and tasted.

Mor-Lath was right; he was skilled. This was delicious. Before she knew it, she'd devoured half.

"Now," he said after she'd eaten a bit, "back to this negotiation thing."

Adrastea looked up at him but preferred to continue eating rather than respond.

"Forget about marriage for the moment. Surely there is something I can do to earn your forgiveness?"

She glared at him then returned her focus to dinner.

"So, ask something of me. Only this time, make it something I can grant."

Adrastea put down her spoon. "All right. Stop killing."

He put his chin on his fist and frowned in thought, his plate forgotten. "You have asked a great thing."

"No greater than my giving my life to you."

"True," he agreed.

She put her hands on the table and leaned forward. "You can't do it, can you? Or rather, you don't want to do it."

"It's not that I can't or that I don't want to. You have put me in a quandary."

"There is no quandary. I don't go around killing. I don't see why you can't do the same."

He studied her for so long she squirmed. "All right," he said. "I'll agree but on one condition."

"No conditions."

"Adrastea. Please."

That simple word, spoken so contritely, took the wind out of her. "Conditions?"

He explained, "Do you know what a mashiah is?"

She mulled over the word and came up with nothing.

"It is a mortal man with the ability to destroy a god."

Oh really? Now this was interesting. She waited for him to explain further.

"There is one who will seek to destroy me. He will hunt me until he finds me, then…" his voice trailed off.

"Oh, come now," she mocked him. "Would death be so bad?"

Mor-Lath did not mock back. He sat there very quiet, very still. "No, you don't understand me. I am a god, the embodiment of Creation's power. I am also immortal. Because I am a god, I do not have the luxury of simply separating my soul from my body.

"I would be utterly destroyed. There would be nothing of me left, no soul, no body, nothing. I would cease to be. Of all the things in Creation, including the Light Themselves, this frightens me the most."

Adrastea sobered. "Where is this mashiah now?"

"He's here in the village."

Adrastea dropped her spoon. "What? Who is he? What's his name?"

He shook his head. "Please, Adrastea. I will solemnly promise that I shall never kill another villager here again. But you must let me stop this mashiah."

"Oh, no. It's not Uncle Natan, is it?"

Mor-Lath allowed himself a small smile. "Relax, betrothed. It is nobody you've met." Then he grew serious again. "For not only my sake but yours, you must let me kill him. If I don't and he succeeds in destroying me, then he shall come after you.

"Please," he begged. "I will give you the lives of your villagers in return for the life of this one man. He is an enemy to us both, whether you like it or not.

"Take comfort in the fact that I will show mercy and kill him quickly.

His soul would go to the Light."

Adrastea took these things and pondered them in her heart. He sounded so sincere. But could she trust him?

Before she could answer, he said, "I will let you have time to think it over. But do not take long. Our very existence is at stake."

Chapter 22

Adrastea's conscience gathered from the corners of sleep. She opened her eyes, her hand moving across the quilt on the bed.

Mor-Lath. The events of the night before hit her all at once. She bolted upright.

To her relief, she was alone in the bedroom. Nothing happened last night to compromise her integrity. Still, not wanting to take any chances, she tossed on her clothes and peeked out the door. No one sat at the table or worked the loom. She was alone.

Relaxing, she came out and took inventory of her remaining foodstock. Her garden was not yet established. How would she get more food? Were her mother's accounts with Rop Storekeeper still valid? Could she continue to subsist from Ari's pantry or would Ari insist that Adrastea develop her own? She would have to ask later.

But not today. Today was Mira's funeral. Adrastea ventured out on the front porch and looked down to the village. If she squinted, she could make out the pyre. It pained her that she couldn't be there to help pile the wood. If she couldn't be there in person, she could at least watch from afar. If only she could see better.

"You can go, if you wish."

Adrastea jumped as Mor-Lath stepped beside her.

"You are not a prisoner in your own home."

She folded her arms. "But I still feel like a prisoner."

"Why? You can go anywhere you wish."

"Not to Sacred Spring," she said with bitterness.

"I don't see you going to Feown either but you're not complaining about that."

She gave a small hmph, more to herself than for his benefit. She made a strong point of observing the village and ignoring him.

Mor-Lath observed it too. "Do go to the funeral if you so wish. I have no reason to stop you. Go anywhere, do anything because you are free."

"Oh, really?"

He nodded. "Marry me?"

"No," she spat.

"See how free you are? True freedom lies in being able to make choices."

"Some choice," she muttered. She faced him fully and put her fists on her hips. "Why do I feel you're playing with me?"

"I'm not. I need you to come to me by your own free will."

She turned away from him. "So why do I feel like I don't have a choice?"

He put a comforting hand on her shoulder. "Because in your heart you've already made your choice. It's this reluctance to admit that choice that makes you feel trapped."

She shrugged off his hand. "That's not so."

He moved closer. "Admit it. What I offer you tempts you. You haven't forgotten your first real taste of Power." He inhaled the fragrance of her hair. "It thrills you in ways you don't dare admit."

Adrastea folded her arms even tighter and hunched down. She was not going to listen to him, not respond. He would only end up playing her with words. In her mind she ran through the map of Ari's garden. She'd spent so much of the past ten years weeding and tending it. She knew exactly where everything was from year to year. "Lavender," she murmured. Ari had hedges around each plot. She knew which plants perennials were, which annuals were rotated where—

His arms slid around her waist, startling her. He pressed his face into her hair. "That won't work," he murmured in her ear. "I can distract you from your thoughts."

She pushed uselessly at his arms. "I don't want to think about you!"

He laughed. "Oh, but you do. You cannot think of herbs forever. Sooner or later, you've got to relax your mind. That's when the thoughts come unbidden. You lay there at night in your lonely bed. In that moment before you drift to sleep, your deepest desires come to the fore. You know you miss the taste of the Deeper Power."

Adrastea focused on the pyre in the village below. What wood did they use, she wondered? Pine? The forest had been stripped of anything useful. The scraps fed the Crossroader's cooking fires.

He nuzzled her ear. "Do you know why they call it the Deeper Power?

Because Power is meant to be wielded." He fed her a taste of it, sweet and alluring. She wanted to melt into its song.

She must not be tempted. Again, she pushed at the hands that held her. "No," she protested. "I... won't!" Rosemary. The rosemary needed trimming.

He distracted her with more Power. It flowed into her like water into a glass. It settled into the corners of her soul as if it belonged there. Her limbs came alive. Her skin woke up, sensitive to every stirring of breeze, the stroke of skin against skin. The song grew into a chorus.

Oh, how she wanted it. What he gave her wasn't enough. How could she get more? There had to be a way to get more without Mor-Lath.

"I don't think so," he told her. "Without me, you are nothing but another village maid, doomed to live out a plebian existence. Do you really want that?"

She didn't care. All she wanted was more Power, to immerse herself in the wondrousness of Creation and not emerge again, ever.

Then he cruelly pulled away that taste of Power. "Sorry," he said, "Power has its price." He released her and stepped back. "Anyhow, you have a visitor."

Adrastea looked up but saw no one. Guilt blossomed in her gut. Mor-Lath had disappeared, leaving her alone. She could still feel the faint thrum of the rhythm of Creation. Now she craved it and cursed the Dark God for that.

She stepped off the porch onto the dirt path leading to the front gate. Kneeling down, she laid a hand to the earth, closed her eyes and listened. It was there, albeit nowhere as strong as when she was with Mor-Lath. Could she pull it from the earth? She reached out and tried to call it to her.

To her surprise, it responded, singing in reply to her request. She lay down and pressed her face to the ground, savoring the song.

"What are you doing?" asked a cool voice.

Adrastea jumped. Looking up, she saw Chloe standing before her but not too close. Hastily, she scrambled from her prone position. She stood facing the Priestess with her hands behind her back. "Nothing," Adrastea replied.

"Continue to touch the Deeper Power like that and you will damn yourself as a Dark Priestess."

Adrastea scowled. "I'm not a Dark Priestess."

"You certainly aren't of the Light. Anyhow, I came to tell you that it is best you do not go to the funeral tonight."

Adrastea took a step backwards. "What?"

"We believe it's for the best."

Who was 'we'? "Who's best?"

"Yours." Chloe was far too smug.

"Why are you doing this?"

Chloe put her hands behind her back and began to pace the garden. "You are so wrapped up in your own problems that you forget that there is a rest of the village. Some of them have ears and others have tongues. Some say you killed Mira."

"Not me. You know that."

Chloe didn't comment on this, but her eyes narrowed. "You're not wanted. They don't want you at the funeral." She stopped and faced Adrastea. "Your reputation is suffering because of this. All the trouble that has been happening here is because of you—"

"Is not," Adrastea retorted hotly.

"—either directly or indirectly. Stay away. Don't make things worse."

While Chloe issued her recommendation, Mor-Lath appeared behind her. Adrastea drew in a sharp breath.

Chloe paused. "Don't bother getting angry with me. It's a decision made by us all."

Before Adrastea could demand to know who "us all" were, Mor-Lath spoke. "My betrothed will go where she pleases."

A startled Chloe spun around and let out a squeak of terror. Adrastea herself felt a momentary flitter of apprehension. This Dark God was different from the one who courted her. His eyes blazed. Around him, Creation bowed to his powerful aura.

Chloe scrambled back, nearly bumping into Adrastea. She scooted to the edge of the porch. Her feet tripped up, setting her bottom down hard on the wooden planks. Even the walls of the house were not far enough away for her.

He advanced towards the priestess, feeding her terror. In fact, Adrastea feared he would kill again.

"You promised," she yelped. "No more killing."

He turned to her and gave her a fierce smile. "Oh, there are worse things than death, as you well know."

Mor-Lath climbed up on the porch and crouched down in front of a trembling Chloe. He drew so close, if Chloe could have melted through the wall, she would have. "Let us get a few more things straight, Priestess of the Light. Adrastea is not a Dark Priestess. She is far more than that. Kindly don't insult her that way."

Chloe trembled, her hands unable to keep still. A single tear ran down her face.

"She will go where she wishes. You will not stop her, nor threaten to stop her. And please don't presume to speak for the Mayor. He is more than capable for speaking for himself, as I well know from experience. As for the village not wanting her around, I know it's your job to speak the truth, but must you be so brutal about it? I hoped to spare her that bitter fact."

Adrastea's knees weakened at that last sentence. That couldn't be true. Could the whole village think she was Mira's killer? Had they turned against her? Was Mor-Lath the only one standing between them and her? She knew what happened to Marta—the attacks and the Innkeeper's final choice to leave the village before things got worse. And that was based on a few unsubstantiated rumors.

Adrastea had been present at Mira's death. Not everyone in the village knew exactly who Mor-Lath was. Even if they did, that would only make things worse. At least Mira's wisdom in keeping Mor-Lath's true identity from the rest of the village had saved her thus far.

But Chloe hadn't been sworn to secrecy. She knew who Mor-Lath was. No vow prevented her from telling all and sundry.

Perhaps the whole village knew already. Did they believe her? She was still an outsider, a refugee. How could they take her word over... over...? She realized there was no one to defend her. The only ones left were Ari and Natan. If either one of them came forth to defend her, the villagers would question their motivations. Their familial connections to Adrastea worked against her favor. The villagers would question why they knew about it for so long, yet kept it a secret.

Chloe was a Light Priestess, one endorsed by both Carles and Mira. Chloe was here to stay, even if the Crossroaders returned home.

Adrastea wanted to sink to the ground, but she didn't dare show weakness in front of Chloe.

Mor-Lath hauled Chloe to her feet and put an arm around her waist. "Here, let me escort you back to the village. I'm heading there myself. You and I can have a pleasant chat on the way."

Chloe could only stare at Mor-Lath. He even had to give her a push to get started. He guided her around Adrastea, down the path and out the front gate. "I'm getting married soon, you know," he told her as they walked along the path towards Sacred Spring. "I'll be needing the services of a Priestess…"

Only when they were gone, did Adrastea let the pain of her new discovery wash her over. She lay down with her face pressed to the earth and prayed. "Oh, Light. Why have You forgotten me?"

⁙

Natan and Ari sat together on a small bench in Mira's house. They stayed near Mira's head, keeping vigil over her body. People from both Sacred Spring and Little Crossroads came, bringing food and sampling the other offerings. Natan forced the memory of his sister from his thoughts. If he allowed her to dwell there, he could, in all likeliness, start shouting at the mourners.

The villagers came in, touched Mira's head then moved away to share their memories of her. Soon visitors crowded the perimeter of the small cottage. They may have wished to pay their respects, but no one wanted to get too close to the body. More mourners entered, offered tokens of sorrow and moved away.

Before the Laying-in, Chloe had removed all small items and personal effects from the room, making it look far too empty for Natan's comfort. Only the quiet murmurings of low conversation filled the room now, and the questions nobody wanted to ask.

He and Ari sat together, holding each other's hands. They nodded their heads as they received everyone's condolences. Mira had no family living but she had Ari. They'd been best friends since forever.

During a lull of mourners, Natan reached across and pushed a small strand of Ari's hair out of her face. Ari didn't handle death well. She'd bottle her feelings up inside while she prepared the body, attended the Lying-in and kept vigil at the funeral. Later, in the privacy of her home or Natan's, she'd find another bottle in which to drown them.

She looked at him after the tender gesture, gave him a tight, too-brief smile. Her walls slammed down again, to remain strong in front of the others.

Natan knew he'd be holding her later and doing his best to restrict her drinking to something that wouldn't kill her. It would take a lot to kill

Ari but that didn't mean she wasn't willing to find out how much that was.

Chloe came stumbling in. She went straight for Natan. "M-m-master Mayor," she faltered. "There's someone outside who wishes to— to speak with you." Her eyes rolled fearfully towards the door.

"Well, can't he come in?"

"No!" Chloe shouted. She apologized, her shame thick and warm. The room fell silent. She dropped her voice. "Just— go speak with him, will you?" Then, waving her hands as if trying to forget what she just said, she muttered something incoherent and headed to the bedroom, closing the door harder than necessary.

Natan grumbled and stood up. "I'd better go see what this is about," he said to Ari. "Probably some Crossroader complaining about something insignificant."

He stepped outside into the morning light and saw no one. Several villagers had also poked their heads out the door and the open windows. When they saw no one, they returned to their more interesting conversations inside.

What game was Chloe playing?

"Master Mayor, I desire a word with you." Natan jumped as Mor-Lath, who wasn't there a moment ago, spoke in his ear.

Suddenly all the sorrow and anger and frustration of the past few days exploded from Natan in a rage of temper. "You bastard!" He slammed Mor-Lath in the chest. "You killed Mira. You dare show your face here?" He yelled it loud enough to bring everyone in the cottage to the door and windows.

Mor-Lath didn't even glance their way. "Well, I was hoping for a quieter conversation."

Natan gave him another shove. It didn't do much toward moving Mor-Lath, so he shoved him again. "You bugger off. I never want to see your face in my village again."

Mor-Lath put his hands up in a diplomatic gesture. "Easy now, Mayor. I come in peace."

"The hell you do. When are you going to leave us alone?"

"When I've got what I came for."

Natan jabbed a sharp finger at Mor-Lath's chest for each word. "You're never getting that."

Mikal managed to struggle between the crowded villagers in the doorway. When he stuck his head out and saw who it was, he drawled in a sarcastic voice, "Oh, hello, Mor-Lath." This set a few people to murmuring.

Mor-Lath gave Mikal a friendly nod. "Good to see you again, little brother."

Natan roared at Mikal. "You! Inside!"

Mikal complied quickly. Natan would deal with his apprentice later.

Mor-Lath took Natan's arm but Natan pulled it out of his grasp. Then he was propelled along by forces unseen. "What the—" He found himself strolling into the commons next to the Dark One. "I don't want to listen to a damn word you have to say."

"Oh, yes you do. Now kindly shut up and let me talk."

Natan sputtered. Mor-Lath ignored his protest. "Well, I must say I'm none too pleased with your new Priestess. Kind of makes me sorry I killed the last one."

"You gonna kill this one too?"

"No. No matter how sweet the temptation is. But she and I have had our little talk together. You'll find her a more tractable woman from now on.

"No," he continued. "I will not be killing her or anyone else. I made a promise to Adrastea."

"I don't believe you." The grass was taller here, muffling their footsteps. A few trees, too spindly for cutting down, offered a scant shade.

"Funny. She said the same thing." Mor-Lath looked at Natan. "However, part of that bargain was that there had to be one needful death."

"Mira's?" Natan spat.

Mor-Lath shook his head. "No. Someone else. You don't know him, but he's got to die."

"Why? There's no reason for all this killing."

"Why? Because this man is a threat to Adrastea." He stopped. "Oh, didn't I tell you before? That's the same reason I killed Mira. Did you know she near killed your niece? She had a shard of sacred glass. She used this to slit Adrastea's throat. Would have died, had I not been there. Carles put the idea into her head. Can you believe it?"

"You gonna kill him too?"

Mor-Lath shook a finger at Natan. "Remember, I promised no more killing."

"I'll believe it when I see it."

Mor-Lath only smiled. "Oh, one other thing. For her protection, I've chosen to spend more time with Adrastea—meaning, all the time."

Natan swore some more.

The Dark God gave Natan a look of mock surprise. "I wouldn't think you'd object, seeing your arrangement with Ari." Then he covered his mouth as if shocked. "Oh, dear. I've besmirched your niece's reputation. I guess I'll have to marry her now to save her honor."

Natan told Mor-Lath what he could do with himself. Mor-Lath only chuckled.

"You done?" Natan demanded.

"There's yet one more thing I think you should know. Someone in Crossroads suffered a nasty bit of interrogation yesterday. An advanced scouting party is on its way here. They'll arrive by nightfall. Something about a story of supplies and an easy target. Put your people on guard and get a hurry-up on those defenses. I have a feeling you'll need them soon."

A nagging fear chewed at Natan's guts. If the god was telling the truth... Natan was more than through with this conversation. He would not let Mor-Lath toy with him. "Bugger off."

"Be nice. And next time, show some gratitude."

As the sun set, Adrastea brought a chair out to the porch. She sat to watch the pyre from afar, her only light a lamp set in the window. She had no wine nor any lactoverosa or anything to help dull the pain of saying goodbye to someone she'd known all her life.

Mor-Lath, who'd been in and out all day, appeared on the porch next to her. She didn't blink. That she was used to his presence annoyed her. He'd tempted her a few more times during the day but not enough to take the edge off of what she recognized to be a growing craving. Her skin craved his touch. How distracting. He was addicting her; she knew it. She didn't dare touch the earth again to see if Creation would answer her need, in case he tried to stop her, or in case he didn't.

She'd have to resist. If she gave in to this craving, he could trick her into marrying him through sheer addictive need. Ari had warned her about the nature of addiction. Some things could take over one's life.

Ari would know. Adrastea did not like to see Ari's life being eaten away by her frustration over Natan and her never-ending need to dull the pain.

Ari's early life hadn't been easy. She and her brothers had lost both parents in the plague that killed Adrastea's own grandparents. In her grief, she turned to her childhood sweetheart, Natan. He had been there for her but then he was apprenticed as Mayor. Mayors could never marry. They served the village and could never serve family.

Ari had ranted that she, as healer, could provide for them both. She never convinced Natan or anyone else to break with tradition. He gave her the love she wanted but only in secret. It had never been enough for Ari. While his clandestine love soothed her soul every so often, the confidential nature of their relationship stressed her.

"I said, you can go to the funeral if you want."

She shook herself free from her thoughts. "What?"

Mor-Lath hunched down next to her chair and laid a hand on her lap. "You really are off with the angels, aren't you? Go to the funeral. Nobody can prevent you."

But Adrastea shook her head. "No. It's best if I stay here. They..." how to explain? "They don't want me down there. I'd bring bad luck. Let them mourn in peace."

"And will you mourn?"

She considered this question. "I will think of many imaginative ways of causing you pain. I will dream of hot knives and vinegar and of how long I can make you scream. I'll think of what interesting little sharp things I can shove under your nails, how slowly I can flay your skin until the pain in your eyes matches the pain in my heart."

He smiled as if she was whispering sweet nothings to him. "I love it when you talk evil."

Adrastea didn't stir. "Some would say I was rising to the Light." Oh, how she wanted to cry for Mira, and again for her mother.

But not in front of him.

She pressed a fist to her lips and focused on the village commons. It was getting dark, almost too dark to see the white shrouded body on the pyre. Chloe would light the pyre soon. That would illuminate the village. It would burn brightly for a few hours then dim down into coals, to smolder for the rest of the night and possibly into the next day.

Mor-Lath's hand moved to her bare arm. She shook it off with violence. "Don't touch me."

"Why? Because of this?" He tempted her addiction.

"Rack off, Mor-Lath," she warned him. She let the desire for the taste of Power wash through her then tried to tell herself it was gone.

"Oh, does that bother you?" He teased her again. This time it was stronger.

She whipped her head around to glare at him. "Stop it," she hissed.

He sat back on his heels. "Or what?" He increased the intensity.

Adrastea launched herself from her chair, tackling him to the porch floor. He laughed as if it was some game. That angered her further. She drew back a fist, fully intending to bring it down hard on his face. He caught it and laughed again.

"Stop mocking me." She had another fist. It landed not on its intended target but sharply against the wooden planking of the porch as he ducked her blow. That hurt.

She gasped at the pain. Using that to fuel her anger, she drew her fist back again. He caught that one as well. With an astounding speed, flipped her over so she was on her back and he on top.

Adrastea kicked and cursed. "Let me up, you mongrel."

"What? And let all this passion cool?"

She struggled and shoved away the feeling that she would never win. She had to win. How dare he ridicule her and make her angry for his entertainment? The world was full of people he could be tormenting, and he had to pick her now.

The fire in her heart lost its flare but continued to sear. He was stronger than her, even if he were not a god. Her hands were useless. The way he straddled her prevented her from using her legs.

But she had other talents. She withdrew into herself and focused all her anger and rage. She remembered the rain barrel and what she had done.

"Oh, what are you planning now, my Darklet?"

She opened her eyes, focused on his face and released the whole of her anger.

A brief flicker of surprise stung down the line on her cheek. He leapt back, freeing her body so she could sit up.

But instead of anger, he seemed pleased. "You clever thing."

She sunk her fist in his stomach and he doubled over, gasping. She drew it back again, but he put his open palm up to her fist, half surrender, half stopping her. His eyes met hers. "Oh, if only you knew the Power that coursed within you now."

She hesitated and turned her thoughts inward. There is was, singing to her, as pure and sweet as it had been when she'd first tasted it just a month ago.

Had it really been only a month? It seemed like she'd felt it all her life. Perhaps she had but didn't know it.

And there was one difference. The addictive quality that had been present whenever Mor-Lath tempted her was gone. This was the Deeper Power as it should be, the same Power that the Light touched, and Creation was.

Instead of leaving her craving, it filled her and satisfied her soul.

She felt sorry for her earlier anger. Guilt nagged her for having let Mor-Lath goad her into it. She wanted to apologize for having struck him. She wanted to make peace, not only with him but the whole of the world. Her heart calmed, and she relaxed, even releasing the fists she had made.

All would be well.

"Adrastea," Mor-Lath barked. "Back to earth."

Reluctantly, she lost her touch with the sweet Deeper Power. In the darkness she tried to focus on Mor-Lath's face in the soft lamp light. He no longer mocked but looked concerned. "Do not let yourself be lost in it," he warned her. "You might not find your way back."

Adrastea didn't answer him. They sat side by side on the porch. His hand covered hers where once he'd been blocking her fist.

A flare of light caught her eye. She squinted down at the village. The pyre lit up, a bright dot in a blot of darkness. The edge of the world held the last faint blues of sunset. Above a few stars had appeared. Slowly she stood and faced the pyre. She could see the silhouettes of people who stood around the fire. Had all of Sacred Spring and Little Crossroads shown up?

Mor-Lath rose behind her. "You should go to the funeral," he said. "You're regret it if you don't."

He was right. Adrastea gave in. She dusted off her clothes and walked down the hill.

Mor-Lath kept pace with her. She let him be, until they stopped just beyond the circle of light. It would not do to be noticed.

Adrastea saw Natan and Ari holding each other and staring into the flames. Their backs turned to Adrastea. Ari's shoulders shuddered.

Mikal stood nearby with his foster siblings. They didn't stir but watched the fire burn, as did most of the villagers. Those whose faces she could see were damp with crying, the light glinting off wet faces. Mourners dabbed at their eyes.

Then a couple turned and moved away. Adrastea recognized Amarice, her form large and awkward. No one could doubt her pregnancy now, for it seemed she'd popped out even more over the past week. She lurched away from the fire. Marlon escorted her back home, supporting her. She must have been tired.

Mor-Lath stepped forward. She looked at him, but he didn't return her gaze. He watched Marlon and Amarice closely.

"What are you thinking?" she asked with warning in her voice.

Mor-Lath observed them as they moved towards home. "Look at them and you tell me what you see."

Adrastea squinted. What did Mor-Lath see? She blinked. The angels that surrounded Amarice appeared. They attended her, stroking her hair, her arms, her belly. So attentive were they, it made Marlon look like one of them, only dark and common.

Mor-Lath prompted, "Look at his soul. What does it say?" He stepped back and left Adrastea to her own devices.

Was there a particular way of looking at someone that revealed what their soul said? Soon the twilight would claim Marlon and his wife. Before he disappeared completely, she felt, rather than saw, what Mor-Lath meant.

"I only feel one thing. 'I am ready'." She turned to him. "What does that mean?"

Mor-Lath only grunted but continued to watch them go home, long after Adrastea couldn't see them anymore. "Come," he said eventually. "Let us move into the light."

Adrastea shook her head and backed up. "We'll be seen."

He nodded. "I'm counting on it."

"But—"

"Forget what they'll think," he insisted. "Believe me, they're not going to care."

Adrastea begged to differ. He snagged her hand and dragged her reluctant self into the circle.

Mira's pyre burned in bright, flickering splendor. What better way to depart this world and return to Creation than by light?

As they stood there, no one approached, no one spoke to them. There were a few glances that Adrastea caught. As her eyes met theirs, the people looked away. Chloe was right. They no longer welcomed her.

She looked at Mor-Lath to her right, and beyond that, saw Natan and Ari. Ari stared at the flames as she bawled like a child. Natan, too, had his eyes filled with tears. He turned and looked at her and didn't glance away. His face spoke only of grief and no more beyond the moment.

Time no longer mattered. While the fire burned, nobody else had any reason to leave. But Adrastea felt she should. The guilt from her unspoken conversation with Natan brought back its bloom to her chest. He would never forgive her for standing so casually with Mira's killer. She had to go.

She turned her back to the pyre, but Mor-Lath stayed her with his arm. "No, you must stay."

"I can't!" her voice quivered. "You have no idea how I feel." She tried to push past him, but he grabbed her arm.

"I am a god. I know exactly how you feel." He pulled her closer to him. "Trust me," he whispered. "Just stay for a moment more."

"No."

"That was a moment, you know."

She felt the rage rise in her.

It never reached its peak.

Beyond the fire, beyond the Mayor's house, someone screamed, then screamed again.

The quietude of grief broke. Gasps and cries of surprise rolled across the village green. "That's Amarice!" someone called.

The crowd dissolved. Everyone scattered like ants.

Adrastea looked up into Mor-Lath's face. "You didn't. You promised!"

"You're right. I didn't. I kept my promise."

Natan came up and jerked Mor-Lath back by an arm to face him. "You bastard. What have you done?"

Mor-Lath remained calm. "I have done nothing. But I did warn you, Mayor. This is not my work." Some of the people had run in the direction of the Poulters. The rest moved about in chaos.

Natan said some choice words to the Dark God.

But all Mor-Lath said in reply was, "Your night has just begun. Go fetch your rifle."

From out in the darkness came a loud crack, whose echo bounced off the buildings. Several people screamed. Natan's expression changed. "What the— that was gunshot!"

Out and away towards the Poulters, someone hollered in surprise. Everyone panicked. The crowd scattered. Mothers hastened children indoors. Men fluttered, unorganized.

Mor-Lath turned away from the sound. He listened for something else. Then he cast out his hand, waving it once.

Amid the noises of panicked people trying to find families, Adrastea could hear these terrible screams of pain.

Natan gave Mor-Lath another shove. "What the hell did you just do?"

"I just saved your village."

Adrastea covered her face with her hands. "Oh, you didn't."

"No, my dear, I didn't kill them. Well, not by my hand. I doubt they will last long, however, when you've learned what they've done to your people, Mayor."

Adrastea looked up. "What did you do?"

"I gave them rather nasty headaches." He stepped away from Natan. "Send your people out to round them up. I dare say you have some questioning to do."

Natan swallowed. Adrastea saw his Adam's apple bobbing several times. "What did they do?" he replied in a hoarse voice.

Mor-Lath didn't answer.

In the moment of silence, Adrastea thought she could hear Amarice wailing. In a moment, she confirmed it. An abrupt need to find out what happened filled her. She ran.

"Adrastea," Natan called out. "It's not safe."

"Let her go," Mor-Lath insisted. "She's perfectly safe."

If they said anything else, she did not hear. Her feet carried her past Natan's house, past the Taylors to the side road. A group of village women viciously attacked a screaming man. They screeched like banshees as they delivered blows and kicks. He was not long for this world. She left them behind and rounded the lane that led to the Poulters. There, three men had beaten another stranger well and truly to death.

Adrastea found Amarice just inside the Poulters' gate, crouched on the ground. Adrastea drew near, she recognized the prone figure of Marlon.

She desperately wished for a light. Looking up, she saw the faint glow of a lamp through the cracks of the Poulters' window, waiting to welcome them home.

Adrastea fetched it and turned up the flame.

Marlon was very much dead, a spreading stain of darkness on the front of his shirt. It stained Amarice's hands and hair as she gripped her locks in grief. She rocked back and forth and wailed loudly.

Jak Carpenter, Rop Storekeeper and Peter Smith dragged the body of the stranger they'd beaten to death over to the gate. They stopped shy of coming in.

"He's dead, isn't he?" Peter asked, gesturing at Marlon.

Adrastea sank to her knees next to Amarice. She nodded.

One by one they came in and stood before the body of their friend. Mack Taylor sobbed.

Why had there to be so many deaths?

Peter echoed her thoughts. "Why have so many died?"

"It's like the plagues again," said Jak.

Rop looked at Adrastea. "It's the Dark One's work, this is."

Adrastea looked up at him, startled. His eyes looked just like Marta's when she was feeling particularly nasty.

"They say your betrothed is a Dark Priest, come to lure you into the ways of Darkness."

What could she say to that?

Peter put a comforting arm around Amarice. "Can't you... you know, like what you did with Dan Mason's leg?"

Adrastea shook her head. "I can't heal death."

"Or you won't?" Rop accused.

Jak put a hand on Rop's shoulder. "Why don't you go fetch Ari? And get Willem too, won't you?"

Rop kept his words to himself. His eyes had more than plenty to say to Adrastea. She narrowed her gaze in return. Only when he was gone, did she dare set the lamp down and scoot back.

Jak turned Marlon's body so it didn't look so distorted. He crossed his hands on his chest.

"It wasn't your fault, lass," Jak said. "You weren't here when it happened."

"I know," Adrastea replied. Her eyes met his. "But I'm going to get accused all the same, aren't I?"

Jak nodded.

She rose. "I think I'll leave now."

"I won't mention anything about you."

She gave him a sad little smile. "Why are you being so kind to me?"

Jak shrugged. "I liked your father."

Others approached, especially that group of women who had been assaulting the other man. Blood spattered their aprons and their arms. They ranted and shrilled. Woe betide any stranger who crossed their path.

Adrastea left the circle of light and slipped out behind the Poulters' house, over the wall into Natan's well-tended garden. She escaped to the deserted road and, without seeking out Mor-Lath, stumbled up the path to home.

Chapter 23

She should never have gone to the funeral. As she fought the bushes alongside the road, she cursed Mor-Lath for convincing her to go. When she got to the front gate of the house, she paused, watching the faded glow of the pyre. There were also smaller lights—lanterns of searchers—moving about, possibly looking for more strangers who had come to the village.

Adrastea wanted to cry. She wanted someone to put their arms around her and comfort her. She wanted it to be someone other than Mor-Lath. But no one waited for her at home. She sunk to her knees in the untended front yard and laid face down on the long wild oats. They crunched beneath her body as she pressed her cheek against their dry grassy coolness.

She let stillness roll over her and she listened. Was Creation listening to her?

It was. The Deeper Power flowed and sang under her face and fingers. She reached out to it and drew it to her. "Why?" she asked it. "What is happening to me?"

The Power flowed into her, clean and clear. She welcomed it. Peace, peace, child, it sang to her, soothing the pain in her soul. She drew on it until the ache in her heart eased. She pulled more to be sure the ache didn't return.

Mor-Lath appeared, as he inevitably would, and sat on the grass next to her. "Adrastea?" He didn't sound too sure at the moment.

She didn't move. "Go away, Mor-Lath. I don't need you."

"That hurts." He sounded serious.

"I'm not falling for any of your games."

He didn't reply to this.

"I've got to leave the village," she explained, "all because of you. I am going by myself. I'm not going with you. I want nothing more to do with you."

"You don't mean that, do you?"

She sat up. "Of course, I do." She could sense, more than see his face. He wasn't happy.

He watched her for a moment longer. "What will you do when you leave?"

"I have skills. I could earn a living."

"Not much call for a country village healer. If only you knew about the great colleges where—"

"I don't care. I have other talents. I will figure out something."

He kept watching her, saying nothing.

"What?" she demanded after the silence grew awkward.

"Have you looked at yourself?" he asked her.

She raised her hands. They shimmered from the Deeper Power. She could see her hands better than she expected in the moonless night. "Yeah? So?"

He reached out a hand. "You're holding the Deeper Power." He laid his hand on her shoulder then snatched it back as if hot. She felt a small ripple where he touched her. "That's a lot," he said.

Was it? Could she hurt him with it?

In a sudden fit of pique, she laid her hand to the sides of his face and held on. All of the Power she held she pushed into him.

He gasped and raised his hands to cover hers. "Oh," he moaned. "That's so sweet..." He reclined to the ground, dragging her along with him. His hands held hers to his face. She couldn't pull free.

The wave of Power from her contact grew stronger. It was as if all the Power she fed to him was coming back, like ripples on a pond. For the first time, she was in control. Was it as addictive to him as when he was feeding her? What would happen if she gave him more? Her capacity was not lessened when she gave him more but seemed to increase.

He whimpered but not from pain. She felt him giving in to the Power. The line on her face throbbed with it. He would reach capacity soon.

Was it possible she could hold more than he? What would happen if she pushed him over the edge?

Before she could find out, Mor-Lath gasped, and his body shuddered as a dire thought occurred to him. A cold wave of realization flowed back through their shared connection. Before she could grasp his thought, it flowed away from her.

"No," he groaned and struggled to get free. He pushed her off him. He scrambled away until his back hit the fence.

Adrastea let go of the Power that filled her. It flowed back into the earth. She gritted her teeth. She was so close to discovering something! She crawled toward him, determined to figure out what it was. If she could control him like that once, surely, she could do it again. Possibly destroy him.

He held up a hand to stop her while he caught his breath. "Oh, no, my Darklet. We are not doing that again without benefit of matrimony."

She frowned in puzzlement. He enjoyed that? Adrastea sat back on the grass in disappointment. So much for having the advantage. Now that the Deeper Power was gone, darkness descended. He became little more than a silhouette.

She heard him draw in a breath. He was going to propose again. She could feel it. She beat him to the punch. "No, I'm not marrying you."

"Then you shall live a very lonely life. Do that to a mortal man, you will kill him. But he will die a very, VERY happy man."

Her disappointment turned into full depression. "Why do I bother?" The ache in her heart returned. The Power didn't eliminate it; it only masked it. "You've set me up well. In effect, you've destroyed my life and then expect me, with nothing left, to flee to your arms and your bed?"

He laid his arms across his knees. "Well, you're half right."

"You and your stupid games."

"What?" he said in all innocence. He scooted closer to her but didn't touch her. "Now, this would be so much easier if you could just tell me what you wanted in exchange for marriage. Every bride has her price."

"I want what you can't give me."

He sighed. "Not the resurrection thing again."

She frowned in annoyance. "What about my soul? I become your bride, I'm forsaken. When I die, off I go for eternal torment. I don't want that."

He considered her concern for a moment. "Oh, didn't I tell you? You won't die."

She nearly fell over backwards. "What?"

"Marry me and you'll be made immortal. Your soul will belong to you. You will never have to worry about dying and eternal torment, whatever that's supposed to mean."

Oh, drat. It would have to make sense. But there had to be a catch somewhere. He was not known for telling the whole truth. "But…?"

"But nothing. You will marry me because it's your destiny. When you do, you become my immortal bride. Everybody wins."

What sheer audacity to claim that everyone would win. No good had come of his presence so far. No way good would come of it, except, perhaps, that he would leave the village. Unless he chose to live near the in-laws. That sounded like something he'd do.

"Ah, you are vexed with me," he cooed.

"Absolutely." She rose to her feet and stamped into the house, slamming the door behind her, not so much to prevent him from following but to further demonstrate her anger.

He pursued her inside where she paced in front of the low fire, muttering about insincerity. Before he could say anything, she vented. "You tell me it's my destiny, yet you tell me I've a choice? I don't see how that works."

He grabbed her hand in passing. She jerked it out of his grasp, so he stepped in and snagged her around the waist. He pulled her backwards until he fell into a chair and she fell into his lap.

"Let me go, you mongrel." Adrastea struggled against him. He evaded her kicks and blows before wrapping his arms around her in a way that all but constrained her from moving. "This isn't convincing me."

"I can't talk with you when you're being unreasonable."

"You mean, when I'm refusing to listen to you."

"Same thing."

"Hardly. I'm most reasonable when I'm not listening to you." She tapped into the Deeper Power without being sure what she was going to do with it.

Mor-Lath put her off his lap. "Now, no more of that. If you're going to play with heat, you might as well do some cooking."

She had no idea what he meant.

"How about I show you something useful?" he offered.

"Oh? Like what?"

"Oh," he mocked her tone, "like using that Power you're so fond of calling upon now for doing something?"

Curiosity replaced the fire in her belly.

He held out his hand. "We need a rock."

"I don't have a rock."

"You've got plenty. We pulled enough out of the garden the other day." He turned to the back door and willed it open. Then, lifting his hand to the open door, a rock flew obediently to his palm. It was a largeish rock that filled his grip.

"Come sit down." He sat on the bench at the table. Adrastea pulled the chair up on the other side.

He placed the rock on the table. "As you know, the Deeper Power binds Creation together. Pull enough of it, and you can unbind as well." He scooted the rock closer to her. "Try it."

She gave him a skeptical look but put her hand to the rock.

"Limit yourself to just the rock, please. I don't want the house to collapse around us."

She lifted her hand from the rock, unsure of what to do. She placed it back down. She felt the Power in the rock and pulled on it. It filled her with its sweet song.

But nothing happened to the rock. She looked at Mor-Lath in puzzlement.

"That's because there's a lot more Power in that rock than you think. Keep pulling."

Resigning herself, she concentrated on pulling Power from the rock. She pulled and pulled. "There's so much."

He nodded in agreement.

And she continued to pull. It flowed and swirled within her until she thought there couldn't be room for more.

"Keep going."

She had to be reaching capacity. Anymore and it would either overwhelm her like it did the night of Feown or possibly destroy her.

"I can't," she cried.

He put both hands on the table and leaned forward. "Don't stop now, you're almost there."

Before her fear could get the best of her, she pulled the last of the Power from the rock. It dissolved into dust. Her stomach clenched.

"Hold onto it," he urged but she couldn't. She had to let go. The Deeper Power flowed out of her to dissipate back into Creation.

Mor-Lath slumped at the table, chin cupped in his hand. "Now you'll have to gather it all back up again. And that won't be easy."

"But it was too much."

He shook his head. "No, it wasn't."

"I can't hold that much." She looked at the pile of dust on the table. Who thought a simple rock could hold so much Power?

"Sure, you can, and more. That's one of the reasons I chose you as my bride."

This gave Adrastea pause. "You mean there were others you could have chosen from?"

"No," he replied plainly. "You are the only one. My choice was whether or not to pursue you. Your choice is whether or not to accept."

"So, why did you choose to pursue me? You do not strike me as the marrying type."

He grinned. "I've been waiting for you my whole life." This his face wrinkled in frustration. "And the Light, with Their vexatious sense of, ah, 'humor', thought to delay your birth until the end of the era. They haven't left me a lot of time in which to convince you. They're up to something." He waved her unasked questions away with his hand. "No matter. Our lesson is not finished."

"But the Light—"

"I said it was no matter. Now," he pointed to the pile of dust that had started to spread across the table. "If you are so interested in talking about the Light, then you can act as the Light and re-create that rock."

She licked her lips. "I can do that?"

"Of course. Granted, destruction is easier and far more satisfying, in my opinion. But yes, you can give Power to the rock and return it the way it was. Rocks are easy because they are simple creations. The sands of the rock remember where they once were. They are easily convinced to return to their former place.

"Try this with something once living and you'll fail, for Life itself is something completely different."

"But I healed—"

"He was still alive. Being such, his body wanted to return to completeness. Had he been completely disassembled, as this rock was, you might have been able to convince his body to be restored but the life itself will have fled." He thumped his finger on the table. Dust slid further. "Now, put that rock back together."

Adrastea felt empty. "But where do I get the Power?"

"From Creation, of course. Had you held onto it like I told you, then you wouldn't have to go find it." He gave her a warning. "However, do not pull it solely from within yourself, or you will end up like that rock. That's how— just fix the rock."

Adrastea drew a breath. Then she put her hands to the table and pulled.

"No, not from the table either. Reach into Creation and pull from there."

"And where is Creation?" snapped Adrastea, getting vexed.

"All around you, you silly woman. Sense the whole of Creation and pull."

After frowning at him, she closed her eyes. She tried to feel the whole world around her.

And there it was. It was far bigger than she expected it to be. Such Power! It could easily afford a comparatively small taste to heal this rock. So, she asked for, and received, the Deeper Power. The sound of it within her had become familiar. Oh, it felt so good.

"Focus," he warned.

Ah, the rock. She concentrated, trying to sense all the dust of the former rock. To her surprise, she found every last speck. Some of it had drifted to the floor. Get back to the table, she ordered. It complied.

Her mind reeled at this. She'd had a taste of what it was like to be a god. She could command the elements. It wasn't so much commanding but convincing. The elements were more than happy to comply with an act of creation, more so than they were when she commanded them to divide.

She glanced up at Mor-Lath, who watched her avidly. A twist of sorrow tugged at her heart. Why did he have to be the Dark God?

Did he catch her thought? He eyes came alive and he sat up straighter. "Adrastea?" he whispered.

She dropped her eyes. Concentrate on the rock. Reform the rock.

However, it took an awful lot of Power to convince the dust to stick to each other. Creation was hard work. As much Power flowed into her, it flowed out and into the rock.

In the end, she did it. The rock returned to a rock, even if not its original shape. Once that was done, the rock seemed satisfied to be a rock. But unlike other times when she handled the Deeper Power, it left a slight tingling taste of Power that didn't evaporate. If she listened very carefully, she could hear it buzzing just under her skin. She closed her eyes and sighed.

She felt Mor-Lath stand beside her. "Adrastea?" he asked, gently taking her hands and guiding her to her feet. He wrapped her hands in his and pressed them to his chest. "Now you know what it's like. Imagine feeling like this all the time."

She opened her eyes and looked into his. There, she saw anticipation and a cautiousness that could almost pass for hope.

"Please," he breathed. "Marry me."

She let out a small sound not quite a whimper but not yet a sigh. Was all this only possible with him? "I— I don't know."

With the back of his fingers, stroked her unscarred cheek. The touch was so gentle, so caring. Her resolve melted away. "Marry me?" He rotated his hand so his palm cupped her cheek. She leaned into it. Her heart knew calm. The Power sang to her, sweet like the voices of angels. This was what it was like to be a god.

He tilted her face up to his. "Marry me." Then his face bent to hers. He gave her a gentle kiss that grew more passionate, more insistent.

Had he not stopped her mouth with a kiss, she would have said yes.

The house began to shake but it was not their doing. They pulled away from each other as the front door slammed open. A fierce wind buffeted them both.

Adrastea watched in horror as multitudes of angels streamed in. As one force, they attacked Mor-Lath. He had only time to curse once before being overwhelmed. So strong was the force of their impact that the back door splintered under the force of their weight. Her hands flew to cover her mouth as she watched the Dark One, borne down by the messengers of Light, fly backwards out of the house. Her body trembled in fear. She ran toward him, only to be caught back by celestial hands.

An angel appeared before Adrastea and beckoned. "Come with me, Daughter of the Light." Adrastea reached out for the hand but her mortal grasp slipped through the insubstantial angel.

She looked back. Where was Mor-Lath?

The angel led her out of the house and down the path of the hill. Adrastea had to run to keep up. Her thoughts flew as fast as her feet. Did divine salvation come at last during her moment of weakness? Was the reason the Light did not intervene until now because she was being tested? Was that the limit of her strength?

Her side ached. She slowed down to catch her breath. What had become of the home behind her?

Up on the hill her house swarmed with angels but also with darker creatures, visible only when they occluded an angel. Mor-Lath had summoned his demons to aid him. They waged a terrible battle with the angels, with shouts and shrieks so loud she wondered if the whole village could hear.

"Come, Daughter of the Light. You are needed."

Needed? "Where are we going?"

"To Amarice. Ari had need of you."

Adrastea followed reluctantly. She had narrowly escaped agreeing to becoming the Bride of the Dark. She had watched angels attacking the him. Now she was being dragged off because Ari had need of an assistant?

"Trust me," the angel said, continuing to beckon. "You serve the Light tonight."

Adrastea followed. The angel guided her through the village where the pyre still burned unwatched. In the air above the commons she saw angels wrestling with demons. She heard their war cries. Was she the only one who heard them?

Several people gathered tightly around the smithy door as if it were full and there was no room for more inside. They did not notice the celestial battle.

She followed the angel to Natan's unlit house and through the back garden. The angel had her climb over the wall, for this was the fastest way to the Poulters, rather than going around the block.

Adrastea arrived at the front door a little worse for wear. Jak Carpenter was still there in the front yard. Someone had given him a chair and a fresh lantern as well. He kept watch over Marlon's dead body, now covered with a sheet. "What's going on?" she asked him.

He jerked a thumb to the closed front door. "Shock was too much for poor Amarice. Ari's in there with her now." He rose from his seat. "Do you know what—"

Adrastea didn't stay for his question. She dashed into the house. Inside, Ari had Amarice squatting by the table, holding on tightly through a contraction. The laboring woman wore nothing but a sweat-soaked blouse. Her hair, still matted with blood, had come loose from her braid to stick to her face in dark tendrils. Splotches of water covered the wooden floor and soaked the hem of Ari's skirt. Ari had built up the fire in the stove and several kettles boiled on top.

Ari acknowledged Adrastea's presence but did not stop coaching Amarice. "Breathe through it... almost over..."

The contraction released. Amarice sank down to her knees. "I can't do this," she wailed.

"I don't think you have much choice."

Adrastea came over to Ari. "What happened?"

"Where have you been?"

"Fighting the Dark God."

"I hope you won. Amarice is in labor. Now go wash your hands and come help me." Ari checked Amarice's progress. "Bloody Light, you're almost there."

Adrastea filled a basin with hot water from the kettle. "When did Amarice go into labor?"

"Hey!" Amarice called. "I'm right here!"

Ari patted her on the lower back. "She knows."

"Well, don't bloody patronize me!"

Ari rolled her eyes. To Adrastea she said, "Tonight's been too much for her. Her back started hurting at the funeral, then..." Ari glanced towards the front door.

Adrastea only nodded. "What do you need me to do?"

"Help me get the sheets off the bed. We're going to need some clean ones."

This was a strange request. Shrugging to herself, she followed Ari into the bedroom.

Once the bedroom door was closed, Ari rounded on her apprentice. "What the bloody blazes is going on?" she hissed, not so loud that Amarice could hear but sharply enough that her anger poked through. "This is Mor-Lath's doing, isn't it? The killing and the such?"

Adrastea shook her head. "No."

"You can't trust anything he says," Ari said. Adrastea caught the faint whiff of alcohol on Ari's breath.

"No, he was with me."

"Oh, was he now?" Ari's tone made Adrastea blush. "I don't imagine I can ask what you were doing?"

Adrastea felt embarrassed. "We were doing nothing like that." Or had they? The Deeper Power had felt pretty intimate. "I'll have you know we went to the funeral."

"Well, I didn't see you there. Besides, he wasn't welcome."

"That's why we didn't let anyone see us," she muttered.

Ari put her fists on her hips. "Oh, is it 'we' now? Does this mean you've made your choice?"

"No!" Her face grew even warmer. She put her hands to her burning cheeks. "That is..." She turned from her mentor.

"You have, haven't you?" Ari grabbed her by the shoulder and spun her around. "Was Mira's sacrifice all for nothing? Or does the heat of his luxurious bed burn hotter than her pyre?"

"It was nothing like that," Adrastea shrieked. She wanted to slap the Healer. She was afraid Ari would slap back and harder. "I've kept my skirts down, thank you."

From the other room, Amarice's panicked voice called out. "Ari? Ari! I'm having another one!"

Ari raised her finger in Adrastea's face. "We will speak of this later, mark my word, girl." She dashed out to assist Amarice.

Adrastea followed, sullen. Perhaps she should leave. "Don't talk to me about luxurious beds," she muttered to the slammed door. "At least I would have the benefit of matrimony."

Amarice shrieked. The table scraped across the floor.

"Adrastea!" Ari bellowed. "Come help me!"

Adrastea obeyed. Before she was betrothed, she was first a healer.

The table had been shoved clear. Amarice rocked on her hands and knees. Ari tried to keep the woman in the crouched position but Amarice fought her to stretch out.

"Lift her back up," Ari commanded. Adrastea grabbed Amarice's shoulders and helped her to a sitting position. Startled, Amarice grabbed Adrastea's hand. She squeezed tight enough to hurt.

"You'll be all right," Adrastea assured her.

Amarice didn't answer during the contraction. She rode it through. Only when it released her could she speak. "No, I'm not all right," she spat. "What the hell are you doing here?"

Ari and Adrastea eased Amarice to her hands and knees. Ari's face over Amarice's back mirrored the same question, unspoken.

She addressed her answer to Ari. "An angel of Light brought me here."

Ari smoothed a tendril of hair out of her face. "Really?" She sounded sincere.

Adrastea wasn't sure how to explain, especially with Amarice there. She licked her lips. "The Light finally came to my rescue." She glanced over at Amarice. The laboring woman was more interested in resting between contractions. "Well, you-know-who came to ask me you-know-what. Then the angels appeared. They attacked him. One led me away. She told me to come here because you needed me."

The howling of the celestial battle outside crescendoed then faded. Adrastea looked up at the roof, glad that the others couldn't hear it.

But she was wrong. Ari looked up as well. "What was that?"

Then Jak burst in. "You've got to come see this!"

Ari turned to him in surprise, glanced once more at Adrastea, then followed Jak outside. Adrastea went too.

Outside, up in the night sky, multitudes of angels and legions of demons battled together.

"Oh," Ari breathed.

"Why are they fighting?" Jak asked nobody in particular.

"Ari!" Amarice called from within the house. Ari remembered herself, cursed and hastened inside.

Adrastea remained outside with Jak, watching the sky. "That man who courts you... is he really the God of the Dark?"

This startled Adrastea. "What do you mean?" she replied, too quickly.

Jak shrugged calmly. "Only that when Natan was here earlier, he cursed Mor-Lath and your name in the same breath."

Adrastea took a step back. "He doesn't think this is my fault, does he?"

"I don't know, lass."

"You don't think he hates me, do you?"

"Who? Your uncle?"

Ari called out. "Adrastea!" It was a call of fright, more than anger.

As she returned to the house, Jak said, "You'll have to ask him, if you have the courage."

When she passed the threshold, Adrastea stopped in shock. Ari and Amarice were not alone. Another woman, dressed in grey, crouched next to Amarice. Amarice clutched her hands, her face twisted in the agony of labor. Ari stood way back. "Oh, Light!" Adrastea cursed under her breath.

Death turned her fathomless eyes to Adrastea. "Come, Daughter of the Light. Our work is not finished." Her voice was a pleasant contralto, soothing and gentle.

"What do you mean?"

Ari spat, "Bloody hell! What's going on?" she asked Death. "I said, who are you?"

Adrastea didn't even glance at the healer. "You're not going to kill her, are you?" she squeaked at Death.

Death shook her head. She leaned forward and whispered something in Amarice's ear. Amarice calmed down.

"I mean to preserve life here tonight. But you must aid me if you wish to thwart Mor-Lath. He has crossed the line twice in this village. I must address the imbalance. If you truly serve the Light, do as I say without question."

The contraction eased up and Amarice relaxed. "Is that true?" she asked Death.

Death nodded. "You will live to see your progeny breathe." She looked at Ari. "Healer, the time is soon. Come help me." She pulled her hands from Amarice's grasp while Ari checked for dilation.

Death pulled Adrastea to the side. "The Light have distracted the Dark for as long as necessary but not for much longer. Sooner or later he will come for his bride."

"But..."

Death laid a finger on Adrastea's lips. "No buts. I do not envy your destiny, Betrothed of the Dark. I cannot say more than this: you will be faced with a different choice soon. Save as many lives as you can. Death will only benefit him."

"She's ready!" Ari declared.

"So soon?" If Adrastea had counted correctly, Amarice had been in labor three hours. Nobody had labor that short, not even Marta, who was known for her intense labors of five hours.

Ari, hunkered down next to Amarice, looked at Death. "What's so special about this baby?"

Death only smiled.

Amarice breathed heavily. "I want to push!"

Adrastea and Death moved to Amarice's side. They supported her upright.

"I see a head," shouted Ari over Amarice's grunts. "It's crowning... the head's out." The contraction eased up but Amarice kept pushing. "You can stop pushing."

"But—" Amarice protested.

"It takes more than one push to birth a baby." Ari ran her finger around the baby's tiny neck to check for loops of cord. "All fine down here."

Adrastea's arms ached with the task of holding up Amarice.

"When the contraction comes," said Ari, "go ahead and push."

Outside, the sounds of battle grew louder. "We need to hurry," Death said softly to Adrastea over Amarice's head. "Don't argue with me and don't hesitate. Obey the angels as you would me."

It wasn't long before the next contraction came. Amarice pushed. The baby slipped out in a shower of water and blood. Ari eased the baby to the floor and pushed it between Amarice's knees so she could see. Death and Adrastea eased Amarice to a kneeling position, so she could lift and hold her baby.

"It's a girl!" Amarice announced.

"Kiss your child," Death told Amarice, "then hand her to Adrastea." Death pressed a small knife to Adrastea's hand. "Cut the cord." She placed a towel and a ball of string on the table. Death straightened the folded towel so it lay perfectly square with the corner of the table and centered the string.

A frown crossed Ari's face. "What do—"

Something hard slammed against the closed door, rattling it and startling them all.

"Quickly, now," commanded Death. She pointed a long finger at Ari. "Your job is not finished tonight. There is another child."

"Impossible. I would have known."

But Death shook her head. "The Light hid them well. Not even Mor-Lath knows there are two." Death glanced back at Adrastea, who held the knife. She hadn't taken the baby from Amarice. "Well, girl?" Death snapped. "Do you serve the Dark after all? Do as I say."

Adrastea shook herself from her reverie. She held out her hands to Amarice's baby.

Amarice continued to clutch the child to her chest. "But—"

"Give her the child," Death compelled her.

Amarice reluctantly turned the child over to Adrastea. Adrastea tied the cord with the string Death had provided. She cut the cord. She wiped the blood and wax from the baby's face and scooped out the mucus from the mouth. The baby startled at this. She opened her mouth and began to grope. "Surely we could—"

"No," sniped Death. "We don't have time." Another loud bang sounded on the door and threatened to splinter it. Death pointed to the storeroom door on the opposite side. "Go there. An angel will come. Follow her instructions if you wish the child to live."

Death all but shoved her through the door. As the door closed, she saw Death place a hand on Ari's forehead and murmur, "Forget..." Adrastea felt a strong surge of the Deeper Power.

The door closed, leaving Adrastea in darkness. What happened?

From the other side of the door came a thumping and an almighty crash as the front door burst open. "Bloody hell!" Ari cursed.

Then a shining light brightened the storeroom. An angel appeared. She held her finger to her lips. "Come with me, Daughter of the Light."

By the light of the angel, Adrastea saw a door opposite her. Out she went.

In the skies above, the battle continued but with fewer angels now. Most of them gathered the Poulters' home. The angel guided her through the back garden. Adrastea climbed awkwardly over the wall, because of the baby, and through Natan's yard.

On the other side of the Mayor's home, the villagers stood out in the commons, also staring up at the skies. They pointed and shouted something about the battle overhead.

The angel laid her finger on her lips once more and beckoned Adrastea onward. Adrastea slipped up the road, hoping no one saw her. She continued up the new path to Little Crossroads, for that was where the angel led.

Its small commons was empty, as most everyone was down in Sacred Spring. All the houses were dark. The angel led Adrastea to one of them. It was one of the original cabins, made of unpeeled logs and dirt floors. The thatching on top would not be enough to keep out the autumn rains.

"What do I do now?" Adrastea asked the angel. The angel faded from Adrastea's sight, leaving no answer.

There had to be a reason she was led here. She knocked on the rough door, quietly, for she did not want to wake anyone who may have been left in the village.

Soon the door opened. Laika peered out. "What do you want?"

Adrastea held the baby closer. "May... may I come in?"

Laika looked her up and down. When she saw the bundle, she moved aside. Adrastea slipped in.

Laika closed the door, plunging them into darkness. She lit a candle.

"Well?" Laika said dryly.

Adrastea gave the baby one last hug, then held her out. "I was told to bring you this."

Laika took the baby. "Whose is it?"

"I think it best I not tell you."

Laika shook her head. "I've seen what happened tonight. I've heard about the bad things. I can't trust you, Healerprentice."

A bright light blossomed in the cabin, brighter far than noonday sun. In the glow a woman stood, white-robed and also white of hair. Her face, in the prime of life, radiated beauty.

Laika backed away. Adrastea pressed herself against the door. A tiny corner of her soul feared this bright being. The rest of her soul wanted to fling herself into Her arms.

"Peace, child," said the bright woman to Laika. Her voice resonated in Adrastea's bones. The bright woman held out Her hands. Adrastea slipped the newborn into them.

"Accept this gift and raise her well." She gave the baby to Laika. She laid her hand upon Laika's head in blessing.

Laika relaxed. She carried the baby to the bed that was no more than a straw tick.

She blew in the baby's face until she drew breath to cry. After she let her cry for a moment, she opened her blouse and put the child to the breast.

The bright woman turned to Adrastea. She smiled but sadness touched Her eyes. "Dear daughter," She said. "I'm so sorry..." Then She placed a hand over Adrastea's eyes.

Chapter 24

Easy there." The grey-robed woman eased Ari to the chair. "You fainted."

Ari put her hand to her head as the dizziness cleared. How odd. Ari never fainted. "What happened?"

Amarice was still crouched on the floor, gripping the table as a contraction consumed her. Her straggled blonde head drooped as the contraction let go. So, she hadn't passed the baby yet. Thank the Light.

Ari lifted herself and moved to the table. "How long was I out?"

The woman shrugged. "Moments." She knelt down next to Amarice and pushed a wisp of hair out of the laboring woman's face.

Ari shook the last of the clouds from her head. She studied the strange woman. It was difficult to see her face, as she was bent down by Amarice. "You're Death, aren't you? Lillybet once spoke of you... I never believed her." A strange bubble of laughter welled up within her. "Of course, you are. If the Dark God is real, why not you?"

Without warning, the door shattered. Splinters of wood flew into the room. Ari and Amarice screamed.

The woman called Death ushered Amarice under the table. She stood between Amarice and the ruined door.

Ari let out a squeak of surprise as a sudden blossoming of luminous beings surround Death. They had to be angels. There were so many around Death that Ari couldn't see past them. "What's going on?"

The angels faced the doorway. Ari didn't need to guess who was there.

The God of the Dark, his countenance washed in his awful glory, grabbed Ari by the neck and slammed her against the wall. "Where is she?" he demanded.

Ari couldn't answer. Spots danced in front of her eyes. A man like this would never make a good husband. She would have to tell Adrastea, assuming Ari lived.

"Mor-Lath," Death warned, "put her down. You promised."

His eyes tightened. He released her. Ari slid to the floor. Her vision returned. She rubbed her throat. "I don't know where she is," she gasped. "I haven't seen her all day. I would have thought she was with you."

"Not Adrastea." He looked around and came face-to-face with Death. "I'm looking for the mother."

"You cannot have her, Mor-Lath," Death said. "She's not yours to have."

Mor-Lath attempted to move Death out of the way. His hands passed through her. Ari wished she knew that trick.

"You can't stop me," he sneered at Death. "You can't interfere like this." He swatted at some of the angels who insisted on swooping him.

"The Light can," Death threw at him.

"They're not here" Between the flurry of angels, he spied Amarice, cowering on the floor. "There you are."

Under the table, she rocked back and forth on her hands and knees, her sweat-soaked shirt trailing on the floor. Another contraction seized her. She tightened in pain.

"Ari?" Amarice whimpered. Ari scrambled across the floor to her. "I want to push."

Mor-Lath tried to skirt around Death, but she blocked him every time. "Get out of my way," he roared.

Ari pulled Amarice out from under the table, trying to keep it between them and the angry god. "Can't push yet," she told her. She reached down and checked Amarice's progress. "Oh, bugger! The cord's prolapsed." Ari tried to push the cord back up inside. "Wait, I can feel a head."

As he tried to move past her, Death tackled Mor-Lath to the floor. "You cannot have them," she insisted. "They belong to the Light."

"The child belongs to me." He scrambled to his feet. "That is the mashiah I've been waiting for." Death pulled him back down again.

The contraction hit Amarice. She grunted as it took hold. Silence claimed her as it completely consumed her being.

Ari felt the head pass through. She checked the neck, bound by the cord. She used her finger to ease it up and over. "Amarice, I promise your child will live."

But then what?

The immortals fought. The table was thrown against the wall where it cracked loudly. Ari dragged Amarice into the corner with some effort. Even if she wasn't pregnant, Amarice was a large lass. With the next contraction, the baby eased out.

It was a boy. She lifted the child and laid him on Amarice's chest. Amarice wrapped her arms around her baby and cried. She rocked back and forth, wailing. The knife Ari had in her pocket was gone but she had a second in her healer's bag by the stove.

The house shook as Mor-Lath threw Death against the wall. He yelled something at her Ari couldn't understand and Death spat something equally nasty back. Ari didn't recognize the language.

Grabbing the bag, Ari helped Amarice to her feet and helped her into the bedroom. Blood streamed down Amarice's legs as she hobbled into the other room.

This had to be the most unusual birth Ari had ever attended. What did Mor-Lath want with Amarice and her baby? And where was Adrastea? If she was here, she could have helped her with Amarice's heavy bulk. Walking is difficult after one just had one's hips split open wide. Then again, if Adrastea was here, she might have had the power to distract Mor-Lath.

Ari cursed the lack of water in the bedroom. All the warm water was out in the other room. Still, Ari did her best to make Amarice comfortable on the bed as she tended to the baby. She tied and severed the umbilical cord. Then, as she set the baby to nurse at Amarice's breast, she gave a gentle tug to see if the placenta had loosened yet.

She had to keep Amarice and the baby safe. That might mean moving them. Until the placenta came, Amarice was going nowhere. "Adrastea, where are you?" Ari muttered.

An almighty crash shook the walls again, a final sound.

Then silence. Ari's heart beat faster. Somebody must have won. But who?

The door creaked open. The victor stepped through.

"Ari," Mor-Lath said. "Give me the woman and her babe."

Ari leapt to her feet. "No." She threatened Mor-Lath with the knife that had separated mother and child. She expected him to laugh at her.

He didn't. He approached, his presence intimidating. If she could have found any strength, she would have stabbed him—wanted to—but her hand wouldn't move. All she could do was stand there, knife upraised while he gently took it from her fingers. "Do not interfere in things over which you have no power."

Once he relieved her of her weapon, he stepped around her.

Amarice screamed and clutched her baby tightly.

Mor-Lath yanked the life from them as if whipping sheets from a bed.

The only movement Ari could manage was to blink the tears from her eyes.

Adrastea woke up on the floor of her mother's home, her head aching. The house was dark but for a patch where the back door used to be.

It all came back to her in a rush. She murmured her first thought: "Mor-Lath." She ran out of the house, heedless of any danger that might be waiting for her.

The remains of the door littered the porch. Splinters lay scattered through the garden but there was no sign of Mor-Lath. Looking up the hill to the mountains and starry sky beyond, she saw nothing out of place. No angels, no demons. Certainly no gods.

She ran to the front of the house. Not much there. Even Mira's funeral pyre was dark. A few remaining angels, spots of brightness, fought demons, whose dark bodies occluded much of the angels' light.

"Oh no," she groaned. "Amarice!" She fled down the hill and onto the commons. A few people huddled in groups near the pyre, whispering fervidly. Someone saw Adrastea and called out to her. She ignored them and fled through Natan's backyard and over the wall to the Poulters. The Lines of the Deeper Power warped into knots, the distortions worsening the closer she moved to the house.

She slipped through the open back door.

Inside, the house was a shambles. The big kitchen table lay tumbled against the wall, cracked in half. The remaining furniture lay scattered about, also damaged.

"Amarice?" she called out, before seeing the trail of blood leading into the bedroom.

Bursting in, she saw Ari standing there, hand raised, a look of utter shock on her face. Slowly Ari sank to her knees and sobbed once.

Behind her, Mor-Lath stood over the bed, his knuckles pressed to his lips in thought. He did not turn when Adrastea entered the room.

Adrastea froze when she saw Amarice and her baby, born alive but reft all-too-soon of that life.

She was too late.

Her knees gave way, dropping her to the floor like Ari. "Oh, Mor-Lath," she groaned. "You promised…"

He studied the dead bodies on the bed. "I did not break that promise."

"You killed a baby." The moment the words were out of her mouth, the reality of it struck her and her anger flared up. "You bloody killed a baby! What sort of monster are you?"

He turned his gaze to her, cold with an emotion she could not identify. "This was all part of your bargain. I promised I would not kill another of your villagers. In exchange, you gave me them." He gestured to the two dead bodies.

"You told me you wanted the mashiah. Not Amarice, and certainly not…" She felt her temper rise. "You never said anything about killing babies!"

His anger blazed. "That baby was the mashiah. Do you realize what he would have grown up to become?"

"A god-killer?" she spat at him.

Mor-Lath recoiled as if slapped hard. "You do not understand what that word means. He would not have just come after me. He would have come after you too. Shall I show you what manner of man I have just killed?" He lunged at her, grabbed her by the arms and gave her a shake. "Shall I?"

Pinning her against the wall, he pressed his forehead to hers. He let the vision of his forthtelling pour into her heart and mind.

Out of the swirling mists of memory-yet-to-be, a man stepped forth, dressed in stained battle leathers. A nasty scar twisted one of his eyes. He looked vaguely like Marlon, but his hair was blond like Amarice's. Unlike Marlon, he had no kindness in his face. His remaining eye burned with a fervent fire that preyed upon Adrastea's heart. The man drew a dagger and approached. "Hello, my pretty," he rasped. "It'd be a shame to part your blood from your veins before parting your pretty legs with a different dagger."

He reached out and snagged her by her bodice. The strings popped loose. She felt his callused hand grope at her bare skin. Adrastea screamed and tried to back away. She could not escape the man who held a dagger to her throat. He slid the tip down between her breasts and then trailed it even lower.

His thoughts, shared with her, of violating her and his joy at the pain it brought her, echoed her very soul, shattering it into panic.

Adrastea couldn't tear herself away. The man's hand was tangled too tightly in her hair. "No!" She searched around but there was no one else in that shadow world but them. She was cornered.

Then she thought of the rock. Adrastea struggled against the man's chest until she could place a hand on his face. Then, as with the rock and the earth, she drew on the Deeper Power, sucking as much of it as she could from him. As she started to pull, the man let go of her and retreated in fear, dissolving into the mist.

Adrastea found herself back in Amarice's bedroom. Ari had scooted as far as the bedroom wall, where she had pressed herself into the wood, unable to go farther. She stared at the pair, eyes wide in terror.

Mor-Lath's hands were still around her arms. That was too much like being restrained by the image of the mashiah. Another wave of panic washed through her and fueled her strength. Without thinking, she drew upon the Deeper Power and sent him flying to the other side of the room.

"I hate you!" she screamed. "How could you do that to me?"

"I had to show you," he insisted, picking himself up from the floor. "You had to be made to understand."

But Adrastea shook her head. "No. You did that because you wanted to. You would say anything—do anything—to get what you wanted."

He opened his mouth to speak. Adrastea called upon the Deeper Power again and pushed him against the wall. By sheer will alone she held him there, her anger fueling her. "For all I know, there is no mashiah. You made that up to trick me into allowing you to kill again." Her whole body trembled from the memory of Marlon's son. Her gaze looked over to Amarice's dead baby. No way they could have been one and the same.

It wasn't enough. She wanted to strangle him with her bare hands. No sooner had she thought that, than her hands were about his throat.

She squeezed. Oh, she tried to squeeze. Within her the Deeper Power wavered. She wanted to call it back. Tears streamed down her face as she fought to strangle a god.

He raised his hand and untangled her fingers from his throat. Her hands shook so much she couldn't control them. He enveloped them in his own. "Shhh," he said.

He sank to his knees. He said words she never thought she'd hear: "I'm so sorry."

So strong were her tears, everything blurred. "What?"

"I never meant to hurt you that way. I... I didn't know any other way to impress upon you the importance of..." His head dropped. He wilted. "If only you understood my fear..." he murmured, almost too quiet for her to hear.

She fought to keep her anger. She would not be manipulated again. "I don't care. You could die for all I care."

"You don't mean that."

"Too sweet I do. You come around with your fine words and your clever tricks. You have me almost liking you. Then you pull something like this?" She flung a hand out towards the dead mother and baby on the bed. "You say you love me and want to marry me but... but..." Her anger grew too strong for words. She shoved him hard on his shoulder. He rocked from the impact. Mor-Lath rose to his feet, a bleak expression on his face.

She pointed a finger at him. "You go too far, Mor-Lath. I..." she drew a breath. "I will never marry you now."

She spun on her heel and stalked out the door, slamming it to emphasize her displeasure. Mor-Lath and Ari stared at one another but did not say a word.

Ari's eyes narrowed. Her hand itched for a knife. She knew exactly where she would plant it.

ഗ⊚ൠⓢↄ

A drastea stalked out the front door, through the yard and past the unattended body of Marlon. She made her furious way down the lane and to the commons. She didn't know where she was going, nor did she care.

"I was such a fool," she cursed to the night air. The darkness hid her shame at having come so close to being tricked into marriage. She had been coerced into a promise that resulted in the death of a baby and his mother.

The night sky held nothing but stars. Even dawn had yet to touch the east. The demons and the angels had fled, or perhaps anger blinded her to the spiritual world. Had the angels come to rescue her earlier that evening? Or did they not care about her?

When they had attacked Mor-Lath, she thought it had been the Light coming to rescue her. She wasn't sure what happened from that point on— she couldn't remember. Then she woke up alone. All other supernatural beings, including Mor-Lath, were gone.

She stopped in the middle of the road, spread her arms wide and addressed the heavens. "Why?!" she bellowed. "Am I not a Daughter of the Light?"

No answer.

She shrieked out all her rage at the Light for forsaking her. She wanted the Light to come down and turn her into a pillar of salt, like the tale of the unfaithful wife, or dissolve her into sea foam, like the forsaken lover. Anything to end this life of pain.

Never in her life had she felt so alone.

She wailed and screeched and rent her clothes and wallowed in the dust until the flare of her anger fled, leaving only sorrow—empty, empty sorrow, draining her of any future joy.

Adrastea wished she had a knife, so she could open her veins and let out the cold, bitterness that flowed within, to finish the job Mira had started.

She laid her face down in the dust and sobbed out the last of her energy. Even the earth felt unresponsive under her touch.

Was there anything left for her here? A dry numbness, when she could cry no more, made her feel stuffed with cotton. She closed her swollen eyes. Perhaps she should let the last of her consciousness bleed away into the ground. If she could pull from Creation, maybe she could bleed back into it, to become lost there forever. Let the coldness of the earth sink into her bones.

Could one will oneself to death?

The canyon breeze danced its cool fingers across her damp skin. She shivered and welcomed the cold. It matched the numbness in her heart. If she was lucky, morning would never come.

Some time later a pair of strong hands found her. They lifted her up and wiped the dust from her face. They picked her up, cradled her close and carried her home without saying a word.

⸙

Adrastea's thoughts gathered from the darkness of oblivion and focused until they became consciousness. She lived?

She felt better, much to her surprise, as sleep had taken the edge off her pain. Even then, her heart felt empty. Something was missing.

At least she felt warm in body.

A hand stroked her face, the side with the scar. It thrummed at the contact. That brought her to full wakefulness. She opened her eyes to see Mor-Lath lying next to her, studying her.

"Good morning," he said in all seriousness.

She gathered the quilts about her, scooting away from him until her back hit the wall. What was he doing in bed with her?

He rose to an elbow and waited for her to speak.

Her face grew warm. "We— we didn't—"

"No. You weren't in the mood." He pushed himself up to sitting. He had a shirt on at least, fully laced up. "And if there had been a single thread of feeling left for me in your heart, any foolishness last night would surely have destroyed it." He raised his knees under the covers and laid his arms across them. "I dare say I may have ruined any chances I have of winning you over."

She clutched the quilts but risked a peek to see, to her assurance, that she wore a modest nightgown. She chose not to question how she came to be wearing it but focused on the fact that it simply was.

"I'm sorry," he said. "I'm sorry for everything. I've handled it poorly. I should have been honest with you from the beginning. I should have told you who the mashiah was. Though I must confess I was not completely sure that it was him until he was born, so well protected he was by the Light.

"I should not have shown you the truth of who he would have become. I was so frustrated with you."

She blinked at him. "Frustrated?"

"I was scared. All you could see was a helpless baby. But I saw his future. I felt frustration that you lacked the foresight to see the man he would become."

He sighed regretfully. "I... I should not let my temper get away from me like that. I should not have shown you your future because upon his death, it ceased being your future. I used it to scare you. For that I'm very sorry."

"You terrified me with a future that will never happen." She remembered him showing her a vision of something, but the details eluded her memory. Where did they go?

He threw back the quilts and swung his legs, thankfully clad in trousers, over the side of the bed. He sat there and put his head in his hands. "I wish I knew how to heal you."

Adrastea didn't know what to say. By his own hand, Mor-Lath had effectively thwarted himself. She drew her knees up and cupped her chin in her hands. "So, why is it you're in bed with me?"

He raised his head up for a moment but didn't turn around. Couldn't he meet her gaze? "You wanted to kill yourself last night. Then, when you had cried yourself out, I brought you home and put you to bed. You spent the rest of the night fighting nightmares. Since they were my fault, I stayed with you and helped you defeat them."

"I don't remember having any nightmares." It was true. The whole night was a blank.

"You're welcome." He sighed in relief and swung around. She sat up straighter. He buried his face in her lap and wrapped his arms around her waist. "Please forgive me," he said. "I will remain with you and defend you. I'll help you any way I can. All this is my fault. I must make amends."

She couldn't push his head off her lap. "I don't want your help."

"I can't leave you to face them alone." He scooted closer to her. "Please don't reject my help just yet."

A tiny alarm bell rung in her head. "Why?" she asked, full of suspicion. "Who's 'them'?"

He lifted his head and took her hands. "Carles Priest will be arriving soon."

"But he's defending Crossroads."

"Crossroads fell three days ago. A rather large contingent of Cithran soldiers came through. They completely overwhelmed the defenses and captured the town. Most men escaped, including your priest. They're coming here now.

"Several men were taken prisoner and questioned one by one. One of the weaker men broke sooner than expected. That's how about your village. He also told about the supplies here and how poorly defended the place is."

"But Uncle Natan is putting up defenses."

He gave her a sorry look. "I'm afraid it won't be enough. We're talking professional soldiers, trained to fight, trained to kill. Farmers and pitchforks will be useless when they arrive.

The blood drained from her face. "They're coming here?"

He held up a hand. "Let me finish my story. When I fail to tell the whole truth, that's when I get in trouble with you.

"The advanced scouting party last night, the ones who killed Marlon Poulter, were sent out just before the Crossroaders' got away. They didn't know anything about the escape. However, what they learned here is far more dangerous to your village.

"Thanks to your little promise, I did not kill them but merely incapacitated them. Two of the seven were killed last night by your villagers, A third was not expected to live to this morning. He might last until evening, but I won't say. The other three are bruised—one has a broken arm—but will live to answer questions.

"As for the last... I'm afraid he got away. He has returned to Crossroads with a tale of a powerful defender. Had I been able to simply kill him, he would have had no tale to tell."

That raised her ire. "Are you saying this is my fault?"

He held up his hands in defense. "Of course not, my Darklet. Just that things don't always go the way we want."

She narrowed her eyes but held her temper and folded her arms tightly. "Go on."

"When the news gets back to those in command, they will call for reinforcements. This means not only more soldiers but Cithran priests. You especially will not like Cithran priests."

He sat up and caressed her stiff shoulders. "I—" He changed his mind. "No, I'm sorry. Wait until Carles Priest arrives and speak with him. I'm afraid you're too upset with me to accept any solution I may offer."

He swung his legs over the side of the bed and stretched before standing. "Would you like me to go with you to your uncle's house?"

"Uh, why?"

Mor-Lath looked around for his boots. "He's not too happy with me; therefore, he's not too happy with you because of everything that happened last night. He thinks that what happened last night was my fault."

He fell to his hands and knees to look under the bed. "I must state in my defense that I had absolutely nothing to do with the presence of the scouting party. However," he said while reaching under the bed, "He does know about the woman and the child, thanks to Ari. I'm afraid that was very much my fault."

Adrastea stiffened. She had been trying to avoid thinking about that. She wanted to cry over Amarice but nothing came—no tears, no pinch of grief. Instead, cold dread settled in her stomach. She scrambled out of bed.

"So." He pulled on his boots. "Your uncle is most unhappy with the situation. As much as he loves you, he is listening to that Chloe woman. He thinks it best you leave the village."

Adrastea stared at him in disbelief. "You're not serious."

"I speak the truth."

Adrastea sank back to the bed. "He wouldn't banish me, would he?"

Mor-Lath put a comforting arm around her. "As an uncle, it pains him greatly. But as the Mayor, which in the end he must be, he must consider the good of the village over the good of one person, even family."

Adrastea heart sunk. Just another reason why Mayors were not allowed family. The conflict of interest could put a village in jeopardy.

"It doesn't end there. Even if you were to flee, it wouldn't stop the army marching this way."

"Isn't there anything we can do?" she asked in a small voice. That anxiety in her stomach tied itself into a knot and sent out roots.

He thought for a moment. "Well, yes. But I think you will feel better about yourself if you discover the solution on your own."

He gave her a tight little smile and a friendly salute, then vanished before her eyes.

She groaned she thought about the inevitable confrontation with Natan.

If she had learned anything from Mira, it was courage. She steeled herself and got dressed, rehearsing in her head all the possible things she could say to ease her uncle's anger toward herself.

A drastea hesitated on Natan's porch. She had to face the Mayor sometime. her anxiety warred with her sense of duty.

If Ari had been correct, Natan's anger with Mor-Lath had grown to near-obsession. No doubt some of that would spill over onto Adrastea. While Uncle Natan must think everything bad happened because of Mor-Lath, ultimately, he would blame Adrastea. He would be justified, of course. But that didn't make it right. It wasn't as if Adrastea had any control over a god.

Natan would shout at her, surely. Would he, as Ari suggested, banish her? When Marta left, did she leave of her own accord or had she no choice? Nobody had spoken of it, at least, not in Adrastea's hearing.

Before she could make a decision on knocking, the door flew open. Mikal bowled into her. They both tumbled to the porch.

"Bloody hell!" He started to apologize, then saw who she was. "Never mind." He picked himself up and backed into the house. "Get in here, quick!"

Adrastea scrambled inside. Mikal closed the door and checked through the closed shutters of the window. "I hope nobody saw you."

Adrastea shook out her skirts. "And what if they did?"

Mikal stared at her in shock. "How can you say that? Do you have any idea what they're saying about you?"

Anger swelled within her. "How can I?" I've been all but grounded to the house for the past few days. I haven't a clue as to what is going on. You going to enlighten me?"

She realized they were alone. "Where's Uncle Natan?"

Mikal folded his arms. "The mayor is interrogating the prisoners."

"What prisoners?"

"Light, Adrastea," he scoffed. "Where have you been?"

"Well, it's not like I've been exactly welcome in the village." Not only did she not have any breakfast, she didn't have any dinner last night as well, leaving her light-headed. "I've got to sit down."

Without waiting for permission, she pulled out a chair. "I guess you don't have anything to eat, do you?"

Mikal threw his hands in the air. "What is it with you and breakfast? Can't you feed yourself?"

Adrastea massaged her forehead with her hands. "It seems I find myself in situations that preclude breakfast."

Mikal snorted. "I've got some three-day bread."

"That'll do."

Mikal's huffiness faded. "You are desperate, aren't you?" He pulled up another chair close to her. "What do you know about last night?"

"I'm not telling you." The thought of Amarice made her feel ill.

Mikal thumped on the table with his finger. "You owe me one favor, remember?"

Adrastea stopped massaging and peeked up through her fingers. "I do?"

"Yeah. Remember how I was your messenger boy a few days ago?"

She gave in. "Feed me and I'll tell you." Maybe her guilt would ease if she shared it with her brother.

"I feed you and you tell me everything. Don't you dare leave a single thing out."

"That's an awfully big ask."

Mikal shrugged. "You've got very few friends at the moment. You let me in. Since I've got Uncle Natan's ear, I might be able to swing things in your favor."

He was right. She had few allies. Her brother might be young, but he was the Mayorprentice, plus he enjoyed a certain level of popularity among the other youths. "All right, I'll tell you all." Every last, sad detail.

Mikal slid a bowl of cornmeal mush with milk in front her. "Eat and talk at the same time."

She nodded, her mouth full. She swallowed and leaned over the table. "You must solemnly vow to never tell another soul what I'm about to tell you."

"Aw, come on, Adrastea. You know I can't do that. I've gotta tell the Mayor everything."

She sighed. "All right, you can tell Natan but nobody else. Not Tom, not anyone." She drew in a deep breath. "I'm only telling this to you because you're the Mayorprentice but you're also my brother. I don't know how everyone will treat you when they learn what I'm going to tell you." She took a quick bite of mush.

He scooted even closer. "This is going to be good. I can tell."

Where to start? When had she last seen Mikal? Without a preamble, she began. "Mira died because she tried to kill me. It was the only thing she could think of to save my soul."

"What?" Mikal squeaked.

"Shh!" She waved a hand at him. "Don't interrupt. Mor-Lath killed Mira because she slit my throat. I almost died. I'm sure I would have gone to the Light. Mor-Lath couldn't have touched me, then. If I was dead, there wouldn't be any reason for him to stay around."

"Isn't that rather extreme?"

"I thought I told you not to interrupt." She took another bite. "Anything to drink?"

"You finish the story first."

"Not even water?"

"Adrastea," Mikal admonished.

She sighed and continued her tale. "So, because she tried to kill me, Mor-Lath took Mira's life."

"That is extreme." He peered at her neck. "Say, where's your cut?"

"He healed it."

"Oooh. Like you healed that leg?"

Adrastea felt uncomfortable when he mentioned Master Mason. If anyone needed proof of her being a witch, that would be more than enough. "Doesn't change my mind about him."

"So, I guess the wedding's off?"

That stung deep. "We were never getting married. Will you stop interrupting?"

"Sorry," he said in his contrition. "Please. Go on. What did Natan tell you at the Spring?

Uncle Natan might not appreciate her telling Mikal everything. She opted for another truth. "That night I met Crozie Priestess."

Mikal gave her a blank look.

She explained, "Crozie was the priestess before Mira—the one who trained her. She disappeared when Mira came of age. Everyone thought she was dead. But she's not."

"Humph." Mikal got up and went to the mantle. He removed a key from a box there and went to a cupboard on the other side of the room. From there, he removed a book, brown and musty with age and brought it back to the table. "She's got to be in here."

"What's that?" asked Adrastea through a mouth of porridge.

"The genealogy book. Everyone who's hatched, matched or dispatched in Sacred Spring is listed in here." He opened it carefully on the table.

She ate while he gently turned pages. "Here she is." He traced her family. "Well. You'll never guess who she is."

"Who?"

He grinned, proud of himself. "She's our great-aunt."

"I know what an aunt is but a great-aunt?"

Mikal waved his hands animatedly. "Uncle Natan explained it to me. A great-aunt is an aunt removed two generations."

"That's a lot?"

"She's Natan's aunt. Our grandmother was her sister."

"I never knew that." If she was truly that old, no wonder everyone thought Crozie was dead. How does a woman that old survive out in the woods, especially without being caught? "It doesn't explain why she ran away, does it?"

He consulted the book. "Nope. But hey, you want to see where we are?"

Adrastea scooted her chair over next to him.

He turned a few pages, then pointed. "Here we are. Mikal, son of Lillybet Weaver (Joe Weaver, outsider), born her twenty-ninth year. Apprenticed to Natan Mayor his thirteenth year."

"And me?"

He turned the book and pointed. There she was, above Mikal in the page. Adrastea, born of Lillybet, born her twentieth year, promised to Ari at birth, apprenticed her tenth year and... to her surprise, a second entry under that: apprenticed also to Mira Priestess her twenty-second year.

Mikal looked up at his sister. "You were apprenticed to Mira as well? Why?"

Adrastea sat back and didn't answer him.

"Adrastea," he prompted. "Was this before or after Mor-Lath?"

"After," she answered him weakly. "I'm listed as an apprentice?" Mira had said nothing of an apprenticeship.

"You are. Nobody sees this book but the Mayor. So, why?"

She sighed. "Maybe Mira thought I needed all the help I could get. Not that it really mattered much. I only had a few lessons, before..."

Mikal nodded. Without a word, he put the book back in its cupboard and replaced the key. "What do you know about last night?"

How much to tell him?

"Adrastea?"

"I don't know where to start."

"From the Spring. You had a talk with Uncle Natan, then decided to go home after all?"

"I thought it would be safe." Her finger traced the wooden pattern of Uncle Natan's table. "When the house was built, our parents put a protection over it so evil could never cross the threshold. That protection ended with our mother's death. After that, he could enter the house as he pleased."

"What did he do?" Mikal breathed. A grin crossed his face. "You didn't do it, did you?"

She slammed the table with her hands. "Mikal Prentice!" Thoughts of intimacy flirted with the edge of her mind. She shooed them away. One did not discuss lust with one's brother.

Mikal didn't seem to know this rule. "Well, did you?"

"No!" She scowled. "Why does everyone think we have?"

Mikal held out one hand. "Dark God..." He held out the other hand. "Sin... It's hard to think of him as behaving honorably, especially with so many opportunities."

"Well, he's not—" she corrected herself, "well, in that matter, yes, he's been honorable but in everything else, he's a bastard."

Mikal put a hand over his mouth. "What's wrong?" he asked. "Can't he get it up?"

Adrastea refused to answer. "Do you want to hear this or not?"

He swallowed his mirth. "Sorry. Go ahead."

"Oh, no," she fretted. "Now I've lost my place. Damn it, Mikal. I told you to not interrupt."

"You were explaining about last night. So Mor-Lath shows up, fails to seduce you and then what?"

Oh, yeah. She felt like wilting, her anger gone. "Um..."

Mikal let out a crow of triumph. "He did seduce you. I knew it." He got up and capered about the table.

Adrastea began to panic. "No, no. He didn't. There wasn't time."

Mikal stopped dancing. "What? You got half your clothes off. In the middle of snogging each other you realize that it's time to make dinner?"

"Mikal, you've got to promise me you won't tell this to anyone, not even Uncle Natan."

Mikal sat down, all ears.

"I haven't told anyone this. Please don't laugh."

Mikal sobered. "I promise."

She leaned across the table. "Mikal, I almost gave in. I almost agreed to marry him."

"So, what stopped you?"

"Angels."

He sat upright. "What?" he yelped. "Like the ones last night?"

"You know about them?"

"Light, yeah. Everyone saw them. They all showed up during the attack. It was chaos. Were they here to save you?"

Adrastea's throat closed up. "They were here to save Amarice."

Mikal grew still. "Oh."

The numbness in her returned. "So, you heard about that?"

He swallowed. "I had to—" he shook his head. "Ari was useless. I think Uncle Natan had to dose her with one of her potions. That left him and me to…"

"I'm sorry." She'd never given any thought to the aftermath.

"Just another thing to deal with. Between Mira and that and these strangers—"

"Soldiers?"

Mikal shook his head. "Dunno. That's what Uncle Natan's trying to figure out right now."

Adrastea finished her porridge. She traced the spoon around in the bowl. "Mor-Lath says they are an advanced scouting troop from the Cithran army."

Mikal considered this. "Makes sense. They all had guns." He said this as if it were a benefit. "We've got more guns now."

"Who knows how to use a gun?"

"Lots of people. Uncle Natan does."

"Just because—"

The door burst open and Natan strode in. Adrastea and Mikal jumped to their feet. "Mikal, I need…" Natan started, then he saw Adrastea. "Bloody hell," he cursed softly. "What are you doing here, girl?"

Chapter 25

The butterflies were back, stirred up by the arrival of Uncle Natan.

Mikal, ever the quick thinker, came to her rescue. "She came here to speak with you. She's heard some rumors and wants to see them cleared."

Natan folded his arms. "You'll have to wait, girl, unless you can enlighten us on who these strangers are who attacked us last night."

Lies and pleading ignorance would never help. Not that the truth was much better. And then there was Mikal, who wouldn't keep his trap shut.

"I believe they are an advanced scouting party of Cithrans. Crossroads fell a few days ago. Those captured told them about Sacred Spring. Despite what happened last night, one of the scouting party escaped. When he gets back to Crossroads he's going to report what happened here. Then they're going to send a large army here to take what we have by force."

Natan spat out swear words that Adrastea had never heard him use. He must have run out of his regular supply last night. "We have no defenses."

"We got the guns," Mikal piped.

Natan scowled at him. "I don't think five guns in the hands of village idiots are going to do us much good. Not that it matters." He turned his displeasure to his niece. "He told you this, didn't he?"

She couldn't deny it.

"And we have no reason to believe anything he says." He held up his hand. "Oh, I agree there may be some truth in his words but how to distinguish it from the rest? Half-truths are the worst lies." He folded his arms. "What else did he tell you?"

"That several of the Crossroaders escaped and are making their way here. They should be here sometime today."

"I'll believe it when I see it. Until then, I'm not putting any stock in anything from him."

Natan took Mikal's chair and made himself comfortable. "I have some words for you."

Adrastea dreaded this. She didn't meet his gaze but hung her head and waited for what he had to say. Mikal had found another chair. He turned it around and straddled it backwards, resting his chin on the back.

Natan folded his hands and rested them on the table. "Ever since Mor-Lath showed up, he has brought nothing but trouble to the village."

Adrastea couldn't help that. She hoped Uncle Natan would choose to go gently on her when considering her punishment.

Or not. Any mercy on his part might be attributed to them being closely related.

"At first, we worried about you, Adrastea. But after having some rather stark examples of his concern for you, we're worried more about the rest of us." He cleared his throat. "For the safety of Sacred Spring, I request that you leave."

Banishment. The news sank like a stone within her. "But… where will I go?"

Natan exhaled. "I'm sorry. I don't know. You will be free to go anywhere you wish. I regret that you must go during a time of war, for that means you may not readily find safe welcome." He smiled grimly. "I know you will not go alone. As much as I loathe him, if Mor-Lath is as fixated on you as he appears, I'm sure he will be your protector in the outside world."

"That's not much comfort."

"Also, as the last survivor of your mother—Mikal being under my protection now—I will arrange with Rop to give to you the balance of her worth in the village in coin. With this, you may purchase what you need on your travels until you can find a place to live. I will have Ari draft you a journeyman's letter, stating that you are free to practice your craft.

"In addition, I will draft letters of introduction to the mayors of the towns nearby, to offer you temporary shelter and aid. However…"

It was more than she expected, the help he offered her. It was better than being booted out with little more than the clothes on one's back.

"I'm sorry, Adrastea but I must recommend in my letters that trouble may follow you in the form of an insistent suitor. While I can vouch for your character, I must warn others that if your suitor causes trouble, to send you on your way. I won't reveal who he is, but I will send warning."

"Thank you," Adrastea said. "I know you can't do more but I'm grateful for what you've done already. I'm so sorry for all the trouble I've caused."

Natan's expression softened. "There's nothing to apologize for, my girl. You've been doing your best standing up to an infinitely more powerful force. I'm proud that you've lasted this long.

"But I must think of the good of the village. We can't help you any more in your battle. I dare say wherever you go, may you continue to resist him. For whatever reason he wants of you, it can't be good."

Tears filled her eyes and a lump formed in her throat, her mouth too dry to speak. She nodded before laying her head on the table to cry. Natan reached out and patted her arm. "I wish we had another solution, but I haven't been able to come up with one."

Her head still down, she nodded. She didn't care what they thought of her sobs and sniffles. She was banished from the home she had known her whole life. She had no idea how to survive in the bigger world. She wouldn't have known how to survive in Crossroads, and she knew people there.

Natan let her cry. "I wish I could offer you more. Maybe someone has a small cart they'll let you have, to carry your belonging. I'm sure Ari's got things she'll want you to have..." He sighed and gave up. "There isn't any other way."

She lifted her head and sniffed. "I wish there was. I don't want to leave."

Grief haunted Natan's countenance. "Your uncle doesn't want you to leave either. But the Mayor's word is final. In all things, it's best your uncle acquiesce to him."

drastea stayed in Natan's house, sitting well away from the windows.

Ari finished laying out Marlon, Amarice and their new baby without her help. The rest of the village was not as understanding as Natan when it came to blame. It was no secret that Mor-Lath, God of the Dark, had killed them. Ergo, the blame also passed onto Adrastea.

When Ari was finished, she collected Adrastea and they snuck away to Ari's home, going around the back way of the village.

Adrastea climbed into the loft she'd called home for the past ten years. Most of her worldly treasures were here. Adrastea had all sorts of keepsakes and childhood treasures—one old doll, a humming button, a wooden recorder of the kind all village children learned to play. These she chose to leave behind for they were of no practical value. There were a few pieces of jewelry that her mother had given her—a slender chain necklace and two bracelets. She took them. Perhaps such things could be sold in time of need. As she held them, she closed her eyes. For a moment, she felt the presence of her mother.

She put the necklace around her own throat but packed the two bracelets away.

Soon everything of hers that could possibly aid her in the lone and dreary world had been packed into a single forlorn bag.

When she was finished there, Adrastea and Ari stole through the back garden, around the village and up to Lillybet's house for the rest of Adrastea's things.

The place was still a shattered mess. Nobody had been there, whether for lack of time or lack of courage. She left the mess. Adrastea had no time to clean up.

Ari offered her advice. "Choose only the most necessary things, for you may very well be carrying your worldly possessions on your back. If we do find you a cart, you can then add more. It's easier to add to than to pare down.

"One thing you must make room for is your book of herbs."

Adrastea had forgotten about it. When she first started her apprenticeship, Ari taught her to read and write by making her copy out every page in Ari's book of herbs—side notes and all. It would come in handy when she plied her own trade.

In Lillybet's bedroom, she sorted through her clothing, choosing the newest and sturdiest, also the warmest, for she did not know when she would find a permanent home.

As she discarded yet another skirt she pondered upon her future life. Was she doomed to run forever? Anywhere that welcomed her would not want her for long. As soon as Mor-Lath showed up and caused trouble, she'd be asked to leave, and not always in a kind way. The thought depressed her.

"Adrastea?" Ari put a hand on her shoulder. "Wake up."

Adrastea let the skirt slip from her hands. "I don't want to go."

"I'm afraid that's not your choice." Ari said it as gently as possible, but the words still stung.

An idea occurred to Adrastea. "Couldn't I live in the forest like Crozie?"

"And do what? Until a few days ago, we didn't know Crozie was alive, much less how she survives. And even if you did figure out how to live, would it be far enough away from the village to keep us safe?"

"Light," came a man's voice from the other room. "What happened here?"

A very weary Carles Priest stepped over the remains of the door. "Oh, hello," he said when he saw the two women. "Have I got a tale for you."

Ari folded her arms. "So do we," she replied dryly.

Several others from Crossroads entered the house, including Ely Mayorprentice. The rest, from what she could hear outside, had happily rejoined their families. Their shouts of joy pushed against the heavy silence of the house.

These men needed a good bath and a change of clothes. Carles definitely needed some sleep. He collapsed onto the first chair he saw. "You wouldn't happen to have any bread, would you?"

Before Adrastea answered, he put his head down on the table and fell asleep.

Ely remained standing. "I need to see Natan Mayor."

Ari nodded. "I'll go get him. I'm sorry we have no food. You're welcome to rest here if you wish." Ari hurried off.

The men looked to Ely. "Go join the others," he said. "I'll come get you if I need you." He collapsed into the other chair. "I need a drink," he said. "Could I trouble you for some water?"

When Adrastea returned from the water barrel outside, Ely, too, had passed into sleep. As she watched him, she saw a nasty gash in his hair on the top of his head.

A drastea draped blankets across the two men sleeping at her table. Her hand hesitated over Ely's wound. How tempting it was to heal him. Should she, or shouldn't she?

Before she could decide, Uncle Natan arrived with Chloe in tow. They sighed over the sleeping men. "They must have been walking all day and night to reach us," Natan said. He sat on the bench at the table. "It's a shame to have to wake them but we need to know what happened." Chloe sat on the bench. She avoided Adrastea's gaze.

Adrastea set mugs of water down near the sleeping men, should they waken while she was occupied. Chloe had brought a pot breakfast mush, the same as what Adrastea had earlier. Ari scooped up bowls for Ely and Carles. "Mikal's cooking?" Adrastea asked.

Ari nodded. "He still makes too much. We've got to teach that boy about proportions."

"Or we could eat breakfast at Natan's every morning."

Ari allowed herself a small little smile tinged with sadness. "That would be good." Adrastea was painfully reminded that she would be lucky to get any breakfast during the next long whenever.

Natan laid a hand on Ely's arm. "Mayorprentice?" he asked gently. Ely didn't stir.

Chloe, watching the proceedings, sniffed. "Carles," she said, as if she were having an unpleasant conversation with him. She hadn't touched him.

He jumped and stiffly raised his head. He looked even worse than when he went to sleep.

Chloe looked smugly pleased about this. If Carles was a light sleeper, Adrastea thought it cruel to use this to an advantage.

"Mayor," he croaked as he eased himself up to sitting.

Chloe pushed the mug of water his way. He downed it thirstily. Even after the drink, he looked like he had a headache.

"What happened?" Natan asked him.

Carles groaned and rubbed the sleep from his eyes. "We'd been expecting small raids at night and had set our guards for that. So most of us were asleep when a whole army came and ran over us. They killed our guards and blasted the walls apart with cannons. We didn't have a chance."

"Most of us escaped. Not everyone did."

A coldness settled between them.

Chloe's gaze darted to Adrastea then back to Carles. "What did they do to the prisoners?"

Carles didn't answer.

Natan looked at the still sleeping Ely. "Where's Sam?"

"He was killed in the first attack. Ely's Mayor now."

The news weighed down Natan's shoulders.

"Poor thing," sympathized Ari, sitting next to Natan. "Not the best time to become Mayor."

"If one can call him Mayor," Carles said. "We've lost Crossroads. I don't know how we're going to get it back."

"How did you escape?" Natan asked.

"When the cannons started, I knew we had to leave. Cithrans kill priests on sight. Ely agreed with me." He sniffed. "We lost several men in our escape."

Adrastea, fascinated by the story, asked, "So, if you were surrounded, how did you get away?"

Carles smiled. "Ah but we weren't surrounded. They'd only blocked off the wall they destroyed. They thought the rest of our barrier would keep us in.

"But they didn't realize how well we knew our town. Did they think we're so backwards-country to not give ourselves an out, even if it's just to bring in fresh water? We learned our lesson from Feown's siege."

He explained how they'd escaped through the cellar of one of the inns and took off through the woods. They would have been found had they remained on the road. He lifted his empty mug and looked mournfully into it. Natan gave him Ely's untouched mug.

After taking a long drink, he continued his story. "So, there's this bloody great army headed this way. They know we're here. Natan, you have no defenses—not that it matters." He took another drink. "You should have seen what they did to the wall. I didn't think that was possible."

"Dark magics?" Natan asked.

Carles shook his head. "No. Purely technology. Something about the Deeper Power doesn't sit right with them. Cithrans kill any priest, Light or Dark, on sight. On suspicion, even."

Natan considered this. "On fear, perhaps?"

Carles gave a half shrug. "Who knows?"

Adrastea pondered this tidbit. Why fear priests, unless one feared the Deeper Power. "I have an idea."

She went into the bedroom and from under the bed brought out Mor-

Lath's book. She's promised herself she'd keep the knowledge of its existence away from others but perhaps it was now time to use it. At the table she handed it to Carles. "If they fear priests, perhaps this would help?"

Carles looked at the book. His expression changed from perplexity to shock.

Ari scooted back against Natan. "I thought I burned that."

"So did I," Chloe added dryly. "Apparently it's indestructible."

"Where'd you get this?" Carles gasped.

Chloe answered, "Where do you think?" She flipped open the cover and pointed out the inscription.

"Ah." He pushed it away. "I don't know if I should use this."

Adrastea scooted the book back to her. "Just thought I'd offer. 'Know Your Enemy' and all that."

Carles looked at her, then at the book. "What have we come to, that I would seriously consider using a Dark book to preserve my own life?"

Natan reached out and snagged the book towards him. "I wish my books were so indestructible." He opened the cover and had a bit of a read, his eyebrows raising every once in a while. "It is knowledge or action which damns us more?"

"Inaction certainly does," said Carles. He yawned. "I've got to get some sleep."

"Good idea," Natan agreed. "We had a Cithran scouting party here last night. Three are dead and the rest are our prisoners. But one scout evaded capture. He will have made it back to Crossroads by now and warned the others. We're going to have to come up with a plan soon. You'll think better fully rested."

Chloe rose. "You come stay with me." Carles rose and followed her out of the house.

Natan and Ari looked at the sleeping Ely. "I guess he'll have to stay here," Ari said.

"What?" said Adrastea, startled. "Where's he going to sleep?"

"We'll stick him in your bed. You come stay with me."

Perhaps staying with Ari would be a good thing. No doubt she had plenty of work Adrastea could do. Keep the hands and mind busy, and idleness, whether of thought or body, could not creep in.

Maybe they'd relax around each other enough to speak of Amarice.

Natan tried to wake Ely again. He wouldn't stir, so he and Ari carried him to the bedroom.

Adrastea wandered through the broken door. She considered picking up the pieces and repairing it the way Mor-Lath had shown her. Splinters and broken planks were scattered all through the garden. As she knelt to pick up the largest piece, she heard a loud Caw! A large crow perched on the edge of the house roof.

There was something strange about that crow. She stepped closer to get a better look.

The crow cawed once more, and launched itself at her, swooping and pecking. Adrastea shrieked and waved it away. It spun around and dived for her again.

Before she knew what she was doing, she'd drawn the Deeper Power to her and put out her hand to ward the crow away. She must have struck it harder than she expected, because it changed angles and hit the edge of the roof hard. Then it fell to the porch with a dull thud.

"Remind me not to surprise you," said Mor-Lath.

Adrastea startled and turned to face him. "It attacked me. I wasn't thinking."

Mor-Lath didn't question her further.

Natan and Ari appeared in the doorway. "Adrastea, what—" started Natan, then he saw Mor-Lath. He swore at him. "What the hell do you want now?"

Mor-Lath glanced at Natan. "Don't you have a funeral to attend?"

Instead of a reaction from Natan, his words struck a raw nerve in Ari. "Bastard!" She launched herself at him, claws bared.

Mor-Lath caught Ari, spun her around and slammed her to the earth, strong enough to knock the wind out of her. It was done and over before Natan could even utter a shout. Adrastea flung her hands over her mouth.

Mor-Lath abandoned the Healer to her gasps. Natan ran to her side. "You could have killed her!" Then he took in a sharp breath when he realized what he'd said. He gathered her close.

Mor-Lath moved to Adrastea's side. "What? And face the displeasure of my betrothed? Believe me, she's not someone you wish to anger."

Adrastea's mouth gaped in surprise. Then she let out her own string of descriptive expletives.

Mor-Lath stilled her lips with his finger. "Now, now, that's not very graceful, my Darklet." He hooked his arm through hers. "Come, let us take a walk to cool your head." He tugged her away while Natan helped a gasping Ari to sit up.

As they rounded the house and set out the front gate to the lane, Adrastea pulled her arm from his. "I don't want to take a walk with you."

"Wants and needs are two different things." He stopped to face her. "You will feel better after a walk."

She stubbornly folded her arms and refuse to go any further. He held out a hand to her, palm up. "Come on, Adrastea. Just a short walk?"

"No."

He dropped his hand. "We could talk here, if that is your wish."

"I can't think of anything I'd want to talk to you about."

"How about your future?" He drew nearer. "The Mayor has asked you to leave. You don't know where you're going to go, nor what you'll do when you get there, or even how you'll get there. You're a country maid. You know nothing about the world out there."

She rolled her eyes. "I suppose you're going to show me all the bad things that could happen out there? Well, I can think of one bad thing that will happen to me out there. You'll follow me."

"I don't see that as a problem."

"I do." She threw her hands in the air. "Already you have ruined my life. Nobody here trusts me. The few who still like me are forced to banish me for the sake of the village. People are dead, and lives ruined because of you. I know you won't stop once I leave Sacred Spring. Anywhere I try to settle down, you'll follow me there and you will cause trouble. You will turn the people against me until they, too, drive me out of their village. I will never have a place to call home, all because I've defied you.

"So, I will become a wanderer, never staying for long in one place. You may have reft me of a home, but I have prevented you from using anyone else against me." She jabbed a finger at him to emphasize her point. "You lose power over me."

"You haven't left yet," he stated coldly.

This sent a shudder of fear through her. "You wouldn't dare." Her eyes narrowed.

He simply closed his eyes and sighed. "I have no desire to play games at this point. If you wish to pack, then go ahead. When you leave, I will go with you. We can continue our negotiations."

She put her hands over her face. "How many times do I have to say no?"

"How many times to I have to ask until you say yes?"

Ari had to put up with Mor-Lath following Adrastea for the rest of the day as she gathered the last scraps of her life. It did not matter whether she was alone or in the company of others. Natan cursed at him a few times and Ari ranted against him, eventually threatening him with bodily harm if he set foot in her house again. Didn't stop him from lurking about. As much as she loved her journeyman, Ari knew that when Adrastea left, Mor-Lath would go with her.

Night fell and Adrastea, fretful and out of sorts, rose from the late supper Ari scraped together. "I'm going to bed. Alone."

Natan looked up at her. He drew in a breath as if he wanted to say something but changed his mind.

"Sleep well," Ari said. The moment the words left her lips, they sounded trite. No doubt this would be the last night in a long time Adrastea would sleep well, if she slept at all.

Then Adrastea stomped her way up the ladder to the loft and to the bed that had been hers for over a decade.

If Mor-Lath disturbed Adrastea during the night, Ari didn't know about it.

The next morning Ari poked her head into the loft. Adrastea slumbered hard. She let her sleep in.

Ari had business in the village. Adrastea would not be welcome.

At the Poulters, someone had moved the bed out of the bedroom. Here, the bodies reposed. Ari arranged Marlon's arm around Amarice who cuddled the baby boy that had drawn only a few breaths of life. They looked so peaceful in death, freed from the horrors that dogged their last hours of life.

The ashes of Mira's pyre were not yet cold. Now the people of the village had to gather more wood for another one. Was this the last of it, or only the beginning?

After the bodies were laid out, Ari cried. She'd had enough of death.

Ari sought out Natan after he decided the fates of a few other lives. He was up at Lillybet's house. For a brief while, it has been Adrastea's home. Now she wasn't sure who it belonged to. Ari's heart ached at the thought of her journeyman leaving the village. The world was different now than when Ari had gone to Feown.

Last night, in a moment of remorse, she had hugged her journeyman and had offered to go with her. Adrastea had turned her down. "It's best I go alone."

"But you won't be able to survive out there."

"I'll manage," came her grim reply. "After all, you did."

Who would the house belong to now?

Natan had been up late with Ely Mayor, Carles and Chloe as they discussed options. She didn't bother to knock on the door but let herself in.

The four were still gathered around the table, looking tired but better than the day before. Had they been up the whole night, or did they get up early? Mikal was there, stirring something in a kettle on the hook in the fireplace. At least his proportions would serve to feed them all today.

"Hello, Ari." Natan yawned. "We don't know what to do."

The others looked at her with the same grimness of features.

Ari paused. "But surely you've come up with some plan."

Carles outlined it. "First we considered abandoning Sacred Spring and fleeing. Then we thought about staying. Then we considered surrendering. Unfortunately, that's all we could think of. Double-unfortunate, none of the solutions we've come up with has any happy endings."

"Well, can't we defend like you did?"

Natan shook his head. "Sacred Spring is too far spread out for us to put up adequate defenses in time."

"And running?"

"Several problems. First, we don't have enough wagons or anything with which to carry our food and belongings. Second, if we did, we'd move too slowly. The army will catch up with us."

"And surrender?"

Carles answered this one. "I'm afraid we've annoyed the army enough for them to want to take revenge on us. They were looking for something. I'm not sure it was only supplies. Otherwise, when they breached our defenses at Crossroads, they would have taken what we had left, and then either abandoned us or killed us. But they didn't.

"When they get here, they will keep looking for whatever it is they're looking for. Those who survive the initial onslaught will be tortured." He swallowed. "No. We cannot surrender."

There had to be something. "What about us staying and fighting?"

Everyone denied this option as well. "If we choose to fight," said Carles, "that will be little better than surrender. It would be a fight to the death. And I don't need to tell you what they'll do to the survivors."

Something clicked in her brain. "Why don't we hide?"

"Hide?" Natan was completely perplexed.

"Yes." She laid her hands on the table. "Crozie's been hiding undetected for a long time. Adrastea and I have been roaming those woods for years in our harvests and have never come across a trace of her. Perhaps we could all hide there too."

"I don't know," Natan started.

"We could make it look like we've deserted the village and have taken everything with us. But the truth is we've only fled to the woods. We hide there, well-camouflaged, and wait for them to leave. Then after they're gone, we can return."

Chloe wasn't convinced. "But what if they leave a party behind?"

"Why would they? There's nothing here. And if they did, I'm sure we could dispatch them."

Carles was not convinced either. "These are soldiers—men of war. Fighting and killing is their craft. I doubt three times the number of us could defeat them."

Ari was getting annoyed. "Unless you've come up with a better plan, I suggest you worry about that when it happens, if it happens. Meanwhile, we've got a village to hide."

Carles looked to Natan. He shrugged. "It's the best plan we've come up with, and the most likely to work."

"We've only got a day," Chloe protested.

Natan rose. "Then let's get started. He turned to the younger man. "Ely, gather your Crossroaders. We need to start packing all our foodstores and clothing and get them to Little Crossroads, in preparation for caching." He called his apprentice over and gave him instructions before sending Mikal on his way.

"How do we know the soldiers won't find us in the woods?" Chloe asked Ari, skeptical of the plan.

"We've lived here all our lives," Ari spat. "We know these woods backwards and forwards."

"Well," Chloe replied dryly. "You couldn't find Crozie."

Ari thought about this. "Crozie Priestess must know some sort of trick or blessing that would hide oneself." She looked to the priest. "Carles, you know of anything like this?"

He thought on it then shook his head in defeat. "I can't think of anything."

"Nevermind. We'll hide first and worry about obfuscation later."

"Or," said Carles, "there might be something in the Book."

"What? Adrastea's book?" Natan asked.

Ari frowned, and Chloe outright protested. "Oh, no," the priestess said. "We cannot stoop to that even to save our own lives."

"Even if it means that you will die? Sure, your soul will go to the Light. Are you ready for that stage in existence?" asked Carles.

Chloe didn't answer that.

"Ari," Natan instructed. "You go scout out some potential hiding places for not only our supplies but our people."

She nodded and turned to leave. He grabbed her arm before she left. "Oh, and get Adrastea to help you. Say nothing about whether this means she stays or goes. All regular business is put on hold until we've completed our plan." He pulled her to him and gave her a strong kiss before releasing her.

"And what about the Poulters?"

"They're not going anywhere. Save the living first, then we'll worry about the dead."

Chapter 26

A drastea, wake up." Mor-Lath sat on her bed and shook her feet. Adrastea pulled her feet in and groaned. She peeked open a bleary eye then muttered, "Go away." She rolled over.

Mor-Lath laid down beside her. "Come on. It's going to be a busy day today."

"Rack off."

"Ari needs your help."

"Ari can rack off."

He sighed and dropped an arm across her. "You know what she'll say when she finds us like this," he teased.

"Like she can do anything about it." Too tired to care, she left the arm there and tried to go back to sleep. If she was going to be banished, at least she could have one good night in a good, clean bed before it happened. At this point, she didn't care who slept with her, as long as he left her alone.

"Oh, come on, my Darklet. You've got a great deal of excitement ahead of you."

"I'm not your Darklet."

"Be my wife then?"

"Mmf."

He smoothed her hair back from her face. "Natan might let you stay."

She didn't respond to that.

He lay there with her, watching her as she tried to snatch a few more moments of sleep. "Ari's coming."

"Rack off, or face her wrath."

"The Cithran army's coming."

"Knew that."

"Natan's got a plan to save the village."

"Don't care."

"You might, if it means delaying your departure."

She rolled over enough to look at him. "Since when do you care about whether I stay or go?" However, a tiny spark of hope ignited inside her.

He shrugged. "I know it matters to you." He pulled her up. "Now, come on. Ari has something she needs you to do. We can't stay in bed all day."

Ari came home as Adrastea, fully dressed, climbed down the ladder and muttered in annoyance, "I can do it myself, thank you!"

"Adrastea?" Ari asked, raising an eyebrow.

Adrastea froze on the ladder, looked over her shoulder at Ari, then relaxed and climbed down the rest of the ladder.

But Ari had guessed her secret. "Damn it, Mor-Lath," Ari shouted up the ladder. "I thought I told you to say out of my house."

Mor-Lath appeared and leaned on the top of the ladder. "Haven't you got more important things to worry about?" He gave her a broad grin.

Adrastea listened while Ari muttered under her breath. If she was backing down from an argument with the Dark God, she had to have something heavy on her mind. "Come with me, Adrastea. We're scouting the forest today." She grabbed her brown healer's cloak and slung her bag over her shoulder.

"Oh?" Adrastea followed Ari outside.

"I'll stay behind," Mor-Lath called out.

"The hell you will. Get out of my house." She slammed the door.

Adrastea chose silence as the wisest course as Ari led her up the hill. The strongest of the village men hauled the food stores up the hill in handcarts, too busy to return greetings. What was happening?

Ari and Adrastea went past Little Crossroads, where nearly all the villagers from both towns had gathered. They listened to Natan and Ely as they explained the plan.

"What's going on?" Adrastea asked. "We're not all leaving Sacred Spring, are we?"

Ari had a smug look on her face. "No but we're going to make it look like we have." She looked at her journeyman. "We're going into hiding." Then she outlined Natan's plan: scout the forest for potential hiding spots for goods and people. "They have to be suitable for a long stay. We may need to hide for as long as a week," Ari explained. "We have no idea how long the army will remain." There were depressions and grottoes everywhere, although no true caves, nothing that would hide a large number of people. "We have to be quick. Ely Mayor says soldiers may arrive sometime today."

"That's not enough time."

"It's all we've got."

The first group comprised the strongest and fastest of the youths. Tom and Martine were there, as were two of their younger siblings, plus Jacob Cutlerprentice from Crossroads and Truesie Taylorprentice.

Ari sighed. They would have to do. "Half go with me, and the other half go with Adrastea. As soon as each party scouts a spot, you tie three rags to a tree nearby, so you can find it again. Then one scout runs back here and takes the first group to be hidden." She handed out handfuls of white cloth strips. "When you return with your group, you must remember to remove the cloth."

After a few more questions, the two parties set off through the forest. Adrastea got Tom, Jacob, and Truesie with her.

Truesie felt a need for conversation. "Adrastea, is it true your suitor is really the God of the Dark?"

"That's just a rumor," Jacob said. "But Chloe Priestess says he's a Dark priest. I didn't know they could get married."

This was not how Adrastea wanted to start her day. "Can we not talk about him?" she snapped. "I'm not marrying him, so it doesn't matter. We've more important things to do. Please try to keep up." She hurried along a faint trail, pulling harder than she had to at her skirt when it snagged on a bush. It tore.

Tom had been sullen all morning. "Perhaps you should marry him. Then you both can leave here and let us get back to our lives."

Adrastea stopped. She could hear the bitterness in his voice. She knew better than to be drawn into an argument. "I thought I said we shouldn't talk about it."

"I hear you're leaving anyway. Good riddance."

Adrastea gave him a narrow look. "How about we save the village first, or I'll be the least of your worries." She took off again and didn't care to check that they kept up with her.

The mood of the party had darkened, despite Truesie's clumsy attempts to change the conversation. Eventually she gave up and tramped after them, subdued.

Ten minutes into their trek they came across the first potential hiding spot, a hollow in the ground over which several large trees had fallen, providing a dark recess. After exploring it to make sure it wasn't already occupied by anything dangerous, Adrastea tied her three white tags high on the trees.

"I'll go first," Tom volunteered.

"I agree," replied Adrastea, more than happy to see him leave.

Adrastea and the other two continued on into the forest. "Why does he hate you so much?" Jacob asked her when Tom was well gone.

"I don't know," Adrastea replied, still not in the mood to talk about it.

"It's because she was the reason his mother left Sacred Spring," Truesie supplied.

Adrastea stopped and rounded on the other girl. "That is so not true."

Truesie folded her arms and hunched her shoulders. "Everyone says it is."

"Why? What are they saying?" A crow flew overhead, cawing loudly.

Suddenly Truesie didn't feel like sharing. "I shouldn't have said anything." She ploughed through the tall grass, leaving a trail behind her.

Adrastea followed. Jacob had no choice but to trail along. Was the reason Natan had asked her to leave due to pressure from the villagers? She caught Truesie's arm. "I want to know what everyone's saying."

"Let go of me." Truesie panicked more than Adrastea expected.

She let her go, surprised. "Why?" she asked, feeling hurt. "Why can't you tell me?"

Truesie had scuttled several meters away. "Don't you get it? Bad things happen to the people around you. How do I know I won't die if I tell you what the others think?"

So that was it. Everyone either hated her like Tom or was afraid of her like Truesie. She looked at the outsider, Jacob but he averted his gaze and said nothing.

A hiss disturbed the air. Mor-Lath appeared next to her, arm outstretched. He caught the arrow aimed for her heart. He held forth his other hand to the forest. To everyone's astonishment, three brown-clothed archers fell out of the trees not more than twenty-five meters distant.

"That was an advanced scouting party," he said without preamble. "The forest is filled with them."

Adrastea gasped. "Oh no. Ari!"

"Ari is safe," he reassured her. "She spotted one of the archers in the trees before they could shoot her. They've returned to the village."

To the other two, he commanded, "Return at once. It is not safe for you out here."

Truesie let out a little squeak of fear. She was not too far behind Jacob in fleeing for their lives.

Mor-Lath and Adrastea followed at a slower pace. "I sometimes forget how young you are, Adrastea."

These words deepened the sourness she felt towards him. "I have nothing to say to you."

He waved the arrow at her. "Not even a thank you?"

"I did not ask you to save me, nor am I grateful that you did so."

He drew in a breath. "Do you truly prefer death? I don't think you do, not really. Should you die now, your life unfulfilled, for the rest of your eternal servitude you will remember the offer I made you and the glimpse of your destiny I shared with you. You will forever wonder, 'what if...' The regret of the path not chosen will burn worse than the regret of a wrong choice and prevent your joy from being whole."

Anger, not regret, was what burned in her now and threatened to spill out her eyes in hot tears. "I will never have joy if I marry you."

He grabbed her hand before she could stride away from him. "Now, that is not true. I don't know who's been pouring poison in your ear but life with me would not be the damnation to hell that you suppose it is." He enveloped her hands in his and would not let her pull away. "Joy is not something that comes and goes like the wind. Joy is a choice we make. Wherever you go, whatever you do, if you find joy, it is because you choose to. Forever is a long time to be miserable, whatever you make your destiny to be."

That was the final straw. Her strength within snapped and the tears flowed. Her knees gave, and she sank to the ground in a freshet of grief. Gently he knelt down beside her and drew her close. She clung to his black shirt and cried in great big sobs. So much had happened to the world as she knew it. People she'd known all her life either hated her or feared her now. The few who still loved her had had to make difficult decisions—had to choose between her and the others. And she lost.

It was only right. Despite what Mor-Lath claimed, she was not more important than the others. They, too, had their lives and their destiny and their right to exist. She could not ask them to sacrifice themselves for her.

How selfish she'd been. She could not expect the others to bear the brunt of the struggle between her and Mor-Lath.

She had to leave Sacred Spring.

While the comfort of his arms was warm, she had to remember who was comforting her. She pushed back from him and wiped away her tears with the edge of her skirt. "I need to return to the village. Natan needs to know about the scouts."

When she returned alone, Adrastea found Little Crossroads in chaos. Men felled trees around the perimeter. They stacked them up in a rudimentary barrier between them and the forest. The children had been gathered and taken down to Sacred Spring to the Smithy, the biggest, strongest and most defensible building.

Both men and women armed themselves with anything that could be construed as a weapon. The food stores brought up from Sacred Spring were loaded into the Crossroaders' homes and the space in them stuffed with straw. Already select youths were making and lighting torches. Should the tide of battle turn against the villagers (as it looked most likely that it would be), they would burn the supplies to prevent them from falling into the hands of the Cithran army.

The army would arrive soon. To the north, several miles away, a column of smoke rose, closer than comfortable. If she was right, that's where the Millers lived... if they were still alive.

A cloud of dust rose above the treeline—the soldiers of Cithra. How many would there be? Two hundred? More? Were so many required to subdue a small village? Only if the village put up a fight.

In the commons of Sacred Spring, people brought out furniture from the homes. They built a barricade around the smithy. There they planned on making their last stand. The hill where her house and Little Crossroads stood was strategically located. The pyre for the Poulters was being disassembled for use in the defense of the town. If the villagers won, by some miracle, there would be plenty of wood for the pyre. If they lost, it wouldn't matter.

Ari spotted her first. She bowled her over in the hug. "I'm glad you're safe."

Adrastea chose not to ruin her joy by mentioning what had happened. Ari would learn soon enough when Truesie and Jacob started spreading their stories. "We saw a scouting party and knew we had to come back."

"So did we. This changes everything. Adrastea, you need to head down to the stillroom and move every medicinal item to the blacksmith. Start with the painkillers and poisons, and then—"

"What? Poisons?"

"Don't argue with me, girl. Poisons will have their use in war. Even as a defeated people, we can strike back." She pushed Adrastea towards Sacred Spring. "Hurry now."

Adrastea took the back path to the village, snaking past the Shepherds house. Ariah protested loudly as men carried out all the furniture from her house. Jak Carpenter tried in vain to reason with her over the need to protect the smithy and she stood her stubborn ground that her house needed defending too. She looked ridiculous to Adrastea in her narrow-mindedness. It pricked her conscience. Was she as guilty of the same ridiculousness?

In the village, the barricade around the smithy was nowhere near ready. Adrastea had no idea what it would take to successfully defend the place. She took the north road past the Taylors' house where even the doors had been removed for the barricade.

At Ari's house, she found Mor-Lath on the porch. He leaned back in one of Ari's chairs, his feet propped up on a porch post, a bottle in his hand. His casualness infuriated her. "That's Ari's beer you're drinking."

He took another swallow and regarded the bottle. "This is really good. Did you brew this? I hope so. I would like more of this." He finished the bottle while Adrastea stormed past him. She resisted the temptation to kick the tilted chair out from underneath him; she had no time for a spat.

As she entered the house, Mor-Lath called out after her, "I took the liberty of packing what you needed."

She ignored him but stopped short when she entered the stillroom. Several small wooden crates sat on the table, bottles and bags in them. She lifted the bottles out and checked the labels.

Mor-Lath followed her in. "Potions and poisons, just like Ari wanted. I like her style."

She lowered the bottle as the anger simmered within her. "Why?" she asked.

He leaned against the doorframe. "Your heart is set on staying. I don't know why. These people will be slaughtered, and you will have to watch them die. But it's no longer your fight. This is no longer your village. When the conflict is over, Natan Mayor will still insist you leave. Why must you cause yourself more pain?"

She slammed her hand on the table, causing the bottles to jump. "Why the hell do you care? You know nothing of feeling pain. If you did, you wouldn't cause as much pain as you do."

Her temper snapped, and she shrieked at her betrothed. "And you don't care about anyone but yourself. You don't care about me; you only care about what I can do for you and I don't even know what that is."

She strode the length of the shelves in the stillroom, looking for anything useful he might have missed. To her consternation, he'd gleaned everything. "I stay and I help because, until I am formally banished, this is still my village. And while most of them may have turned their backs to me, every single person who ever cared for me in this whole miserable world is here, even the ones you've killed."

Curse him for his infuriating efficiency. There was nothing left to pack. "I will stay and I will fight until the bitter end. I may, like you said, end up watching every single one of them die but when they do, it won't be because I didn't stand up and do something. I will defend them to the very last, because in the past, those who cared about me the most stood up and defended me when faced with an enemy more terrible than the whole Cithran army. Even if it meant their lives." Memories of Mira caused tears to well in her eyes.

She turned from him, put her hands on the table and bowed her head. She would not let him see her cry. Mor-Lath leaned in the doorway, arms folded. He said nothing to her tirade, did not mock, did not smirk.

She had no time to cry. She sniffed and gathered her courage from the various corners to which it had fled. Picking up a box, she said, "I must deliver these."

"I will help you."

"I'd rather you didn't."

With fluid grace, he moved into the stillroom, picked up a box and grinned wickedly. "Not your choice." He disappeared before her very eyes.

Could no one stop him? If she were able, she'd turn him over her knee and give him such a thrashing.

"Mongrel," she muttered as she hefted her box and departed the stillroom through mortal means.

When she reached the Smithy, she had to knock to be given

admittance. Once inside, a flustered Mikal greeted her. "Oh good, you're here. Go put that box with the rest."

"What rest?"

Mikal pointed to the stalls. Two boxes of supplies stood there already. She sighed and turned to leave. There were about a dozen back at the stillroom.

Sheelagh came down the ladder. "Is this all of them?" she asked.

"No. There's a dozen more back at the stillroom."

Sheelagh sat on the bottom rung of the ladder. "I've just carried ten of the blasted things up there! I'm not looking forward to another ten."

Ten already? "You mean…" Oh, drat him! "I'll go back to Ari's and see how many are left." She made her hasty departure.

Outside the men of the villages finished dragging the last of the available furniture to the smithy. The barricade was inadequate.

She stalked her way back to Ari's house through the commons. The ashes of Mira's pyre had not been scattered. Adrastea scooped up a handful to sprinkle in the wind.

They were still warm. She lifted her hands and let the ashes drift down and away, saying a silent goodbye to Mira.

A small plume of dust rose just beyond the trees. A small party of red-clad riders on horses came around the bend.

A smaller figure, a woman dressed in green robes, led them. She carried a tall polearm on which several strips of white fabric had been tied. They streamed out behind her as they galloped into town. Five heavily-armed men on big, nasty warhorses surrounded her, dwarfing her horse to the size of a pony.

Adrastea froze. They were here already?

One of the men working on the barricade shouted a warning. Soon all of them came running, armed with sharpened tools-turned-weapons.

The woman and her escort rode up to the front of the Inn, not far from Adrastea. They stopped short enough to see each other clearly but far enough away to prevent any skirmishes.

The villagers gathered around and brandished their pikes, pitchforks and scythes.

"Parlay," the woman demanded. Her voice was low-pitched, almost a growl and she had a strong accent. "We come under the flag of truce."

"Don't believe her, lads," one of the Crossroaders shouted. "That's what they said last time." They had sized up the soldiers of the escort. They would not be much of a match. No doubt the soldiers, who all wore livery of red, had done the same and picked it an easy battle.

Adrastea, having no weapon for her hands, drew on the Deeper Power. If she could turn a rock into powdery sand, what could she do to this woman?

The woman must have been a priestess, for her eyes turned to Adrastea. "Who are you?" she demanded. "Are you the witch of this village?"

Adrastea folded her arms but did not release the Deeper Power. It calmed her soul and gave her enough peace to think clearly. "No, I'm the Healer."

The woman snorted. "Hmph. Liar. I see the aura about you."

Adrastea wanted to blast the woman then and there but checked herself. She would be no better than Mor-Lath if she killed. "Who the hell are you, to come riding here without a welcome?"

"I am Sister Mydala. I serve the One True God in defense of the True Faith. I am here to cleanse the world from evil." She lowered her flag of truce to point it to Adrastea's heart. "I can see into your soul, witch. You're of the Dark."

The men around Adrastea shifted nervously.

"I walk in the Light," Adrastea countered. Flush with Power, she knew what to say. "I do not recognize your authority or your right to be in this village."

Sister Mydala laughed. "I do not recognize your right to deny me passage." She leaned forward on the pommel of her saddle. "In fact, I don't think you have the right to speak for this village."

Adrastea looked to the men around her. Most of them were Crossroaders but a few, like Jak and Tam, were from Sacred Spring. They returned her gaze and each one nodded.

She turned back to Sister Mydala. "I have as much right as any man here to speak for the village. And we all say you're not welcome." The men nodded their agreement.

Sister Mydala shrugged off their statements. "Go fetch the Mayor, little girl. I have an offer to propose."

Jak Carpenter said, "Give us your offer and we'll take it to the Mayor."

"Yeah," shouted a Crossroader. "We know what you did to the Mayor of the last town you rode through."

She considered them, and then raised her standard high again. "So be it. Tell him we will let the people of your village live if every man, woman and child of you be baptized into the True Faith. You shall swear allegiance to the One True God. You will tithe your goods to the True Faith.

"In return, we shall offer spiritual guidance to all and ensure your safety with a military presence here in your village. As a further token of our generosity, we shall cleanse this village of all the evil witches and warlocks." She held out her arms. "You shall be free. We know you are hiding those who have sold their souls to the Evil One. We have felt their presence here."

The men murmured among themselves.

"They don't mean you, do they, Adrastea?" Jak asked. He shuffled closer to her and tightened his grip on his scythe.

Adrastea's eyes never left Sister Mydala. "Me, and Chloe and Carles too."

"But they didn't kill Carles last time."

"Perhaps they didn't know who he was. And I don't blame him for not revealing who he is."

"Do they know he is here?"

Adrastea knew Jak meant Mor-Lath. She shrugged.

Sister Mydala rose in closer. The soldiers of her escort spread out, half-encircling the villagers. "You." She pointed her standard at Jak. "You're the Mayor. I can tell. Your witch defers to you. Accept our generous offer."

"And if we refuse?" Jak asked calmly.

"Then we shall have no choice but to cleanse the entire village of all men, women and children to save their souls from Evil."

"How generous," muttered a Crossroader behind her. Adrastea turned to see whom it was, for she thought she recognized the voice. It was Master Mason, whose leg she'd healed recently.

"Should we take it?" Adrastea whispered to Jak.

"That's for Natan and Ely to decide. But I say no."

Before they could declare their intent to consider the offer, Sister Mydala's horse reared up in fright, throwing her. The other horses panicked. The soldiers, being better horsemen, clung to their mounts a little longer. One was thrown. A terrified horse rolled on another. The others fled, taking their riders with them.

The armed villagers rushed the fallen Cithrans. The rolled man was dead. The thrown one held up his hands in surrender. He knew his odds.

They approached the fallen Sister Mydala with weapons ready. Who knew what kind of tricks a foreign priestess would get up to?

She lay in the dust, gasping for her lost wind. Adrastea stood over her. She held onto the Deeper Power, not sure what to do with it should she feel the priestess draw on her own.

Sister Mydala looked up at her, eyes burning with hatred. "Your kind shall be cleansed from the world. And we shall start with your village and the black coven you hide here."

Adrastea sank to one knee. "So much for offering us a choice."

She grasped the front of Sister Mydala's robes and gave her a shake. "You threatened to kill us all. And you threatened to kill me regardless. Did you think we were going to stand idly by and let it happen?" She drew in more Power until she felt her very skin glow.

Sister Mydala's jaw dropped open and her eyes wandered to Adrastea's cheek. "The Mark..." She panicked. "You're the Bride!" She struggled until her clothing tore, leaving a scrap of rag in Adrastea's hand.

Sister Mydala scrambled to her feet. "My master's been looking for you." She turned and ran.

Adrastea watched her go, stunned at her pronouncement. Her Power dissipated, leaving her feeling empty. The villagers, who stood around her, stared at Adrastea. Tam Innkeeper stepped back. "Adrastea, is this true?"

She looked at him. "No. I walk in the Light."

But Tam shook his head. "He really is Mor-Lath, the Dark God, isn't he? You've betrayed us all."

"No," she said, dread rising within her. "I'm not his bride. You must believe me."

"You've destroyed my family," he wailed. "My wife had to flee. Now my children are going to be slain."

Adrastea backed away. "I'm sorry," she said, too little too late. "I never meant any of this to happen."

She fled. Her feet found their way up the hill. Instead of fleeing blindly into the forest, she slowed down enough to think rationally.

She had to warn Uncle Natan. But as for herself, it was too late. Even if Sacred Spring survived the coming battle, she would no longer be welcome here.

Everything had been her fault. They would all die. It would be because of her.

The barrier around Little Crossroads was nowhere near ready to defend them.

"Natan Mayor!" she called. "Uncle Natan!"

He stood up from a small circle of men holding war council and approached her. "Adrastea?"

"The army's coming." She quickly relayed the events of the failed parlay, leaving out unnecessary details about herself. He would hear the rest, should he survive the battle. And if he didn't, it wouldn't matter. "As we were considering bringing the offer to you, the horses spooked. I swear it wasn't one of us. But they took that as an affront. They are going to attack us."

Natan swore. He ran back to the circle. "They're coming!"

The men rose as one and scrambled. The villagers armed themselves. Those with hunting bows and rifles ran to the crest of the hill for first shots.

As Adrastea stood on the naked hill, she wished they hadn't cut down the trees; they could have used them for shelter. She saw the road leading into town and the fallow lands lying behind Ari's walled garden. That house would be the first they would destroy, then the Tanners and Tailors and maybe Mira's cottage, before they reached the barrier protecting the smithy.

How foolish it had been to put the children in there. Sure, it was the biggest building in the village. She now saw how weak it was, how easily it could be pulled down and the inhabitants slaughtered.

They'd sent the children to their deaths.

As they watched, columns of soldiers marched into view. They did not come by the road but across the fields, heedless of the crops nearing harvest. Beasts of burden followed, dragging odd-looking wooden contraptions. Adrastea had never seen such things before, with their tall towers and long arms. Definitely machines of war.

"Bugger me," uttered Natan as they watched them move into place. "We can't defend against that."

Carles and Chloe came forward. "That's what they used to harass Crossroads before they breached our walls with cannon fire," Carles said. "They called them," he paused to sift for the word, "trebbushay? They lob these little iron balls that explode when they land." He shook his head. "We'll not survive."

The villagers watched as more soldiers arrived. Ely started counting. When he reached three hundred and more came still, he gave up. Behind him, a few of the women wept. "Why so many for such a small village?" he asked.

"They're looking for something," Mor-Lath said as he joined their ranks.

Natan looked at him. "What are they looking for?"

Mor-Lath didn't answer but turned to Adrastea. Everyone's eyes followed until they rested on her.

"Me?" she squeaked. "But why?"

"The priestess recognized you for who you are."

Natan scowled at his niece. "You didn't tell me this."

Adrastea looked abashed. "I didn't think it was important."

"Nor should you have," Mor-Lath said. "They didn't know. Oh, they knew there was a powerful presence here in your little village. Aware of the amount of Power but not its source, they thought they'd stumbled across a secret coven of the witches. They burn witches."

Carles said, "They burn priests, too."

Mor-Lath shrugged. "Witches, priests. Same thing to them."

Chloe whimpered, clutching to Carles' arm.

"That's why there are so many soldiers and so many of their priests of the so-called 'True Faith'."

Adrastea felt alarm. "If it's me they seek, what if I leave? Then maybe they'll leave us alone if I'm gone."

Mor-Lath shook his head. "It's too late. They'll destroy the village first and then search the bodies for you. It won't matter if you're here or not."

Adrastea's stomach knotted up. She closed her eyes and fought the sensation of nausea. It would not do to throw up in front of everyone. After she'd swallowed excessive spit, she whispered, "So we're all going to die? Is there—" She stopped. She couldn't ask anything of him, not without him wanting something in return.

He inclined his head. "Is there something I could do, you mean?"

She bowed her head even lower and clutched her arms around her, wishing she could curl up into a ball so tight it disappeared completely. Everyone who stood on the hill—Natan and Ari, Carles and Chloe, Ely and more—watched her. The others stood ready with weapons, praying to the Light as they faced what looked to be certain death. Their fear rolled along the Lines like a relentless wave.

"Oh," Mor-Lath continued, as if discussing the plot of a garden or the strategy of a game, "I could delay them a bit, give you a chance to come up with another useless plan. I could even kill them, should you choose to release me from my promise.

"But what's half a thousand deaths? This is but one small snippet of the whole of the Cithran army. Your little Mydala has already dispatched messengers. More will come. I might be able to delay them, but more would come after that, and then more. The Cithran army is half a million strong. And then there's the rest of the Empire. They'll breed more.

"I couldn't do it. Not alone." He leaned over and whispered into her ear. "But there's you."

Her eyes flew open. "Me? How?"

"You? I didn't say you could. Alone, I can't. Alone, you certainly can't. But us together, we could stop them for good."

She turned to him. "What are you saying?"

"Marry me."

She opened her mouth to say no but realized that was out of habit. "I don't understand."

"I don't have time to explain." He pointed out across the village to the fields that lay beyond. The Cithrans primed their engines of war. "If you do not make your decision soon, they will make it for you."

There were too many 'ifs' involved. "It's not enough," she blurted. "You yourself said that more would come. So, what if we destroyed that army there, and the army behind it, and the one after that. It would never end."

Mor-Lath thought for a moment. "How about this for a bride-price: Marry me and not only will we together stop the whole Cithran army, but I will set a protection over your village. Evil shall not touch Sacred Spring for three generations. All who approach with evil intent shall not be able to enter."

"And the good?"

"They can enter freely," he conceded. He took her by the arms. "Agreed?"

A war engine launched. After the great arm swung back, there was a distant crack. "Heads up!" One of the villagers shouted in warning.

A moment later something exploded to the left of the villagers on the hillside. Those in proximity fled in fear. The rest who had witnessed Mor-Lath's offer shuffled in nervousness.

Mor-Lath laid his hand on her cheek. "You are running out of time. Marry me?"

"You put the protection on the village first!"

He stepped back. "So be it."

He summoned a knife from Ari's pocket. It flew, hilt-first, to his hand. He applied it to his left hand and sliced sharply. Then he held his hand out over the ground. Everyone watched at the blood—far more luminous than mortal blood—dripped from his hand. With each drop that hit the earth, a ring of light spread out. The first ring from the first drop only went as far as a meter from where he stood, before disappearing into the earth.

The second ring flowed a few meters wider than that, and the third even further. His blood sent out rings of powerful protection around the village.

Another exploding ball struck the hillside, sending dirt flying. The Cithrans' aim improved. The next ball would reach Little Crossroads. At least they hadn't attacked the smithy yet.

When the entire village was protected, Mor-Lath held out his bloody hand to Adrastea. "Heal that, if you please."

She did not hesitate before drawing on the Deeper Power. With a touch of her finger she sealed up the cut, leaving only a red scar behind. It made her think of the scar on her cheek.

"That protection will prevent them from entering here but it will not stop their artillery. Stay true to your promise, Adrastea. Marry me."

Adrastea hung her head. She had agreed after all. She steeled her heart, telling herself it was for the best. She'd saved not only Sacred Spring but the remains of Crossroads. If they could stop the whole Cithran army, she could save countless other villages and maybe even Feown.

Perhaps it was a good bargain after all, she tried to convince herself.

Mor-Lath pointed a finger at Carles. "You're a priest. Hear our vows."

"B— but I'm a priest of the Light," he stammered.

"I recognize the authority of the Light to bind me in marriage." He took Adrastea's hands and went down to his knees. "Kneel down."

Another canon ball struck the village green.

Adrastea sank to her knees.

Carles, quite shaken, came forward. A missile flew overhead, missing Little Crossroads and striking the trees on the other side. People ducked and screamed. Carles cringed but remained where he stood.

"Our vows, priest," Mor-Lath insisted rather forcefully.

Carles took a breath and wavered. Natan came up from behind and held him steady. "Do it," he whispered in his ear. "We have no choice."

Carles nodded. "Repeat after me.

"I, Mor-Lath take you, Adrastea as my wife..."

Mor-Lath looked into Adrastea's eyes. "I, Mor-Lath, God of the Dark, take you, Adrastea Healer as my wife." His eyes burned fierce. Not with the teasing light or the tolerance he'd shown in the past but sheer determination. This was a god who was getting his way. He was not going to let anyone or anything, not even Light or Creation to stop him.

He continued, not needing any prompting. "All that I have I give to you. All that I am, I am for you. I shall hold you above all others. In this I plight my troth."

Carles looked at him with doubt. "You forgot something."

Mor-Lath calmly returned his gaze. "No, I did not."

The priest frowned but continued the ceremony. "I, Adrastea take you, Mor-Lath as my husband..."

Her voice shook but she said the words. "I, Adrastea take you Mor-Lath as my husband."

Carles prompted, "All that I have, I give to you."

"All that I have, I give to you."

He prompted and she repeated: "All that I am I am for you. All my love I give to you and none other. I shall hold you above all others. In this I plight my troth."

She did it.

Natan's head bowed. His hands dropped from Carles' shoulders.

Carles Priest pronounced, "Stand as husband and wife."

Mor-Lath rose to his feet, guiding Adrastea upright. Carles turned away, hunched over. Ari drew in a ragged sob and her knees quivered. Everyone else stepped back as they rose, too stunned to speak.

Mor-Lath stroked Adrastea's left cheek. She gasped as a sharp line burned into her skin. She put a hand to her cheek and steeled herself for the pain. It burned but only for a moment, nothing like before.

He'd marked her twice. Then he lifted her chin and gave her a kiss.

This was no kiss of seduction, as he'd given her before. This was a kiss of possession, hard and demanding, leaving no doubt that she now belonged to him.

Another launched ball flew overhead and smashed through the

barrier built behind them.

"And now, we go to fulfill my promise," he murmured to her. He turned her to face the villagers she'd saved. "Say your goodbyes."

Her throat was too choked up to speak. She raised a tentative hand but dropped it. All the people she'd known her whole life stared back, shocked. Tears streamed down Ari's cheeks. Natan looked up, his eyes full of grief and guilt. They clung together.

Mor-Lath wrapped an arm about Adrastea's waist. He smiled in a satisfied way. "Mine," he uttered, before they disappeared together.

End of Book One

A Note from the Author

Thank you so much for reading **God of the Dark**. I hope you enjoyed it and want to read the rest of the books in the series.

If you did enjoy this book, please leave an honest review on the site where you purchased it. Alternatively, leave a review on a reputable review site like Amazon, Goodreads or LibraryThing. Reviews are not only the highest compliment you can pay to an author, they also help other readers discover great books. Share the love. Thank you!

Acknowledgements

I've spent a long time in the arms of this book but I've not been alone. So many, many people have read bits (or all) of this, giving their invaluable feedback. Without their help, this series would not have become what it grew up to be, nor would I have been the writer I became. It astounds me how many early readers, critters and general cheerleaders have laid eyeballs on this. I know I've forgotten some names. For that, I beg your forgiveness.

Kathryn VanRoosendaal, the very first reader. Anne Wingate, the second.

And in no particular order:

Far too many critters from the Online Writing Workshop, Michael Staton, Erica Chandler, Erin Fitzgerald, Nicole Minsk, Christian Crowe, Andrew, Ellie Comeau, Rose Black, four different Johns, the entire Vicious Circle, most of the Stromatolights, Satima Flavell Neist, Melody LeBaron, Gary Herdsman, Samantha Holmes, John Wood, Jason Ventner (always!), Robert Flowers, Elizabeth Glover, Dianna Lang, Paul Carter, James Horak, Larry Payne, Robert Pickering, Jan Herdsman, Elizabeth Burton, Mike Dumas, Jen Kilshaw, Hannah Whitehead, Richard Armitage, Hilary Gratwick and everyone else. While I may have forgotten your names, your impact remains on these words. Also grateful to industry professionals Janet Reid, Kristin Nelson and Tricia Skinner, who all had nice things to say. Much gratitude to you all.

As for those who didn't have nice (or constructive) things to say, those who told me I shouldn't be an author, and/or who disparaged commercial fiction... guess what? You were wrong. Very much so. Somewhere someone needed this book. I am glad to defy you so they can have it. Nyah.

Finally I acknowledge the Whadjuk tribe of the Nyoongar people, past and present, who are the traditional owners of the land on which I live and write.

Bride of the Dark

Book 2 – Of The Dark

Read on for a sneak peek into "Bride of the Dark"

Chapter 1

She'd done it. Adrastea had married Mor-Lath, God of the Dark. A strange haziness overcame her as soon as the vows had left her lips. The world wavered up and down.

Married. Wait...

Had this really happened?

This was not how she had envisioned her wedding—certainly not in the middle of war. Adrastea looked out from the hill above the village of Sacred Spring to the army that surrounded it. Tall machines, their poles high in the air and dangling with ropes, stood sentinel over so many soldiers. The crops were gone, trampled to dust.

Plumes of smoke rose from the village below. Cries of young fear echoed up from the smithy. As she looked at the incredulous faces of Uncle Natan and Ari, her heart ached. She'd done it to save them. She'd done it to save everyone. Her face stung. She put a hand to her cheek, but the pain did not last long. Had she imagined it?

Did she imagine this whole thing?

She shook her head in a vain attempt to knock the haziness out of it.

Mor-Lath's arm slid about her waist. He drew her close to his chest. "Mine," he murmured in her ear. His triumph washed over her.

Adrastea shuddered. What had she done? Her throat ached from smoke and tears.

Mor-Lath called upon the Deeper Power, letting it fill him. The lines on Adrastea's face—there were two now—sang in harmony with the Power he held. He reached... somewhere distant... and grasped onto something.

Shift.

Adrastea's heart felt like had been tugged from the inside out, the rest of her following through. Her head spun as she lost orientation. The image of Sacred Spring wavered and blurred as if disappearing. If it were not for Mor-Lath's arm about her waist, she would have fallen.

Her feet connected to something solid, not the grass she stood upon moments before. The scent of different air filled her nostrils, also smoke but of a different kind.

They were no longer at Sacred Spring.

When Creation resolved itself, she looked down onto a vast city. How high up were they? Her head swam with vertigo and she clung to the strong arm around her waist.

In the distance, a mighty silver river snaked its way by the city. A smoky pall covered the sky, muting out the sun.

Outside the city walls wall a multitude of small white patches, like tiles, filled the empty spaces between the fallen buildings and across fields. Adrastea squinted for a better view, for she did not recognize them at first through the blurriness.

Tents. Thousands of tents pitched before the wall, scattered about like confetti. And the miniscule moving figures? Horses, possibly. Or people. So many!

"Welcome back to Feown," Mor-Lath murmured, his baritone voice touched with excitement. It nagged at her, as if she was supposed to feel it too.

Well, she didn't.

He buried his nose in her hair and inhaled. All she smelled was smoke.

"Where are we?" Her head had recovered from the sudden change of height.

"It's called the Maiden's Tower. Interesting story but we don't have time. It's the highest point in Feown." He breathed warm air into her ear. "I believe part of our bargain, my Bride, was the salvation of your little village?"

Sacred Spring. Her heart thumped. Was it all right?

"Feown, too. You belong to it by right of blood. You are very much the daughter of this once-august city. You can save it as well."

Feown? Hers? Except for the last time Mor-Lath had brought her here she had never been to Feown. The city was too far away, at least two weeks' travel. Ari had been there before as a journeyman.

But for a country girl like herself? The furthest she had ever been was Crossroads.

Now she was the Bride of the Dark. She looked beyond the walls of Feown, to the vast pallor of smoky and speckled camps of the army. Surely this was not the same army that threatened Sacred Spring? "What do I do?"

Mor-Lath pressed his cheek to hers, sending the new line on her cheek singing. "Every life in Creation is connected to it by a thread of Power. In turn, each person is connected to others by more threads.

"Below us, in the depths of the palace is a man by the name of General Miniver. He is in charge of the force invading Feown, and ultimately, those who are currently battering your village. Right now, he is doing terrible things to the Duchess of Feown—things that would make your innocent heart cringe."

Oh? The memory of a memory, a blond man, his heart full of ill intent, drawing bloody lines on her skin with a knifepoint before— What could possibly be worse than what Mor-Lath had shown her?

"Focus on him. Concentrate on the Lines that connect him to his war council, his captains and lieutenants, his sergeants and so forth."

Adrastea closed her eyes. She drew on the Deeper Power. With him behind her, it came to her easily. "How do I find the General?"

"Think of his name. It is by our names we are connected."

General Miniver. As she focused on the name, the bright sparks of people's lives within the palace opened to her. Everything else faded but those little spots of humanity. They flew past her awareness like fuzzy little mayflies as she sought the spark called General Miniver.

Every spark was an individual, with its own personality of being, its own mix of emotions and thoughts. She wanted to stop and explore. She wanted to reach out and stroke them, for each one sang its own note. Together, their song called to her.

Mor-Lath warned, "Stop that. We're running out of time."

She found General Miniver. His spark burned fierce and red as he tortured a woman. Her spark flickered and fluttered, an angry simmer of water droplets on a hot grill that refused to evaporate. Immediately Adrastea's heart went out to the woman, to comfort her.

"Don't waste time!" Mor-Lath snapped. "You'll end her suffering soon enough. Focus on the General."

She felt the Dark God's personal strength flow into her as his arms tightened about her waist. "Focus on the General, then follow the Lines that connect to him. Soldiers will feel different from everyone else. Their song sings of battle."

Adrastea saw what he meant. She had never noticed before but each Line that connected the General to the Duchess to the soldiers to the others in the palace, to the palace itself and to her, each Line had its own song.

The Line between the general and the woman had its own feel. It was different from the Line between him and the other men. The general fought the woman. The antagonism between them was strong. Between him and the men—subservience, obedience, and something else.

Mor-Lath murmured his approval. "Now, follow that Line and all the others like unto it until you have reached every last one. Be warned; there are many."

Her consciousness skipped along the Lines, locating bright sparks of life like beads on a string. She kept a hold of the strings as more were added. "How many?"

"There are half a million."

"Half a million?!" She nearly dropped the Lines. Adrastea had no idea there were that many people in the world, much less that number of soldiers. But if this army was that huge, imagine how many people there were in the world beyond that.

His arms tightened once more. He gave her a little shake. "Don't lose focus. Every second you let your mind wander is another second that army has to assault your Sacred Spring."

She increased her efforts. Soon, her mind raced over the sparks until they became a blaze of light. Every spark was found. Was it a moment or was it a year?

"There," Mor-Lath said. "That's the whole army."

How did he know? Adrastea refocused her mind. Have to save Sacred Spring. "Now what?"

"Imagine yourself grasping the Lines of Power that connect you to everyone you've touched. When you are ready, pull on those Lines. Imagine lifting each life up and through you. It's important that you imagine every single Line going through your heart. They must go through you, or it won't work. Are you ready?"

She trembled. Her hands tightened on his arms. Her heart thumped hard. She felt his heart beating in parallel with hers. Why couldn't it slow down?

Are you ready?

She nodded.

"Good. Let's begin." He pulled on the Deeper Power.

He called to Creation. It answered him, flowing through her, to him and back. His hands slid, one moving down around her belly while the other reaching upwards across her bodice to her collarbone until he enveloped her whole body with his. As the Power enveloped them, they blended together, no longer her and him but them. He poured all the Deeper Power he held into her, giving it to her freely.

She gasped as it overwhelmed her in its warmth and sweetness. This was very different from the times he'd tempted her with Power before. Before, was a mere sip of water. This was a torrent that threatened to pull her down. "Don't let it overpower you," he urged. "Stay focused." There was a hint of desperation in his voice. She brought herself back. "Ready? Can you see them all?

The Lines. She redirected her attention there. A half-million lives pulsed, their multitudinous symphonies sang to her through the Deeper Power. So many but she could count each one.

"Now pull."

Adrastea pulled. She imagined every single one of those half million lives being lifted up and away from where they were. An unimaginable amount of Deeper Power came away from them. It flowed down the Lines until it contacted her. But instead of flowing through her, the Power poured into her. So much! Who knew there was so much Power?

Did she scream? How would she hold it all?

Somewhere she thought she heard a voice of protest but then Mor-Lath's voice was in her head. "Do not let yourself be distracted by anything. Keep pulling until you are finished."

She felt the Power of a half-million lives pour into her until all was contained in her. Oh, how it burned! Once inside, it shrieked and twisted as if not sure where to go. She wanted to cry out in pain, in passion, in surprise but too much was happening. Voices chattered in confusion, adding to the chaos.

She felt the Power in every speck of dust that was her. The intensity increased, if that was even possible. The specks of dust began to melt, to move.

Adrastea began to change.

Her spine straightened ever so slightly. Her limbs lengthened. Her eyes focused and she felt her skin move like the vibrations of a hummer toy. Her teeth slid to their proper places and her voice changed a few notes deeper. Her waist narrowed, and her hips rounded. Something within her tuned up until the song she had gathered to her vibrated in perfect harmonies. Oh, the beauty of the song.

It felt too much. Her knees buckled. The very world felt as if it would tear apart. She grasped at Mor-Lath to keep from falling.

Panic rippled through Mor-Lath, washing over Adrastea...

About the Author

Heidi Kneale is an Australian author of moderate repute. She is best known for her escapist fiction—especially Fantasy and Romance. Like most humans, she's got a family. She also keeps company with the World's Most Boring Cat. When not writing novels, she can be found composing music or staring at the stars.

Find her at:

Blog: http://RomanceSpinners.blogspot.com
Twitter: @heidikneale
Web: http://tinyurl.com/heidikneale/

Want a free story?

Of course you do!

Get Heidi Kneale's short story "Within Her" when you sign up for her quarterly newsletter at http://tinyurl.com/heidikneale/ plus get news of upcoming releases, special deals and more.

When I've had too much of reality, I open a book.

www.ingramcontent.com/pod-product-compliance
Lightning Source LLC
Chambersburg PA
CBHW071144100726
47908CB00002B/247